FIREBORNE

ROSARIA MUNDA

putnam

G. P. Putnam's Sons

G. P. PUTNAM'S SONS

An imprint of Penguin Random House LLC, New York

Visit us online at penguinrandomhouse.com

Library of Congress Cataloging-in-Publication Data
Names: Munda, Rosaria, author.
Title: Fireborne / Rosaria Munda.
Description: New York: G. P. Putnam's Sons, [2019] | Series: [Aurelian cycle; book 1]
Summary: "Two dragonriders must go head-to-head for the top position in the Callipolan fleet, and protect the new regime from those who lost power"—Provided by publisher.
Identifiers: LCCN 2018052935 (print) | LCCN 2018057220 (ebook)
ISBN 9780525518228 (ebook) | ISBN 9780525518211 (hardcover)
Subjects: | CYAC: Dragons—Fiction. | Orphans—Fiction. | Fantasy.
Classification: LCC PZ7.1.M825 (ebook) | LCC PZ7.1.M825 Fir 2019 (print) | DDC [Fic]—dc23
LC record available at https://lccn.loc.gov/2018052935

Printed in the United States of America
ISBN 9780525518211
1 3 5 7 9 10 8 6 4 2

Design by Lindsey Andrews
Text set in Sabon LT Pro

For my mother and my grandmother,
fellow writers

PROLOGUE

Later, he would be known as the First Protector, and under his vision the city would transform. Serfs would be freed, schools would be built, and dragons would, for the first time, be ridden by commoners.

Before that, he was the leader of the bloodiest revolution his people had ever seen.

He never doubted that he would create a just city. Nor did he doubt that the families of the old regime deserved to die. But he did, sometimes, regret the way it happened, the day the palace was finally overrun.

He remembered in particular one of the ruling families, their tormentors still at work when he found them. The dragonlord had been kept alive, to watch; his youngest son was the only child left. A boy of about seven or eight, his expression blank beneath a mask of blood. The remains of their family lay around them.

"Stop this foolishness at once," the First Protector said, when he and his guard found them.

The revolutionaries let go of the boy, whom they had been

hurting, and began to protest: This man is Leon Stormscourge, don't you know what he's done—but they fell silent when the dragonlord spoke from his knees on the bloodstained carpet.

"My son," he said, in the language he and the First Protector shared. "Please, Atreus."

The First Protector took a half glance at the child. He said, "Leo will be looked after."

He gave one of his guards a murmured order. The soldier started, hesitated, and then lifted the dragonlord's son in his arms. When the boy had been carried, limp and silent, from the room, the leader of the revolution knelt before the dragonlord.

"Those—animals—" the dragonlord rasped.

The First Protector did not disagree. Instead, he put a hand to the knife on his belt. When he met the dragonlord's gaze, it was in an unspoken question. The dragonlord closed his eyes and nodded.

Then, to the First Protector's surprise, he spoke.

"Your vision," he said. "Do you think it will ever be worth this, Atreus?"

The First Protector drew his knife.

"Yes," he said.

The dragonlord's question returned to him often in the years that followed. Even as many of the other details of the Revolution began to fade from his memory, he remembered Leon Stormscourge.

Leon's son, on the other hand, was a detail he forgot.

1

MESSAGES FROM THE MINISTRY

Nine Years Later

LEE

Morning is our favorite time to fly. Today, even with the tournament looming and the empty arena below us a reminder that soon we'll be watched, for the first time, by thousands, it's still possible to savor the city sprawled beneath a dragon's wings. When we pull tight on a turn, I glimpse one of Pallor's black eyes, depthless, turned on me. The line between us, of shared emotions and thoughts that are usually latent in the saddle, goes taut. Yes. Today it begins. Today we'll rise.

But in order to do that, I'll need a clear head. I gently extricate myself from Pallor's simmering anticipation and refocus on the arena. Two other dragonriders fly with us, each riding one of the other two breeds: Crissa and her skyfish are in the air above us, while Cor and his stormscourge glide below, bellowing ash over the arena stands. We're on our last rehearsal, this time with just the squadron leaders.

I lift my voice over the wind. "You're taking her too low, Cor."

Cor grunts, frustrated, and urges his stormscourge higher. We've rehearsed the choreography of the tournament's opening ceremony over and over with ministry officials, and every time, the question of how to demonstrate the might of the storm-scourge breed becomes tricky. Before the Revolution, the dragons of Stormscourge House—of my family—were known for terrorizing the countryside; but in even older days, they were our island's greatest defense against aerial invasion.

"They told us to fire low," says Cor.

"Not *that* low. It's risky for the audience."

Our dragons are immature, barely horse-size, and can't yet breathe fire. But the smoke they produce can still burn.

Crissa and her skyfish, long, slender, and pale enough blue to blend with the morning sky, circle above us. "You want to impress the people," she calls down to Cor. "Not roast them."

Cor waves a hand. "All right, all right . . ."

The fleet is still in training, dragons and riders both. Known now as Guardians, the new regime's dragonriders are lowborn, commoners, even former serfs. No longer the sons of dragonlords.

Except for me, though I'm the only one who knows that.

Because in the wake of the Revolution, to be dragonborn is to be wanted for dead. I was born Leo, son of Leon, dragonlord of Stormscourge House and Drakarch of the Far Highlands—but, since the orphanage, I've been Lee. Not even the First Protector, who saved my life and then welcomed me, without recognition, into his Guardian program two years after that, knows the truth.

That a Stormscourge tested into the meritocratic dragon-riding program designed to replace everything his family stood for.

Even though I know I'm lucky to be here—lucky to be alive,

4

lucky to have escaped the orphanage—memories of the old life have a way of intruding and twisting. Especially today, as Pallor and I circle above the Palace arena, open to the public for the first time since the Revolution. The old regime had tournaments here, too. Tournaments I watched my father compete in, dreaming of the day it would be my turn.

I lean forward and rest a gloved hand on Pallor's silver-scaled neck as his wings, translucent in the morning light, tighten in a dive. Pallor is an aurelian, a smaller breed known for being careful and maneuverable, and the aurelian formation for today's ceremony is the only one complex enough to require coleaders. I can rehearse alone, but to do the thing properly, I need—

Annie. There she is.

Another aurelian, this one amber-toned, has emerged from the cave mouth at the base of the arena, and on her back rides my sparring partner, Annie. She and I have trained together for as long as we've been in the Guardian program, and we've known each other since the orphanage before that.

It's a past life's worth of memories that we're both pretty good at not talking about.

"Annie!" Crissa calls with a cheerful wave. "There you are."

"Lee's been flying like an idiot out here without you," Cor says.

Pallor and I fire ash downward. Cor dodges the stream with a bark of laughter.

Annie's lips curve at Cor's remark, but instead of answering, she rolls seamlessly into formation opposite me, her dragon, Aela, mirroring Pallor's movements. Annie's red-brown braid hangs low on her back, her pale freckled face set in concentration. I've thought of Annie as beautiful—strikingly beautiful—for almost as long as I can remember, but I've never told her that.

"Take it from the top?" I suggest.

There are calls of assent from the other three.

We right ourselves only when the bell rings the hour. The arena below, the Palace to one side and the karst pillar supporting Pytho's Keep on the other, the jagged rooftops, the plains stretching out to the sea—for a moment I feel a protectiveness, almost a possessiveness, of the city and island spread below. The vows that we took when we became Guardians echo in my mind: *All that I am belongs to Callipolis. By the wings of my dragon I will keep her . . .*

Today, eight of the Guardians will compete in the quarterfinal tournament for Firstrider, commander of the aerial fleet. I'm one of those eight, along with Annie, Cor, and Crissa. Qualifying rounds have been going on among the thirty-two dragonriders for weeks.

It will be the first time since the Revolution that Callipolis names a Firstrider, one of the few titles it's kept from the old regime. The dragons of the revolutionary fleet are finally old enough, and their riders well-enough trained, to vie for a position that's been vacant since the Revolution. For the other Guardians, the Firstrider Tournaments are a chance to prove themselves; for me, it will be that and something more.

Because *Firstrider* is a title I've wanted since before the Revolution. It would be all the recognition, power, and respect that my family lost over the course of a single bloody month when I was eight years old, regained.

Firstrider.

Distantly, below, the bells of the Palace clocktower are tolling.

I rouse myself. "We should get in for breakfast. Goran said he'd have the tournament bracket ready by then."

We land on the Eyrie, the jutting stone platform that rises from the center of the arena, where we dismount, unsaddle our dragons, and dismiss them to their nests in the caves below. Back in the Palace, we find the rest of the Guardian corps, thirty-odd students in all, trickling into the Cloister refectory from the dorms. The walls of the refectory are bare stone, the windows high and narrow, breakfast the usual slightly burnt porridge. Though we are technically Palace residents, we live in what were, before the Revolution, servants' quarters.

"You're up early."

Duck, Cor's younger brother, has scooted on his bench to make room for us where he's sitting with some friends. Though Duck and Cor share olive skin and wavy hair, in manner they're opposites, Cor tending to scowl where Duck wears an open smile. Annie slides comfortably onto the bench beside Duck. They're both sixteen, a year younger than most of us. While it was the first commonality that brought them together, they remained friends because Duck seemed to like the challenge. It's hard to get Annie to smile, and Duck's good at it.

Duck lifts his spoon from his porridge and cocks it in Annie's direction. "Ready for your big day?"

Annie snorts, but all the same, color enters her cheeks. A rare glimpse of ambition she usually keeps close to the vest. She is hunching again: Always, on the ground, Annie hunches, as if hoping to take up less space. It's a jarring contrast to her confidence in the air.

Crissa tells Duck, in the bracing voice she pulls out whenever she's encouraging riders in her squadron: "Your big day, too."

Duck lifts his shoulders, grin flagging. "Let's not get ahead of ourselves."

Like the four of us, Duck made it into today's quarterfinals. He'll do great—depending on how he handles his nerves, and who he's up against.

"Nervous, Dorian?"

Speaking of which. Power, one of the qualifying storm-scourge riders, has passed us on his way from the serving counter. He drapes an arm around Duck's shoulder, as if he were encouraging him, and flicks a spare palm over close-shaven black hair as he locks eyes with me. Power is around my height and weight, and this has always been the kind of calculation I make, and can tell he's making, when we look at each other.

Duck has gone rigid. "Get your hands off me," he says through gritted teeth.

Cor sets down his glass with a click on the hardwood table. I return my spoon to a resting position in the bowl of porridge.

It's almost disappointing when Power withdraws his arm. He's become more careful in recent years. "Jumpy, are we?"

He wanders back to the empty seat between Darius and Alexa, who have been watching our interchange apprehensively. The tension slides out of Duck's shoulders, and he makes a gut-tural noise of disgust.

"Sometimes," Cor muses, "I miss the days when patrician kids like Power got away with stuff, and it was up to us to keep them in line."

"I don't," Duck mutters.

In the old regime, my family was among the ruling dragon-born, and the patrician families like Power's were a tier below, wealthy but dragonless. Power holds the usual patrician disdain for commoners like Cor and Crissa and, most damningly, Annie, who is not only a commoner but a former serf.

Crissa murmurs, "I'm sure Goran misses those good old days, too."

Her eyes narrow on the doorway of the refectory, where a single adult has entered the room. Goran, our patrician drillmaster, is a ruddy-faced, aging, formerly fit officer gone to seed, with traces of a Dragontongue accent that he thickens when he wants to intimidate lowborn riders. The sight of him has always been unsettlingly familiar. We must have crossed paths in the years before, but he's never recognized me, and that's all that matters. Goran's loyalty to Atreus is apparent; to the ideals of the Revolution, less so. Before Atreus put his foot down, Goran let Power and the other patrician Guardians get away with almost anything.

"Morning, Guardians," Goran tells the room. "Ready to hear the bracket for today's matches?"

The tables go silent. Goran begins to read from his list. "We've got Annie versus Darius—"

Darius, one of Power's patrician friends in the stormscourge squadron, turns around to look at Annie, and I'm pleased to see that his usual easygoing bravado has been replaced by a furrowed brow. Annie folds her arms and glares back.

"—Cor versus Rock—"

Cor scowls despite the fact that it's a decent pairing, no doubt calculating the possible combinations left to be assigned. Specifically, who might be paired with Duck.

"Next we'll have Lee and Crissa—"

Crissa lets out a groan and presses her palms to her forehead in a theatrical gesture of dismay, then locks her eyes on mine. Crissa has the kind of face—perpetually sun-flushed, framed by dark gold curls streaked with blond—that, when you stare at it, you end up allowing your gaze to linger on too long. She lifts an eyebrow playfully.

"Do your worst, Lee."

I can feel myself blushing for reasons that have nothing to do with the match. Crissa smirks. Cor rolls his eyes.

After ours comes the final pairing, the one we all saw coming as soon as Goran paired me and Crissa.

"Finally, we'll have Power versus Duck."

Power lets out a trilling drumroll, but he's the only one who looks pleased. Duck has sunk low in his seat; Cor's face has tightened. Annie's arm moves ever so slightly, as if squeezing Duck's hand beneath the table. Duck is one of the only people I have ever seen Annie touch voluntarily, and she does so often. Now, as she takes his hand, he perceptibly swallows.

According to Cor, they're not together. But even if they're not, it's pretty clear Duck's smitten. He has been for years and yet still Annie touches him like this, casually, as if they're still kids—oblivious, as far as I can tell. Annie used to touch me like that, in the orphanage. She stopped when we came here.

I realize that Duck is staring at me, staring at him. We look away from each other at once.

"You've got a little over an hour till the opening ceremony," Goran says, "so I'd recommend you get moving. How many of you have family coming today?"

There's a show of hands. Pretty much everybody; Annie and I are the predictable exceptions. But then I see Annie's fingers lifted a bit off the table. She is studying them as if surprised herself.

That doesn't make sense. How could Annie have family coming?

"Save the greetings for the end," Goran says. "But feel free to take the rest of the day off. Madam Mortmane will be doing sign-outs by the Cloister entrance. Any questions?"

When there aren't, he catches my eye. "Lee, Annie, a word."

I can't remember the last time Goran wanted to speak with Annie. We wait, seated, as the others take their leave and Goran assumes a vacant chair at the head of the table. I can almost feel the tension riddling Annie's body at his proximity. Although years have passed since he's outright bullied her—the extra chores, the arbitrarily low marks, the ridicule on the Eyrie— Goran has never stopped treating Annie's presence on the corps as particularly offensive, as if her status as a former serf, compounded with her gender, were one too many of Atreus's innovations to be tolerated in one person.

"I've got notes from the ministry, one for each of you."

He hands me mine, then Annie hers. As usual, he avoids looking at her, like she's a perversion to keep in his peripheral vision.

My note is stamped with the seal of Atreus Athanatos, the First Protector.

"Read them later," Goran says. "You're dismissed."

We stop together in the corridor outside to tear open our notes. Atreus has handwritten a single phrase. I read it, and for the first time today, the acid jolt of nerves hits my stomach.

Good luck, Lee.

I look up. Annie is still reading, frozen. Then her shoulders go up, and she tears her eyes away from her note.

"We should get to the armory," she says.

By the time we arrive, the rest of the corps are getting ready to head underground to the dragon nests. Annie and I make our way to the aurelian squad's cubbies amid riders shrugging on flamesuits, hooking on their last few plates of armor, and slinging tack over their shoulders to carry down to the caves. The room smells of leather, sweat, and ash: the smells of dragonriding.

I feel something pressed into my hand; Annie has passed me her note and turned away. Inviting me to read it but unwilling to watch as I do.

Our cubbies are side by side; in recent years I've trained myself to stare at anything, anything in the *world*, other than Annie when she's changing uniforms. Today, I stare at her note. Her message bears the seal of the Ministry of Propaganda, not the First Protector. It says:

> THE MINISTRY WOULD LIKE TO REMIND ANTIGONE SUR AELA OF THE INTENSELY PUBLIC NATURE OF THE OBLIGATIONS OF RIDERS OF THE FOURTH ORDER, AND TO URGE HER TO CONSIDER CAREFULLY WHETHER SHE BELIEVES HER VOWS TO SERVE THE STATE WOULD BE BEST HONORED BY PURSUING SUCH A PUBLIC ROLE.

They want her to throw the match.

Beside me, Annie has finished putting on her flamesuit. Black leather, treated for heat and fire, hugs her slender frame from neckline to ankles, her braided hair a burst of red above the suit's dark silhouette. She makes no attempt to discuss the note, not while others are still around us, and so we finish arming in silence, strapping plates of armor, forged out of repurposed dragons' scales, over our flamesuits, and tightening them one by one. After the last riders have headed out and we're alone in the armory, Annie takes back her note.

"What did yours say?" she asks.

Atreus's note is the last thing I want to show her. I hesitate.

"Please," she says quietly.

Without waiting for my answer, she takes my note from the cubby. After reading it, she sinks down onto the bench beside me.

"Congratulations," she says.

She doesn't sound bitter, or even jealous—just tired.

"You're the peasant they want," she adds.

Peasant was one of the words banned after the Revolution, except in historical context. I don't think I've ever heard Annie say it. Not in reference to herself.

Nor in reference to me, though it's been my official identity for as long as she's known me. It is an omission on her part that I've been conscious of since the orphanage, when I was less skilled at hiding where I came from, and that she's only ever since acknowledged with certain silences.

I speak through a rising discomfort. "That's not how—Atreus would never think of it like that—"

Annie's head is tilted back as she studies the ceiling. "Atreus would. He needs riders in the Fourth Order who pass muster with the elites."

The Fourth Order will be the rank given to the four riders who win today, signaling that of the thirty-two riders in the corps, they are the four most skilled. It's the highest ranking in the fleet below Firstrider.

"You're talking about—"

"I'm talking about succession."

I freeze on the word; Annie sounds short of breath to utter it aloud.

Before he ends his stewardship of the new regime, Atreus's successor will be chosen from among the best and the brightest of the Guardians. The next Protector. All but officially, that selection pool will be made up of the Fourth Order.

"He's thinking about succession," Annie repeats, "and he needs peasants who don't still—act like it."

I speak through gritted teeth as I yank the straps of an arm guard tighter on my forearm. "You don't *act like it*."

Annie lets out a faint laugh. We both know I'm lying. I can guess as well as she what the ministry probably has on file: that Annie is known for being too deferential, too reserved, for having trouble with situations that require public speaking. She's been at the top of the class for as long as I can remember but almost never raises her hand.

She could train past that. She could find the confidence if she tried and had the resources. But how is she supposed to look for that, to think she even *should* look for that, if the ministry sends her letters like this?

Something else, then. Something that has nothing to do with the ministry.

"You said you had family coming today?"

I ask the question gingerly, unsure whether I should ask it at all. Annie blinks, then shakes her head. "Not family. Friends . . . from my village."

My village are two more words Annie usually avoids saying. She enunciates them carefully, as if they're foreign.

"They wrote," she goes on. "A letter. Not from the parents— they don't read." I risk a quick glance at her; her face begins to redden at *read*. "But their son's been in school since the Revolution, so he wrote. That they'd be coming. They were the family who I was with for a bit before Albans."

Albans was our orphanage. She hasn't mentioned her circumstances before it, at least in front of me, in years.

She fiddles with her hair, pushing a few strands out of her eyes and behind her ear. "I haven't seen them since—" She looks up and I realize I'm staring at her; I look away and she does, too, seizing her boots, jamming one foot after another into them.

"I bet your making Fourth Order would mean a lot to them," I tell her. "It would probably mean a lot to anyone coming in from the countryside to watch the tournament. You'd be—"

Still bent over her boots, Annie prompts me softly.

"I'd be what?"

I hear myself say it. Words that would have shamed my father to hear said by anyone, let alone by me.

"You'd be making history."

Annie has reached for her helmet, the other gloved hand braced on her knees, about to push to her feet. There's a strange curve to her smile, a lift to her eyebrows, as she looks at me. When she speaks, she doesn't counter that I would, according to the lowborn identity I've assumed, be making history, too.

As if she knows I'm not. As if she knows that I am simply hoping, desperately, hungrily, to repeat it.

"Let's go, Lee."

2

THE FOURTH ORDER

Before he met the girl, the boy in the orphanage moved like a sleepwalker. Tasteless meals, hard beds on cold nights, the bullying and the beatings—he passed through all of it unseeing. Let them bully him. Let them beat him. They were nothing. Their language was the one he had listened to as he watched his family die.

Instead of listening, he remembered. He remembered his family around him, his sisters' laughter, his brother's teasing, his mother's voice. A world of light and warmth, great fireplaces tended by servants, ornate glass windows overlooking the Firemouth, chandeliers hanging low over tables piled high with food. He remembered the sight of his father at court, resplendent as he received his subjects. He remembered lifting aloft, the city falling below, his father's arm steadying him as the wings of his stormscourge beat the air. Her name was Aletheia, and sometimes, his father allowed him to bring her scraps from the table.

"One day," his father told him, his arm around him as the highlands of Callipolis stretched below Aletheia's wings, "this

will be yours, if a dragon Chooses you. You will learn to rule, just as I did."

"Did your father teach you?"

"What he could. But much of it came naturally to me, Leo. Just as it will for you. We were born to rule, just as the peasants were born to serve."

He found that he could live in these memories for hours. And when they ran out, he invented futures: a dragon he would be Chosen by, dragonfire he would have power over, the people who had taken everything from him helpless and awaiting punishment. He imagined making them pay.

When he did this, it kept the real world, and the other memories, out. Nothing hurt so much as being forced back to the present.

That was what happened when he met the girl.

He could see through the doorway that it was one child against two larger ones. The girl struggled. It was all familiar.

But then, for the first time since he'd come to the orphanage, he found himself walking toward the violence rather than away from it.

He pulled a kitchen knife out of his pocket as he approached. The words in the other language came slowly, but they were there. "Go away."

At the sight of his knife, they fled.

As he knelt beside the girl, he realized he recognized her: She shared courses with him at school, despite the fact that she was at least a year younger than him and his classmates. She had scrawny limbs, scraggly red-brown hair, and clothes that were well-worn even by orphanage standards. He was struck, as he looked at her, by how small she seemed.

*It was the first time he had ever found himself thinking this
about someone else: In his family, he had been the smallest.*

"*You shouldn't have fought them,*" he said. "*They only
make it harder for you when you fight them. They only hurt you
more—*"

He stopped himself.

*The girl shrugged and looked up at him, her face wet with
tears, and he saw a bitter ferocity and determination there that
he recognized.*

"*Sometimes I can't not fight,*" she said.

ANNIE

No amount of practice prepares you for the sight of the arena's
stands completely full, banners flapping in the wind, trumpets
sounding the Anthem of the Revolution as the drums keep time.
Aela and I delight together in the searing blue horizon, the sharp
late-spring breeze, the city cheering below us as we perform the
opening ceremony. Moments like this, it hits me like it did the
first time: that the life I have begun to think of as routine is, in
fact, extraordinary. Today, in the stands below, the people are
watching commoners like themselves ride dragons. It's the kind
of thing that can't help making you feel proud of your country.

Even if it turns out that your country is not so proud of you.

But as that thought threatens to overwhelm, I feel Aela's
body, warm through the saddle, her presence soft at the back of
my mind. *Hold. Be still. Not now.* For as long as I can remember, Aela has been able to temper the feelings I couldn't. Even
in the very beginning, when I was still a child with lingering

nightmares of dragonfire. With Aela, they fell away. A dragon's comfort for a dragon's crimes. What would people from my village think? What would my parents have thought, my brothers and sisters? Questions I've never had answered, but when I'm with Aela, they don't matter anymore.

Together with Lee sur Pallor, we lead the aurelian squadron over the heads of the audience while the shimmering skyfish dart back and forth across the arena above us. As we practiced this morning, Cor keeps the stormscourge squadron high, their ash safely out of range of citizens in the stands below.

Atreus begins his speech after we've landed and dismissed our dragons. Even at a distance from the Palace Box, it's impossible to miss Atreus's presence, his close-cut steel-gray hair, his confident pose that more than makes up for his simple, muted garb. The only thing lost is the way his gaze makes you feel powerful. Important. Needed. When we first met him, as children freshly Chosen by the new regime's hatchling dragons, a shiver went down my spine when he said my name. Bound for the first time to Aela's, in drakonym, like a dragonlord's. *Antigone sur Aela, make your vows.*

What would it have been like, I can't help wondering, to receive a note of good luck from *him* this morning, instead of one of caution from the Ministry of Propaganda? What did Lee feel as he read those words? And is that why, standing beside me, he is able to look so unabashedly confident as he regards the waiting crowd—

But confidence has never been something Lee's been short on, notes from Atreus or no. That's been apparent from the beginning.

A lot of things have been apparent from the beginning, with Lee.

"Men and women of Callipolis," Atreus proclaims, "welcome to the quarterfinal Firstrider Tournament. Ten years ago, you made a historic choice. You chose to test everyone equally, to choose the best among you to become dragonriders, and to train them to lead. To bring Callipolis into a new era of greatness, of air power in the service of what is right. Of virtuous leaders and just rule. For the years between the old way of dragons and the new, you have allowed me to be your steward. Now I ask you to look to your future. To your Guardians. Four of whom today will become semifinalists for Firstrider, and members of the Fourth Order.

"In a few years I will say: May the most virtuous Guardian rule. But today, I say: May the best riders win."

The cheering goes up, resounding. It sets my blood on fire.

I take a seat on the stone bleachers beside Duck to watch the first match: his brother, Cor, against Rock, who rides a stormscourge like Cor, and comes from a highland serf family, like me. Rock has stubbly gray-blond hair, fair skin, and a hulking frame that earned him his nickname years ago. When the announcer uses his real name, riders on the Eyrie act surprised.

"Good luck, *Richard*!" they call.

Rock takes the ribbing in good cheer, exchanging a last few shoulder pumps with Lotus and Darius before heading down the stone ramp to the cave mouth alongside Cor.

For the first time since our conversation, the cool reassurance of Lee's voice saying what I already knew wavers. Lee was right—I'd be making history if I made it into the Fourth Order today. But so would Rock. And who doesn't like *Rock*? Boisterous, steadfast, confident? The kind of peasant even the patrician kids like . . .

It's not like my note said anything that isn't true. It's not as though I'd like public roles. Or want that much attention. I like winning, and I'm good at it, but there's more to this than winning a match. Making the Fourth Order would put me on display. I'd hate that. I'd be *bad* at it. Right?

But—

Beside me, Duck's leg hammers the bleacher, expelling nerves for his brother. Cor and Rock, down at the cave mouth, are blowing into the summoning whistles built into their wristbands, filling the cave with a sound that human ears cannot hear but their dragons have been trained to recognize. It is said that in the early days of dragonriding, riders could summon their dragons mind to mind—but that hasn't been done in centuries.

Their dragons emerge; Cor and Rock mount and take off. They stall above the arena at ten meters apart, level with the wall of the Outer Palace, the Inner Palace rising still higher, and the karst supporting Pytho's Keep towering over them. The bell rings, Cor advances, Rock swerves, and the realization hits me.

Rock's not good enough to beat Cor.

It wouldn't be an obvious call to the audience, but it's easy for me to see the signs: Rock sur Bast moves too slowly; Cor sur Maurana keeps getting within range. Though Cor's shots are going wide, as soon as one aims true, Rock won't have time to dodge. Tournament sparring is won by hits of unsparked dragonfire—a smoky substance called ash, which has enough heat to burn and blackens tourney armor on contact. The torso counts as a kill shot, the limbs as penalties; three penalties serve as a kill.

"Come on, Cor!"

Duck has gotten to his feet beside me, leaning against the railing of the Eyrie, squinting upward against the glare of the sun.

When Rock lands the first penalty—a lucky shot that blackens Cor's arm—Duck inhales like he feels the burn.

"Stormscourge fire. Nothing burns so bad, they say," says Power, who's joined us on Duck's other side. His movements on the ground are like his flying: lithe and predatorial as a slinking cat. His helmet is tucked under his arm, the sunlight glowing on his bronze skin and the shaven edge of his hair. Duck stiffens but doesn't look left.

"Care to comment, Annie?" Power adds.

Asking for my expertise on stormscourge fire is one of Power's favorite ways to taunt me. He likes to study my face while he does it, as I stare back woodenly. After so many years, it feels like a kind of tradition.

Duck's fists are curling. When we were kids, Power's allusions to what happened to my family got Duck riled enough to fight. Fights that he lost. Power's muscles are compact, his tactics in fisticuffs closer to a street rat's than a patrician child's.

"What do you want?" Duck growls.

Power leans close, too close, to Duck. His voice is a low murmur. "A long, slow roast."

Duck stiffens, and I place a restraining hand on his arm.

"Get away from us," I tell Power.

Our conversation is quiet, but it's caught the attention of riders on nearby bleachers. Lee and Crissa are closest. At my quelling glance, Lee remains where he is, but continues to watch. Waiting, poised to move.

Now Power's turned his attention from Duck to me, like a dragon on a new scent. Dark brown eyes bore into mine, teeth flashing in a smile. He inclines his head in a mockery of old regime obeisance, as if I were dragonborn.

I can feel heat in my face. As Power slinks away, Duck shrugs my hand off his arm. Though his eyes have returned to his brother's match above us, his breathing is light. "Hey, Annie?"

"Yeah?"

"Want to come with me to see my family during the break?"

"I thought we're supposed to wait till the end—"

"I think I'd better do it before."

I think of Power's eyes, fury-lit, and feel the helpless ache that I associate with watching Duck get hurt. Power sur Eater has hospitalized other riders before.

"All right."

Duck takes his eyes off the match long enough to smile crookedly at me. The wind tugs at his wavy hair as a sheepish but stubborn shrug pulls his shoulders up, like his good humor is itself an act of defiance. When I first met him, he took my hand and led me onto the roof of the Cloister, just to look at the stars. At the time, I hadn't understood. Just to see the stars? We can see them anytime. *Not like this,* Duck told me. *You'll see. They're beautiful.*

And I wasn't prepared for how beautiful they were, so close and still on that crenellated rooftop that they seemed near enough to touch. We got caught, but it was worth it. It was the first detention Goran ever gave me that I completed smiling.

The crowd is erupting. Cor has dived down, swept close, and landed a third penalty shot against Rock. Duck lets out a triumphant yell, his fist pumping the air.

Cor sur Maurana landed a kill shot. The match is over.

I'm the only highlander left in the running.

On the Eyrie, Cor and Rock dismount with the telltale stiffness of fresh burns. The announcer proclaims Cor sur Maurana as the first member of the Fourth Order, and Cor waves his arm in the air. An adrenaline high makes his grin seem a little crazed. Rock is welcomed off his dragon by his friend Lotus, who helps him limp over to the railing while his stormscourge takes off for the caves.

"You put in a good fight, friend," Lotus says. The son of a celebrated patrician poet, Lotus's wiry hair, brown skin, and lanky frame are a study in contrast to Rock's highland build.

Rock dusts his hands together. "Now, for our wager on Lee and Crissa?"

As Guardians, we've taken vows forswearing the earthly pleasures of money, marriage, and offspring—but gambling still finds a way, at least where Rock and Lotus are concerned.

"Yes indeed," says Lotus. "I'll raise you a Dragontongue translation that—"

"You know we can *hear* you," Crissa interrupts them. "And I assume you'll be betting on me, Lotus. Since I'm your squadron leader?"

Lotus gulps. Crissa smirks, then catches Lee's eye and pounds a fist into her palm. "Ready, Lee?"

Clad in scale-plated tourney armor, unsmiling, with his dark hair, gray eyes, and high cheekbones, Lee looks more like a warlord from a tapestry of the Bassilean Wars than an opponent to trash-talk. But Crissa is undeterred. And to my surprise, Lee lifts an eyebrow at her. A minute rejoinder that is enough to make Crissa blush.

Another bet going on, in the girls' dorm: how much of Crissa's flirting it will take for Lee to—in Deirdre's words—*succumb*. Deirdre and Alexa started it, and even Orla joined in eventually.

Crissa knows about the pot and thinks it's funny. I avoid conversations about it. There have been no payouts.

Lee and Crissa make their way down the ramp to the summoning point, and the sound of Deirdre's and Alexa's giggling from a nearby bleacher grates in my ears. But when they launch into the air, the Eyrie falls silent. All concerns with Crissa, her flirting, and Lee's inscrutable responses to it fall away at the sight of Lee flying.

I'm Lee's sparring partner so often that I rarely get the chance to watch him. Lee and Pallor move with a perfect balance of fluidity and precision, never overshooting, never falling short, never holding back. It's so beautiful that I find myself holding my breath, aching to get in the air myself. I want to be the one responding to their attacks and retreats, to feel the intoxication that comes from sparring with someone who pushes you to fly your best, your most daring, your hardest.

Crissa is probably our strongest skyfish rider. She knows how to turn her skyfish's natural speed and flexibility to her advantage. But even this does very little against Lee's pinpoint control.

"Why does he keep missing openings?" Rock murmurs.

But he doesn't know Lee's style as I do. Lee isn't missing openings. He's just not going for anything less than a kill shot.

Finally, Crissa grows impatient, veers in a roundabout, and charges. Lee swerves left a split second before Pallor fires. Pallor's first breath of ash is the one that wins the match: The front of Crissa's cuirass blackens. Lee won without a single penalty.

When he lands and removes his helmet, his face—in contrast to Cor's startled euphoria—is completely calm. He finds Crissa, who smiles with contained disappointment as she shakes his hand. Lee maintains a look of stone-faced tranquility as the sound of cheering comes from the stands and the announcer declares him the second member of the Fourth Order. It's like he's been waiting for it.

I feel a twinge of something between bitterness and admiration: It comes so naturally to him. Not just winning—but thinking he *should* win.

And then the rejoining thought, unwanted but undeniable: *Of course it does. Of course it comes naturally to him.*

It'd come naturally to you, too, if you were dragonborn.

The term feels dirty. Like *peasant*, banned, except rather than from the lexicon, it is banned from my mind in reference to Lee. Sneaking into my thoughts now only because he looks so bloody *poised*.

Of course, his birth was never *substantiated*—

But it never really needed to be substantiated.

And it never mattered. What matters is, Lee flies well. He's a good leader, and he's my friend. He deserves to win. Why should I begrudge him the comfort he has in doing it?

Why should I begrudge him the First Protector's favor, this supposed slum orphan with all his unexpected confidence and grace—

A twenty-minute break has been called before the final two matches: Duck's against Power, and mine against Darius. The riders who've already sparred are making their way down the Eyrie stairs to the Palace entrance, where medics are ready to treat their burns during the break. Duck touches my arm.

"Coming?"

Duck's family is sitting in the Bronze section, reserved for *skilled labor*; below them is the Iron section for *unskilled labor*;

high above them, on either side of the Palace Box, are the Silver and Gold sections, for the *spirited*—meaning military— and *philosophical* classes. Before the Revolution, your family determined your class—commoner, patrician, dragonborn—but under the new regime, class is something you're tested into.

"Looking for someone?" Duck asks.

I'm scanning the crowd, ignoring the stares that our armor is attracting, looking for faces from my village. Where are they? Aren't they here? They would definitely be class-bronze; farming counts as skilled labor. This is the section where they would be sitting.

"Dorian! You're here! And Annie!"

The Sutters surround us. I'm embraced by Duck's mother and his two sisters while his youngest brother jumps onto a bench and launches himself into Duck's arms. The Sutters, much like Duck, have always been unquestioning in their welcome.

"Exciting about Cor, isn't it? Do you think he could make Firstrider?"

Duck squints: I wonder if we're both weighing the likelihood of Cor having a chance when Lee's a semifinalist, too. "Maybe. But Firstrider's more of an honorary title in times of peace."

"There might be a war," Duck's younger sister Merina points out. Her pigtails flop as she bounces on the balls of her feet. Like all of the Sutter children, Merina has her mother's tan complexion and her father's hazel eyes and wavy hair.

Duck laughs and shakes his head. "Probably not." He ticks off, comfortably: "We've got a good relationship with Damos, the dragons of the Iscan Archipelago are sworn neutral, the Bassilean Empire's been in decline for centuries . . ."

Duck has said nothing more than the baseline of what we've

learned in class about the geopolitics of the region, but his family stares as if he'd jarred them. The Sutters own a bakery in Highmarket. They've always taken pride in Cor's and Duck's advancement, but with a certain wary incomprehension.

Mr. Sutter says, with an odd strain in his deep voice, "There's New Pythos. They've got it in for us, haven't they?"

It's an attempt to keep up in displays of knowledge, so awkwardly delivered that I feel peripheral shame. Duck hoists his little brother Greg up onto his back, lines appearing on his forehead as he considers how to answer. Mr. Sutter doesn't realize it, but he's just betrayed his educational level. For years, New Pythos has been rumored to harbor survivors from the Three Families that escaped the Palace Day massacres, but its military might is known to be negligible. The island doesn't have dragons. Or air power. Not even a naval fleet, because the karst pillars that surround it make its waters nearly impassable. But the Ministry of Propaganda keeps up rumors of a New Pythian threat among the lower class-metals all the same. They are— as the propaganda officials tell Guardians in class—*useful*, for inspiring patriotism.

An explanation that's easier to take in stride before your class-bronze dad repeats it to you.

Duck agrees slowly. "That's true. There's New Pythos."

Mrs. Sutter's arms, perpetually flour-dusted, are placed on her hips as if to ward off the tension that she senses rising between her husband and son. "War or no, Fourth Order's an honor in its own right."

Merina pipes up eagerly. "We were learning about that in school this week. Fourth Order means they're considering you for next Protector. Cor'll be doing more rounds and speeches and going to fancy parties with the class-golds and sort of auditioning—"

They're learning about the Fourth Order in *school*? The thought of children across the country talking about us fills me with anxiety. Even as I remind myself that of course they are. It's relevant to them. *We're* relevant to them.

The ministry would like to remind Antigone sur Aela of the intensely public nature of the obligations of a Fourth Order rider . . .

Ana, the oldest girl in the Sutter family, shudders. "That sounds terrifying. Better Cor than me."

Tall, bony, plain-faced, Ana has just summed up my own feelings. I feel a rush of fondness for her.

"Have you taken your metals test yet?" I ask her.

A year younger than us, Ana is in her final year of school, when the metals test is usually administered. She nods, then flicks her bare wrist. "Results aren't back yet. But I don't test well like Duck and Cor."

When the results are returned, Ana will wear the wristband her test assigned her. Her parents' bronze wristbands flash in the sun, the mark of skilled labor. Duck's and mine, the rarest in the city, are gold entwined with silver, indicating that when we took the test as children in the Guardian talent search, we tested as both *philosophical* and *spirited*.

The bells are ringing. Duck's shoulders set at the sound as he remembers what comes next. Power. "Time to be getting back."

Mrs. Sutter hugs me farewell, an unthinkingly maternal act that leaves me flustered. "Good luck at your match, dear. You'll come for Midsummer this year? No excuses this time."

"We will drag Annie and Lee bodily from the Cloister if need be," Duck assures her.

On the way back up to the Eyrie, I crane my neck to search the crowds in the Bronze stands. But there's still no sign of anyone from my village.

Maybe they didn't come.

It'd mean a lot to the people in your village if you made Fourth Order, Lee said this morning.

It's funny how much the thought of it mattering to them matters to *me*.

I'm so absorbed straining for a sight of them that I practically stumble into Darius, my match opponent, descending from the bleachers in the Gold section. He's blond, tall, well-built like a statue of white marble. He has friends with him, other patrician boys who've tested Gold. I know most of them by sight; Guardians attend many of their classes with the Gold students— they're our future peers, coworkers—underlings. Many of the officials I do rounds with when I tour the Inner Palace and other branches of government are their parents.

And all of them would love for Darius sur Myra to make the Fourth Order.

Darius sees me, stops dead, and then gestures at the stone archway we're both about to walk through, the picture of gentility. "After you, Annie."

Dragons. I'll throw it. I've got to throw it. What were my vows for, if not obedience to the will of the state? And the state wants this boy. It hurts but I don't *blame* them. I just went cold from the thought of mere *schoolchildren* talking about me, didn't I? Darius isn't my favorite person but he's decent, he'd do a fine job—

Duck and Power are up next; Darius and I will close the tournament.

On the Eyrie, Duck, who is now rigid with nerves, submits to his brother's check-over of his suit and his murmured advice. Power's stormscourge is large enough that he doesn't have to worry about fire conservation and precision; Eater pretty much never runs out. Duck's best strategy is to move, move, move, and hopefully wear them down.

"And no—bloody—spillovers," Cor hisses.

Most of the time, the line between our emotions and our dragons' is dim, subliminal. But with violent flares of emotions, the walls break down, and you share everything. Spilling over can be a rider's greatest advantage or greatest weakness. Some riders, like Power, spill over on purpose; Lee and I don't, though I'm more comfortable sharing minds with my dragon than Lee is. Duck's the sort of rider who spills over easily and shouldn't. In his and Certa's case, it never ends well. They lose control.

Duck and Power walk down the ramp; Lee goes to stand beside Cor and Crissa, and though I don't usually seek his company when he's with the other two squadron leaders, I find myself moving toward him as if pulled. Stress reaction, orphanage behavior—I diagnose it even as I let myself do it. When he sees me approaching, he breaks away to join me at the Eyrie's edge. Side by side, we lean against the rail to watch.

Duck and Power assume position overhead. There's silence on the Eyrie again, as there was for Lee's match, but this time it's silence of a different kind. Even Rock and Lotus have forgone making bets.

And then it begins. Power sur Eater attacks; Duck sur Certa retreats; and then Duck sets off, Power in pursuit. But Power must figure out Duck's strategy soon enough, because we hear him shout: "Running? Brings me back to the good old days, Dorian!"

"Tune him out, Duck," Lee murmurs, his gray eyes fixed on Duck's mother-of-pearl skyfish, his fingers tight on the Eyrie railing.

But Duck has never been good at tuning Power out. Sure enough, a telltale ripple goes through his skyfish. Not something the audience would notice, but we can tell it's the first sign of a spillover.

And then Duck makes a jackknife turn and fires. Power dodges; the ash passes harmlessly over his shoulder; and he takes advantage of the close range to fire himself. He hits Duck on the leg, full heat.

The audience gasps in appreciation and the bell rings to mark the penalty; but on the Eyrie, muttering has broken out with a different realization. Duck's opening was wide; Power could have made a kill shot. Instead, Power went for a full-heat penalty.

A long, slow roast. Power's going to draw this out.

The two of them back out of range while Duck opens the coolant shafts on the leg of his flamesuit, a temporary pain reliever that will delay his reaction to the burn. Then they reset and advance again. By now, Duck has unmistakably spilled over; Certa is twitching at odd moments, her movements uncoordinated. Whatever emotions Duck is experiencing are now reverberating, dragon-size, between the two of them. Power scores his second penalty hit barely a minute later, this time across Duck's arm and side. Again, avoiding a kill shot even though he had the opening; again, full heat.

I'm beginning to feel sick to my stomach.

Stormscourge fire. Nothing burns so bad.

I can feel memories rising like a coming storm. Predictable.

I should have seen it coming, the one way this morning could get *harder*. Not this, not now, of all times—

But once it starts happening, it always *keeps* happening. And so I clutch the rail and will the world around me to stay in focus.

I can feel Lee's eyes, which should be on the match, on me instead.

Behind us, Cor says, "Master Goran, call a foul."

"It's not a foul to make a kill shot and miss, Cor."

Cor rounds on our drillmaster. His voice is shaking. "Power is playing with his prey before he eats it."

Goran's tension with the three squadron leaders has never exactly been a secret, though none of them has ever acknowledged it: Atreus, not Goran, appointed three lowborn riders, one of them female, to leadership positions within the corps two years ago.

"Power has done nothing illegal," Goran says.

Cor makes a choking sound. He turns from Goran. Crissa lays a hand on his arm.

"I'm going to fetch the medic," she says. "Why don't you come with me?"

He shrugs her off. "*No.*"

I'm pretty sure my face is showing nothing, betraying *nothing*, but all the same Lee has stepped closer to me so our sides are touching and places his hand beside mine on the rail. A silent invitation, where no one will see it but me. For a second, I fight the urge. But the world is going in and out; the memories are closing in; the thought of Duck up there, hurting, with no way out, threatens to overwhelm. I give in. Seizing Lee's hand and holding, focusing on his grip. I'm pretty sure my nails are digging into his skin, but he doesn't pull away, only returns the pressure. I don't look at him.

Overhead, Duck seems to have abandoned—or perhaps forgotten—his original strategy of keeping distance. He and Power are circling each other, Duck's skyfish rippling with their shared emotions. Within seconds, Power takes his third and final shot. Though it need only be a partial hit to finish the match, he makes it a kill shot anyway. Duck is engulfed in thick black smoke. When it clears, his silhouette is stiff on his dragon. They descend slowly behind Power and Eater to the Eyrie. Power dismounts. He's smiling.

"Hope he's all right," he says. "That came out a bit more forcefully than I intended—"

Cor launches for him with a wordless cry. Lee's hand tears free of mine to help hold him back.

Goran and the medic cut the straps tying Duck's boots to his stirrups and ease him from Certa's back. Her gaze is vacant: the expression of a dragon whose rider is unconscious. I take in the sight of Duck's limp figure, the smell of smoke, and feel the panic roll over me in cold waves.

Nothing burns like stormscourge fire.

Lee steps forward and then, when he realizes I am moving with him, turns and catches me across the waist, holding me back. He turns me toward him, seeking my eyes.

"Annie."

"I have to—"

I'm straining to get past him, unable to speak, barely able to see Duck for what I can no longer fight remembering. The memories of stormscourge fire engulfing my whole world while I watched and could do nothing.

Then Lee's blazing eyes find mine. The world stills. Everything else falls away.

"I'll take care of him. You need to go."

At first I don't understand. And then it comes rushing back: my match. I still have a match.

A match that I'm not supposed to win. A match that no one in my village came to see. A match that, if I win, will thrust me into the kind of spotlight that makes me ill to imagine.

The ministry would like to remind Antigone sur Aela of the intensely public nature—

—vows to serve the state—

I look from Cor, as Crissa strains to hold him back, to Duck, unconscious as the medic removes his armor; to Power, watching with a satisfied smile. Then I look to the cave mouth, where Darius waits for me, wrist lifted to his mouth to summon his stormscourge as his family and friends watch from the Gold stands.

And then all those things fade away, and all that is left is a single thought:

Like hell am I throwing this match.

I look up at Lee and nod. Whatever he's searching my eyes for, he seems to find. His hands drop from my shoulders and I turn from him to walk toward the cave mouth.

"Annie," says a different voice.

I stop again. Goran's hand has taken my shoulder. I look back at him.

"Remember what the ministry wrote you about," Goran says.

He towers over me, broad-shouldered in his uniform, the figure that for years I've associated with the sour taste of my own inadequacy. For a moment I feel a clarity that's piercing and bright. The kind I usually only feel with Aela, except this time, I find it alone. Crystalized within it is an anger I had forgotten I possessed.

I turn my back on him without a word.

LEE

There is a moment when it happens, usually somewhere between summoning and launch, where Annie transforms from the person she is on the ground to the one she becomes in the air. Where the hesitation vanishes, the awkwardness falls away, and suddenly she's free. Unleashed.

As many times as I've seen it happen, today I am struck by it as if it were the first time. As she and Darius rise into the air to take their positions, I can practically feel the surge of energy rising.

Duck is stirring, groaning; the coolant that Master Welse applies is beginning to do its work. Keeping my eyes on Annie's copper-toned aurelian, I rise from their sides to go and stand beside Goran.

"Looks like it really did the trick," I tell him.

His eyes remained fixed on the dragons above us, and he responds with irritation.

"I'm sorry?"

"Whatever you just said to her."

The bell rings. Darius and his iron-gray stormscourge charge forward, while Annie and Aela turn upward and begin to rise.

Racing the pull of gravity, charging full speed into the

cloudless sky. So fast, so sure, so beautiful that the hair on the back of my neck stands on end.

The others might not see the difference, but I do. Annie flies like something out of the old order. She always has. The instincts that were trained, for me, by a childhood of watching dragons with their riders are, for her, instincts she was simply *born with*. After all, the riders of the new regime have no role models of mature riders. We do not have the luxury of being trained by our dragonriding fathers, whose own training came from their fathers before them.

Whatever guidance my father could have given me died with him. But Annie has never needed guidance at all.

Darius realizes what's happening a split second later and urges his stormscourge up after her, to regain the vertical distance, but she's already taken the lead, and in any case Aela is faster and lighter than Myra.

There are whistles of delight around us as the other riders realize what Annie's doing. Height is always an advantage; gravity is a weapon. But the most obvious way to use it—descending from on high with double the speed of your opponent—is the kind of maneuver very few riders have the skill to pull off. I feel a smile breaking my face. Goran is silent, his brows scrunched up as he stares upward into the sun.

The gap widens as they rise; slowly, as they become mere points of darkness against the sky, each begins to slow. And then Annie, a mere pinprick above us, stalls.

For a moment everything is still.

She dives.

Darius, hovering below her, wavers and stalls, preparing for her attack. There are screams around us: from the other riders, from the stands. Aela's wings are beating at full force, maximizing her speed in free fall; she is hurtling toward Darius. And then when they are in range, it happens in a blurring instant: Darius fires, she swerves, it misses, and she fires into an opening that only she can see. And then she's hurtling past him, toward the Eyrie, and Darius is following behind. The front of his armor is blackened with a kill shot.

Annie won her match in a little under two minutes.

The bell is ringing as Aela skids and clatters onto the Eyrie edge. Annie slices the straps fixing her boots in their stirrups and leaps off. She takes off her helmet: her red-tinged hair, the same color as Aela's scales, glints in the sunlight, streaked and flattened with sweat. Her expression is defiant, almost angry. But then at the sound of the screaming and cheering it changes: Slowly, haltingly, as she makes sense of it, she begins to smile.

Darius dismounts laboriously. Annie goes to him and offers her hand. She seems surprised when he shakes it.

Antigone sur Aela, the final member of the Fourth Order, the announcer tells the crowd.

I have moved toward her, pulled by the magnetism of her beaming smile; as I congratulate her and our eyes meet, I see her smile change and briefly soften. As if she recognizes, in a fleeting moment, the same thing I do: The tournaments aren't over; the bracket is narrowing; she and I are, after today's results, set on an increasingly likely collision course.

But that's still a long way off and possibly not a future at all. The way the penalties from today add up, the next tournament, in a month, will place me against Cor; Annie will face Power. And then still one more tournament to determine Firstrider.

Together, the four of us mount the stairs for the concluding ceremony. Duck has been taken to the Palace infirmary; Cor is reasonably calmed, but nevertheless, I take care to walk between him and Power. Annie's breath is still heaving, the sweat on her face undried.

It's not until we enter the Palace Box that I feel the familiarity of it roll over me in a wave I'd forgotten to steel myself against.

I have memories of this place.

Atreus is seated on the dais that once held the seats of the three triarchs who ruled together before the Revolution. Arcturus Aurelian, Kit Skyfish, and my uncle, Crethon Stormscourge. Now there's only the First Protector. Around him—in the seats that were once reserved for the most powerful members of the dragonborn families—now sit the members of his council and other officials of the new regime. The jewels and sumptuous gowns that I remember have been replaced by the simple uniforms of government functionaries. Instead of the triarchy's infinite loop of the circling dragons of the Three Families, the red banners rippling above us bear the Revolution's dragon, wings spread, breathing the four circlets of fire representing the four classes of the new regime.

There's an aisle down the length of the box, from the stairs we've mounted to the dais where Atreus waits. The last time I was in this place, I watched my father walk down it.

Beside me, Annie inhales the faintest breath. She looks from me to the faces of the adults turned toward us—the same ones who revealed themselves, this morning, to doubt her fitness for this moment. Annie's letter was unsigned, but the Minister of Propaganda, Miranda Hane, is standing in this audience, three feet away from Atreus, and her eyes are on Annie.

There's no time to exchange more than a glance, so all I can do is give Annie a smile and a nod forward as we begin our walk down the aisle. Annie's steps are paced with mine; her gaze, like mine, set straight ahead. I can practically hear her holding her breath as she imitates me.

This is how you do it. This is how you own a victory.

My father's rugged smile, his tired but triumphant gait, his sparking eye catching his older brother's with a muted shrug as he knelt to accept his laurel, return to me as I walk. The last tournament I saw him in, I was seven years old. A melee against the Aurelians, a bit of spring entertainment that was their calm before the storm in a year of growing unrest. Unrest that would become a revolution.

Now, ten years later, I bend a knee before the man who betrayed my father and my people. He places the laurel of the Fourth Order on my brow. Beside me, Annie takes a knee to accept her own laurel in turn.

In a concluding speech, Atreus refers to the tournaments ahead that will move us one step closer to the title of Firstrider of Callipolis, and after that, to the naming of Atreus's successor. One step closer to solidifying the institutions of a revolutionary regime that replaces the one held by my family for centuries.

The revolutionary regime that struggles to undo their centuries' worth of wrongs.

Annie stands beside me, her expression frozen, her breathing light and rapid, as these words wash over us. I marvel, with the part of my mind not lost in memories of another life, at the fact that this girl, who can stare down a dragon twice Aela's size, can be stricken by the sight of a few dozen functionaries' scrutinizing faces.

My father's voice returns to me from another lifetime: *It will come to you naturally, Leo. We were born to rule.*

No. That world is gone now, and I'm done with it.

And then, with a surging sorrow that I thought I had outgrown: *Forgive me, Father.*

ANNIE

Rock is waiting for me at the foot of the stairs, blocking the exit with his great frame, and he's beaming. It is not an expression I'd expect from someone who just lost his match.

"They're here," he says.

His highland accent has thickened inexplicably.

My stomach flips. "Who?"

"That family. From your village. Got here just before your match started; they're sitting next to my folks. You didn't tell me you had highlanders coming!"

He seizes my arm, and I follow him into the Bronze section, pushing through the crowds of people who part with excited congratulations as we pass. I register, only in afterthought, that the congratulations are directed at *me*.

And then I see them. A burly, graying man, a stout woman with her hair wrapped under a faded scarf, and a line of children beside them who share their parents' sunburned faces and yellow hair. They're older and taller, and also *fatter*—their bodies full and well-fed, no more jutting bones or too-taut skin.

"Annie," Mr. Macky croaks, with the highland accent that still brings me warmth, though it faded from my own speech long ago.

Mrs. Macky says, "Annie, darling, you did wonderfully. We're so proud."

"Thank you," I start to say.

But the words don't get all the way out, because I've choked on them.

And then Mr. Macky, whom I haven't seen since I was six, who last knew me as a freshly orphaned child sleepless from nightmares of dragonfire, puts his arms around me the same way he did ten years ago, and says, "That I lived to see the day when Silas's daughter rode a dragon. We've never been prouder of anything, Annie."

It's not a long reunion, but every minute of it feels like water on parched earth. They tell me how Holbin has changed since last I saw it—the houses rebuilt, new herds raised, wool sold to the city textile houses as a part of Atreus's push to grow trade and alleviate Callipolis's dependence on subsistence farming. At first, the Holbiners had been nervous of these innovations. But now, well-fed even in winter, their memories of the old famines long faded and their children attending sporadic schooling down in Thornham, Holbin has more to hope for and little left to fear. "Except dragons," Macky jokes, and then hastens to add: "But that's just people being backward. They'll see they've nothing to fear with you riding one, Annie. One day."

The Mackys' oldest son, whose letter reached me a week ago, hands me a bouquet of wildflowers that smell like home. When I compliment his writing—a childish script, poorly spelled and not punctuated at all, but for all that something I beheld as a miracle—he blushes. I remember him as a toddler; he's thirteen now.

Too soon, it's time to bid them farewell. They mean to drive back today alongside Rock's family, who offer to have them stay the night with them in their home in the Near Highlands at Thornham, on their way back to Holbin.

I weave toward the Palace entrance through a lingering crowd whose congratulations I receive with dazed gratitude in passing. Thumped on the shoulder, bronze and iron wristbands flashing on wrists as craftsmen and day laborers beam at me and usher me through their midst, calling out in the hard vowels of the urban accents. I'm shorter than most of them by a head.

"It's the highland rider! Antigone sur Aela!"

"How's that for a win!"

"*Told you*, Geoff, told you the girl riders could hold their own . . ."

"You flew very well."

I stop at the sound of the last voice. Low and toned with an accent that sounds faintly foreign, cutting through the murmur of the crowd easily. A young woman's voice. When I turn to look, I see that she's barely older than me, perhaps Crissa's age. Long, dark hair frames a narrow face and piercing gray eyes above a dark, full-length cloak.

"Thank you," I say.

"You are Antigone?"

"Yes."

"A worthy name. Uncommon. Are you from a patrician family?"

I shake my head, surprised that she doesn't know. "Holbin," I say. "The highlands."

A victor's laurel on my forehead, highland wildflowers in my arms, the words fill me with pride.

The girl's eyes flash in surprise.

"Extraordinary," she says. "And what about the other rider, the other talented one. What is his name?"

The other talented one. I don't need to ask whom she means, though I feel it would be inappropriate not to. "On the white aurelian?"

The traditional description of Pallor's color mutation, silver where most aurelians are shades of amber and gold.

"Yes."

"Lee. Lee sur Pallor."

"Lee," the girl repeats thoughtfully. "Where is he from?"

She is studying me intently. My pulse accelerates, and it is suddenly difficult to provide the needed answer.

"Cheapside," I tell her. "A slum orphan."

The Guardians' neighborhoods of origin is publicly available information. I cannot shake the impression, as I say it, that I am telling this girl something she already knows; that what she's really interested in is my face as I say it. But that makes no sense.

She must be from Damos. That's why she's asking these questions any Callipolan would know. Although she is pale, almost as pale as a Callipolan highlander . . .

"Indeed?" the girl says, her eyes still traveling my face. "Well. Congratulations again, Antigone."

And then she turns and walks away, pulling her hood over her head as she does. Below the hem of her cloak I can make out riding boots.

But then I look at the boots more closely. I take in the leather reinforced to resist heat, shafts for coolant, slits for bootknives, and slots for straps to tie in to stirrups . . .

Those aren't just riding boots. They're *dragonriding* boots.

I am still puzzling over her footwear as I reenter the Palace and return to the Guardians' Cloister, whose disjointed collection of repurposed servants' quarters and former dragonlords' studies surround a small central courtyard in a wing of the Outer Palace. This afternoon, the Cloister is deserted. The rest of the Guardians are out in the city with their friends and families, celebrating.

Except, of course, Lee.

"There you are," he says.

He's washed, put on his ground uniform, and taken off his laurel. But he's still flushed with triumph, his face lit by a half smile that makes him seem younger, less guarded, less tired. The face of someone who's glimpsed the future and found it bright.

"I was just about to check on Duck in the infirmary," he says, "want to come?"

Duck. How could I have forgotten? "Yes. Let me change first."

In the empty girls' dorm I pause before entering the washroom. Apart from the Guardians' banner, an entwined circlet of silver and gold, hanging above the doorway, the room is austere. But the Guardians' proscription from possessions doesn't prevent us from decorating our spaces in small ways. Crissa covers the wall of her desk with her drawings and bits of shells and sea glass from her hometown on the coast; some of the others tack up assignments they're trying to memorize or bits of their favorite Dragontongue poetry.

I go to my bare desk and place the wildflowers in my drinking glass. Then I remove the laurel from my brow and hook it on the wall.

I pull the ministry's letter from my pocket and read it again.

The ministry would like to remind Antigone sur Aela of the intensely public nature of the obligations of riders of the Fourth Order . . .

Maybe I read it wrong from the start.

Maybe it's a challenge.

And even if it's not, I'm going to tell myself it is.

Let everything that intimidates me about the Fourth Order be another test, another training hurdle, another set of skills to master. Even if I don't make Firstrider, even if I'm never chosen for Protector—I'll serve the state better by bettering myself. One step at a time.

I can make history one step at a time.

I tack the ministry's note to my wall, too.

3

FIRST SIGHTING

He and the girl were in an unofficial alliance. He didn't think of it as friendship, because it mostly consisted of sitting near her at meals, in the yard, in class, and—at first—not talking. After the episode with the knife, he'd gained a reputation for being deranged and dangerous, and that reputation was useful. People left him alone, and when he was in her vicinity, they left the girl alone, too.

He didn't really consider why he was doing this, nor did he realize that it helped him. She was a foothold out of the months of sleepwalking. Their silence turned into conversations. Sometimes she would repeat what he said, slightly differently, as if his pronunciation bothered her. At first, he was terrified that she'd realized what the accent meant. That he was someone other people wanted dead.

But she never seemed suspicious. Not even when he imitated her corrections, repeating them under his breath until he could say them right. When teachers called on him in class, he began to answer. The girl remained silent.

"You can read Callish pretty well, right?" he finally asked.

They were in the schoolyard. He handed her what he had learned, recently, was called a newspaper. It was an invention of the new regime.

"Read this to me."

By then he'd learned a few things about the girl: that she taught herself to read without a teacher, because no one in her village had been literate. And that she came from the Far Highlands, from a village that had been in his father's land holdings. He felt good about this. It justified his looking after her, because she belonged to him.

The girl took the newspaper and said, "Which part?"

He could think of no way to request news about the Three Families that wouldn't seem suspicious, and instead he just said: "Everything."

So the girl read to him. That newspaper, and others, too, as he found them. It was a time of great change on their island, and they couldn't help being swept up in what they read. The boy listened raptly to all news of the First Protector, the man who had saved him. And he couldn't help being infected by how excited the girl was about it all, even the things neither of them fully understood.

The most important event that they struggled to understand was a referendum that Atreus's post-revolutionary People's Assembly held concerning thirty-two dragon eggs that had survived the Red Month. Should the eggs be destroyed? Should Callipolis do as neighboring Damos had done centuries before, and become dragonless and democratic?

Or, if their dragons were hatched, and Callipolis remained an airborne nation, how would they decide which children would be offered to the dragon hatchlings for their Choosing?

The First Protector proposed a merit-based dragonrider selection process. Delegates from the coast supported this, arguing that air power was necessary to the island's military defense. But delegates from the inner countryside and the city's poorer districts argued that dragons had only ever been used to oppress and control. Still others argued that this third way would become something new, unknown since the beginning of dragonriding on the Medean: Guardians would be the dawn of a new era, of dragons in the service of justice.

The boy and girl shuttled back and forth through these arguments, debating them in echoes of what they read. The girl tended to oppose keeping dragons; the boy tended to favor them. But each was not without their wavering moments.

"I suppose it would be different, if the people riding dragons were good," the girl allowed.

The boy's concern, meanwhile, was one he didn't confide: Of course the dragons ought to be kept, he thought—but what would it mean, to have them ridden by commoners? The idea unsettled him deeply.

Atreus's proposal passed, narrowly. The Guardian program became something their teachers talked about in class, as well as something they read of in newspapers.

Its purpose served, Atreus dissolved the People's Assembly. He did not call it again.

Instead, the newspapers began to tell of a test that would be administered to all, giving the lowest a chance to rise, the highest to prove their worth, and the children of all an opportunity to test into the dragons' Choosing ceremony that had, historically, been reserved for the sons of the Three Families alone.

Finally, the article the boy had been hoping for came. It said *that not all members of the Three Families had been accounted for during the Red Month. Some of the dragonborn were missing. The article suggested that they had survived. That, their identities hidden, they had escaped to New Pythos and been given refuge. Though the boy's name was not on the list of missing dragonborn, others he remembered were.*

The boy told the girl: "I have to leave."

"The basement?"

"The orphanage."

The girl looked up at him. They were doing dishes over a basin of nearly frozen water, their fingers raw and shaking from cold. The girl had by now started doing her chores alongside him. She was teaching him how to work more efficiently, so he would be punished less often.

"Don't bother washing the backs of those plates, they're not the dirty part. But why would you want to leave the orphanage? There's food here."

"Yeah, but everyone here are just peasants."

The girl's brow furrowed. The boy turned his plate over and began to scrub its other side. He hesitated, and then confided what the news article had given him confidence to finally share with her: "The point is, I've got people who're probably waiting for me."

"In the city?"

"No. Somewhere else. Another island."

"Can I come with you?"

"Sure," he said. "Maybe you could be my maidservant or something."

"I don't know how to be a maidservant."

The boy considered: He didn't know how to be a maidservant either.

"I think they just wash things," he said. "You're really good at that. Want to plan the trip with me?"

It was winter, so they agreed that they mustn't go now. Spring maybe, or summer. And then there was the question of provisions and a backpack and what you put in the backpack. Sometimes they wrote lists of things they'd need, which was exciting. Sometimes they actually acquired items on the list, which was even better. They began to build a stockpile in an unused closet on the third floor, and sometimes they would go there and make inventories, or just sit next to the pile of goods and read newspapers together.

LEE

It's a relief to resume our usual routine after the weekend of the tournament. An early breakfast in the Cloister, bread and cheese tucked in my satchel for lunch later, then Cor and I head out of the Palace for a rounds session down in the Manufacturing District. Cor nods at the fourth pair of silver dragon's wings, pinned on the shoulder of our uniforms, signifying rank of the Fourth Order.

"Dapper, aren't they?"

"Yeah, I say we keep them."

Cor lets out a bark of laughter. I wonder if he, like me, is strategically avoiding the thought that in a month we'll be back in the arena, facing each other.

Early in the morning, this late in spring, the city is in full form. We leave the Palace through the gardens, opened to the public since the Revolution and overlooked by Pytho's Keep and the

Janiculum Hill, the patrician neighborhood on the Palace side of the river. Crossing the bridge over the Fer, Cor takes us along his favorite routes through his native Highmarket, quieter than the main thoroughfares where bustling shopkeepers hawk their wares to wealthier customers from across the river. But even on the quiet streets, Guardian uniforms attract attention. This soon after the public tournament, a few people actually point. A fruitmonger stops us to press cut melon into Cor's hands, bobbing his head in a half bow. It's an urban courtesy left over from Aurelian rule over the city, and we've been taught to ignore it.

"For the two Guardians as a thank-you for their service to the city . . ."

Cor thanks him for the melon, grinning lopsidedly. Outside the Palace, in his home neighborhood, the hard Highmarket vowels return to Cor's speech. He begins to gnaw his slice as we continue walking.

"We're not supposed to accept that kind of thing," I tell him.

"Do you want your half or not? I'm happy to eat it if you're too noble."

I wrest my melon from him.

Thanks to regular rounds with the Ministry of Propaganda, I'm primed to notice the posters changing as we pass through the city: In Highmarket, with its high concentration of skilled laborers, the posters tacked on walls laud the virtues of citizens who've tested Bronze: BRONZE IS BORNE OF STRENGTH AND SKILL. But as we pass into the poorer neighborhoods, Southside and the Manufacturing District, where unskilled laborers live and work, the posters change. IRON IS THE STRENGTH OF THE CITY, they read, and in addition to praising the virtues of Iron class, they praise the metals test itself and the wisdom of Atreus for instituting it. ANYONE CAN BECOME GOLD, these posters read. SCHOOL FOR EVERYONE MAKES OPPORTUNITY FOR ALL.

"Laying it on a little thick, don't you think?" Cor mutters.

"The posters aren't *wrong*," I point out.

I saw enough, during my years at Albans Orphanage, to mark the changes that have been made in the poorer neighborhoods over the years since the Revolution. New housing has been erected, roads are now cobbled, schools have been built in neighborhoods where literacy had been unheard of. For the most part, the people we pass seem well-fed—if a little poorly dressed—and they walk with the purposeful stride of the employed. The posters might be heavy-handed, but they're heavy-handed about changes that are real.

Cor *tsks*. "All the same," he says, "you'll notice that they don't bother putting up this stuff in Scholars Row or the Janiculum."

Scholars Row is the other Gold-heavy neighborhood besides the Janiculum. It contains the Lyceum—Atreus's university for the Gold students—as well as the War College for the Silvers. When the Guardians aren't on rounds sessions as a part of our government training, we split our classes between the two academies in Scholars Row. Cor's never stopped noticing its differences from the poorer neighborhoods, including the one he's from; my answer, that his home neighborhood is still better off than it used to be, has never been enough for him.

I stop at the door of a hulking warehouse off a dusty, windowless street, its sign faded over an oversize door. "This is it."

Fullerton's is one of the city's most successful new textile houses, on our rounds schedule to tour today before class. Rounds have a way of filling Cor's and my daylight hours where homework would best be done, leaving classes as something we're perpetually treading water to keep up with, but that's not the kind of thing you complain about. Heavy rounds are a sign of favor; and anyway, they're the real education. They're the part of the day you see what the city actually does, instead of hearing about it.

The Fullerton foreman is carefully dressed, closely shaven, and begins to sweat through his outer jacket as he gives us his tour. Afterward, we shadow him as he goes about his morning routine among the workers tending looms, bent over dyeing vats, filling stockrooms with shipments bound for Damos and Bassilea. Then Cor goes into his office to occupy him with additional questions while I pull aside one of the class-iron workers. In a lowered voice, I double-check the numbers the foreman gave us: wages, hours, breaks, days off. It's a system Cor and I devised years ago after we began to notice discrepancies. This is not, technically, part of our obligations on rounds, but it's become our common practice.

The girl I've pulled aside twists her iron wristband the whole time I talk with her, stammering her responses, eyes not traveling higher than the Guardian circlet emblazoned on the breast of my uniform, until I ask her where she's from. She gives me the answer I can already hear in her accent: Cheapside. I tell her I grew up there; she finally meets my eyes to answer, "I know." And then I'm able to get more out of her. How she's treated; if she has any complaints. She's close to my age, but the accompanying observations—that she's full-figured, pretty, wisps of brown hair escaping her scarf—I push away with discomfort. Power and Darius might enjoy the high of flirting with awestruck class-irons, but their vulnerability makes me want to do anything but. I pretend I haven't noticed the flush growing along her neck as we speak.

"Overall, how do you find your work?"

She seems surprised by the question. "It's honest, and I'm glad I've got it."

Sometimes, with class-irons, you can feel the resentment burning because of their test result, but most Cheapsiders are grateful for Atreus's programs. The Manufacturing District, the public works programs, the quarries and the mines all provide wages—albeit low ones—for those who previously struggled to find work at all.

Afterward, as Cor and I head back through the dusty streets to Scholars Row for class, we compare the notes from the worker with those of the foreman.

"Her numbers matched his."

"Did she report anything?" Cor asks.

"Nothing unusual. Her feet hurt, her back hurts. But overall, she's fine."

Back on Scholars Row, we enter the gate of the porter's lodge to the Lyceum. Coming from the barren, oversize proportions of the Manufacturing District, full of grim-faced workers hurrying down dusty streets, the serene beauty of the Lyceum is disorienting, with its intricate stone courtyards and carefully tended greens full of laughing, carefree scholars. Gold students are encouraged to pursue government work after finishing their schooling, but not obligated. Many go on to careers in academia, the arts, in trade. Cor sees a few other Guardians lounging under an oak and goes to join them; I head inside. We've got a spare half hour, enough time for me to finish up my reading for Diplomacy in the empty classroom before it starts.

I'm already walking into the lecture hall before I realize I've been hearing someone speaking inside it. Too late, I stop.

A single person is in the room before me: Annie. Sitting in her usual seat midway up the hall. She's staring at me, frozen. The room is silent now.

Annie was projecting, I realize. Talking as if she were answering a question, to the empty room. Her voice was raised louder than I've ever heard it in class. Practicing.

Good.

She's beet red. I back out of the room.

"I'll see you in a bit," I say.

"No—you can—"

"I'll finish my reading in the library."

A half hour later, I return to the lecture hall, where I take my seat beside Cor and Crissa, toward the front. Duck, stiff with bandages and still only allowed out of the infirmary for class, has taken his usual seat beside Annie in the back corner. The rest of the class is filing in, a combination of Guardians and Lyceum students, along with the occasional adult class-gold who's dropped by for the intellectual exercise. Gold students seated in the row below us twist around to congratulate me and Cor for our performances in the tournament while Crissa looks on, smirking. With anyone but Crissa, being congratulated next to the person you bested in a match would be uncomfortable, but Crissa's ability to laugh things off is legendary. After we're done fielding compliments from Gold girls, she leans over.

"Enjoying yourselves?"

"We are doing our civic duty," Cor says.

We all rise as Professor Perkins enters; when we've resumed our seats, he asks for a volunteer to summarize our reading assignment. Fresh off finishing it in the Lyceum library, I know better than to raise my hand. The reading was about New Pythos. It falls solidly into the category of discussions I don't volunteer to participate in.

For the first time in my memory, Annie's is among the hands that go up. Perkins's eyes, clouded with age and accustomed to her region of the classroom being a dead zone for volunteers, passes right over it.

"Lee?"

My stomach lurches. I watch Annie's hand droop.

"That was some fine flying at the tournament this weekend," Perkins adds, his light brown wrinkles doubling with a smile. A few appreciative whoops go up around the room, Cor thumps me on the shoulder, and it startles a grin out of me that lasts a half second.

"Thank you."

Then I look down at the reading, take a half breath, and steel myself. "The article says there's no way to prove the rumors about New Pythos having dragons aren't true, and suggests reassessing them as a threat."

Perkins nods and provides the counterargument: "But New Pythos has never been allowed access to dragons and lacks the hot springs that make for fertile hatching grounds. How could the ha'Aurelians have air power, Lee?"

Ha'Aurelians—half Aurelians—are the dragonless branch of Aurelian House that colonized New Pythos generations ago. Palms sweating, I answer again. "Offshore egg stockpiles. The author suggests that the Three Families might have hidden eggs. The dragonborn who escaped to New Pythos could have taken that knowledge with them."

The dragonborn who escaped.

I could practically recite the names of missing dragonborn in my sleep, and the ones I think of most often are my cousins, Ixion and Julia. Ixion was a little older than I, Julia closer to my age. After Palace Day the bodies thought to be theirs were too disfigured to be conclusively identified.

"Very good. Thank you, Lee." Perkins turns to the class in general. "What do we make of this theory?"

"Rather tenuous," says a girl with an accent of the liquid melody of the southern vassal islands.

"An excuse for warmongering," says another boy. Patrician, judging by the fine cut of his tunic and the clipped tones of his Palace-standard accent. "More fodder for the *People's Paper*."

There are chuckles around the room; the *People's Paper* is the paper that circulates among the lower class-metals, heavily regulated by the Ministry of Propaganda, and most Golds don't deign to read it.

Perkins nods. "Perhaps," he allows. "But the real difficulty with such theories is that, given our diplomatic situation with New Pythos, there is no way to prove them right *or* wrong. Callipolis and New Pythos have never recognized each other's sovereignty, and their only means of communication is through embassies of neutral third-party states. With such a lack of transparency, how can we know what they intend? Much less what they are accomplishing, shrouded by all that North Sea fog."

I leave class lost in memories. It's rare that I let my thoughts linger on New Pythos these days. The escape I used to plan so eagerly in my spare time with Annie, the distraction that was so welcome amid everything else . . .

The plans that ended up coming to nothing.

"Hey."

Present-day Annie has materialized in front of me, in the middle of the Lyceum courtyard, Duck at her side. Cor and Crissa are at mine. From Annie's purposeful expression I half expect her to bring up our encounter before class, but instead she jerks her chin sideways, toward the Lyceum Club.

"I want to have lunch."

The sounds of laughter come muted through the club's latticed windows. Neither of us has ever eaten there, though there's nothing preventing it—the only requirement for admission is a gold wristband.

Duck swings round to look at her, but she isn't looking at anyone but me. I've stopped walking. "You won't like it."

Annie has stopped, too, and her arms are folded. "We can go. Other Guardians go."

Certain other Guardians go. The Lyceum Club has a reputation for being more welcoming to certain Lyceum students than others—in other words, the ones from patrician families. Lotus, Power, Darius, Alexa, and Max, who grew up on Janiculum Hill and like to meet up with their grammar school friends, dine there regularly. For my part, I've never been interested in observing how the new aristocracy of Callipolis entertains themselves. The patricians from the Janiculum were intimately involved in Atreus's Revolution, their betrayal of the dragonlords key to its success—and now the metals test is something they benefit from. They tend, overwhelmingly, to test Gold.

I like the opportunities Atreus has created for the poor from neighborhoods like Cheapside. The opportunities he's made for the patricians of the Janiculum, I care less for.

"I want to try it," Annie says.

Then try it without me.

But that doesn't seem to be an option she's willing to consider. She looks furiously determined and at the same time frightened—as if, more than the club itself, her own initiative scares her most of all. It hooks me against all reason. I push away my foreboding.

"Fine," I say.

Duck, Cor, and Crissa are looking between us, mystified. Because, after all, why should *I*, Lee the slum rat, be the gatekeeper for this rite of passage Annie seems to have created for herself?

"You coming?" I ask Crissa and Cor.

"Got that thrill out of my system ages ago," Crissa says, hoisting her bag higher on her shoulder. "Cloister for me. Cor?"

Cor shifts, squinting at the club with apprehension. "Yeah, maybe some other time . . ."

"I'll go," Duck says to Annie.

The three of us mount the steps of the Lyceum Club. In the foyer, I stare down the host whose job is to check wristbands. Though we've never met before, he seems to recognize me and lets us in without even glancing at my wrist.

We enter a dark, wood-paneled dining room full of arguing students, aging professors filling the room with pipe smoke, and all ages in between. Class-golds of any age are welcome to dine in the club whenever they please, regardless of whether they're attending classes. The polished wooden tables are scattered with today's edition of the *Gold Gazette*, the preferred paper of the class-golds because of its greater editorial freedom. It circulates only within Palace and Lyceum walls.

"Lee! How are you?"

A Gold student I know from Damian Philosophy calls my name from a table in the center of the floor, where he sits with a few friends. Their meals are half finished, fluted glasses of summer wine nearly empty. They've turned and are smiling in my direction, beckoning.

"Care to join us? We can pull up chairs—"

I can almost feel Annie recoiling beside me: Sitting with barely known acquaintances seems to be more than she bargained for.

"Thanks, Ian. Don't trouble yourselves. Good to see you all . . ."

I return their smiles, clasp Ian on the arm, then lead Annie and Duck past them. As we cross the floor, I note the presence of other Guardians in the room, easy to spot in their uniforms: Power and Darius, unsurprisingly, with a few girls from rhetoric class; more surprisingly, Rock, at a private table with Lotus in a far corner. I lead us to an empty booth. Annie takes the seat with its back to two walls and scans the room as though she were on dragonback surveying hostile terrain; Duck eases himself in after her, with the care of someone trying not to aggravate burns beneath his uniform.

"Where's the serving counter?" Annie mutters.

"There isn't one."

"So how—"

Annie falls silent. A young woman has appeared at our table, wearing a variation on serving attire I haven't seen since before the Revolution. Hers is the only iron wristband in sight.

"May I take your orders, sirs and miss?"

Duck looks at the server in fascination; Annie goes red, as she does whenever she interacts with servants.

"What's on the menu today?" I ask.

The serving girl tells us; it all sounds better than anything I've had in years. I order, and then Duck, looking even more stunned by the choices she's listed, asks for the dish that incorporates bacon. Annie, who does not seem to have processed any of what we've said, mutters that she'd like the same as me, please.

"I'll be back with your drinks in a moment."

We watch her walk away. Then Annie twitches.

"What do you think her wages are?"

Because I do rounds with the Labor Draft Board, I know exactly what her wages are. "Decent. More than most class-irons make in the textile houses, and loads better than mining."

I'm beginning to acclimate enough to listen in on conversations around us, and the number of them happening in Dragontongue is startling—in most parts of the city its triarchist associations mean that Callish is preferred. But here, with so many patricians for whom Dragontongue is their native language, it's used freely. Heard colloquially outside language class, it sounds like a parody of the old life.

It's not that I'm opposed to censoring, per se, but wouldn't you agree that he goes too far . . .

I'd take a Damian red over a Callish any day, no question . . .

Our food arrives. We've always been well-fed in the Cloister, and coming from Albans I've never thought to question its quality; but this is something else entirely. Greens perfectly seasoned, steak that is seared on the outside and pink within, potatoes overflowing with butter. Annie takes one look at her meal, then attacks it with her knife and fork as if determined to consume it before it disappears.

It's been a long time since I've noticed how Annie approaches food—in the earliest years, she *scarfed* it, and I learned to imitate her—but in this context, a glittering dining room designed for laughter and leisure, it's hard to watch. As Duck begins to rave about his lunch, how it is the *best meal ever*, I slide a hand across the table and touch her wrist.

"Slower," I murmur.

She looks up from her plate. Her eyes widen and blink rapidly. She nods.

It is one of the strangest meals I've ever had. I'm aware of how it tastes—*good*, the way I remember expecting food to taste, before I learned to be grateful to eat at all—and I'm aware of Annie's eyes tracking me, determined to learn despite her flushed face. I become conscious of every habit of polite dining as I struggle to demonstrate them slowly, clearly, without comment, so Duck doesn't realize the lesson is taking place at all. Annie imitates how I pace myself, how I place a fork into the steak and a knife beside it to cut, how I don't let it grind against the plate, how I use the knife to guide peas onto my fork and place the utensils alongside one another when I've finished. The things you're taught to care about, when you're not afraid of starving.

By the end, I'm sick with shame.

"And how was it?" says the serving girl, returning to ask if we'd like coffee or dessert.

"It was the most amazing meal I've ever had," Duck says, so solemnly that she actually laughs. As we watch her take our plates back to the kitchen, his voice lowers.

"Do you think she finds it strange, being surrounded by people who . . ."

Annie finishes his sentence immediately, like she'd been thinking about it, too. "Who tested better than her?"

"Or were born into the kind of privilege that *made* them test better," I mutter.

Fresh off a meal spent demonstrating that privilege, the observation smarts particularly.

Annie's eyes remain on the dregs of her cider as she tilts the glass back and forth. Her reply is mild, but has a tone of finality to it.

"I like to think that everyone had to get here on their own merits. No matter where they came from."

I lift my eyes to her, willing her to acknowledge me in this reprieve by looking at me, but she only glances across the floor again. "In any case, most people are speaking Callish. A lot of it's Palace-standard, but there are Southside accents at that table over there, and Harbortown accents behind us."

I hadn't noticed, focused as I had been on the sounds of my mother tongue.

"Even if the Dragontongue representation is a little . . . more than proportionate to the Callipolan population," Annie adds grimly.

"I hope my sister's metals test went all right," Duck mutters.

Annie's hand slips over his on the table and squeezes it gently. She doesn't notice the way Duck goes still at her touch.

Then her wandering gaze catches on someone across the room and her hand drops. I twist around in my seat. Power has noticed us, and he's beckoning Annie over to his and Darius's booth. Some of the girls from rhetoric class are giggling behind their hands, catching each other's eyes.

"Don't do it, Annie," Duck says at once.

Eyes on Power, Annie tilts her glass of cider back and drains it. She returns the empty glass to the table, rises, and makes her way across the floor.

Duck watches her depart with a line between his eyes. "And she tells *me* to ignore him?"

ANNIE

In a month, Power and I will be facing each other in the air. But today, I approach his table in the Lyceum Club as if we're facing off already. When I stand in front of it, he spreads his arms and leans back, his gesture taking in the entirety of the smoke-filled, wood-paneled room.

"Welcome," he says grandly, in Dragontongue, "to my domain."

The girls sitting with Power look avidly between us, like they're getting a pre-tournament sampler for free. When I don't say anything, Power adds, in Callish, "I just said—"

"I understood you."

"Good for you!"

Power turns to the table. "Antigone, having beat my mate Darius here"—Darius glowers at him—"will be my opponent in the upcoming match." He switches to Dragontongue and lowers his voice conspiratorially. "She's a very ambitious serf."

Titters go around the table. One of the girls actually lets out a suppressed shriek, scandalized. Power turns back to me, his eyes glittering.

"Isn't that right, Annie?" he asks in Callish.

I can practically hear those watching us hold their breath. I know how this scene is supposed to go: I've seen Crissa stand Power down in front of others, smoothly dousing his ego with a few well-placed words. The delighted guffaws of those listening, to see him burned. I know that's what the table's waiting for.

But my mind draws a blank.

You idiot, what did you think *would happen if you came over here? You think just because you won a match you'd get better at* this?

"Yeah," I tell him, bitterness filling my mouth both at my words' inadequacy and the fact that they're in Callish. "That's right."

I turn on my heel and walk away.

That taste of bitterness continues throughout the day. My rounds schedule has never been as extensive as Lee's or even Duck's, and this afternoon I have only a single session shadowing Ornby, an elderly researcher who's vetting old Dragontongue literature for the Censorship Committee. Together in his dusty office we go over which texts should be banned, which should be translated for the general public, and which should be limited to Gold consumption.

"Feeling lenient, are we?" Ornby says as he reviews my choices. "I'd have banned the sympathetic portrait of a dragonlord entirely. You'd make it available to the general public?"

Still prickly from my lunch in the Lyceum Club, I shrug and offer one of Ornby's favorite phrases back to him. "It could help the people grow in sympathy."

Ornby's blue eyes crinkle as he shakes his head. "The Golds, maybe. But we can't complicate the narrative too much for the lower class-metals, or they'll get confused. Might even start wanting dragonlords back. You're cleverer than most people, Annie, you've got to remember that! Maybe you can handle the nuance of this piece, but they wouldn't . . ."

Usually, Ornby's mention of my cleverness—flattering and

always slightly conspiratorial—is enough to stop me from questioning censorship practices, but today my thoughts go to Duck's father spouting propaganda about New Pythos, and I feel a twinge of unease.

By the end of the day I've lost the good mood left over from the tournament entirely. Afternoon training begins with Goran spending a good half hour on the Eyrie praising Lee's, Cor's, and Power's tournament performances and not mentioning mine at all. It feels like evidence that life, far from changing since gaining the Fourth Order, is going to proceed with exactly the same frustrations as before.

After dinner, in another resumption of routine, I help Rock through his aerial-tactics homework in the Cloister solarium before study hall, where Guardians are getting a start on homework at shared tables and easy chairs. I'm more impatient than usual today, and it's setting us both on edge.

"You've got to keep the third dimension in mind. It's not a *field*, Rock."

Rock's problem set is spread between us, a web of diagrams I'm correcting as I talk him through them; at the other end of the table, Crissa sits doodling on her history reading and Duck applies aloe to his burns, sleeves rolled up to his forearms. The fading sunlight glows on potted plants lining wall-size windows and creeping along a glass ceiling, opened to let in the breeze. The solarium is the only part of the Cloister set aside for recreation.

Rock's hair is on end, his eyes bloodshot from squinting at my scribbles. "I get it in theory, all right? You're worse than Goran sometimes."

"You don't like how I explain things, go find Lee."

"I tried," Rock says. "He was busy."

Lee's busy schedule is the last thing I want to hear about. I glare at Rock. He folds his arms and glares back. A voice behind us interrupts.

"Annie! There you are."

I turn in my chair. The formidable, iron-haired Mistress Mortmane, directress of the Cloister, is on her way to our mailboxes. She hands me a memo that bears the ministry's seal of the four-tiered city, concentric rings of iron, bronze, silver, and gold.

"I'll just give you this personally, shall I?"

Her eye flickers in what might just be a wink before she moves on.

The memo, addressed "ATTN: Fourth Order Riders," contains a list of schedule changes for me, Lee, Power, and Cor, effective immediately. The sight of my name next to the words *Fourth Order* sends a jolt down my spine.

BEGIN ATTENDING:

ADVANCED DRAGONTONGUE POETRY

WEEKLY HIGH COUNCIL MEETINGS (IF NOT ALREADY ATTENDING)

ADVANCED ETIQUETTE AND DANCE LESSONS (TO BEGIN TWO WEEKS BEFORE LYCEAN BALL)

PRIVATE CLASS WEEKLY WITH THE FIRST PROTECTOR

I feel a smile spreading of its own accord across my face.

It's happening. Whatever Goran or Power might say or not say, however scanty my rounds schedule might still be, the ship has pushed off from the shore and I'm on it.

I arrive at Dragontongue Poetry the next day a few minutes

early; the classroom door is still shut. Of all the changes from the memo, this is the one I'm most certain I'll like—and do well in. Our study of languages of the Medean has been purely conversational classes until now, but I've always been interested in Dragontongue poetry, which is renowned for its beauty. The dragonborn—and Aurelians particularly, whose language it was first, before they came to Callipolis—are known to have lived and breathed their poetry, speaking as often in quotations as not, and began learning it by heart as children.

As far as the Inner Palace is concerned, knowledge of Dragontongue poetry is a form of literacy patrician families of Callipolis still value—and will expect of its rulers.

Lee is waiting outside the classroom, too. Far from sharing my excitement, he's fuming.

"I don't believe this. Of all the ways to waste our time—"

There are circles under his eyes; since his promotion to squadron leader he often looks tired during the school week. Cor appears at the end of the hallway, looking similarly sleep-deprived and similarly indignant.

"Is this a joke? *This* is our reward for making Fourth Order?"

Gold students have begun to arrive, giving us curious glances as they make their way inside the classroom; the Guardians are so outnumbered by Gold students at the Lyceum that our presence in new classes tends to be treated as a novelty. Neither Cor nor Lee moves to follow them; they seem to be agreed on lingering in the hallway for as long as possible.

"It's a cultural literacy thing," I tell Cor.

Cor lowers his voice, eyes tracking the arriving Gold students.

"Maybe for you. I haven't got your knack for Dragontongue. I'll just be embarrassing myself in front of a bunch of patrician kids . . . ah."

Power is sidling down the hall, already looking amused.

"Such long faces."

Cor scowls at him. "Piss off."

Power drops his bag with a thud between Lee and Cor. Two passing Gold girls glance our way, and Power rakes a hand over his close-cut hair, catching their eyes with a lifted eyebrow. They disappear into the classroom, giggling. "Word is, this class is pretty easy. *If* you've already got the *Aurelian Cycle* memorized, that is—"

Lee is leaning against the wall, arms folded. His lip curls. "Didn't know you were such a Dragontongue scholar, Power."

"I had tutors."

Lee tosses his head back and laughs. Then he smiles at Power. "Good for you."

The force of Lee's disdain makes Power flinch. He recovers with a startled shiver, gives Lee a strange look, and regains some of his confidence to share more Lyceum gossip: "I've heard the class is taught by a former court tutor, anyway. Got his start teaching Stormscourge brats before the Revolution. Guess he wasn't so loyal in the end—"

Cor snorts in spite of himself. Lee's smile hitches. For the instant before he fixes it, his whole body stills. As far as I can tell, I'm the only one who notices.

"We're going to be late," I tell them.

Inside the classroom, the four of us take empty desks at the back; the only other Guardian already enrolled in this class is

Lotus, whom I recognize even before he turns and waves by his curly head of hair. His connection to Dragontongue poetry through his father probably means he's here by choice.

The girl whose desk is next to mine leans in my direction. "Are you Antigone? Antigone sur Aela?"

The way she says it, I feel like she's talking about someone neither of us has met. I nod and she beams.

"Your flying this weekend was *amazing*," she says.

I return her smile with surprise, and the girl extends her hand. Her brown dress, a muted color against her tawny complexion and spiraling black hair, shows the signs of a comfortable patrician life: cut to knee length with the precision of a Janiculum dressmaker, and carefully pressed. "Hanna," she says. "Hanna Lund. Though I guess there's no reason you'd want to know who *I* am!"

I shake her hand, too startled to think of a polite way to disagree with such an unexpected remark.

"Our new students. Welcome."

The professor, a pale, balding, bespectacled man in his midthirties, has entered the room last and notes our presence with a gracious smile as he takes his place at the front of the room. "My name is Richard Tyndale, and I am absolutely delighted to have the four of you in my class. Let's see"—he consults a list, then looks at me—"you must be Antigone sur Aela?"

"Yes, but I go by Annie."

"We will use the full Dragontongue in this class, I think, Antigone. Very unusual name, for a highlander. And then we have Power sur Eater—"

Power lifts his fingers to indicate his presence. Tyndale smiles.

"Welcome. I'll be glad to tell your father that I've finally got you as my student. Cor sur Maurana—?"

Cor nods. Tyndale's eyes slide to the only remaining new student and he stills.

"Leo?"

Dragon's bloody sparkfire.

Lee's eyes widen for a fraction of an instant. "Lee," he says. "Lee sur Pallor."

Tyndale twitches. He hastens to correct himself. "Of course—my mistake—"

Leo. The unfamiliar name reverberates in my ears with the shock of an unexpected obscenity.

I want to hide it away and never hear it again.

As Tyndale turns from us, a few students glance at one another, exchanging looks of perturbed amusement. As if they're wondering how Tyndale could forget the name of a Guardian in the Fourth Order. Lee has sunk low in his seat beside me.

"I trust the four of you received the assignment I sent along with your primers? Good. Then let's get started. Volunteers to read the Dragontongue?"

The class is midway through translating the *Aurelian Cycle*, the epic poem considered the foundational text of Dragontongue literature. Hanna volunteers and begins to read. Her Dragontongue is without accent—the mark of a native speaker. I register in surprise that someone with such a background would ever think of me as *amazing*.

But then, as she begins to read about Uriel sur Aron, leading his people into exile from the destruction of the sun-bright island of old Aureos, Lee closes his eyes and grips the sides of his desk. It's hard to know whether the sight of his face or the sound of the words I'm listening to provokes my rising sorrow. Even if some of the words escape me, the tragedy of the line is clear enough, and still piercing.

"Antigone, why don't you translate first."

I practically jump. Tyndale is smiling in a way that makes me wonder whether I'm imagining the tone of challenge in his voice. I flip open my notebook, conscious of being watched by a classroom of strangers, and look down at my homework. The sight of my translation calms me at once: I've triple-checked it. I begin to read, and then, as Lee clears his throat loudly beside me, I remember to raise my voice. The way I've been practicing, in empty classrooms, at every spare moment since the Fourth Order tournament. When I'm finished, I look up to find Tyndale staring at me.

"Good," he says. But he doesn't sound pleased so much as surprised. "Did you notice anything interesting about that last line? Any figures of speech that caught your eye?"

Hands are going up around the room. Tyndale glances on them, then back at me. Giving me a chance.

Figures of speech aren't something you learn in conversational Dragontongue classes, but they were listed in the glossary at the back of the primer, and I read that glossary last night. I look down, twisting my hands together beneath my desk. "Ascending tricolon. Chiasmus with the nouns and adjectives. And an enjambment to the next line."

The hands are going down. Tyndale is nodding.

"Good," he says again. "What about the form of the verb. Anything interesting there?"

"A historical infinitive."

"Well spotted. And its paradigm?"

I recite it.

Tyndale catches Lotus's eye. "Looks like our poet's son has competition."

For the remainder of the class, Tyndale calls on me several more times and on Power and Cor enough to determine that Power's translations are from memory and that Cor's grasp of the grammar is rudimentary at best. He doesn't call on Lee.

At the end of class, when he dismisses us, he adds:

"If you have a minute, Lee."

Lee remains hunched, face downturned, while the rest of us exit the classroom.

In the hallway, I hesitate, foreboding coiling in my stomach. Should I wait for Lee? Make sure he's all right after whatever conversation Tyndale wants to have with him?

Would he even want that?

Would *I* want that?

No. I'm pretty sure—actually I'm absolutely certain—I wouldn't.

"Hey . . . Antigone?" Hanna Lund stands in front of me, bent to one side to counterweigh her book bag, tucking a stray curl behind her ear. A few of the other girls from class wait for her a little apart from us, watching. "Some of us go do homework in the library together, after class? If you want to join?"

It takes me a second to understand what she's asking.

A Gold student—an almost certainly *patrician* Gold student—is inviting me to do something with her friends? And nervous to do so, as if she fears *my* rejecting *her*? I shift my own book bag higher on my shoulder. She's taller than me—they're all taller than me—consistently, patrician kids are. I have to look up to meet her uncertain eyes.

"Yeah . . . I'd love to."

Hanna grins.

Lee will have to figure out the business with Tyndale on his own.

I don't begin to worry about him until he starts missing meals. Absent from dinner that evening, absent from breakfast the morning afterward. The first time I see him again is in class later in the morning, and the bruises under his eyes have grown so dark that he looks haggard.

What did Tyndale say to him?

The Fourth Order riders attend our first High Council meeting that afternoon—or at least, it's a first for some of us. I'm pretty sure Lee's been going for over a year already. We listen, take notes, and are told to ask questions later, at class with the First Protector.

His class is held in a conference room off his office. Like so many rooms in the Inner Palace, it overlooks the Firemouth, the cavernous central opening to the dragons' caves that, for the old regime, connected the Three Families' apartments directly to their dragons, a mere summoning whistle's blow away. On the other side of a wall of rippling glass, a stone balcony that once doubled as a lord's dragon perch looks out over the encircling windows of the Inner Palace. In other parts of the Palace, especially the halls repurposed to public use, the original dragonborn heraldry has been effaced, but here the stained glass edging the windows in red roses remains, a traditional symbol of Aurelian House. Atreus's own additions to the room are austere: simple wooden furniture, unadorned but well-made, and hard-backed chairs.

We rise when he enters.

"Please. Be seated," Atreus says. "We will not waste time with formalities in this setting."

We resume our seats, and Atreus takes his own, straightening the collar of a simple tunic that emphasizes his severe, hawklike features and a gray face weathered by experience. Atreus's monastic lifestyle is almost as legendary as his career: an orphaned patrician; a scholar in Damos; an advisor to the triarchy; and finally, the leader of the Revolution that brought it down. He's been known to say that Callipolis is his wife, the Revolution his child. That the Guardians will be his legacy.

"I have heard nothing but praise of the four of you," Atreus tells us, "and consider it a privilege to take part in the final stages of your training. I intend for our class to cover subjects ranging from the philosophical to the poetic. Both will serve a purpose to you as future statesmen: theory for the mind, beauty for the soul."

He sets two books on the table in front of him: his own *Revolutionary Manifesto*, written the year before the Revolution, and the *Aurelian Cycle*, in the original Dragontongue.

"But practical matters to start us off. Do you have questions about the High Council meeting?"

I raise my hand, all the way up.

This time, unlike with Perkins, Atreus's eyes do not pass over me.

"Antigone?"

LEE

There's a certain irony, after years of going unrecognized, to being noticed by your family's old poetry tutor.

After the other students are gone, Tyndale walks to the door, looks out in the hall in both directions, and closes it. His foot-falls echo in the empty, stone-walled classroom.

I'm racking my memory for anything about him that points to what he'll want to do with me now, but there's nothing. I was only six or seven the last time I saw him, and he mainly taught my older sisters.

"You're alive."

He says it with unmistakable relief. He stands in front of me, his palms braced on the desk at the front of the row I'm sitting in, and looks at me like I'm some sort of apparition.

So he doesn't mean to turn me in. I realize I've been holding my breath for the last minute, and exhale.

"How did you survive?"

He's switched to Dragontongue. Even as my breathing returns to normal, I feel a twinge of irritation. If he's so happy to see me, so happy to see I survived, why is he risking my safety for a *language preference*? Anyone could be listening outside the door. They would be more than surprised to hear a Cheapside orphan speaking native-level Dragontongue.

"Atreus intervened," I say in Callish.

Tyndale's eyes widen. "He saved you?"

I nod.

"And your family—did he save any of the others?"

He's still speaking in Dragontongue, and this question has an urgency to it that surprises me.

"No."

He's still waiting, staring at me, but for a moment I can't think of anything more to say that I can put into words. "It was too late for the others."

I try to say the words without thinking about them, but

images flash across my mind and empty it, and for one moment the whole classroom fades away.

Tyndale has turned away, as if swept by a similar emotion. "I'm sorry. I wouldn't usually say—but I suppose there's no reason not to, now. I was"—he gives a little half-lost laugh—"I was in love with your sister."

My sister. *Which sister?* I wonder for a second, then realize who it must have been. As if hearing my thoughts, he adds, "Penelope."

Her name, her face, everything about her comes flooding back. It's strange to hear her name on another's tongue—as if, after years of not speaking about my family to anybody, some part of me had stopped believing that anybody else could have known them.

He keeps talking, not like he wants to but like he can't bring himself to stop. "It obviously wasn't something that—had a future. I was lowborn, even if I was a scholar, and she was on her way to being betrothed to some Aurelian, I don't remember his name . . . but I loved her. Dragons, I loved her. Even though I knew she would never love me or be able to have me. I've never loved anyone like I loved her."

Penelope was sixteen when she died. I had not known about a betrothal; I hadn't thought of her as the sort of being that men fell in love with or married. She had simply been my oldest sister. My beautiful, joyful sister, who was always abandoning grown-up conversations to come and play with me. Her hair was dark, like mine, but it was long and wavy and used to fall around her shoulders like two curtains when she crouched to my height.

I realize that I'm a year older now than she ever got to be.

"When I heard—what happened on Palace Day—I just—"

He doesn't finish, just stops, and for me everything stops, too.

I sit completely still, feeling the ground beneath me slipping. I lean forward, brace my elbows on the desk, place my head in my hands, and wait for it to stop. Worst of all are the sounds that come with the images.

Tyndale is so lost in his own thoughts, I don't even think he notices my response. When he speaks again, his narrative has skipped forward. I let the words wash over me, and slowly the other sounds in my head recede and the images fade.

"I think I went mad for a little while, after it happened," Tyndale is saying, his voice hoarse, cracking a little. "Palace Day was one of the most terrible massacres this city has ever seen. Yes, the guilty were punished—but so were countless numbers who were completely innocent—just for being born into a particular family."

"Atreus punished them," I say, my voice sounding distant in my own ears. "Death penalties, life sentences. For the people who . . ."

I don't finish.

"Yes, he locked them up," says Tyndale, almost impatiently. "But he still has us celebrate it. Palace Day, a commemoration of *the brave beginnings of a new regime*. It's—a blight, a stain on the new regime that Atreus should never have allowed. When he did, that was when I knew."

"Knew what?"

"That he would be no better. That in the end, he might even be worse. The dragonlords—at least there was nobility in them. Not this cowardly, bureaucratic hypocrisy."

Tyndale doesn't speak in the tone of someone interested in a more nuanced point of view. An unexpected resentment comes to me. I remember feeling these things, or something like them. I remember the old dream and the old failure. But I was a child then; Tyndale was an adult. If he was so certain at the time, he could have done something.

"You could have set off for New Pythos, if you'd wanted. If you were so certain the old order was better."

"I tried," Tyndale says.

That stops me short. I prompt him.

"But—?"

"But I was told to wait."

That's not the reason I expect.

"By whom?"

"By people I think you would like to meet. People," Tyndale adds, with delicate emphasis, "who have been biding their time."

The sun is low enough in the sky to send orange rays horizontally across the room, lighting up the desks and Tyndale's silhouette, strewing jewels of color where it pierces through stained glass.

"You're talking about New Pythos. The ha'Aurelians."

I hear my own skepticism, despite my accelerating pulse: I've read too many bloviating editorials in the *People's Paper* full of such conspiracy theories. The nationalist sentiment they foment is too easily tracked, a predictable chemical reaction that the Ministry of Propaganda sets off when desired. "That's an idle threat. They're powerless."

"Or so they've led Callipolis to believe."

We look at each other, and I say nothing. Though my heart,

by now, is pounding. Perkins's words from Diplomacy return to me: *We have no idea what they're planning, shrouded in the North Sea's fog.*

Tyndale asks, "Does Atreus know who you are?"

I shake my head.

To my surprise, Tyndale smiles. "Perfect," he says. "You'll be well-placed."

Well-placed for what?

But there would only be one *what*.

"Would you like to meet them?" Tyndale asks. "I'm sure they'd like to see you again. I'm sure they've missed you."

My throat is tight.

Who? Which ones survived? Would they even know me—?

"I'm sure they would appreciate your help," Tyndale adds.

* * *

Lashing rain and dark fog blanket the North Sea. We're drilling by squadron: Crissa leads the skyfish drills; Cor the storm-scourge, and I the aurelian. My squadron tails one another through the rain, struggling to stay in formation through the poor visibility, and we race to break the surface of the clouds one after another. The blue sky and glaring sunlight are blinding when we burst through the last layer of rainclouds. Pallor twitches water from his wings with a snort of satisfaction; I can feel his heaving breaths through the saddle as I yank off my helmet and wipe rain from my eyes. We count off, one by one, as the aurelian riders breach the cloud cover, soaked and shivering, but with our formation intact. When all are accounted for, Pallor and I take a moment to regain our breath.

And that's when I notice it: other dragons on the horizon.

At first I think nothing of it; the squads have divided, and some could have flown farther north than planned.

Until I see a gleam of gold.

Aurelians.

All of my aurelians just counted off.

Which means that the ones on the horizon are not in the Callipolan fleet.

And then gleams of other colors: flashes of blue, blotches of darkness. A full fleet, with all three breeds.

They're approaching. Growing larger, their outlines becoming clearer against the sky.

The hair on the back of my neck rises.

A full fleet, announcing itself.

They've been biding their time.

With the force of an explosion, my emotions—a mixture of surprise and joy and *longing*—spill into Pallor, who lets out a screeching cry. My feelings, erupting from his mouth.

Then as his cry fades, there's noise above the whistling of the wind: Annie, shouting.

"Everyone *get down*!"

Her fist forms the signal for those too far to hear her voice; the rest of the squad begins diving back into the cover of the stratus clouds. It occurs to me, distantly through the fog of our spillover, that I've never heard Annie call out orders before, because, as aurelian squadron leader, that's my job. But I'm transfixed, unable to tear my eyes from the fleet that bears down upon us. What thoughts I can unravel from Pallor's are focused on a single point.

My people. My family. Close—

"Max, Deirdre, find Cor and Crissa and tell them to call off their squads, the drills are over! Tell them we have a foreign fleet sighting, possible sparked dragons two miles north!"

And then Annie has reined Aela round, facing Pallor, blocking our sight of the Pythian fleet. She, too, has pulled off her helmet, and beneath it her face is white, her eyes wide. Her rain-darkened hair is plastered across her forehead, water still trickling down the sides of her face. For the first time, looking at me, she seems frightened.

"Lee, let's go!"

4

ALETHEIA

A year had passed since the boy entered the orphanage. Though he and the girl continued to plan for their trip to New Pythos, the idea gradually lost its urgency. He had gotten good at school, better at chores, and the nightmares were coming less often. New Pythos was as far away in his imagination as his family was becoming in his memory.

Then, on the first anniversary of his family's murders, there was a parade through the city. The day had been named a national holiday. "Palace Day" commemorated the turning point in the Red Month, the day the people finally breached the walls of the Palace, after the dragons had been poisoned.

Standing in the main square, the boy had a clear view of the one surviving dragon brought forth for the final spectacle, and could easily recognize it.

His father's dragon had been one of the largest in the old fleet. Aletheia had a coloring unique among stormscourges: red-tipped wings and a red crest. The boy remembered running his hands over her hard scales, laying a hand on the bridge between her great black eyes.

Today, the mighty beast was almost unrecognizable. She had long since had the sparker cut from her throat, her wings clipped, and now she was barely more than an exceptionally large, cart-size beast with fierce jaws. These, too, had been chained shut. The boy watched the dragon being led up onto the dais, the chains cinched back so her head was forced down. Then the man who had saved him, who now called himself the First Protector, spoke about the things this dragon had done. Villages burned, innocent blood spilled, senseless and undeserved violence suffered by countless hundreds under this dragon, and countless thousands under other dragons, for centuries. He said that such times would never come again.

But the boy didn't listen. He was watching his father's dragon struggle to breathe.

Then he heard a sound to his right and looked down. The girl, standing next to him, was weeping. She did not take her eyes off Aletheia, and tears were streaming down her face.

He put his arm around her and pulled her close. He assumed that she was feeling the same sorrow he felt as he watched the once-great beast be humiliated.

Standing like this, holding the girl, he watched the axe cut off the head of his father's dragon.

* * *

Out in the yard, later that day, the boy found the girl sitting under one of the few trees, her eyes closed. He thought she was sleeping until she opened them.

"You were crying today in the square," he pointed out.

He felt compelled to say it, as if he needed some confirmation of the grief that they had, for that moment, shared.

He was on the brink of telling her everything. It was time, he had decided. The sight of Aletheia's execution had galvanized him. It was time to go. And he was going to bring the girl with him.

She looked up at him from where she was sitting and seemed on the verge of speaking, as if she were trying to decide whether or not she wanted to. But slowly she gathered courage. Her face stiffened, became determined, and she spoke in a low, controlled voice.

"That dragon killed my family."

LEE

Annie keeps Aela close beside Pallor during our flight back to Callipolis. The rest of the squadron follows close behind. In the silence that Annie leaves me, I struggle to extricate from Pallor's mind. I'm holding him by the neck, leaning low on the saddle, fighting the desire for his closeness, and Pallor only makes it harder. He senses my distress and tries to stay close, struggling to offer me comfort. Meanwhile the thoughts are buffeting:

Tyndale was right. All this time, while I convinced myself that the blustering of their threat was nothing but cheap shots fired by the Ministry of Propaganda for the consumption of gullible class-irons—

Who were they, those riders who were almost close enough to speak to?

Were there other Palace Day survivors?

Were they *kin*?

When we're within sight of the Palace, Annie speaks. Her

words are muffled, her expression hidden beneath her visor. She raises her voice over the pounding rain.

"Lee. Have you extricated?"

The problem of *her*, of what she knows or doesn't know, is too great a problem for my mind, still fighting free of Pallor's, to assess. I've never been the kind of rider who spills over easily, much less the kind that lets it last. This was irregular, and Annie knows it, and she saw what triggered it clearly enough.

I grit my teeth. "Nearly."

"The sighting needs to be reported to the Inner Palace directly."

I realize what she's getting at and balk. The thought of military counsel, of sitting down before Atreus Athanatos *now*—

"Are you—"

Are you going to report me?

I would, in a better state, know to swallow the question that gets halfway out before I bite my tongue. But this lost in spill-over, enough of a rising note of panic escapes with it. Annie's helmet turns briefly in my direction. She doesn't ask me to finish my question.

"It would be irregular if you're not there. Pull yourself together."

When Annie tugs at Aela's reins, breaking away from the rest of the fleet, I follow numbly. The Inner Palace lies below us, a tower of inward-facing windows encircling the Firemouth entrance to the dragons' caves, blurred by rain. Annie stalls after entering it, looking from one Aurelian balcony to the next, uncertain which leads to the First Protector's office. I speak for the first time, pointing.

"It's that one."

Atreus works from apartments that, in my childhood, belonged to the Aurelian triarch; I was taught as a child to recognize the balcony that doubled as his dragon's perch.

Annie's shoulders stiffen at my knowledge, but she doesn't question it.

We land, dismount, and dismiss our dragons. For a moment, Pallor resists, the aftereffects of the spillover still linking us. I lift my helmet, pull him close, and rest my forehead against his dripping silver-ridged brow before wrenching my mind free. He lets out a whimper at the extricating that makes my fists curl.

And then he follows Aela down into the darkness of the Firemouth. As the two dragons are swallowed in the rain-lashed shadows of the cavern, a headache grows with his distance.

And then the thoughts return.

Alive. Some of them are really alive. And as Tyndale hinted, they have *dragons.*

They have a chance of taking Callipolis back.

I hear the pronoun in my thoughts and test its alternative, the appeal of it humming in my blood: What if not *they* but *we* . . .

I raise my head to find Annie looking at me, her helmet tucked under her arm, her wet hair plastered on her forehead, her face twisted with an expression I cannot begin to divine.

Disappointment? Disgust? Anger?

She turns from me, steps forward, and hammers on the door built into the glass wall. A second later it opens. A very surprised assistant takes in the sight of us, two drenched teenagers in flamesuits, standing on a balcony that has no other entrance.

"We need to speak to the First Protector and General Holmes immediately," Annie says.

The meeting passes in a haze: Annie takes one look at me, then does the talking herself. We sit in the Council Room with Atreus and General Holmes, the Minister of Defense, at the great oak table usually reserved for members of the High Council. Though I'm familiar with Holmes from rounds, I'm almost certain Annie isn't. Where Atreus is perpetually clean-shaven and modestly dressed, Holmes wears a close, curling brown beard and keeps the many decorations of his uniform well-polished. He made a name for himself in the Revolution at Atreus's side, an infusion of lowborn vigor in contrast to Atreus's high-minded principles, and the reputation he gained was for ruthlessness.

I've always considered it best not to learn the details. Holmes likes me; I've worked with him for years; it's never been relevant.

But today, as I look at him and think of dragons from New Pythos, it feels relevant.

Far from betraying intimidation in such formidable company, Annie sits up straight and describes the Pythian fleet with precision; she managed to count them while also issuing orders to the squad. In total, she accounted for five skyfish, nine aurelians, and seven stormscourges. Too distant to make out their ages.

Holmes finally asks, "And after you saw them. Did you engage?"

He is looking at me, I realize. Waiting to hear how I responded, as leader of the squadron. I feel a dull flood of panic hit: This is it. This is the end. A single spillover to undo almost ten years of pretending, and reveal me as the potential traitor that I am.

But when Annie speaks, it isn't to say that.

"Lee told everyone to get below cloud cover and back to Callipolis."

I swing a sideways glance at her in amazement.

Covering for me. Annie's *covering* for me.

Pinpricks of pink on her pale cheeks are the only evidence of what this is costing her: After years of being underestimated, written off by the ministry of this country and, by extension, the men sitting across from us, Annie has just proved herself competent in a crisis, capable of leadership, and worthy of the kind of promotion she was recently told not to pursue. And she's sweeping her actions under the rug, for my sake.

Shouldn't you have turned me in instead?

Because surely the kind of visions that have been slithering through my mind are those of someone who deserves to be turned in, not sheltered. Surely these fantasies of triumph and retribution, abandoned since my childhood but now back with all their seductive force, are enough to damn me.

Annie meets my gaze and lifts an eyebrow. I clear my throat. And then, for reasons I cannot even begin to understand, I hear myself accept her gift and offer the explanation she and Holmes are waiting for.

"We had no way of knowing whether they had sparked, and we were unarmed."

Sparked, meaning dragons mature enough to breathe fire rather than ash, as ours are still too young to do.

"Good call, Lee," Holmes says.

His deep voice is warm, approving. Annie swallows hard. I feel sick.

Atreus drums his fingers on the table and speaks for the first time.

"It's clear we've made a grave error in overlooking New Pythos," he says. "We were content to dismiss rumors of dragon sightings off the northern coast as idle gossip, useful for our propaganda and nothing more. It appears we have misjudged."

"We should have attacked them years ago," Holmes murmurs. "When their dragons were weak. Stormed that god-forsaken rock with the full navy and wiped the rest of those inbred little bastards out . . . Now it's too late."

Inbred little bastards. The kind of slur I'm usually all but numb to, but today causes my mind to burn, as if fevered, with visions of vengeful dragonfire.

What if I never had to sit stone-faced through such slurs again?

Atreus hums his dissent. "Let's not jump to conclusions. We'll dispatch word to our ambassadors on Isca to seek an audience at the New Pythian embassy immediately. Perhaps Rhadamanthus can be reasoned with."

Rhadamanthus ha'Aurelian, the current scion of New Pythos. Atreus turns to an aide sitting at the end of the table. "Summon the two fastest skyfish riders, tell them they're needed as messengers. That would be—"

He looks at me.

"Crissa, Dorian," I answer, supplying Duck's rarely used full name.

The aide bows and leaves. Once he's gone, Holmes leans forward. "You think *diplomacy* will settle this?" he asks Atreus.

"I am bound to consider it if it might prevent a war."

Holmes's face is dark with skepticism. I remember the fleet approaching, the full force of their numbers spread against the sky, and can't help but share it. Those were not the demonstrations of a nation seeking a diplomatic solution.

The corridor outside is quiet after our dismissal, its few windows letting in rain-smothered light. For a moment, after we've closed the door behind us, Annie and I stand side by side. The foot between us feels like a great distance, and the silence feels loud.

The past hour is reverberating within me in flashes: the sight of their fleet; the desperate longing; Annie's voice crying my name and tearing me away. The sound of her voice describing the job I should have done, as if I had done it. And all the while my thoughts straying to dreams of revenge that would mean the betrayal not only of her but of her people.

She turns and walks away.

"Annie?"

But I have no idea what I'm about to say to her, and she doesn't turn back.

* * *

"That dragon killed my family."

For a second he stared at her, not understanding. And then he thought he must have misheard. He asked her to say it again, and she did.

"You're lying," he said.

She did not expect this. Her eyes widened.

"My family was killed by a dragon," she said. "Soldiers locked them in the house and our dragonlord set fire to it."

"How come you're alive, then?"

She blanched. "Because he made me watch."

He remembered the feeling of an adult's hands on his shoulders, forcing his face toward things he didn't want to see.

"That doesn't make sense," he spat.

She seemed to be struggling to find the words to explain herself. It was clearly the last thing she'd been expecting to do. "He said one of us had to watch so they could tell the rest of the village—"

Her voice was starting to waver. He cut her off, because he didn't want to hear her crying. "How do you know it was the dragon from the square?"

"Because it was a stormscourge with red on its wings—"

"Then they must have deserved it!"

He practically shouted at her.

Her head went back against the tree behind her as if he had struck her. For a moment, they just stared at each other, her head tilted back, looking at him with bleak disbelief, him staring down at her, feeling his chest rising and falling and something like hatred coursing through him.

She spoke first, her voice very quiet.

"They were killed because we didn't meet a food quota during the Famine."

"There was no Famine," he snapped.

She blinked. "Excuse me?"

"It was a bunch of lies. Everybody knows that. Exaggerated so people could get away with not paying what they owed—"

"My mother," she said, "died during the Famine. So did my baby brother. Because we didn't have enough food. And we lived on a farm."

Her eyes were bright, but she seemed so angry now that she was past crying. She pointed a thumb over her shoulder, at the children playing elsewhere in the yard. "And in case you haven't noticed, the Famine is why most of them are here."

She pushed from her knees up, so she slid to her feet with her back still against the tree. Even standing, she was more than a head shorter. She was looking at him as though she'd never seen him before. All the fury and disgust that she had for her tormentors was, for the first time, turned on him.

"Stay away from me," she said.

ANNIE

My feet take me away from Lee with the force of physical repulsion. If I have to spend another moment in his presence, the emotions that have been simmering will turn to a boil. I need space to think, and I need to do it without having to look at those gray eyes and those cheekbones that are just a little too fine and high.

Stay away from me.

Should I have turned him in?

That's the question that locks itself in my mind as I walk away.

I'd be a fool to trust him.

But all the same, I couldn't bring myself to do it.

I don't blame Lee for spilling over, and I don't blame him for the look of longing that transformed his face when he first saw them. It doesn't take a stretch of the imagination to understand what he must have felt. I know the ache of an orphan's loneliness; I know what it is to crave the comfort of kin. All that was—natural.

I blame Lee for what followed. For listening to me when I told him to turn around, though it seemed to tear him apart. For sitting beside me as I reported a military threat of dragonlords on the horizon to the leaders of Callipolis and then hoarsely offering his counsel. For giving me the faintest hope that, maybe, I hadn't just lost him.

I blame him for the fact that I still want to trust him.

I want it so hard, it hurts.

And the fact that I just forwent credit in front of Atreus Athanatos and Amon Holmes for the sake of this fool's hope makes me sick to my stomach.

Back in the Cloister, I go to the boys' dorm in search of Duck, who's packing. A sealed message has been given to him and Crissa to bear to the New Pythian ambassador on Isca, the sworn neutral archipelago federation on the northwest edge of the Medean Sea. He and Crissa have been told to wait until Rhadamanthus's answer is returned.

"Please be careful. Ride fast—"

"It'll be fine, Annie," Duck says. "We're heading south, anyway . . ."

But it doesn't seem like enough, after you realize the skies contain dragons other than your own. Two unsparked skyfish is precious little defense against a hostile sky. Somewhere during our conversation, he took my hands in his, and now, though I know I'm supposed to, I don't want to let go.

"It's time, Duck."

Crissa has appeared in the doorway of the dorm, her helmet under her shoulder. Her braid is still wet from the rain; we haven't been on the ground long enough since the first sighting for it to dry. She casts an eye on our entwined hands but makes no comment.

"I know." Duck withdraws his hands from mine. Then he clears his throat. "I'm not sure how long we'll be gone, but I wanted to say—Midsummer, when we get back. You'll come?"

He's offering more than an invitation, I realize: He's setting a fixed point on a vanishing horizon, something for me to focus on. The realization nearly brings a lump to my throat.

"Yes. I'll come."

"Good. And make sure you invite Lee."

Lee.

I think of that silent corridor, standing beside Lee in the

rain-thick darkness as he said my name. When I found myself unable to look at him, much less speak to him. The lie comes out as if of its own accord.

"I already asked him. He said no."

I haven't asked him. I haven't even brought up the idea. As far as he knows, we're spending Midsummer in the Cloister together, like always.

But that's unthinkable now.

Duck's eyes narrow as he looks at me. Even Crissa looks a little surprised.

"Okay then," Duck says. "Just the two of us?"

He sounds uncertain, but not displeased.

"Just the two of us."

* * *

After their fight, the other children resumed the torment they had stopped in his presence. The boy watched them steal the girl's meals, trip her, tear apart her homework before class so she'd be punished for not doing it. He did nothing.

All the while, her words gnawed at him. He tried at first to dismiss them as a child's joke, some kind of willful lie gone too far. He told himself she was little, too little, and had not understood what had happened to her family. But this was not enough. She wasn't much younger than him, and he knew she was smarter. She understood everything.

He struggled to comprehend the story she'd told. Even here he protested: She must have been ignorant of something. Even if there had been a famine of some sort, his father would never have punished his people without good reason—

But this was a dead end, too, because he couldn't think of any reason good enough to make a girl watch her family burn to death.

He kept trying to reconcile his father and his dragon with a burning house, a family dying, a girl being held and made to watch. He could not think of anything that could have merited it.

How could his father have done such a thing? His father had been brave, noble. His dragon made him a leader of men—not just a good man, but a great one.

These beliefs, taken for granted before his father's death, were one of the few comforts he had left.

Now these comforts were stained. Try as he might, he could no longer think of his father without a sickening sense of doubt. It infected all his memories. Even memories of things like dinner with his family and stories before bed were no longer safe.

He lost his appetite, stopped sleeping, was unable to focus in class. His thoughts went round and round as he tried to find a way of preserving the father he'd remembered before he learned the girl's story.

In the end, after their desperate circling, he arrived at a simple solution.

He could go.

He had the provisions; he had a plan. He was ready—as ready as he ever would be. New Pythos was waiting. He need not succumb to the girl at all. He need not choose. He could simply leave.

ANNIE

It's beginning to feel like the whole world is tearing apart, and that part of what I'm losing is Lee.

Instead of dinner and homework, I sit in on meeting after meeting alongside Lee, Cor, and Power in the Inner Palace. At a debriefing Holmes holds for the entire corps, we're given a new patrol schedule for the northern coast of Callipolis and told that our training will narrow in focus. To air combat, exclusively— and not the kind performed in tournaments. Meanwhile the tournaments themselves have taken on a sinister new significance.

"In times of peace, the titles of Firstrider and Alternus are little more than honorifics," Holmes tells us. "But now, we need to be prepared. We need a fleet commander leading the offensive. And an Alternus at his back, defending."

Both titles will be determined by the final tournament. Cor and Power straighten with excitement as Holmes says this, and Lee hunches in his seat, like the words press too heavily on him. In the wake of the sighting I've begun to notice him as if a line connected us: I hear every word he utters and, even more, I hear his silences.

Every word and every silence a tally on a ledger I despair of making but know I must.

Because time and space give me the coolness of resolve that shock did not. If it comes to a choice, I need to choose according to my conscience and my vows. Friendship will not justify treason.

If Lee is compromised, it's my duty to report him.

That night I lie awake, imagining Duck, unsheltered and exposed as he crosses the Medean Sea on dragonback; and I think of Lee, the boy I know better than anyone and at the same time have felt, since the sighting, that I know not at all. I ache from missing them both.

The following morning our new life starts: Excused from class, we return to the Eyrie for intensive drilling of contact charges, weapons charges, the quick and dirty ways to win when winning means a kill, not a kill shot. When you might not have the benefit of sparked dragonfire to do the job for you. Though a lack of demonstrated dragonfire at the sighting suggests that the other fleet is also unsparked, we must prepare as if they are.

A steadiness settles over the Eyrie as Goran tells us: *This is how you open the throat.*

Not because he hasn't given us these kinds of lessons before, but because this is the first time we've listened and known an imminent reason we might use them. Lee sits silent, head bowed, elbows crooked over his knees as he listens to Goran describe the ways to mutilate and kill an enemy rider.

Enemy, Goran says. Not *opponent.* Even the language has changed.

Lee's fingers are clenched on his knees so hard, the knuckles have gone white.

And then we separate by squadrons, as we usually do, and the drilling begins. I rein Aela away from Lee sur Pallor. Instead, I pair with Max, one of the aurelian riders from my halfsquadron. Lee, realizing what I've done, pairs off with Deirdre.

It's the first time I've voluntarily chosen a sparring partner other than Lee in years. Usually, Goran has to remind us to separate.

Sparring starts. Aela and I get in Max's guard once. Then again, and again, and again. Max made it into the Sixteenth Order—the upper half of the corps' flight ranking—but that's not enough.

"Dragons, Annie, at least wait for the reset," he mutters, massaging his arm where I've rammed him.

"You asleep, Lee?" I hear Goran shout from down on the Eyrie.

Though I tried to claim a spot over the arena far from them, I can still see Lee and Deirdre's sparring. Goran's criticism wouldn't make sense for most riders: Lee is, after all, getting inside Deirdre's guard and landing hits. But I see the difference, too. Lee isn't trying. He's doing the minimum—enough, in Lee's case, to win. Because in Lee's case, halfhearted is still good.

Watching him, I feel my despair shift to anger.

Goran seems to be sharing my short temper.

"Aurelian squadron, time out. Annie, Lee, trade partners. Wake him up, Antigone."

It's always while I'm in the air that Goran forgets to discount my ability.

Pallor and Aela space out, ten meters apart, above the arena, wings spread to coast on the breeze. Lee and I eye each other through the slits in our visors, gripping blunt-headed jousting pikes and fireproof shields. We've practiced with both before, but because they're considered to be a complementary weapon to sparked dragonfire, they've never been a priority in our training. Now, with the threat of unsparked fleet engagements, they're the next best alternative.

Aela has begun to simmer with my anger herself; she is snorting, eager. Pallor, like Lee, is just a little too calm. Like he's not really there.

Goran calls the advance and we charge.

Our momentum surpasses theirs; the force of our contact

ripples through Lee sur Pallor. As they ride out the shock, I lean over Aela's wing and ram my pike home. Lee moves his shield to block it but not quite fast enough; it skids left and rams, not into his chest, but his shoulder.

Lee grunts in pain. He pulls Pallor out, to disengage, and as he does, I feel my anger bursting its restraints. Because I know what just happened. I have no illusions about my strength; Lee's and my abilities are level in traditional sparring, ash against ash; but when it comes to hand-to-hand combat I'm half his size and have half his muscle. I should never have landed that penalty at all.

We slam into each other again, and this time, despite an opening that I shouldn't have bared, Lee's pike doesn't make contact and mine does again.

Fight back, you bastard. Fight back, you bloody coward, don't you leave me like this—

I feel the explosion of anger course from me into Aela, at once a relief and an escalation into greater fury. We've spilled over. Through the haze I hear Lee shouting.

"You are *out of order.*"

The world sharpens back into focus, though Aela's and my shared anger still gives it a liquid edge. The echoes of the words I was thinking vibrate in my ears; that's how I realize I was doing more than thinking. Lee's ripped off his helmet, his eyes white-rimmed as he stares at me. Around us, other pairs have paused in their sparring. I can only imagine what they must be thinking if they heard what I shouted.

"There a problem?" Goran calls.

"I'll take care of it," Lee says. "*Ground*, Antigone."

The sound of my full name at the end of his order snaps

me back into my senses, even as the rage changes flavor. I yank Aela's reins down and descend toward the deserted ramparts that gird the arena walls. We clatter onto the flagstones. I cut the straps that bind my legs to the stirrups and leap off. A moment later, Lee sur Pallor lands beside us. He dismounts, every line of his movement tense with fury, and dismisses Pallor back into the air with a flick of his wrist.

We glare at each other. Behind me, Aela, still riding my emotions, growls. Overhead, the aurelian squad resumes sparring.

"What the *hell* was that?"

"I should report you. I should have reported you right then—"

Lee stands perfectly still. For a moment all I can hear is the wind and Aela's hard breathing at my back.

"Then why didn't you?"

My eyes are stinging.

"Because I wanted to trust you, and I was a fool for it."

I know my eyes must be too bright. Lee takes them in, then tilts his head back and looks up at the cirrus clouds high above us. When the silence has lengthened to the point that I'm on the verge of breaking it, he inhales slowly, pushes dark hair back from his eyes, and looks at me.

"You weren't."

"I wasn't?"

Lee shakes his head. And then, as his face fills with pain, I understand at last.

The white knuckles, the silence, the bowed head: Lee isn't planning to defect.

He's steeling himself to stay, as I should have known he would.

* * *

When he went to the closet on the third floor, to the stockpile to pack his bag for New Pythos, he realized that instead of escaping her, he had stumbled across her path. She was inside, the door closed. And she was crying. He'd heard her cry before, but he'd never heard her cry like this. Not like she was frightened or in pain: like she was in despair.

He stood on the threshold and thought, I can come back later, when she's gone.

Because he knew that if he crossed the threshold now, he'd never leave. He would not get the backpack or the provisions. He wouldn't escape. He'd sink down beside her and do the only thing left to do. He would comfort her.

He remembered his father's teachings and tried, now, to convince himself: She's just a peasant. She doesn't matter.

But even as he told himself this, he found himself opening the door.

She was sitting against the opposite wall, where he usually sat, her face buried in her knees, her hands gripping her hair. As if his body were acting of its own accord, he slid to the ground, placed his palms on the floor, and hung his head.

He waited for her to say something, to demand an apology, and he thought of the words she would wring out of him: "They didn't deserve it." *He would say it; he would hate himself and her and his father for it, but he would say it. She'd won.*

But she didn't ask him to say anything.

He heard floorboards creak as she shifted forward, and then he felt her hands reach out, clutch him, and pull him toward her. She buried her face against his shirt and held him like she thought he might disappear.

Then she let out a dull sob, and he realized that he wasn't the only one who felt defeated.

He wrapped his arms around her and began to utter phrases he'd never said before, only heard others say to him: Don't cry. It's over now. I'm here. *She was too thin. He could see the bruises the other children had left on her, and he felt responsible. The stockpile he'd come to pack was left unmentioned, unthought of, in the corner. He held her until she fell asleep, and when she woke, he took her to find food.*

He never spoke of the voyage to New Pythos again.

She never asked him why he didn't.

Though he didn't note it consciously, this was the first day he tried not to think of his family when they surfaced in his mind. He pushed them away, and only realized, months later, that he'd begun to forget them.

LEE

A day has passed since we spoke on the arena ramparts. Annie sits across from me in class with Atreus, so when the First Protector asks us to propose discussion topics and I raise my hand, I'm acutely aware of her eyes on me from across the table. And then I volunteer a topic I've never brought up in any class before: I ask about the old regime.

"Why is the new regime better than the old?" My throat, closed from a long silence, has to unstick itself to speak.

Atreus leans back in his chair, smiling mildly at the challenge.

"Is it?" he asks.

"Of course it is," Cor says, as if even considering the alternative were offensive.

"How?"

"The new regime has fair trials," Cor says. "A trade-based economy that supports a growing middle class. Universal education. Opportunities for advancement that don't depend on birth. Compare that to the old regime—we've all heard the horror stories."

Atreus nods slowly. "I'm sure you have. And some of you have even lived them." Though the reference is oblique, I feel the room's awareness of Annie rise. I can practically see Cor making a point not to glance at her, while Power actually does. Her face reveals nothing. "These stories aside," Atreus goes on, "what can you tell me about their failings?"

This time, both Annie and I raise our hands.

I've been conscious, since the Fourth Order tournament, of refraining from volunteering when Annie wants to participate. But today I keep my hand in the air and seek her eyes. They widen ever so slightly as they meet mine, her lips parting.

I need this.

She lowers her hand.

"Lee?"

I grip the edge of the table and speak slowly, working it through as I say it. Years' worth of readings and homework assignments and class discussions that can be distilled into a few sentences of difficult truth.

"Thousands died in poverty and starvation under the triarchy. The dragonborn feasted while their people starved and denied the famines they found inconvenient. They operated with almost no legal restraints, cruelly and without mercy, and then they justified the wrongs they committed by claiming it was their blood-borne right."

In my peripheral vision, Annie shifts in her chair.

Atreus is nodding. "Indeed. And how could such unbridled power not ultimately lead to corruption? Can you see the flaw in it, Lee—the premise that lay rotten at the core?"

I nod. This flaw I've been aware of since I first began to consider such things at all.

"Their power was inherited."

"Exactly. Power did not correspond to worth. And that distance—between power and worth—is something rule under dragons has been grappling with from the beginning." Atreus indicates, with an open hand, the *Aurelian Cycle* that remains on the table, ready to be referred to, in every one of our classes. "There was greatness in them. But with that greatness came arrogance, and with that arrogance corruption, and with that corruption downfall.

"Now. How are you different?"

Power's answer is ready, smug. "We deserve it."

The irony of his answer does not seem to be lost on Atreus, whose mouth has curved into a thin smile. "Do you?"

"Don't we?"

"That depends on you," Atreus says. "You only deserve this mantle as long as you can be more reasonable and more virtuous than what came before. And that's important to remember now, more than ever, in the face of what may come."

When I look up, I find that Annie's too-bright eyes haven't left my face.

* * *

Tyndale keeps office hours in the literature department of the Lyceum. I find my way there quickly; I want to give him my refusal while the resolve is still hot.

Because I know that when the answer from New Pythos comes back, these words will be harder to say, even though their answer can't change mine.

I'll swallow this cup. What remains to be seen is how bitter it will be going down. Depending on the answer Crissa and Duck bring back, it may turn out to be bitter indeed.

"I've thought about it. Your offer. To join—them."

"Yes?"

"No."

Tyndale grimaces, then motions toward the chair across from his paper-laden desk. The room is sun-soaked, the open window letting in the smell of mown grass from the courtyard.

"Sit."

Aging leather upholstery creaks under my weight. Tyndale's tone becomes avuncular. He is, as before, speaking in Dragontongue. "I worry that you haven't fully considered your situation, Leo. Perhaps this seems like the easiest answer right now. But in the long run, in your position—it will not be easy. Selling out now means paying the price later."

"I'm not selling out."

Tyndale cocks his head. Then he rests it on a propped palm.

"Then what exactly are you doing?"

"I'm choosing Callipolis."

I've switched to Dragontongue, too. We are, after all, behind closed doors, and for this I feel the need to use it. There is an exhilaration in speaking it again after all these years. It seems to lend the words power.

"I believe in Atreus. I believe in what he's doing. Even if it was born in blood."

Tyndale's expression has transformed from skepticism to pity.

"You think Palace Day was the end of the bloodshed?" he asks. "You've just chosen to start it all over again."

Three days later, Crissa and Duck return from Isca, and I watch Annie fold Duck into the kind of hug she hasn't given me since we were children. Her smile is simple, easy, happy as she looks up at him. The kind of smile—carefree, unstained by old memories—that she's never given me.

I turn away, because I have no business feeling this sudden ache, and Crissa hands me the message she bears from New Pythos.

It was waiting for us: That's why she and Duck were able to return to Callipolis so quickly. By the time our message reached them, the Pythians' own was already waiting for us in the embassy.

THE RIGHTFUL TRIARCHS OF CALLIPOLIS HAVE TIRED OF THEIR EXILE.
THEY WILL SOON BE COMING HOME.

The message is more or less the blow I was expecting; the cup to be drunk every bit as bitter and slow-acting as Tyndale had implied. Steeled against the shock, I feel still the clear pressure of purpose, the focus of a charted course: Train; prepare; await the plunge.

What I don't expect is the note, two weeks later, tucked inside the homework Tyndale hands back to me, in the well-worn script of practiced Dragontongue.

My dear cousin—

I'd hardly dared to hope it was you in that first tournament. But now my joy is confirmed. Find me in the Drowned Dragon, Cheapside, on Midsummer, at three hours past midnight. Leave your stubbornness for the night: Midsummer is a time for family.

Julia

5

MIDSUMMER

LEE

Julia was a nurse's nightmare. The kind of girl who always managed to escape, to find the boys and join whatever game we were playing, who always returned covered in dirt, priceless dresses torn, knees scraped. Against all expectations, it was Julia—destined to a suitable match and the domestic confines that came with it—who controlled the orbits of our play with the magnetism of the sun. When Julia arrived, the day began to matter. The trees in the Palace gardens became karst we scaled, the ponds became seas we flew over, the lawns became fields we scorched in great duels to the death by dragonfire.

The fight was always who would be Firstrider and who would be Alternus. It was a fight Julia usually won.

"When I grow up, I'll be Firstrider and Triarch, like my father," she proclaimed. "Like Pytho the Unifier, like Uriel sur Aron."

"You can't, Julia," the older boys scoffed. My brother, Laertes, recently found in his ceremony to be a *passus*, forsaken by dragons; Julia's brother Ixion, Laertes's age; and Delo, one of the Skyfish eldest-born. "Girls don't ride."

I remember hauling her away as she screamed after them, purple-faced. The most biting swears she knew were centuries-old, phrases we had learned from the *Aurelian Cycle*, so antiquated that our brothers, who were old enough to learn real swears from our fathers, only laughed harder.

"My father said they'll change it," she told me afterward, eyes streaming with fury as we stood in the shade of a copse to regroup. "My father says he'll change the rules for me. I'll ride."

One never disagreed with Julia, but I also played pretend with her enough to know when she was pretending about herself. I knew the power of her lies, which felt so much like life that they were enough, for hours, to convince us both, though we stood squarely on the ground, that we were flying.

"My father," Julia told me, gray eyes wide as she confided her faith, "can do *anything*."

The last time I saw Julia was during the Red Month.

The chronology of the period between the fall of the old regime and the rise of the new is hazy in my memory; flashes are vivid and the rest is lost. When I last saw her, the dragonborn families were under house arrest in the Great Palace. My father's summoning whistle had been confiscated, Aletheia confined to her nest. The militia who'd taken control of the Inner Palace had sworn themselves loyal to a Revolution and then made the dragonlords they'd captured swear their loyalty as well, in a farce that was all but openly acknowledged, but whose charade remained propped up for weeks. The militia were there, by their own explanation, for our protection—for during those weeks the sounds of protests, of commoners rioting, clamoring for bread and blood outside the Outer walls, could be heard all the way inside the Inner Palace.

During those weeks, my uncle, Crethon, the Triarch of the West, tried to flee to his highland estate with his wife and children. They were caught. When they'd been returned to the city, revolutionaries brought Crethon's wife and children to our apartments in the Inner Palace and demanded an audience with the Drakarch of the Far Highlands and his family.

My father received them in our parlor. Our cousins showed the signs of rough travel and recent beatings. Julia was, like me, the youngest, but she hadn't been spared the bruises that darkened all of my cousins' faces. It was the first time I'd ever seen evidence of violence inflicted on a dragonborn. The rage that filled me was not only at her pain but at the sheer gall of it—to strike a Stormscourge, to strike a dragonlord's child. It was still, even that late in the Red Month, unthinkable. My aunt, being held by one of the guards, was uttering a moan so low in her throat that I hadn't immediately realized it was a human sound.

Our chief guard told us, in labored Dragontongue: "This is the fate that will be met by any dragonlord's family who tries to escape this Revolution."

At that point I could barely distinguish him from the rest, but his pockmarked face was one I would learn, on Palace Day, to remember. He held Julia, then seven, by the shoulders and shook her, to prove his point.

"Good citizen," my father answered, rising to stand between us and the guard and employing the egalitarian address then fashionable for the revolutionaries, "my family has no plans to leave the Palace. But where is Lady Helena's lord? She is distraught."

I remember noting how wrong it was to hear my father use a tone of deference with such a person. And I remember Julia, holding my gaze from across the room where she was confined beneath the man's dirty hands. Her eyes were clear, defiant, full of a fury that I wouldn't feel in its full force until Palace Day.

The guardsman said, "The lady and her children will never see their lord again."

Julia's sobbing mother was led away first, Julia after her.

That was how I last saw Julia.

* * *

That was nine years ago. Now the Palace gardens that we once played in are full of city children. The children of cobblers and bakers and blacksmiths, who are free to enjoy the blossoming summer-smells that were, in my childhood, the privilege of the dragonborn alone. Though the children here today are playing in a different language, they laugh the same way we did and play the same games. They're still pretending to fly on dragonback.

All the same, as I watch them from the bench I've sunk into halfway across the grounds, I find it hard to believe that Julia and I ever acted the way they do. Without a care in the world.

How did she survive?

And the worse thought: *What* did she survive? What horrors did she witness or endure when the walls were breached—

"Lee?"

I look up, and it takes a moment for me to focus. Crissa is approaching. We're on our way back from Atreus's address in the People's Square across the river, where he broke the news to the public of the Pythian threat and assured them of Callipolis's readiness to fight. Like me, Crissa is dressed in the ceremonial armor, silver under a black mantle, the Guardian's emblem a twined circlet on her breastplate. The Guardians and their dragons stood arrayed behind Atreus during his speech as a display of Callipolan air power.

It was the same dais where, eight years ago, Aletheia was executed. The Callipolans in the square today were roaring with the same wild fury, a sea of colors and faces that became, at Atreus's raised arm, a thunderous single voice. I listened, and remembered Aletheia, and fought nausea.

I shift, making room for her, and Crissa takes a seat beside me. "Hey."

Three days have passed since I received Julia's letter. Midsummer, when Julia will come to look for me, is a few days away.

Though I've incinerated the letter, its every word remains etched in my memory. Julia's handwriting has matured, no longer a child's block letters but a practiced, adult script, comfortable in an alphabet I only use for translation homework.

My mind goes blank when I try to think of what will happen come Midsummer. And then, in that blank, I remind myself: I spend Midsummer with Annie.

Crissa is sitting close enough for her knee to brush mine. Even sweating under layers of thin-plated ceremonial armor, this added heat becomes the most sensitive point on my body at once. The contact is surprising, but not unpleasant, and I don't pull my knee away.

"Beautiful, isn't it?" she says. "I love the Palace gardens at this time of year."

The sky is blue, the air is sweet but not too warm, and a gentle breeze cools our faces. Crissa sweeps her hair free from her neck so the dark gold curls cascade down her back, radiant against the black of her mantle. When she breathes in, taking in the smell of earth, of roses and honeysuckle, her smile is so full of such simple pleasure that I feel a pang of remembrance. *That* is what it looks like, to be able to enjoy freely, without the constricting binds of old griefs.

That is what Julia and I used to be.

Though I would not be able to articulate the connection, it's that thought that leads me to the question I ask her next.

"Do you still draw?"

When we were younger, Crissa drew all the time. Dragons, people, seascapes of her home in Harbortown. At my question she smiles, a little pained, and shakes her head. Her knee is still against mine.

"Not since we were made squadron leaders. But I'd draw this if I had the time."

The laden oaks, the burbling fountain, the terraced rooftops of the Janiculum leading to the karst of Pytho's Keep rising magnificent against the cloudless sky.

Crissa sighs, taking it in. Then she rouses herself, produces a folded paper from her pocket, and holds it out to me. "Have you seen this yet? From Propaganda."

The memo notifies us of a schedule of new obligations for Guardians: morale visits, where we make appearances alongside our dragons before the people, delivering motivational speeches and showing proof of our nation's strength to defy the Pythian threat.

"I don't fancy rallying mobs, to be honest," Crissa mutters.

I share her hesitation. Amid increased training, ramped-up patrol schedules, and back-to-back rounds sessions with the Ministry of Defense, it's hard to stomach the idea of wasting time with propaganda. And then there's the crudity of the campaign itself. *By the wings of my dragon I will keep her, let my reason guide her to justice,* we swore as children becoming Guardians. They were vows that seemed to encompass something nobler than promoting patriotism from dragonback with a bit of cheap rhetoric.

But it's been a long time since we were children, and if this helps allay the people's fear, I've no reason to balk at it. Even if it feels vulgar.

"We've trained for it. We knew this would be a part of our job eventually."

The lines in Crissa's brow remain unsmoothed. "I know."

Implicit in the assignment is its secondary purpose: auditioning which Guardians are best received by the people. A question that will be particularly relevant for the riders of the Fourth Order.

Although the list makes it apparent that the audition has already been under way, not all Guardians have been given an equal number of assignments. Those who routinely do well in oration practice—Cor, Power, Crissa, Rock, and I—have been assigned multiple visits. Those who do poorly have been overlooked.

Including Annie, who despite being a member of the Fourth Order has not been assigned any visits at all.

"She's going to be furious."

I realize only after I've murmured this that I've not used her name. But Crissa doesn't have to ask whom I mean.

"Won't she be relieved? Annie hates public obligations."

I remember Annie alone, practicing a raised voice in a Lyceum lecture hall, and shake my head. "I think that was before she made Fourth Order."

Crissa takes a last look at the list before rolling it back up. "Good for her."

Crissa was no-nonsense about the brief hell she experienced when Atreus first promoted her to squadron leader. Goran's vitriol, his determination to make her pay for it, slid off her back like water. Or at least it did in public. In private, she hyperventilated. When Cor and I found her doing it, she made us swear not to tell anyone.

She must know almost exactly what Annie struggles against, within and without.

"They won't be able to ignore her forever," Crissa adds. "Not at this rate."

In other words, not if Annie beats Power for finalist. The tournament will take place ten days after Midsummer, when the city has returned from its holiday.

I hand the paper back to her and our hands snag on it. For an instant longer than necessary, the tips of Crissa's fingers linger on the back of my hand. Even after she removes her fingers, the memory of the touch—minute, but for its deliberateness it might as well have been words—leaves my skin burning.

"We should get back," she says. "Find Cor and do squadron meeting."

She pushes hair from her face, and I realize she's flushed, too.

Back inside the Cloister, half the Guardians are still in ceremonial uniform from Atreus's speech. The other half are on their way out to air patrols, or to classes, which have resumed. Cor is in the boys' dorm with Duck and Annie. The sight of the Sutter brothers together is enough to tell me that something's wrong: They only confer in crisis. Then, as I take in Cor's ashen face and the fact that Duck, sitting on his bed beside Annie, is sniffling, my first thought is that someone in their family died. The dormitory is otherwise empty, its long row of beds crisply made, its desks cleared and clean, ready for evening inspection.

"What happened?"

Cor looks up at me and then away, as if ashamed to be seen in such a moment. It's Duck's voice that bursts out in answer. A letter lies, half crumpled, in his lap.

"Our sister's metals test results came back. She got Iron."

It's strange, with my thoughts so often now on the skies and the threat from the North Sea and Julia returned from the dead, to remember that something as banal as the metals test still has the power to upend a life.

Eyes on the ceiling, Cor adds an explanation. "She's always had this . . . problem where she switches letters around when she tries to read. Vocabulary like you wouldn't believe, though. Anyway, she was hoping to get passed as Bronze for an apprenticeship as a baker, so she could work in the family shop, but apparently she . . . wasn't good enough."

He sounds a little light-headed.

I think of that girl in the Lyceum Club, calling us *sirs and miss* as she took our orders. The ones from the textile houses, twirling their iron wristbands, not meeting my eyes when I'm on rounds.

"Does she have a work assignment yet, or—"

"Fullerton's."

The one we so recently examined, whose workers we were relieved to find had no causes for complaint except for aching feet. But now the memory of that relief makes me feel ashamed. Cor places a hand over his mouth, like he's catching something. He removes his weight from the desk he's been leaning on.

"Excuse me."

The door to the dormitory slams after him, and in its echoing wake Duck sags dully against Annie's arms.

"I need to go home."

"Midsummer is in just a few days," Annie says.

"You're still coming, right?" Duck asks.

Annie looks up at me, over Duck's head. She swallows.

Duck feels the change in her and looks up, too. He sobers instantly.

"You're still welcome, Lee. I know you told Annie no, but the offer stands—"

I cast my mind back, over conversations we might possibly have had in which Annie asked such a thing and I declined. I have to cast back far; it's been a while since we've properly talked. Since before the Pythian sighting. Even since reconciling, words haven't come easily.

But then I realize why I'm coming up empty. Annie's closed eyes are evidence enough.

I hear myself say, "Thanks, Duck. But I'll be all right here."

Duck looks frustrated, doubtful, but also fundamentally unsurprised; he's tried before, and my answer has been no. But this is the first time he's invited us home for Midsummer.

Annie's eyes, when they open, are bright, and now she cannot look at me.

I spend the next two days preparing myself to spend Midsummer without her.

It's not that spending it with Annie was ever what either of us would describe as a good time. Unlike the national holidays celebrated in Callipolis, Midsummer and Midwinter center on the family. People go home, wherever home may be; the city—and the Cloister—clears out. The evening is spent at dinner with loved ones, under the summer's longest sky.

Except for people like Annie and me, who while away the long dusk trying not to think. Not to remember. Not to *miss*.

I can't blame her for wanting to upgrade. I certainly don't feel justified in resenting her for wanting to do it without me. But that doesn't make the thought of spending one of the hardest holidays of the year alone easier to contemplate.

It also doesn't make it any easier to contemplate Julia's offer with a clear head.

Because the fact of the matter is, Annie's being gone means it would be easy—absurdly easy—to make my way to Cheapside and meet her.

The morning of Midsummer, I head to the armory to suit up for the skeleton-crew patrol that will run today along the north coast, to find Crissa suiting up as well. Windows have been thrown open to let out the gathering heat, and the lazy trill of cicadas from the courtyard outside is the only sound in the room aside from Crissa's boots as she stomps her feet into them on the skyfish bench.

"You're not going home?" I ask as I take a seat opposite her and reach for my flamesuit.

Crissa is one of the riders who most vocally misses home— the shore, the docks, the gulls of Harbortown. She always takes leave when it's offered.

She shakes her head. Her fingers are twisting her hair, with mesmerizing speed, into a braid. "No one else signed up for this shift. And I wasn't going to ask Cor to cover it, what with the business with his sister. Perks of being a squadron leader, huh?"

She tosses the braid behind her shoulder and lets out a

self-conscious laugh. I recognize it as a variation of the response I've been making about family holidays for years: laughing off homesickness in the hopes it'll put a stop to the unwanted pity. I change the subject.

"Good day to fly."

And that it is. A brisk summer breeze lifts the dragons' wings; not a cloud is in sight; and visibility on the North Sea stretches for miles. It's not the kind of skies that bring ambush. The New Pythians probably want to spend this day with their families, too.

And Julia wants to spend it with me.

Surely, whatever side I've committed to, whatever regime I've chosen—surely I could *see* her—just this once?

The thoughts are too volatile; I push them away and let the open sky fill my thoughts. Crissa insists on taking the dragons low, the talons of her skyfish practically tickling the crests of the waves as she laughs in delight. Pallor doesn't have a skyfish's love of water, but he enjoys chasing Phaedra all the same, and Crissa's high spirits have a way of catching. The hours pass quickly; before we know it, the day is done, the sun setting, and we're able to head home.

"Hey."

We've rejoined in the empty solarium after separating to rinse off brine. Crissa, in her ground uniform again, is toweling her glowing hair dry; a lowered sun fills the room with long shadows. I'm suddenly conscious that we're completely alone and that we've both just emerged from the bath. Two facts that should not seem related but suddenly do.

Crissa takes a seat on the opposite side of the empty room. Instead of diminishing the tension I'm feeling, her distance heightens it. As if now, the tension is a thing acknowledged.

"So," she says. "You told Annie you didn't want to go to Duck's."

"Yeah." And then, for no good reason at all, I add the truth. "Apparently."

I regret saying it at once. But Crissa's nodding like this is what she expected.

"Did something . . . happen, between you two?"

I could say yes, and it would be more than true, but not in the way I know Crissa to be asking.

"Not like that."

It's only after I say it that the feeling of emptiness hits. Annie's absence, tonight of all nights. Perhaps Crissa sees something in my face that betrays me, because she doesn't press the question.

"With anyone else, then?" Crissa says, releasing her hair from the towel and looking at me from under the wet curls.

It's startling to find that this kind of turn in conversation, amid everything else on my mind, still has the power to make my mouth go dry. This isn't the kind of discussion I've ever had in the Cloister; it's as if in this space, the vows we took as children overshadow any such reference. No children, no family, no marriage. Not explicit on anything else, but that never seemed the point. Ten feet apart, alone, phrasing our meanings obliquely, it feels like Crissa and I are doing something forbidden.

"Me?"

"You."

To my horror, I feel myself blushing. Crissa, maddeningly, does not. She just smiles.

"No." Then I ask, defensive: "What about you?"

"What about me what?"

My consternation must be showing because suddenly, Crissa laughs. Like she's releasing me. And then I'm laughing, too. Sheepishly.

She asks, "Do you have plans for tonight?"

A flashing awareness again of this whole wide-empty Cloister, its unchaperoned dorm rooms, and just the two of us. Even Mistress Mortmane has gone home. I take in Crissa's face, pink from the bath, and her eyes, blue as the Medean, direct as they hold my gaze.

Mouth shut tightly, I shake my head.

"I was just asking," Crissa goes on, watching me steadily, "because I was wondering if you'd fancy coming to a dinner party with me."

"Oh."

Crissa's eyes twinkle with a mischief she doesn't acknowledge as I adjust my expression.

"My friend's in her first year at the War College," she explains. "She's not going home either, because Harbortown's too far. Anyway, she and some of the other Silver cadets are putting together a dinner. Might be fun."

Annie gone, Julia's note incinerated, I feel a strange recklessness take hold of me.

"Sure. I'll go."

* * *

The War College is where Callipolis trains its future military officers, and it lies across from the Lyceum, on Scholars Row. I've been inside the War College before, but tonight is my first experience of the Silvers' austere barracks on the edge of the campus. In honor of Midsummer, a fire has been lit on the flagstones for a roast, mismatched chairs and tables have been brought from inside, and an odd assortment of personal dishes and repurposed military gear have been supplied for crockery. The evening shadows are long across the yellowed green as the sun waits out its longest day.

Crissa and her friend Mara embrace with shrieks of delight, golden hair mixing with black, tan arms enfolding brown. I'm welcomed with enthusiasm by Mara's classmates, who refill my and Crissa's goblets often as we prepare dinner, and demand our insights about the situation with New Pythos, though most of the questions are ones neither Crissa nor I have answers to.

"What did the Pythians *look* like? Were you able to see their dragons' call markings?"

"Do you think their fleet's sparked?"

"Is there some way to *make* our fleet spark?"

"I've got this theory, about where they'd want to strike first—"

The first-year's friend elbows him. "Shut up, Lee sur Pallor doesn't want to hear your *theory*—"

When the meal is finally cooked—about two hours later than we were aiming for, and several bottles further along than planned—the conversations are uproariously loud, echoing in the courtyard, under the light of candles that have been added to the tables as the sun set. They have by now moved on to less grim topics. Among them is the upcoming Firstrider Tournaments.

"Who are you rooting for to win Firstrider, Crissa?"

There are guffaws around the table as Crissa and I lock eyes. Crissa smiles, seems to greatly enjoy taking her time considering her answer while the cadets snicker and look from her to me.

Finally, with the air of making a narrow call, she says: "Oh, probably Lee sur Pallor."

The cadets cheer; I'm thumped on my back. Crissa is still smiling at me, teasingly; I am returning the smile against my will.

"Don't tell Cor."

"Why Lee?" someone shouts.

"Because I think he'd do a fine job leading the fleet. I'd follow him into war."

My stomach skips again, though this time it is not just because of Crissa's smile.

Because since Julia's note, even if the vision of making Firstrider is clearer than ever, the thought of war with New Pythos has become something I can barely imagine, let alone imagine leading.

Three in the morning, Cheapside . . .

More thumps on my back; a toast goes up to *Lee sur Pallor, future fleet commander of Callipolis.* Then to the coming war. Then to the summer, to Atreus, to the Revolution, to the Guardians; then to the cadets' mothers, to the highlands and the lowlands and the vassal archipelagos, which some of them hail from. And then, well into their cups, the cadets start complaining about the Gold students in the Lyceum. The rivalry between the schools runs deep, and the cadets take the time to assure me and Crissa that though our wristbands contain gold, they consider us an exception to their slurs: "You ride dragons. You don't just sit on your asses reading books all day. Plus, you're not snobs."

Crissa and I raise our goblets. "To not being snobs!"

The complaints about Golds begin with tall tales of school

pranks administered and suffered, but it gradually degenerates into more serious accusations. The first stars are winking into life when Crissa's friend Mara says:

"The Lyceans are a bunch of Dragontongue-speaking triarchist traitors."

Crissa, who's been listening to the Gold-bashing with an expression of detached amusement as she gnaws the last bits off a chicken bone, sits up at this with a noise of indignation.

"Okay, that's just not true."

There are a few wolf whistles around the table, encouraging a confrontation between the girls. Mara folds her arms and tosses her hair. She has the long vowels of Harbortown that Crissa began to clip years ago.

"How many of them speak Dragontongue? We all know who tests Gold. With their hoity-toity Lycean Ball and all their old-regime traditions . . ."

Crissa sets her chicken bone down to make a dividing motion with her hands.

"Speaking Dragontongue does *not* make them triarchists."

"It makes them patricians from the Janiculum Hill, which is as good as triarchist—"

Crissa snorts. "The Janiculum *brought down* the triarchy. Then it purged the patricians who'd stood in the way."

"The *people* brought down the triarchy," Mara insists. "It was a people's revolution."

There are a few cheers of affirmation from the other cadets at this. Crissa waves them off.

"Oh, spare us the class-iron propaganda sheets," she snaps. "It was an inside job. Who do you think poisoned the dragons? Farmers and fishermen? The Red Month came about through servants, advisors, courtiers. Atreus's peers, the patricians who speak Dragontongue. The mob was only let in at the end."

At the end means Palace Day. Pressure is building in my temple.

There's silence after Crissa's pronouncement, and for a moment all we can hear is the chirping of cicadas. One of the cadets, a jocular second year named Gaven, takes it upon himself to dispel the tension Crissa's passion has left behind. He raises his glass, sparkling in the candlelight.

"To Palace Day!"

I should have seen that coming.

The toast goes round, and I raise my glass like everyone else, though I imagine smashing it into the table and ramming it into Gaven's neck.

I'm expecting that to be the end of it, but then Gaven leans back and says, "What it must have been like to have been there that day, you know? Making *history*. The glory of it."

There are nods around the table. Crissa is the exception; her nose wrinkles as if she's caught the scent, yet again, of the work of the *People's Paper*. Because in the Cloister and the Lyceum at least, the narrative of Palace Day is not glorified.

For the rest of the class metals, it's touted as the proudest day in our history.

"My brother was there," Gaven goes on. "The stories he tells about it—"

Crissa lifts up her palms, as if to ward something off.

"If this is the part of the conversation where we start sharing Palace Day stories," she says quietly, "let's just not."

"No, let's," I say unexpectedly.

Crissa swings around and looks at me, her face full of

surprised disappointment that the long shadows of the candlelight accentuate. In other circumstances I'd appreciate her decency, but mention of Palace Day puts me past appreciating anything. I grin back at Gaven, so wide it feels like my face is splitting.

"Let's hear it. Tell me, Gaven, about your brother's glorious achievements on Palace Day."

Gaven tells me.

Three hours later, I'm in Cheapside.

* * *

I haven't been back to the slums since the year and a half in Albans, but my memory of the walking route between the orphanage and the neighborhood school is just enough to get me to the alley where I know the Drowned Dragon to be. It's strange to navigate in the dark, on Midsummer, with nothing but blurry childhood memories to guide me. Fires are lit here and there among the crumbling buildings, clusters of class-irons gathered at tables set up on street corners and alleyways to drink and feast through the night. None of them takes notice of a cloaked figure passing through the shantytown.

Now that I'm on my way, it seems incredible that I could ever have considered not coming. The path can't be taken fast enough; anticipation fills me with unbearable impatience.

Until finally, I'm there.

The tavern is so poorly lit that, when I first enter, I have to let my eyes adjust. A few candles light the tables here and there for the handful of patrons with nowhere better to be on Midsummer night and the solitary barman who barely looks at me as I enter.

And in the back, in the booth farthest from the door, sits Julia.

Her long dark hair is loose around her shoulders, her riding cloak still pulled around her. But even shrouded and seated in shadow, it's plain to see that like her handwriting, Julia has grown. Nothing drives home how many years have passed like seeing the child I remember turned into a young woman.

Nine years, I realize. It's been nine years since I last saw kin.

Tightness has taken hold of my throat.

"Julia," I say.

She rises.

"Leo."

There's a moment where we stand looking at each other; and then we both take a step forward. When we embrace, the tightness closes in my throat and I choke on it. Julia tightens her embrace and makes a low, murmuring sound. Somehow it's enough to convey comfort, and at the same time a shared understanding of a bone-deep sorrow. The grief that I've grown so accustomed to quieting alone rises from forgotten depths. I have no strength to fight it.

When we finally break apart, she's smiling, her eyes wet.

"I thought you wouldn't come," she says.

"I thought I wouldn't, either . . ."

"Come, let's sit . . ."

The booth is tiny, so that even seated across from each other we're still leaned close. Julia has reached across the table and taken my hands again, like she can't bear the thought of letting me go. I return her hold tightly.

"You're all grown up," she murmurs, her eyes raking my face. "You look like them . . . Leon, of course, but there's also so much of Niobe . . ."

It's the first time I've heard my mother's name spoken aloud since the Revolution. I want to beg Julia not to talk about her, and at the same time, to keep talking about her and never stop.

We're speaking in Dragontongue, I realize. I hadn't even noticed.

"How did you get out?" I ask.

I hadn't meant to ask it first, but now, sitting across from her, it's the only question that matters.

Julia's fingers squeeze mine.

"We hid," she says. "Ixion and I. Until it was . . . over."

Palace Day. *She's talking about Palace Day.* Not as an exultant revolutionary, like the cadets from dinner, but as another survivor. Her voice is steady, the pain muted, as if she's had practice talking about it, and the talking helped her. The kind of practice I've never had.

"We could hear—everything. Well, Ixion could hear everything. Ixion"—her voice trembles and rises higher—"covered my ears. He's never really been the same since that."

I remember Ixion as someone who had everything before him, and knew it.

"He got us out afterward, to New Pythos. I can't remember it very well. We don't really talk about it."

It's my turn to tighten my fingers over hers.

"And you?" she whispers.

And me.

Nine years of silence stand between me and the memories like a wall. The words come out in the only way I can think to say them.

"We didn't have time to hide."

Julia's slow breathing, her hands in mine, her gray eyes liquid. The parting of her lips as she swallows.

I try to say more. For once in my life, I want to say more. For once in my life, it's *safe* to say more. I'm with kin at last, with the one person in the world who would understand—

But I can't.

I've hit upon the spot where the words stop, and there's no penetrating it. I look up at her and shake my head, and she understands this, too.

It's strange, after years taking refuge in silence, to suddenly feel trapped by it.

"Oh, Leo . . ."

Her voice is soft as a caress, and for a moment I think the sound of the name I lost, uttered with such sorrow, will be enough to send me over the edge. I drop my head and wait for the waves of grief to ebb, feeling the steady pulse of her hands in mine. One of them pulls away and returns with a handkerchief, which she slips into my curled palm.

Softly, anticipating my shame, she quotes the *Aurelian Cycle*:

By my own pain's knowledge will I comfort the sufferings of men.

It strikes me how often I used to hear the Cycle quoted in conversation, in *our* conversation—and how rarely I do now.

I dry my face downturned, return the handkerchief, and raise my head. "Thank you."

Julia nods, tucking it away. "Should we speak of other things?"

"Yes."

Julie smiles, the lines of worry easing from her face. The next words she offers me like gifts she's prepared.

"I was at your last tournament, Leo. You fly beautifully."

No compliment has ever filled me with such warmth.

"That was when you first recognized . . ."

"Yes. Or at least, that was when I first hoped I did. It wasn't until the tutor contacted us that I knew for sure."

Julia's hands are burn-smoothed, her cloak partly disguising the leather of what can only be a flamesuit. I offer, in return, the only conclusion that makes sense.

"You ride, too."

Julia nods. The corner of her lip quirks as she looks at me. A smirk I remember. The smirk Julia has when she's won.

"The families started allowing female riders?"

"Desperate times," Julia says mildly.

But her lifted shoulder doesn't bely the fact that she moved a mountain, and the smile that plays at her lips shows she knows she did. There's something gladdening about the realization that, after all we've lost, this at least Julia gained.

The next question is stranger, but I can't fight my curiosity. "Have you had a ranking tournament, or . . . ?"

Julia hesitates for the first time, then nods. "I'm Firstrider."

Again, the careful nonchalance, and beneath it a pride born of years of anger to which I stood witness. As my thoughts return to the old Julia with her scratched knees and her torn dresses and her stubborn defiance as she stared our brothers down, a smile breaks across my face.

"You did it," I say.

Julia's mouth curves with triumph. "Yes. I did it."

But then, like a settling cloud, I remember what it all adds up to—if I do what I've committed to and the set trajectory continues as planned.

Because Julia's ranking will not just have made her Firstrider, it will have made her commander of the Pythian aerial fleet.

Sworn not only to go into battle against Callipolis but to lead those who do.

Our hands have remained entwined throughout the conversation. Julia seems to have the same wakening discomfort as I do; she shifts, in the guise of pulling her cloak tighter around her, but it doesn't seem coincidence that our hands pull apart and neither of us moves to rejoin them.

Julia breaks the silence first. "The families sent me, Leo. You can imagine what they want. The tutor told us about your reservations. Rhadamanthus wants me to help you see reason. Before it's too late."

For a moment I only register her words with a distant pang of longing. *The families.* Who else—?

And then I hear the rest of what she said.

Too late.

I find my hands reaching forward on the narrow table, seeking hers again in desperation. "Julia, I can't—you have to talk to them. Please—whatever they're planning—"

But then Julia's fingers take one of my own reaching hands in hers and lifts it to press my own fingers against my lips. I fall silent.

"I told them I'd come for that," she whispers. "But the truth is, I haven't seen you in nine years. There will be time for those conversations. Do we need to have them so soon? It's Midsummer, and I've *missed* you, Leo."

I'm stopped short. "I've missed you, too."

It suddenly hurts, the force of how much I've missed her. Them. All of it. Surely that's allowed, for a little while—just to miss them?

"Let us spend tonight talking of other things," Julia says.

I see her request for what it is: an offer to pretend together one last time.

And as it was when we were children, the force of her believing is still enough to make the real world fade, for a little while, to nothing.

ANNIE

I've always loved Duck's house—bustling with children, full of laughter, never quiet or calm, but welcoming to you even if you are. It's the kind of place that feels so immediate that it makes everything else seem less real. The concerns that consume me in the Cloister—the threat of New Pythos and classes and training and that godforsaken list of morale visits on which my name was so noticeably absent—feel like problems from another life. Even the guilt I've felt since Duck broke our Midsummer plans to Lee becomes distant. I'd meant to invite him, after we reconciled. I'd been planning on it—

But I'd delayed. Delayed because, if I'm honest with myself, the thought of a weekend with Duck's family, Lee out of my mind and my sight, was what I wanted more.

I've been coming to the Sutter house on leave days since I was nine. It was the first home I'd come to since the Mackys took me to Albans. At first it was overwhelming. All the ways it was good made it hard. Family meals, children screeching and laughing, parents telling you when to go to bed—they were things I'd forgotten I missed. As if sensing my discomfort, Duck buffered. Kept me busy, so the memories couldn't crowd in. Made sure I was laughing, because when I wasn't laughing, I wanted to cry.

It got easier over time. Not for Lee. He came once and never again.

Tonight, the house is less full of joy than usual. Ana is packing bags for a new life in the boardinghouse attached to Fullerton's, where she'll start in a week. When we talk about it, briefly, in the morning, Ana is matter-of-fact. It was a better posting than most, and she'd never expected to test well. Some of her friends' postings were worse. All the same I sense her reluctance to meet my eyes. The greater resentment comes from Mr. Sutter, whose anger hangs over the Midsummer dinner like a cloud with the comments he can't stop making to Cor: *What's the point of our daughters going to school if this is what they get? Before, we'd just have found her a suitable match . . .*

Cor drinks long and deep from his cider and lets his father's dissatisfaction roll over him in waves, the lines growing between his eyebrows as the night wears on. He doesn't attempt the rebuttals that we've learned to such complaints, and I don't blame him. The arguments justifying class-iron labor postings are offered patly in class—but when you look at Ana, imagine her toiling in a workhouse because she answered a few questions wrong on a test, words like *the good of the state* begin to make less sense.

After the long dinner outside has finished and the table's been brought back in, Ana, her father, and Cor sit down to go over her preparations for Fullerton's.

"Let's go over your rights as an Iron worker again. I want to make sure you know them."

"Cor, really—"

"Really."

Duck has lured his younger siblings out of their hearing; he's roughhousing with Greg and Merina on the rug between the sofa and the fireplace. A strained line is barely visible between his eyebrows as he distracts them. I watch their scuffling from the sofa, an old quilt pulled up to my chin.

"It's past their bedtime, Dorian," Mrs. Sutter calls from the kitchen.

"Can I read them a story first, Mum?"

Duck has leapt without warning onto the sofa, which creaks as he adds his stocky weight, and scoots close to tug the quilt over both of us. His hair is disheveled from Greg's yanking on it.

"Budge up, you blanket hog," he tells me.

I'm suddenly conscious of Duck's body pressed against mine beneath the quilt. Merina plops down on the sofa next to me and tugs the quilt over herself, too. So there are bodies warm on either side of me, and I'm in the middle.

I'd almost forgotten what this feels like.

The book Greg fetches, entitled *Tales of the Medean*, is one of two books his family owns; the other is Atreus's *Revolutionary Manifesto*. The fairy tales are illuminated, images of dragons and lords and ladies alternating with text.

"I learned how to read with this," Duck tells me.

He shifts his weight so he can see better, and as he does, his arm goes around my shoulders to steady himself, and then when he's steady, I wonder if he'll remove it or if I want him to.

His arm remains around me. He begins to read.

It's not reading aloud like you do in class: It's a style I've never heard before. Duck reads each character with a different kind of voice, some low, some high, some raspy, some thunderous. This is something parents must do with their children, I realize. Parents who know how to read.

Merina and Greg are giggling with delight and within minutes, I am too. By the end of the story Greg has fallen asleep and Merina's head is slumped against my shoulder. Duck surveys them and then looks at me.

"I should probably put Greg down."

"One more," Merina demands sleepily.

Duck resumes reading, more quietly this time. Beneath the quilt, the fingers of the hand not wrapped around my shoulder find mine and slip into them. The patter of my heart as I listen to him read becomes something I can feel and hear.

These feelings—happiness, safety, warmth beside Duck—what do they add up to?

Do they add up to something more than that?

Do they add up to something more for *him*?

Merina has fallen asleep, too.

"I'm off to bed, dears. You'll put Greg and Merina down?"

Mrs. Sutter is on her way upstairs. Her eyes are crinkled permanently at the corners, the same that form around Duck's when he smiles. She kisses Duck on the forehead, and from Duck's long-suffering expression I sense this is a nighttime routine he considers himself to have outgrown, but will endure for her sake. My school-level Damian is just enough for me to understand her mother tongue.

"So good to have you home for a night, darling. We've been worried about you these past few weeks."

Duck's Damian is rusty, mumbled. "It's good to be home, Mum."

Before she turns away, as easily as if she's always done it, Mrs. Sutter kisses me on the forehead, too.

There's silence after she leaves us, except for the crackling fire: Merina's weight against me on one side, her breathing soft as she sleeps; Duck's body wrapped around me beneath the quilt; the children's book open and heavy on my lap; the feeling of a mother's kiss tingling on my forehead.

Duck speaks first.

"It's funny," he murmurs, "when you remember the vows mean we can't ever have any of this."

The Guardian vows forswearing marriage and family.

I replay the sentence, and my mind fixes on the ambiguity of a single pronoun: When Duck says *we*, does he mean the Guardians in general? Or just—?

I've looked up at him; our faces are inches apart. His hazel eyes widen as if he, too, realized the ambiguity of what he just said.

And then, suddenly, I feel *panicked*.

"I meant—"

"The Guardians in general—?"

"Yeah—"

Another feeling, wrong: relief. As if he can read it, Duck untwines his fingers from mine beneath the blanket. I nearly release my breath.

"I'm glad you came, Annie," he says abruptly.

"I'm glad I came, too."

And that's true. I've loved every bit of this visit, every unchecked burst of laughter and moment of unfiltered happiness—

Then why this *panic*?

"Do you think you'll stay tomorrow, or—"

I hesitate, and though I should be thinking only of Duck in this moment, of the faint lines that have appeared between his eyebrows as he studies me, I realize that I'm thinking about Lee instead.

Lee, who told me, on the arena ramparts, that he would stay, against every reason he had to leave; and whom I've now gone and left.

I say, "I'll probably head back to the Cloister tomorrow morning. I just—"

I have no words to explain the rest of it. But Duck seems to understand from how I swallow.

"I'm glad we could have you for this long, at least," he says simply.

LEE

I wake in the Cloister dorm disoriented. Slowly, the surroundings resolve themselves: the same long row of beds as always, but the sunlight slanting in at the unfamiliar angle of late morning. It takes me a moment to distinguish the feeling of splintering joy and sorrow and loss that's mingled with the physical sensation of a headache. Fragmented memories of the conversation with Julia, of the parting that seemed too soon even though it happened hours later, of a dazed walk through the silent predawn city back to the Palace return to me slowly.

"Morning."

I raise my head, focusing slowly on the small figure perched on the bed next to mine.

"Annie?"

It is the first time she's sought my company since the Pythian fleet was sighted.

She holds out a muffin.

"From Duck's mum."

I sit up and wince, raising my hand to rub my forehead.

"I should be on patrol," I realize.

"Don't worry about it. Cor came back early, too; he's out with Crissa. They decided to let you sleep it off."

Sleep off having met with one of the riders whom Cor and Crissa are now patrolling our skies to guard against. I feel the weight of guilt, the greater for its delay, settling over me. Except, fresh off of a night spent in the company of Julia, it's hard to know what I feel most guilty about: that I just had drinks with a cousin who wants to kill my friends; or that my friends want to kill my cousins.

This is why you shouldn't have met with her.

When I look up at Annie, I see guilt in her expression, too.

"You're hungover," she says.

"I went to a Midsummer dinner at the War College. With Crissa."

"Oh." Relief, mingled with something else, battles across Annie's face. "Good," she says. "I'm glad you did."

I take the muffin from her and take a bite. It is the most satisfying thing I've ever tasted.

"How was Midsummer with the Sutters?"

It sounds like a bad poem. Annie fiddles with auburn wisps of her hair, averting her face slightly. "It was nice."

"You're back early," I observe.

She hesitates. It feels like she's teetering on the edge of saying something that will embarrass us both. I can't decide if I want her to. But then, instead, she just says: "We need to train. The tournament's in a week." She curls fists in her lap as she adds:

"I want to make finalist. And I—really want to beat Power."

I look at her in surprise. Both at the desires she's admitting, and what she's proposing.

"You came back so we could spar?"

Annie, looking just a little bashful, nods. Her braid is freshly done, ready to tuck under a helmet.

The mere thought of taking Pallor out on a morning like this is enough to start clearing my head; and then the thought of sparring with Annie, of feeling the blood-singing clarity of reflex and instinct that it takes to match her, of slipping into the all-minded focus that relieves the need for conscious thought— suddenly that's the only thing I want.

However complicated Julia has left my thoughts about the Pythians, my thoughts about the tournament are simple. I want to make finalist, too.

"Great. Let's suit up."

Last night and the confusion of emotions left over from it are already passing like the memory of a dream.

6
—
SEMIFINALS

ANNIE

I wait with growing dread for another message from the ministry in the week leading up to the second tournament, but nothing comes. I do get a letter from Holbin: Macky's son writes, *Dear Annie, we hope you beet them were sorry we wont be their this time but were all rooting for you in Holbin,* and I pin this letter on my wall, too, next to the dried laurel from the first tournament.

In the preceding week, the Fourth Order riders are exempted from coastal patrols in order to train; the other three are also allowed to delay their morale visits. Since I haven't been assigned any, I have nothing to reschedule. I tell myself it doesn't matter; that morale visits are crass, cheap experiments in rhetorical manipulation; but I still know that being excluded from them means I have, yet again, been written off by the Callipolan ministry.

Let them write me off. I'll train.

I spend every free minute drilling with Lee or with Cor and Rock, whose stormscourges make them good preparation for Power. I've never felt a desire for victory quite like this. All Power's jokes about highlanders and peasants, all the entitlement he brags about among his patrician friends, all the ministry's misgivings about me and their favor for riders like him—I finally have a chance to throw it back in their faces, in public. Because Power may be more polished leadership material on the ground, but the air is my turf.

In the lead-up to the match, many of the Janiculum riders stop talking to me, while Rock and the other riders from the countryside sit with me at nearly every meal. But not all loyalties divide along such lines. To my surprise, in Dragontongue class the day before the tournament, Hanna Lund and the other patrician students I've been doing homework with in the library pass me a handmade card signed by most of the girls in the class. They've written a quote from the *Aurelian Cycle* inside: *And as she turned, it was revealed by her tread that she was fireborne.*

"Power's a jerk. We'll be cheering for you, Antigone."

The day of the tournament dawns overcast, fiercely windy, with thick gray stratus blanketing the low sky, hiding the top of Pytho's Keep. Despite the gloomy weather the stands are full. Power has stationed himself on the far side of the Eyrie, surrounded by stormscourge riders, to watch Lee and Cor's match. They glance occasionally in my direction, where I stand with the aurelian riders beside Duck, and I return their stares: I feel the coming match has turned my blood brazen.

Duck grimaces as his brother and Lee set up overhead and launch into forward attack. I wonder, but don't ask, if he can decide whom he's rooting for. In any case, he doesn't have much time to consider the question. Cor has always been an erratic flyer; on good days he flies as well as Lee or better; but on bad days he can't hold a candle to him. And stress almost always means that Cor will have a bad day. Lee lands a penalty hit early and it goes downhill from there: Cor spills over, which makes him and Maurana fly worse, and then it's only a matter of time before Lee gets inside their guard.

"No surprises there," Lotus mutters to Rock, when the bell is rung in Lee's favor after about five minutes.

Lee sur Pallor, finalist for Firstrider, the announcer cries.

They land, and Cor shakes Lee's hand sloppily amid roaring applause, then strides off the Eyrie to nurse his disappointment privately. Next to me, Duck sighs, frustrated but not exactly disappointed. As if even he can't resist rooting for Lee, family ties to the contrary.

Goran's voice calls: "Power, Antigone, you're up."

Duck's fingers tighten on my shoulder, a silent encouragement, before releasing it. I start to make for the cave mouth before pausing: Lee is moving purposefully in our direction, his helmet under one arm, his hair plastered in sweat, his face still lit by adrenaline. Right before he reaches us, Power crosses Lee's path. He leans in, clasps Lee's shoulder, and I can only just hear him over the whistling wind.

"You know what the dragonborn used to say. Peasants burn best—"

Lee's gray eyes, still blazing from his own match, focus on Power's. Though his expression doesn't alter, a chill emanates. Power's grin falters and he takes a half step backward, seemingly unconsciously.

Then as I turn for the cave mouth, Lee's hand reaches out and catches my arm.

"Let me check your armor."

He speaks through gritted teeth. I feel myself warming beneath my helmet.

"My armor is fine."

But he ignores my protest, and though I should try to stop him, I don't. He begins to pat me down, yanking on each buckle of my helmet, cuirass, and limb guards, roughly and quickly, as if determined not to let his hands linger. But when he raises his face, it's reddened.

At the sight, an answering heat awakens in my body. Blooming from every inch of me that his hands brush, spreading up my neck with warmth. He's standing so close that I can *smell* him, his fresh sweat mingled with the scent of Pallor's smoke. Although I know we're being watched by thousands, all I really notice is that Duck and Crissa are looking over, and I wish they weren't.

Finally, he nods and steps back. His face, usually so pale against the dark hair, glows red even at a distance.

"Go," he says.

Power is waiting for me at the cave mouth, grinning as I approach. His gaze travels down to my bare neck, still flushed enough that the summer breeze feels cool against it.

"Do you think he got everything?"

I ignore him. We blow into the whistles built into our wristbands, waiting for a sound that's inaudible to us to call the dragon who's been trained to respond to it. Power raises a canteen to his lips as he waits, and I do the same: Now's the time to drink as much water as possible.

A stillness settles over me as I feel Aela approach, and one by one my senses confirm it: the sound of her wings; the brush of the cave-draft on my face; the sight of her amber scales glinting in the darkness as she emerges. The nerves that have been twisting my stomach all morning fall away, replaced by an awareness so clear, it is a kind of absence of thought. This is Aela. It's time.

I tighten Aela's saddle, check her reins, and she twists her head round for one last check, finding my eyes with her slitted golden ones. I scratch the ridge of her nose and she flexes her neck back. Her eagerness for the match, mingling with mine, charges a rush down my spine. Aela's thirst for the fight has always been a high I ride with pleasure.

"Let's do this."

She folds her wings close as I mount. I strap my boots, one by one, into their stirrups. A few meters away, Power has done the same with Eater. We put on our helmets and, after an exchanged nod, pull our visors down.

And then, with a leap that breaks from gravity, we're in the air, great wings beating to lift us higher. The gray blanket of clouds, the crowds, the glistening river fill my vision once again: On Aela, the world always seems hyperfocused.

Then the bell rings, Power charges, and we dive.

A week ago, when we first talked this match out, I told Lee the strategy I wanted to take and he tried to talk me down. Eater's lungs don't *run out*, he said, it would take too long, run too high a risk of injuries, and given Power's proclivity for full-heat hits, the injuries risked would be too debilitating.

"Eater's range is twice as long as Aela's," I answered. "*How else* should I do it?"

Lee, rather than offering alternatives, just said, "It's suicide."

The reply I gave was one I wouldn't think of making to anyone but Lee.

"Not for me."

Lee didn't argue with that.

It's known as the gadfly approach: teasing in and out of range long enough, provoking enough shots from your opponent, that they run out of ash. But for Eater, that will take a long time. Not to mention that Power is one of the few of us who's mastered using spillovers to his advantage: Where anger and excitement spilling into your dragon disorients someone like Cor, they just make Power unpredictable. It's a tactic historically favored by stormscourge riders. He and Eater ride their emotions like a roller coaster whose direction only they can predict, and Power gives him rein to fire at will.

But Aela and I can dodge almost anything.

So as the match starts, I let Power take the offensive, Aela and I playing hopscotch between Eater's jets of ash, staying close, keeping him firing, keeping him busy. The minutes tick past, and Aela and I dodge, weave, and dodge again.

But even if you're flying at your best, you can't help tiring eventually, and mistakes happen. After about ten minutes we turn just a little too shallowly, and I feel a blistering heat across my left calf. I can't contain a hiss of pain: It's a full-heat burn, the kind we aren't even allowed to dole out in training. The shining armor blackens, reacting to the heat, and a bell for the first penalty rings out across the stands. Aela senses my pain even if she's impervious to the heat. She pulls out of range and waits as I unplug the coolant shaft set in the calf of my flamesuit. Cool liquid pours down my leg, soothing the burn, though it's severe enough that the pain doesn't fade entirely. But the coolant will hold off the worst of it for another half hour, which is all I need.

Every second I spend out of range is one gained by Eater, and I need to keep him firing if I want to deplete him, so I bring Aela round without further pause. We begin a second round. Minutes blur together into dodging and gamboling and shots fired to my left and right and back as I focus only on reaction and response—

Until the second penalty hits. I fail to dodge Power's jackknife turn, and Eater's ash, full heat, sears my arms. In the time-out before reset, I fumble to open the coolant shafts at my elbows with fingers stiff in their gloves, then twist the reins around my wrists, relieving my fingers of the need to clench. Even as I struggle to master the reins, I feel the adrenaline and pain loosening me, pushing me closer to Aela. The heightened connection fills me with a different kind of calm. Aela and I are on our last chance: Three penalties counts as a kill shot.

We reset for a third round.

"It's over, Annie," Power calls.

He's grinning as he replaces his helmet; the emotions he's freely spilling over are, clearly, verging on euphoria. I reenter his range. He resumes firing. As Aela and I begin, once more, to swerve and dodge, I note what Power, in his transported state, has not. Eater's ash has begun, every few meters, to sputter.

I turn Aela and pull her to a halt. Power and I are facing each other. I'm exposed, within Power's range. I can make out his glittering, triumphant eyes through the visor of his helmet. The arena is spread below us, and the clouds obscuring the top of Pytho's Keep hang low and close.

Eater opens his mouth for a kill shot—and nothing comes out.

Power's eyes widen. In the split second that it takes me to surge forward and fire, he launches upward. My shot misses everything but Eater's trailing tail. And then Power and Eater disappear into the cloud cover.

For a moment Aela and I are stalled, looking up into the clouds where Power has vanished.

Power's intention is as clear as if he'd announced it. Two rules of tournament sparring that both of us know: first, that contact charges are off limits between dragons of different breeds during sporting events. Second, that whatever happens out of sight of the referee is considered fair game.

If I go into those clouds, Eater will tackle Aela. He's more than half her size.

But if I wait, his lungs will recover. And every moment that I wait, the coolant wears off a bit more, and the pain becomes just a little more consuming.

"Are we doing this?" I say to Aela.

But Aela is already rising, and I don't have to urge her with anything more than a shared determination.

The passage up through the stratus cloud is quiet, disorienting in its seamless uniformity of gray. I can feel Aela's heart pounding in time with my own. When we break through, I have a split second to realize that there's an altostratus layer of clouds blanketing the sky still higher, and that we're between layers, lost in a strange, gray-white light. The only remaining sign of land is the top of Pytho's Keep, a few hundred meters away, rising out of the stratus like a floating fortress.

I see all of this in the half instant before Eater slams into us from behind.

Aela shrieks and twists while Eater's talons sink into the pauldron protecting my shoulder, puncturing the armor and flamesuit, sinking into my skin. The talons of his other forearm are sinking into Aela's back. She screams and *I feel it*, her pain bursting in a haze through my own. And then I feel her fury.

Fine. You want to play dirty? We'll play dirty.

I reach with burn-clumsy fingers for my bootknife and slash, over and over, against the inside of Eater's forearms, and he shrieks and pulls his talons out of us.

Aela twists us round and then, though she's gained the leverage to break free of Eater, she doesn't. She claws her way up his torso, scrabbling with him arm and leg. Both dragons' wings are beating madly, keeping us aloft and stalling, blocking each rider's sight of the other as they lock in their embrace.

Then Aela sinks her talons into the membrane of Eater's inner wing. He shrieks, Power cries out, and Eater curls the wing into his side—and then, *finally*, as we begin to free-fall with only three wings holding two dragons aloft, Eater's folded wing gives us an opening straight onto Power's crouched form.

Aela fires, full heat. Power disappears in the smoke. Then she kicks off from Eater and Power with a shriek of disgust.

The smoke clears. Power's armor is blackened; he sits dazed, lost in the shock of a full-heat blast. Numbly, automatically, he begins to open his torso coolant shafts.

"Do you yield?"

We're poised, at firing distance, to hit him again, and Eater's still empty. Power's voice comes out in a low gasp.

"Yeah."

"Helmet," I demand.

Proof and guarantee of a match won, in the absence of a referee.

Power lets out a hoarse laugh but doesn't question my precaution. With shaking hands, he lifts his helmet from his head. His hair is glistening with sweat, his face scudded with tracks of ash. For one inscrutable moment, he stares at me, eyes so dilated from spillover that they look black. Then he tosses his soot-covered helmet through the open air.

I catch it.

We descend together through the stratus. When we burst back into sight of the arena, there's an explosion of noise. It takes me a moment to realize: It is cheering, and it's for me.

Like someone else has possessed my body, I lift Power's helmet above my head and shake it for the world to see.

There's a confusion of shouting once we land on the Eyrie. Duck is jumping up and down, Crissa is screaming in delight, and Lee is there, helping me cut my boots free of their straps, guiding me off the saddle, and taking stock of my injuries with careful fingers. I can no longer move my fingers or my left leg, and my shoulder, which is dripping blood, is stiff with pain. I can still feel Aela's pulsing heartbeat and searing wound like my own. Lee's arm grips me below the shoulder, steadying me.

"Annie, are you all right?" Goran's voice seems to come from a great distance. He sounds concerned. It's so surprising that I laugh out loud. Power is nowhere to be seen, so it's into Goran's hands that I push Power's helmet.

"I'm great."

Lee's grip on my arm tightens as he turns me toward him. "Annie, we've got to do the concluding ceremony. Can you make it through?"

The concluding ceremony.

For the finalists.

"You and me," I realize.

Lee is holding me upright, one arm around me, the other steadying me, his face just inches from mine. His gray eyes are piercing and proud and just a little pained. The sweat and ash have dried in tracks down his face.

"You and me," he repeats quietly.

All of a sudden, I feel like crying.

I waver again. The coolant is definitely wearing off, as is the adrenaline. The Eyrie is starting to fade in and out.

"Can she fly up?" Goran asks.

"Not with Aela being tended. I'll walk her, that'll be easier . . ."

Lee's arm against my back, firm and purposeful. Down to the arena stands, then up the stairs to the Palace Box. People are cheering, screaming when they see us, but the sound feels muffled.

"I could have killed you when you went into the stratus after him," Lee says as we mount the stairs, admiration battling with exasperation in his voice. "That *sneak*, pulling a contact charge . . ."

When we reach the Palace Box, he releases my side so none of the waiting ministers can see that he'd been supporting me. The last time I stood in this place, I was numb with terror; today, I have no thoughts for that. Let the ministry think what it thinks; let Propaganda write me another memo. I've done it. I've beaten Power. For the moment, I have to focus all my attention on walking. One step after another, with Lee beside me, down the aisle to where the First Protector stands, smiling.

"My two finalists," he says, with warmth in his voice. It does not seem to be a scripted line.

There are more ceremonial words, then the weight of the laurel placed over my head. And then Aela's presence, close, as I slip a laurel down her long neck and she rumbles with pride.

"A week before Palace Day, we will gather for our last, and most important, tournament," Atreus tells the audience. "One of these finalists will become Alternus, lieutenant and defender of the people, and one will become Firstrider, their champion.

"Lee and Antigone, we wish you luck in your final months of training."

* * *

Later that evening I lie half awake in the darkened Palace infirmary. Master Welse has already headed home for the night; the infirmary is deserted when the door to my ward creaks open. Hushed voices, giggling, a few silhouetted heads peering in. Crissa's voice comes out low and playful.

"Aaaannie . . ."

I sit up from my pillows, my burns twinging. "What are you *doing*?"

Crissa flings open the door, and light from the corridor spills in. Behind her stand the other girls: Deirdre and Alexa, inseparable for as long as we've been in the program, and also Orla, who usually avoids group activities in favor of her books. Her presence particularly signifies that something unusual is afoot.

"We're here to take you to your party," Crissa announces.

I'm so startled that my first thought is why she isn't at *Lee's* party. She is, after all, his friend. "What about Lee?"

"The aurelian squadron's taking care of him. *We're* taking care of you."

We, the female Guardians. A few of the boys, too, behind them, though I can't make out their faces. My heart constricts, touched and surprised that they're here at all. I hadn't thought of celebrations, and if I had, I'd have assumed they'd be for Lee. But then I remember my burns.

"I can't really . . ."

Walk. For a day at least. Physician's orders.

"Not a problem," Crissa says, unperturbed. And then, with the air of summoning a dragon, she bellows: "Richard!"

A tall, sturdy figure makes his way through the girls and crouches by my bed. Rock. And then he deploys the brogue he usually pretends not to have. The brogue of home.

"Up you get, finalist."

I burst out laughing. "You can't be serious—"

But they are serious indeed. Deirdre and Alexa hoist me onto Rock's shoulders, and Crissa hurls what looks like a blanket over my back, but it turns out to be a Callipolan flag, its wing-spread dragon breathing four circlets of fire against red. Orla seizes the laurel lying on the bedside table and reaches up on tiptoe to mash it on my head. Duck, standing in the doorway, holds one of Goran's training horns to his lips and blows. The silence of the infirmary breaks like an explosion.

"To the Pickled Boar!"

The Pickled Boar is a tavern on the other side of the river in Highmarket, popular among the lowborn Guardians. I've never been before.

Duck's shout is taken up by the other girls, and I'm marched out of the infirmary. The passage through the Palace gardens, across the river, and into Highmarket passes in a blur: the moon-lit gardens crossed with loping speed that I mark from Rock's great height as I cling to the Callipolan flag around my shoulders; the silhouettes of Deirdre and Alexa and Orla streaking around us, shrieking and screaming and giggling in the darkness as Crissa cries *onward!* like she's leading a charge, and Duck blowing the horn like he's determined to destroy the Palace's usual peaceful silence.

Highmarket is awash with noise: We're not the only ones

who took the tournament as an excuse to celebrate, and it seems that in the wake of the threat from New Pythos it has a lot of steam to blow off. Callipolan flags everywhere, *horns* everywhere, being sold by enterprising street merchants and blown from the streets and the balconies, amid a cacophony of shrieking and choruses of drunken singing and even the occasional low throb of a street drum. Ale sloshes in toasts and forms sticky puddles on the cobblestones; sheets have been painted with messages and hung from second-story windows: LOWBORN TAKES THE LAUREL; LONG LIVE THE REVOLUTION; DOWN WITH NEW PYTHOS.

At the door of the Pickled Boar, when Crissa helps me to the ground, I protest the flaw I've just realized in her plan.

"Crissa, we've all sworn vows of poverty, how're we supposed to buy ourselves *drinks*—"

Crissa and Rock let out thunderous laughs.

"Trust me," Crissa says, throwing her arm around my flag-draped shoulders and not noticing as I wince, "you're not going to have to buy yourself a drink tonight."

And then she ushers me into the tavern. Candles and sconces light a room full of laughter, faces painted with the Callipolan colors, a group of musicians in the corner hammering on drums and plucking at fiddles that send not so much music as rhythm into my blood. As soon as we're inside, Crissa leaps onto the closest empty chair and summons up the voice she usually reserves for commanding her squadron from dragonback, spreading an arm wide in my direction.

"Ladies and gentlemen of Callipolis, I give you your highland finalist!"

Amid roars of applause that deafen, Rock seizes my fist and

thrusts it into the air. And then I am surrounded, my shoulders—still tender with burns and a talon's piercing—thumped by complete strangers. It hurts, but even so I'm beaming.

"Whiskey for the highlander!"

I'm passed a drink whose fumes alone makes my eyes water, and as I set my lips to it, I begin to splutter. But the bristle-bearded man who's handed it to me only cheers the more, those around us laughing with delight as they applaud.

"Antigone sur Aela's first whiskey!"

"Drink up, lassie! Drink to the Revolution!"

"Another!"

And then the musicians begin playing the Anthem of the Revolution, and it's hard to say whether the strength of the whiskey or the shivers of the melody down my spine makes my eyes fill, and I raise my glass and sing with the rest the song of my country.

We rise, we rise, for the glory of Callipolis . . .

7

MORALE VISITS

LEE

The first class with Tyndale after the tournament, I find a note tucked into the homework he returns to me.

Cousin—

I gave him two letters; this is the one for if you made it.

Do you remember how the dreams of glory sang in our blood as we were children, when we pretended to wage war? They were the dreams that I remembered when I made Firstrider of New Pythos.

We have so many things to discuss, you and I. But before we do, I want you to know this: that I, your cousin, your blood, hope you make Firstrider as much as I hoped I would myself. Perhaps it's madness to wish such a thing, with the future looming over us as it does. But the truth is that however it ends, I want you to taste it. My kin, my first friend—I want you to know what it's like to feel the might of the world at your feet. Not in pretend: in earnest.

And then I hope you let yourself imagine how it could go from there. You and I, retaking what's ours. Making those bastards pay for what they've done. Setting things right.

Our fathers may be dead, but their blood runs in our veins. We were born to this.

Give me the time and place for our next meeting.

The day I receive Julia's letter, the Firstrider Tournament is a month away, set for a week before the Palace Day anniversary and two weeks after the Lycean Ball. I reread it even as I appreciate it for what it is: a temptation. Julia's words awaken the old hunger and trace it to its starting point. To wanting Firstrider, for as long as I can remember, as any dragonlord's son would, *as my birthright.* It's easy to slip into such thinking.

It's easy to yearn after thoughts of revenge.

We were born to this.

I can't think of any answer that wouldn't be a lie in its denial, so I don't acknowledge the temptation at all. I propose a meeting at Wayfarer's Arch, a dragon perch built on an island arch that's midway between the karst pillars of New Pythos and the Callipolan northern shore. Midnight, on the next full moon, a week before the Lycean Ball.

I tell myself that I do it in Callipolis's name, even if it's without Callipolis's knowledge. I tell myself that the more information I can gather about the Pythian fleet, the better.

And I tell myself that I will make Firstrider with a different set of principles.

ANNIE

The burns from the semifinal tournament have begun to itch, and the dressings still require changing and ointment several times a day. On the first patrol I run with Power after the tournament, I expect him to be taciturn and possibly even in the mood for retribution. I have my pike—sharpened for real combat rather than the blunt kind we train with—gripped loose and ready under my arm, Power sur Eater on the outside of it. But as we leave the city behind and steer the dragons toward the northern coast, Power reins Eater to chatting distance and pulls his helmet off his head.

"So what's your plan?" he calls.

I raise my visor, too.

"What?"

The fields of the lowland plains roll out below us, emerald green from summer crops freshly burst from the earth; here and there, the spires of dragon perches, mounted with bells and unlit beacons, tower over toy-size villages.

"For beating Lee. In the final tournament. I could be your training partner."

I laugh aloud. The last time we were in the air together, Eater's talons pierced my shoulder and Aela's side in an illegal charge that we're still recovering from. The burns that they gave me itch badly enough that sitting still—in class, in the saddle—takes concentration.

"You think I'd train with you?"

Power slings his reins into one hand, twists a shoulder back to face me, and cocks an eyebrow. "I think you'd better. If you want to beat him. I could teach you spillovers; you'd be suited to them. We can start after the Lycean Ball. Our schedules will be clearer then."

For graduating Gold students, the Lycean Ball marks their transition to contributing members of the elite; for the Guardians this year, it will serve as our debut to Gold society. Between now and then, many professors have been setting end-of-year assignments and final exams that the Guardians—expanded military and public obligations notwithstanding—are still expected to complete.

"You're going to have to train for this tournament . . . He's pretty good," Power adds. An understatement, but the closest thing to a compliment he's ever said about Lee. "You should have some sort of plan."

Some sort of plan.

The problem is, I don't. Making finalist and finding myself opposite Lee was like breaking the gray-white nothingness of stratus clouds and bursting into the sunlight above them: blinding. And I'm still dazed by it.

It's strange how you can fight your way to a door, even through it, without thinking about what lies on the other side.

Fourth Order, finalist—titles I've clawed my way into and have found, upon seizing them, that I like how they settle. But *Firstrider? Commander of the Callipolan Aerial Fleet?*

Firstrider and Fleet Commander instead of *Lee?*

"You must really want Lee to lose," I observe.

The North Sea approaches, a gray swath on the horizon, punctuated by cliffs. But Power is watching me, not the ground below, and flashes a sudden grin. "Maybe I want *you* to win. Because I think you'd do a better job than that self-satisfied ass. Because I think you've got the head and the guts for it and that you'd do a good job, period. That too hard to imagine, Annie? That somebody wants you to win?"

Even though he seems to intend it as a compliment, in tone it feels more like an insult. When he realizes I'm not going to answer, he keeps going. The disgust in his voice is apparent even when he's lifting it over the wind.

"*You* probably don't even want you to win. You'd rather be his Alterna than go for commandership—"

"You don't know anything *about* me, Power."

"Yeah? I know what they say about you."

"About *me*?"

"They say serfs are always happiest when they have a lord."

I haul Aela to a halt midair so hard that I rock forward in the saddle and she hawks against the bit. Power has to circle round to face us. The northern coastline, Fort Aron and its harbor, stretch below, and the rising cliffs of the highlands spread west, green grass and violet heather both bleached silver under the cumulus-laden sky.

"I take it back," Power says easily, spreading his hands in surrender.

Aela's startled anger is quivering in time with my own like a sustained, high-pitched note.

"We're done talking."

"Sure, sure—"

"We're *done*."

His words eat at me in the silence that follows.

The day after our patrol, I receive a memo from the ministry, summoning me to the office of Miranda Hane. My walk to the Inner Palace is spent trying to calm an elevated heartrate. This is it. That memo I ignored before the Fourth Order, the morale visit lists my name has been absent from—this is when I face the person behind it. The Minister of Propaganda.

Still seething from Power's insinuations, I'm almost relieved for this change. Here, at least, is something I can *face*.

"Antigone, hello. Thank you for coming."

Miranda Hane has risen and, to my surprise, is smiling. The Ministry of Propaganda is the only ministry headed by a woman, and my first thought, meeting her, is of Skyfish ladies from the dragonborn tapestries. She has the same warm brown complexion, regal posture, and dark curls framing a clear gaze—although unlike the ladies of those tapestries, Hane wears trousers and her hair is cropped chin-length. Behind her, a floor-to-ceiling window overlooks the Firemouth, lined with potted plants that diffuse the sunlight.

There's stiffness in my arms and fingers that have nothing to do with tournament injuries, and I find myself unsure where to place my hands—at my sides? in my pockets? Hane extends her own hand and I realize, belatedly, that she expects me to shake it. Like we're adult males.

"Please sit."

After I've taken a seat across from her—on the edge of it, because I can't make my body relax—she studies me from under dark eyebrows. I remind myself to sit straighter; I realize that my arms are crossed; I unfold them and then clench my fingers in my lap. My burns twinge.

"Congratulations on making finalist. You flew very well."

"Thank you."

Sitting across from her, my courage is flagging like a sail on a dying breeze. For the first time, it occurs to me that I must have been mad—a stubborn, reckless fool—to take that note as a challenge. This woman helms one of the most powerful branches of government and I took it upon myself to defy her?

"I've been reviewing your file."

My racing thoughts pause. Hane taps a folder in front of her, the only item on her otherwise clear leather-topped desk.

"You have nothing but the highest marks in all your classes, but your teachers routinely note that you don't speak up enough. The exceptions are your new Dragontongue professor and the First Protector, who find your participation over the last few weeks more than satisfactory. Your only low marks are in oration, but your rhetoric professor observes that since making the Fourth Order you've been applying yourself with more— determination. Would you agree with these assessments?"

Mouth clamped shut, I nod.

"The Cloister directress Jillian Mortmane reports that you get along well with others and are not without friends. Your drillmaster, Wes Goran, describes your abilities in the air as *dubious at best* and your tendencies *subservient*, though I can only assume, given your performance in the last two tournaments I've observed, that his reporting has been . . . misleading."

Power's question returns to me, biting. *Do you know what they say about you?* I hesitate, then nod again.

A look of distaste passes over Hane's face.

"Just with you, or all the girls? Or is it your birth—?"

I've never been asked about Goran like this before. I open my mouth, but no words come out. Hane speaks first, sounding tired.

"You don't have to answer that."

She looks me over with a twisting frown. Then exhales, slowly and audibly, through her nose. I will my face not to go blotchy, as I can feel it's on the verge of doing.

"All right, Antigone."

I think I must be imagining the tone of concession in her voice. She's opened my file and begun flipping through it. Past reports from teachers, work samples, flight pattern analyses, test scores, medical history. She stops on the page titled "Bio" and glances it over; I watch her eyebrows rise, a line appear between them. She blinks, shakes her head a little like she's clearing it, and looks up. She doesn't comment on what she's just read.

"I'm going to assign you a morale visit."

I let out the breath I didn't realize I'd been holding.

The details of the process wash over my numb ears: My first morale visit will be to Holbin Hill, my home village; I'm to assist Lee's morale visit to Cheapside first, to *get an idea of what they're looking for*; I'm to draft a speech, if I so choose; and I'm to pick another Guardian as a visiting partner.

It will be the first time I've been back to Holbin in ten years.

"Do you have any questions?"

A single doubt is nagging; I hesitate. Hane prompts me with a motion of her hand.

"Do we have to bring dragons?" I ask.

Hane tilts her head at the question, like it perplexes her.

"Yes," she says. "That *is* the point of these visits, Antigone. You're appearing as a dragonrider. Which means showing the people your dragon."

She's looking at me expectantly, like she expects me to explain myself, but all I can feel is my fluttering stomach. Finally, *finally* I've been given a morale visit—a single morale visit, a *chance* to prove that I deserve it—against what must be this woman's better judgment and certainly her first inclinations. And now I question her?

Nevertheless the words blurt from my mouth.

"Mightn't we make an exception—"

I close it abruptly, look down, feel the blotchiness starting up my neck. But Hane's voice contains nothing but understanding.

"That was years ago, Annie. And this is you, one of theirs, weeks after Callipolis has been alerted to the threat of Pythian dragonfire. Whatever Holbin voted in the original referendum regarding dragons—they'll know this is different."

Over the next few days, I try to convince myself that Hane is right. And I try to find the words to tell Lee that I'll be coming with him to Cheapside, but none come. In any case, speaking of any kind has become oddly weighted, since we both made finalist for Firstrider.

The morning of our visit, I find him in the armory, dressed as I am, in ceremonial uniform, looking unusually grim.

"What are you doing here?"

"I'm coming, too. They're . . . having me do a morale visit. But I've got to watch this one first."

Lee raises a finger to the bridge of his nose and rubs it. Like he likes the idea of doing Cheapside together as little as I do.

"Annie, look, when I'm doing these, I—"

He breaks off. Shakes his head, drags his fingers through the side of his dark hair as he avoids my eyes. I understand abruptly.

"You put on the show they want."

For a second, he looks miserable. "It . . . means something to them. That's what I've realized. Even if it feels—hollow to us. It's not, to them. You'll see."

We land with our dragons in the cordoned-off part of the main square of Cheapside, next to the rising spire of the neighborhood's dragon perch. It's the first time I've been back since

Albans. While the representative from Propaganda makes introductions, I study the crowd gathering in front of us. It's strange,
years later, to notice the things that I didn't as a child: Their
clothes are worn, their bodies dirty, thin. Appearances I used to
take for granted but now see as signs of poverty. The wristbands
are nearly all iron. With a start, I see a face I recognize: To the
edge of the square, a crowd of grubby, downtrodden-looking
children are waiting next to our old orphanage master.

From the corner of my eye, I can see Lee watching me.

Gibbon finishes his introduction and gestures Lee forward,
and Lee's attention turns to the audience.

"Citizens of Callipolis," he begins. "I come to you now in the
wake of challenging news for our nation . . ."

I've watched Lee speak in class for eight years; he's always
been confident and well-spoken and poised. But this is the first
time I've seen him address a crowd as a representative of the
state. His shoulders are thrown back, the silver breast of his uniform gleaming in the sunlight, his black gold-trimmed mantle
falling carelessly off one shoulder as he lifts a hand to invoke his
audience. A dragon behind him, the crowd in front of him, Lee
holds the square captivated like he owns it. The address probably
began as a canned text provided by the Ministry of Propaganda,
but it's easy for me to detect Lee's doctoring: We've proofread
each other's writing for too many years not to recognize the
other's style. The ministry's trite phrases become heart-sure and
meaningful as he breathes them into life. His speechmaking, like
his flying, is beautiful.

Gibbon, who's come to stand beside me, is smiling a little.
"Every time, he's like this," he says.

Lee has them roaring by the end, in a kind of rising crescendo with his words, shrieking their approval as he says that we will never surrender *this glorious revolution, this people's revolution,* and that *we will defend Callipolis by land and by sea and by air.*

I try to imagine myself standing where he's standing, doing what he's doing, and can't.

They're always happiest when they have a lord.

I push the thought away with revulsion.

When his speech is over, I stand beside Lee and watch as he receives each citizen in the greeting line. He puts them at ease, listens patiently, and focuses on each person with his whole attention. Nothing throws him off—not when they tell him their grievances or ask him to place his hand on their child or even weep with fear about the coming war.

"I just keep thinking, what if they spark before ours—what if they've already sparked—"

"We're training for that very possibility every day."

The mother's voice goes strained, wild. "But how can we stand a chance if—"

Lee lets out a laugh—gentle—and takes the woman's sun-burned hand. Her face is lined, her brown hair streaked with gray. At his touch, she looks up at him. "Have a little faith in your fleet, madam."

She takes in his face like she's looking into the light. For a moment I see Lee as she must see him: his kind smile, worn by old sorrows; the gray eyes that are both intelligent and full of concern; the dark hair, shining in the sunlight, blown back from his forehead by the breeze. The Guardians' emblem of the circlets of silver and gold entwined on his breastplate, the filling shoulders of a boy in the prime of his youth and strength.

The face that is beginning to transform into a man's.

The man's face that grows, day by day, more familiar—

The woman raises his hand to her lips, kisses it, and breath leaves me like it's been sucked from my lungs. Because it is unmistakably a politeness from before the Revolution. From a time when subjects showed their gratitude to dragonlords, in the ways they'd been taught.

Lee has gone rigid. And then, when he looks up, it's at me, watching him. His face has drained of color.

There are conversations I wish we'd never had as children. Things I hope we'll never say again. Realizations I wish I need never have had or have.

But the realization I most regret, the one I hate and resist most of all, is that while I've always known *what* he is, the worst thing is not what he is but *who*.

That even if I've never been told exactly who *Leo* was, I've begun to recognize his maturing face.

Lee, Leo, *Leon*—

The greeting line moves on, and the thought is pushed back to the silence where I prefer it. When those in the line want to speak to me, I do my best to imitate Lee, even though I feel self-conscious and tongue-tied. When it's nearly over and I feel as drained as if we've been doing it for hours, I hear a familiar voice say our names.

"All right, Lee, Annie?"

The orphanage master uses a chummy voice, as if to make clear to those watching that he's on a first-name basis with us.

He prods the first children forward. Lee guides them to Pallor, and I bring the next group of children to Aela. She huffs and, at my clucking and snapped fingers, lowers her head reluctantly to their height. The children reach out with trembling, tentative fingertips to brush her amber scales. It's strange to realize that these children, who seem so tiny, are the same age we once were at Albans.

One of the girls in my group bursts into tears.

I go cold with panic. Why is she crying? What did I do? How do I make it stop? *There are people watching—*

"Trade?"

Lee has appeared at my side, nodding at his own group of children. None of them are crying. Leaving them with me, he approaches the crying girl from my group, scoops her up as if it's the most natural thing in the world, and says, "Hey."

Like he's shed one skin and slipped into another, and this one, too, I recognize. Not the man growing visible under his ceremonial armor like a molting bird of prey, but the boy I knew in Albans. The boy who had no father, who reminded me of no one, who mattered to me only because in a world where we had no one, he was kind.

I lead the others back to the Albans section as snatches of Lee's conversation with the girl come from behind me: *I know, they can be scary, can't they? But that one wasn't going to hurt you*, and then, after she says something else, too incoherent for me to understand, he adds: *I'm sorry you miss your mum.*

My eyes are beginning to burn with the memories. His words of comfort are gentle, practiced. Because of course, he has practiced them. When he passes me, and our glances catch for a brief moment, I realize that his eyes have reddened, too.

Back with the others, he sets the girl on her feet and tells her, a firmness entering his voice, that it's time to stop crying.

And, to my surprise, she does. Steels herself, wipes her face, nods with determination.

Was that me?

And the worse thought, that has me sick with shame: Is that me still?

What would it be like to serve as Alterna to this boy, whom of all people I should refuse to serve? And what perversion of upbringing or nature makes that easier for me to envision than becoming his superior? A revolution was fought to undo these patterns, and yet here I am, unable to picture any future but one where I repeat them.

That won't do. That *can't* do. I won't let it.

I will not let Power be right. Not about my people. Not about my desires. Not about me.

* * *

Three days before my morale visit to Holbin, Crissa finds me working at a table in the solarium after we've gotten out of training. Specialists in dragon biology have begun inspecting the fleet, offering suggestions for ways to trigger the dragons' spark-fire. So far, none of their recommendations have had any effect. We're left training with pikes and shields.

"What are you working on?"

Crissa's smiling, using her most cheerful squadron-leader voice, the one that I now associate with clinging to Rock's shoulders as we raced through the moonlit Palace, a flag around my shoulders and joy in my blood. She takes the seat across from me and nods at the paper in front of me as her fingers rake golden hair back from her face.

"My speech."

"For your morale visit?"

I nod, remembering Lee in Cheapside. As far as I could tell, he didn't even bother to write his down. The speech I'm star-ing at has taken me three hours of drafting and redrafting to compose.

"Do you want me to look it over?"

Crissa makes this offer so promptly that I realize it must be the real reason she's taken a seat across from me. The problem is, the idea of having anyone read the thing makes me feel like throwing up. I assess this reaction and decide it's probably a bad sign. Anyway, as far as my options go, Crissa's aren't a bad set of eyes. She gets good marks in oration, and even if we're not best friends, I do trust her. I push the paper across the table, defying my roiling stomach.

When she finishes, she has to clear her throat before speak-ing, and I realize that her eyes are a little bright.

"It's really good, Annie."

I unfold my arms, which I realize have twisted together as I watched her read. "Oh. Thanks."

"Have you practiced it, at all? Saying it?"

I shake my head. Crissa looks down at the speech and then back at me, her forehead wrinkling.

"You probably should. It's going to be important that you stay composed. Nobody likes watching girls cry—it makes them too uncomfortable. And saying this aloud would probably make *me* cry."

That's been my worry, too.

"Maybe I shouldn't do it."

Crissa shakes her head. "No. You absolutely *should* do it. But you should practice the hell out of it first. In front of someone."

"Did you . . . practice? When you first started doing morale visits?"

She's been doing visits as frequently as any of the higher-ranked boys, and far from surprising me, it fits the pattern I've observed from afar for years: Crissa's charm and confidence give her a success within the system that slips past most unnoticed, but that I've always regarded as a kind of miracle.

Crissa nods. "Of course I practiced."

She seems to sense my surprise and adds, with a roll of her eyes and a flick of hair from her shoulder: "I mean, I'm no cult leader, I'm not *Lee*. But when I put in the work, I like to think I get the job done."

I let out a startled laugh. After brooding for so many days on what I saw at Cheapside, it's strange to hear Lee's charisma joked about so unceremoniously. For the first time since I stood next to him during his morale visit, I feel the knot in my chest loosen a fraction.

Crissa does this. People who aren't Lee *do* this.

She gets to her feet.

"Come on," she says, tugging my arm.

"What?"

"I'm going to coach you."

* * *

Over the next three days I move from training to class to patrols to rounds in a haze of anticipation: sometimes excitement; sometimes foreboding. I push away the unimaginable thought of Aela at Holbin and focus on the speech, which I go over and over with Crissa until I know it cold. I think of the Mackys, how they embraced me and brought me highland flowers the day of the Fourth Order tournament and their letter to me before my match with Power. I tell myself that the pit of doubt and shame left in the wake of Power's insinuations will soon have its answer. Whatever uncertainty I've had about ascending to Firstrider in place of Lee—surely it will be cured by the sight of home, the faces of those for whom it would mean so much if I succeeded. Surely Holbin will give me the strength to prove Power wrong. For the first time in years, I allow myself to remember everything I miss about it. The jagged rocks protruding from impossibly green fields, the wind off the North Sea rippling the grass like waves.

I choose Duck as my visiting partner; the ministry's reply suggests a preference, in not so subtle terms, that I take Lee instead, and I ignore it.

No. Absolutely not. I know enough to know that *Leo* has no place in Holbin.

"Don't be nervous," Duck tells me, in the armory, the morning of. "You'll do great."

"Duck, it's . . . not going to be as easy as it was for your and Cor's neighborhood."

"I know."

It's a half-hour flight to Holbin, and on the way, as we ride in silence, I can feel all the nerves I've been suppressing for the last few days take over. When we land, Duck says simply, "It's beautiful."

Holbin Hill is in the lower ranges of the western highlands, on the base of the mountains. As I dismount, I inhale air that's cleaner than anything I've breathed in months. The light this high on the mountain is tinged with silver, and the wind smells of cold rocks and heather. We're on a stony clearing a little south of the village, awaited by the Macky family, whom I haven't seen since the first tournament; and Miranda Hane herself, who made the journey on horseback, alongside a small contingent of ministry officials.

"I decided I would see to this visit personally," Hane tells me, smiling.

I feel a flutter of a different kind of nerves at the sight of her. How much is her presence meant to be a support, and how much is it a test?

"Annie, you remember Don Macky?" Hane goes on, still smiling at me. "He's the village leader who helped organize this visit. He said his family came to see you at your first tournament?"

I nod, and Macky smiles. "Hello again, Annie."

His eyes flick past me toward Aela and Certa, their folded wings rippling in the wind, then return to my face with determination.

"There they are," says Macky's son.

A trail of people are trickling down the path from the collection of buildings that make up the village. Their buildings look new and well-made: Atreus took special care in the years after the Revolution to fund reconstruction of villages destroyed by dragonfire. Flocks of sheep, visible as ambling spots of white on the surrounding hillside, have multiplied since I was last here, evidence of Atreus's incentives to grow textile exports and wean Callipolis off reliance on subsistence farming.

My heart's begun to race, my palms to sweat. Eventually, they're all standing level with us, but they keep to the far side of the clearing, farther back than even Macky.

"Please, come closer," Hane says.

People glance at each other like they're trying to decide if this is an order, and what might happen if they don't comply. Some take a few steps closer. I recognize almost everyone, though I've forgotten a lot of names. I search the villagers' expressions for any sign of welcome, and though there are a few smiles, most have their eyes on the dragons and look wary.

Hane steps forward, introduces us, and then invites me to begin.

My stomach, which has been lurching, goes still at her cue. I remember how easily Lee stepped into this moment, as naturally as a dragon kicking off the ground. But there's no point comparing it with that. *Stand straight,* Crissa told me on the arena ramparts where we stood ten meters apart to practice, *hold your head up, remember that you fly a dragon and try to look like it.*

I begin. I describe the first attack on Holbin, then the second. I can tell it's surprising them that I'm talking about it at all, and whispering breaks out, but I'm in no place to stop or second-guess myself, so I keep going. Describing the attacks is the hardest part, but my voice is steady and clear, just like it was on the ramparts with Crissa. Then I describe the Revolution, how Holbin took part in the overthrow of the old regime. I describe the changes that Atreus has made, in and out of the city. I describe the education I'm receiving, thanks to a merit-based test. I describe a government where dragons abide by laws rather than create them.

I tell them that the Pythians have declared their intentions to retake Callipolis. I tell them that I've seen the Pythians and their dragons myself. I tell them that the Revolution was not the end of it after all; that it seems it was only the beginning of a whole new war. A war we must, at all costs, win.

"As a Guardian and dragonrider, I've sworn to defend this island. As a finalist for Firstrider, I'm contending for more than that. I am contending to lead the Callipolan aerial fleet."

Though I've said it over and over in rehearsal, it is only now, in front of the villagers of Holbin, that the shiver goes down my spine at the words. The realization, all over again, of the sheer miracle of it. Me. A serf, a Holbiner. Contending for Firstrider.

"I am also a farmer's daughter, a villager of Holbin Hill, an orphan. I know how it feels to be hungry. I've seen dragon-fire take everything I cared about away. I am one of you. So are every single one of my fellow dragonriders. We're here to protect you, as the old dragonriders did not. Even if you can't believe the words, please remember the facts: My family died at the hands of the old regime. And I would sooner die than see its crimes repeated."

I'm finished. There's just silence.

I look over at Hane and she gives me a small nod. As far as she's concerned, I did it right. She steps forward and begins to introduce the next stage of the visit. I permit myself to close my eyes, reach out, and place a hand on Aela's neck, taking in a calming breath.

"If you'd like to come forward, Antigone—Annie—and Dorian will receive you. I'm sure you must be glad to see Annie again after so many years and want to wish her good luck in the final tournament."

I look up from Aela.

No one has moved.

Macky and Hane look at each other. Macky says, "Now then, don't be shy. Boris, you and Helga want to start us off?" And quietly to me, he adds: "Annie, take a few steps forward from that dragon of yours, there's a good girl . . ."

A trickling line of villagers begins to form, moving toward us with unmistakable reluctance across the rocky clearing. When

Boris and Helga, with their three children, arrive within speaking distance, I see Boris's knees soften at the same time Hane does.

"Please remain standing," Hane says sharply.

I feel the back of my neck ignite with heat, flowing into my face.

"Thank you for coming," I say.

It occurs to me, for the first time, how I must sound to them: the highland accent gone, the clipped vowels and flat tones of Palace-standard speech. Austere and sterile, like a ministry official.

Boris and Helga look at each other. Their children are gathered at their heels, the youngest peering at our dragons from between his mother's legs. They incline their heads, without a word, and turn away.

It goes on like this, the silence and the stiffness, until I'm greeted by a woman whom I remember was widowed in the second Holbin attack. Now, ten years older, her face lined with care, her graying hair bound with a faded black scarf, she approaches me, glares, and says:

"Your father would be ashamed of you, girl."

And then she spits. She is taller than me; the wind and gravity carry it easily across the short distance between us, onto my face.

For a moment the shock of it leaves me frozen. And then, behind me, Aela lets out a low whine. I clench my fists to prevent a spillover, willing my head clear, willing Aela to calm. But then I hear other noises: growling, hissing, another dragon's wings snapping open. Duck has spilled over; Certa feels his outrage. Hane steps forward on one side of me, Macky on the other, their eyes wide and panicked. And all the while the widow still stands before me, glaring and defiant, like she's daring me to prove her right.

I look behind me. Duck's pupils are dilated; one of his hands has reached up to seize Certa's reins, the other is a balled fist at his side. I tell him, "If you cannot control Certa, please remove her."

And then I turn back to the widow, wipe my face, and force the words out.

"Summer's blessings on your house."

The next villager spits, too.

LEE

On the day of my second meeting with Julia it's difficult to focus on anything but what I'll say when we see each other. Her letter, its vision, has a way of twisting and reshaping whenever I try to grasp at what is wrong with it. But when I'm summoned from class and sent to Atreus's office, all thought of Julia slides from my mind. I remember, with foreboding, that Annie's visit to Holbin was scheduled for today as well.

Inside Atreus's office, Annie is perched on one of the dark-stained chairs facing Atreus, making a report in a quiet voice. Duck sits beside her, head in his hands. Miranda Hane is standing to the side, her arms folded, her expression stony, but it softens when she sees me.

"Lee, please, come in," she says, beckoning.

I have the impression she intends my presence and name to offer some comfort to Annie. She looks surprised when Annie cringes instead. She doesn't turn her head, doesn't look at me. I realize, as I come closer, that tears are coursing silently and steadily down her cheeks while she speaks. A handkerchief is clutched in one hand, forgotten.

And then I hear what she's describing.

"And you used only words of courtesy and kept Aela calm to the end?" Atreus asks quietly, when she seems to have nothing left to say.

Annie nods. This high in the Inner Palace, sunlight is still able to pour long swaths across the room from the windows looking out of the Firemouth, and it glows on the red-brown hair of her downturned head and trembling shoulders. Atreus and Hane exchange a look that Annie doesn't notice. After years of straining for the rare demonstrations of Atreus's approval, I see the signs of it now, though only the faintest lifted eyebrow betrays it.

But Annie does not seem be in a state to appreciate the approval of anyone.

"Was it the speech?" she asks in a whisper, clutching her knees with whitening fingers.

Hane's eyes are full. "Oh, Annie, no," she says. "You delivered your speech beautifully. It was my mistake for thinking it would be enough. There are just some wounds that run too deep for words to heal."

Atreus adds, heavily: "And the anger of the people can be often cruel and ill-placed. Today you paid the price for wrongs you didn't commit."

Wrongs you didn't commit.

Atreus can't know how those words implicate me, though it's clear that Annie does. Her shuddering shoulders shift on his last words, her back twisting, as if to turn herself from me completely. Though no one else notices, I perceive the movement as if she had shouted *get out*.

I begin to back toward the door.

"You behaved in every way befitting a Guardian, Antigone," says Atreus. "Thank you."

Annie's shaking shoulders go up to her ears.

"Is there anything else you require, Protector?"

"No. You and Dorian may go. And, Antigone? Please take any time you need before returning to class. Your superiors will be notified."

Annie and Duck rise. Annie passes me in the doorway as if she can't see me at all.

When they're gone, Atreus shifts his gaze to me.

"So. You've heard the problem. If you were the administrator, what would you do?"

I realize, at last, why I'm here: to play pretend. Atreus has done this with me before. Though this time, it's with a village whose particular history I have pondered for the last eight years.

"I would call off further morale visits to the highlands," I tell him, "and leave Holbin alone."

"Good," says Atreus, nodding slowly, as if we're in class. "Why?"

"Because the coming war will teach them what we can't."

* * *

Pallor and I arrive at Wayfarer's Arch early. We wait for Julia among the moonlit crags in the stone clearing of the ancient dragon perch, mounted atop an arch of karst that rises so far above the moonlit North Sea that the waves look, from this height, like still water. Pallor throws himself onto the stones at the ledge like a cat curling into its bed and lowers his head onto his crossed forelegs to wait. I sit beside him, looking out over the dark, karst-studded sea, scratching under the joint of his membranous silver wing, where it often itches. He ruffles his wings and shifts his weight closer, uttering a snort of contentment.

"You like it up here, don't you?" I murmur.

I like it up here, too. It's easier, looking out over a view like this, to revisit the welcome Annie received in Holbin. The sight of her stricken, tearstained face, and the exhaustion that set in afterward. I've watched Callipolis transform year by year into a better place than the one the old regime left—and still, the old wounds are so easily reopened. The wounds the dragonborn left behind.

The wounds *my father* left behind.

How does the thought still have the power to make me lightheaded, this many years later?

Pallor nuzzles the back of my head, which I've lowered into my knees, and I reach out to notch my fingers between his horns and hold. Like I'm on the deck of a swaying ship and he's the rail.

I lift my head at the whisper of wings overhead. A passing shadow across the stars makes Pallor and me lurch to our feet. His wings cock half opened, tensing as another dragon circles in descent.

Julia's stormscourge is midsize for an adolescent, unusually slender, her wingspan exceptionally long. It's impossible to make out, in the night, how she handles, though I find myself irrepressibly curious. When they land on the opposite side of the perch, Julia slides off her back with fluid comfort and the stormscourge eyes Pallor curiously, her horned tail lifting. Pallor paws the ground, shifting weight from side to side, as if to compensate for the fact that she is almost half again his size.

"Easy," Julia and I both say at once, though Julia says it in Dragontongue. "Erinys, meet—"

"Pallor."

"Pallor," Julia repeats, testing it.

We watch Pallor and Erinys approach each other like skeptical but curious dogs, sniffing and sidestepping.

Julia muses, her mouth twisting: "Pallor, the aurelian who Chose a Stormscourge."

I wonder what she makes of that. The virtues of the old houses and their dragons are shorthands we've grown up knowing: Skyfish House, known for their moderation and mercy; Stormscourge, for their discipline and strength; Aurelian, for their judiciousness and learning. She must look at Pallor and wonder what was lacking in me, and what found, that I was passed by the stormscourge and Chosen by an aurelian when I was presented to dragons.

When Pallor and Erinys have circled each other and parted again to stare from a distance in what seems to be a mutually agreed upon ceasefire, Julia turns to me.

"Hello again, cousin," she says in Dragontongue.

As she approaches me on this moonlit night, it's easy to see what a tavern booth concealed. The seabirds' detritus of broken shells crunches and cracks beneath her boots at each step, her cloak streaming behind her on the salt-spray wind. Julia walks with the unmistakable air of a Stormscourge: confident, poised, with a lingering note of danger that persists even when weapons are laid down. A brooch of highland heather, the symbol of Stormscourge House, clasps her cloak at the breast.

Everything about her that should be intimidating makes me feel at home.

"Did you like my letter?" she asks, when we stand feet apart.

Our fathers may be dead, but their blood runs in our veins. We were born to this.

"Yes. It was beautiful. Like something out of the old poetry."

Julia smiles thinly at my choice of words.

"You didn't find it compelling?"

I look at our two dragons, eyeing each other at a distance as their wings, ever so slowly, ease back into resting position. I think of the fantasies that have danced across my vision since I read her letter, of Julia and I, side by side, on dragonback, *taking back what is ours*. The kind of narratives we explored in play as children, but now, we should be old enough to know better. For us, dragons may have meant glory; but for most everyone else, they were what Annie experienced today. Something to be feared, hated, and at the soonest opportunity, spat upon.

"I find reality compelling."

Julia scoffs. "Fine. Let's discuss reality. Our fleet will attack soon. We intend to make this a war, and we intend to win it. We will not be sparing."

The girl from the Drowned Dragon, familiar and full of sad understanding, has vanished. The new Julia is fierce, her businesslike tone enough to make my blood chill.

I hear my own voice take on coldness and issue the conclusion that is really a question.

"Your fleet hasn't *sparked* yet. This is an idle threat."

For a second we just stare at each other, and then she tosses her head back, lets out a laugh of abandon, and breathes a word.

It takes me a moment to understand that it's a command, and it's for Erinys.

Erinys lifts her head like a wolf to the moon and *fires*.

For a brief, blinding moment, sparked dragonfire warms the night like a beacon.

Pallor rears, reverses, and for an instant I feel his intimidation twist in time with my own sinking heart. Erinys lowers her head and watches his retreat, cool and confident, her tail flicking idly back and forth across the stones. At a distance of ten meters Pallor bares his teeth and growls. The acrid smell of dragonfire lingers sharp on the air.

"It's all right, Pallor." I turn to Julia. "How long?"

Julia shrugs. "A week or so?"

"Congratulations."

She is smirking, an eyebrow lifted. "Thank you, cousin."

"Just Erinys?"

Erinys is likely to have been the first; sparking tends to spread hierarchically among fleets, from higher-ranked dragons to lower ones.

Julia only smiles at that question, as if to say: *Do you really think I'm going to answer that?*

"Are we really such an idle threat, cousin?" she asks. "Even if it were just Erinys. One sparked dragon is enough to level a town. What do you have right now? Pikes and shields?"

Her words wash over my rising incredulity. *Level a town? Does she hear herself?*

"Julia, *this is madness*." The coldness has been stripped from my voice as the desperation hits. "Thousands of innocent people will die. You quote the old poetry? You must see that these are the kinds of mistakes that brought down the Aurelians, that finished the dragonlords—"

"You can stop it."

This stops me short.

"If you turn, and help us bring this usurping regime down from the inside, none of those deaths need to happen. If you keep rising—to Firstrider, maybe to Protector—you can hand it over like a plucked fruit."

I take a step back from her, and shells crunch beneath my boot. To turn was a request I'd expected—but to betray from the inside is a step baser than I'd even considered.

"You balk," she observes. "Why?"

As if of my own accord, my arms open, my palms spread. She studies me with cool gray eyes.

"They've raised you," she surmises.

"More than that."

"You believe in their vision," she realizes. Her voice is cold with disgust. "You believe they're better. Even after everything they've done. You'd be loyal to the man who betrayed us."

I lift my shoulders, lower them. "I think there's more to this than questions of vengeance and birthright."

A strange, bitter smile twists Julia's face. The moonlight glints silver on her dark hair, on her cloaked shoulders.

"I was warned that you might feel this way. What exactly about Atreus's vision do you find so appealing? His generous but ill-implemented meritocratic process, his efforts to rewrite the past with his censors? Do you think it's *noble* that he lets peasants vie for Firstrider? She rides well, I grant, our little highland serf."

Julia's disdain drips on her words like acid, and I recoil from it. *Our* rings in my ears, the casual possessive of Stormscourges discussing land holdings.

"The other finalist is not *our* anything."

Julia's voice lashes her response. "*And you are not naïve.* Wake up. You think his regime is better because it calls serfs by another name and teaches them to read? Maybe it is. *For now.* In a time of plenty, without pressure or strain. But watch and see how that vision splinters when we exert pressure. Then we can revisit whether you think it's noble. Whether you have the stomach for more."

Exert pressure. The possibilities for interpretation there are open, but the purport is clear. Pressure will come in the form of violence.

For a moment there's no sound but the gulls crying sleepily from the edges of the karst.

"When?" I ask.

Julia tilts her head back, rakes her hair back from her face, and smirks at me. "Don't look so *worried*, cousin. The first time will be just a taste."

Her tone is playful. A mockery of the tone she used to adopt in the garden, when she was teasing. What does *a taste* mean, for someone who speaks so casually of leveling a town? I look out over the edge of the karst, at the flattened sea blurring a reflection of the stars, and reach for words out of a sudden feeling of emptiness. With nothing but the ocean to bound it, the dome of the dark night feels infinite.

Julia, what have you become?

It seems I'm not the only one who's troubled by the distance. Julia speaks first, her voice softening to a murmur as she changes the subject.

"Do you want Firstrider so much you can taste it?"

The moonlit karst comes back into focus, and with it the silver outline of my cousin with her streaming hair and riding cloak, her feet planted on the rock beneath them like she owns it, as she waits for my answer.

Do I want to breathe? Do I want to eat? This has been a dream in the fabric of my longing for as long as I can remember. Less a desire than a need. I've lost everything else from the old life, but this I can keep. This, I'm still allowed to want.

"Yes. Of course."

Julia nods, relieved by the strip of common ground that we still share.

"That's how it was for me, too. That's how I won. Good luck in the final tournament, Leo. I pray to the long-dead gods that it brings sense to you."

8

THE LYCEAN BALL

ANNIE

There's a time, after my morale visit to Holbin, when the world goes dark. I remain in bed for hours, skipping meals, refusing conversation.

Your father would be ashamed of you, girl.

Would he have been?

My father died a year before the Revolution. When I search through the handful of memories that I still have of him for an answer, I realize that I remember him too poorly to know.

"Annie. Lee's been asking about you."

Crissa's voice rouses me from a half sleep where I've been lying in bed, cocooned beneath the covers and willing my own existence to stop.

For a moment, all I can think of is how it felt when Lee used to hold me. Warm, and safe, the only thing that could make the crying stop.

But not now. Not for Holbin.

"Tell him I'm fine."

I won't be that child anymore. I can do this without him.

And eventually, I do. I get out of bed, brush my hair, eat a meal. The world slowly returns: patrols, training, classes. I'm not assigned any more morale visits, and in the wake of Holbin, I can't say that I wish otherwise. Propaganda now avoids visits in parts of the countryside that have particularly fraught histories with dragonfire.

Overshadowing our usual obligations is the Lycean Ball's approach, our last public event before the Firstrider Tournament and Palace Day. Though we remain tensed for the Pythians' first move, the ministry has determined that this tradition, at least, should proceed as planned. Eventually it feels like every spare minute is filled with its preparations: fittings, etiquette sessions, advanced dance lessons. Though in most ways it's a welcome respite from worse pressure and darker thoughts, it's not without its own kind of stress.

Especially when, in advanced dance, I'm told to pair off with Lee.

"As the Guardians will be the Lyceans of honor for the event this year, the finalists will lead the opening dance," the dance instructor tells us as we stand in the vaulted grand hall the Lyceum uses for ceremonies. His accent has traces of Dragontongue, his tunic trimmed with delicate embroidery more fashionable in the old regime. "Shouldn't be too difficult for either of you since you're both so light on your feet."

The instructor moves on, to prepare and position the other practicing partners, leaving silence in his wake. It's strange to stand so close to Lee after hours spent listlessly in bed, relearning how to do without his comfort. But the person I remembered comforting me in the orphanage bears little resemblance to the one I stand beside now: shoulders full beneath his uniform, toned from years of training on the Eyrie; tall enough that I have to tilt my head up to look at his sunburnt, wind-chapped face. This is a boy who eats until he's full, who reads into the night, and spends summer days on dragonback.

Although, on closer inspection, Lee's gray eyes are lined in a way that I didn't remember them being before my morale visit.

"Have you started training yet?" I ask.

Lee looks startled. "For the Firstrider Tournament?"

I nod, thinking of Power's offer to train and my refusal. The compliments like insults, the words that cut because they hit home. *You probably don't even want you to win,* he said. I haven't spoken to Power since.

Lee shakes his head. "Not yet."

Will Lee bother to train? I wonder. Or will he just assume, with that same confidence that leads him from class to rounds to training with such grace, that Firstrider is his for the taking?

Before the morale visit I thought my ambition would make Holbin proud. Now I know better. Whatever history I make as a dragonrider, they have no interest in. Those words that I spent bedridden hours trying to unhear: *Your father would be ashamed of you, girl.*

For all I know, the widow was right. For all I know, my family would have had no interest in my ambition either.

It's a relief when the instructor's voice pulls me from my spiraling thoughts.

"You're all familiar with the standard waltz by now," he tells the class, standing in the center of the polished floor. "Today we're going to work on a slightly trickier variation."

Lee emits an exhale of understanding.

"The Medean," he murmurs.

His eyes have lit with the beginnings of a smile as he watches the instructor assume position with his assistant.

"I'm sorry?"

"It's a waltz."

The instructor explains: "One of the oldest dances across the dragon-birthing sea, the Medean waltz has long been a favorite of the airborne courts. It was designed to imitate a dragon in flight."

At his prompting, partners join together. Lee extends a hand, palm up, and I place my fingers over his. His other hand goes to the small of my back. Although it's a position I've practiced with other dance partners before, never until this moment have I felt the intimacy of being held *here*, the center of my gravity, where his slightest pressure lights every nerve of my body, and my only instinct is to respond.

I've watched Pallor be calmed by this same hand, this same touch, light but firm, for the last seven years.

The instructor goes on: "The Medean is faster, syncopated, more expressive than the waltz you're used to—and harder to pull off. But, when done right . . . there's nothing more beautiful."

Lee adjusts, bringing me closer, clasping my hand more firmly in his, craning his neck to track the first few demonstrated steps that the instructor models with his assistant. We stand so close now that my gaze is level with the neck of his uniform, the shadow where his throat meets his collarbone.

When I realize I've been staring at it, I jerk my face back and up, to look at his.

"Why are you smiling?" I mutter.

Our turn to imitate. Lee exerts pressure and I move to his

touch. The step is long, the catch delayed so it snaps a forceful turn. I feel the delight of its motion the way Aela delights in a dive. Lee studies my face and his smile softens. For a moment, his expression contains something that looks like longing.

"That's right, Lee's got it," the instructor observes, moving between us.

Lee is holding me close enough for his breath to brush my ear. That same easy confidence that I was, moments ago, contemplating in bitterness is now turned on me like sunlight.

"Because this one's fun."

The next half hour is a blur of motion and lightness guided by Lee's touch, and it leaves me with a spring in my step for the first time since Holbin and a lingering warmth in the small of my back where he held it.

In addition to the general lessons offered to the rest of the corps, the Fourth Order riders also receive special etiquette instructions. Lee, Power, Cor, and I attend a private session in one of the small conference rooms of the Ministry of Propaganda, conducted by Miranda Hane herself. I haven't seen her since my morale visit.

"Good to see you, Antigone. How are you?"

From the way she asks, I realize that she's remembering how we last parted, when I was—the thought makes me cringe—making a report to the First Protector while crying. But she speaks with a warmth that feels genuine and without condescension.

"I'm better, thanks."

Hane smiles, then moves to the center of the conference room to address the group as a whole. Cor and I have taken a seat, Lee stands with arms folded, and Power lounges against the side of one of the tables, looking bored.

"Hello, everyone, and thank you for coming." She goes on to explain that after the Lycean Ball's dinner, the four of us will be introduced to some of the most influential elites of the class-golds, individually. "This is your first official public appearance as future leaders of the city—and you four will be of particular interest as candidates for next Protector, whom the Golds will take part in choosing. Unlike the other metals, Golds are not just your subjects: They're also your constituents."

At Hane's mention of the Protectorship, Power flashes a brief, crooked grin; Cor looks a little alarmed; Lee's expression does not alter at all; and my stomach sinks. The upcoming Firstrider Tournament has been a daunting enough prospect without adding this. New ways to be evaluated, new hoops to jump through, more people to impress. At least in the arena, I have Aela.

"We urge you," Hane goes on, "to make a good impression. Regardless of what your personal political ambitions may be, it's critical to put your best face forward—especially during these uncertain times. You've paid morale visits to the class-bronzes, irons, and silvers; now is the time to reassure the class-golds."

She gestures forward her assistant, who's been waiting at the side of the room.

"To that end. Let's rehearse."

The introductions are highly formalized, a script that we're expected to master and perform. We'll be paired with ministry escorts who will introduce us in Callish, but we practice the Dragontongue variation as well, in case any guest changes the language. Hane drills Cor's pronunciation of the Dragontongue phrases repeatedly, until he's flushing with embarrassment but can produce them a little less harshly. When Hane works with Lee, she has to remind him not to mutter his Dragontongue and then compliments him on his accent. Power produces the phrases in both languages with great flourish, and Hane seems torn by disapproval and amusement. When it's my turn, she introduces me to her assistant, who's impersonating the third party.

"And it will be polite in your case to curtsy, Antigone—"

As soon as I do it, Power lets out a snicker. I look up. Hane's face is clouded, and Lee's gone red.

"Not like that," Hane says softly.

Confusion makes me struggle to defend myself: "This is how my mother—"

I stop, understanding abruptly. I begin to color, too.

"Like this," Hane says simply. "This is how you'll do it from now on."

She demonstrates. It's strange to watch someone curtsy in trousers. Hane's neck remains erect; the motion is slight and airy, and contains none of the sweeping obeisance that my mother's curtsy did. I imitate, wishing my face would stop burning, wishing Power would stop smirking. Wishing Lee would stop staring at the floor.

Hane proceeds with the role play. "May I introduce . . ."

I need no prompting to produce the phrases that I've watched the other three practice before me. But when Hane prompts a switch to Dragontongue, I cannot stop my voice from lowering in shame.

"From the stomach," Hane reminds me.

I say the Dragontongue again, at full volume. It sounds alien, my own mouth producing the language that I'm so much more comfortable hearing than speaking. I can hear the sound of the

Callish accenting my words, rough on the phonemes that, for a native speaker, would sound flutelike and liquid. I wonder whether here, too, Hane is cringing at a peasant's lingering crudities.

But instead she says, "Excellent."

For the female Guardians, there are also fittings, dresses occasioned for the first time in years and commissioned by the ministry. I pass the session at the dressmakers with my tongue thick in my mouth; the fabrics that they're asking us to choose between are luxurious enough to delight Deirdre and Alexa, but leave me speechless with unease. Crissa, who seems to straddle the other girls' delight and my discomfort, stays by my side and keeps up a steady stream of commiserating commentary to put me at ease—*Oh, these city dresses are so fancy, aren't they, my family would never dream of going to dressmakers this nice*—and I appreciate it, though I don't tell her that the idea of going to a dressmaker in the first place would, to my family, have been unfathomable. We're assigned colors by squadron, but the cut and textile are left to our choosing. Crissa worms preferences I'm surprised to find I have out of me while the dressmakers are in the back room, then demands them on my behalf when they return.

"Having a dress you feel good in can make all the difference," Crissa tells me sagely afterward, when I attempt to thank her.

I don't really understand what she means until the night of the ball. Then, barricaded in the girls' dorm, I pull on a dress that looks like something out of Duck's book of fairy tales and allow Crissa to arrange my hair. When Alexa passes me the mirror she's smuggled in from her home on the Janiculum, I take in my appearance with surprise. It's strange to see that with the right kind of clothing and hair, I don't look like someone who would ever have been called a peasant. Almost reflexively, I pull my shoulders back and stand a little straighter. Deirdre and Alexa are letting out shrill exclamations of delight, and for once I don't mind. Even Orla, lying on her bed and reading as usual despite her ball gown, takes the time to glance over the top of her book and give me a thumbs-up.

"Our Annie, all grown up," Deirdre says to Alexa, wiping an imaginary tear.

Crissa takes my hand to spin me toward her, the half step of a dance, and I let out a laugh of startled delight. At the sound of my laugh she presses her finger against my lips like she's pausing something.

"That's it. That's the face you need to wear. Smile the whole time, Annie. Show those wrinkly old Golds how much fun you're having. That'll impress them more than anything."

I haven't told her any of what Hane said to us in the private session for the Fourth Order. But maybe Lee or Cor did. Or maybe Crissa just guessed.

When we join the boys in the solarium, I hesitate on the threshold. It feels ridiculous to be wearing a formal gown in front of people who've never seen you in anything but a military uniform. But then Duck appears in front of me.

"Annie?"

I let out a half-embarrassed laugh. He wears the same delighted expression he once turned up to a starry sky when he insisted I *see* it. Warmth fills me. Surely this is a gift greater than any other, to be able to enjoy the world so openly, without apology.

"Not bad yourself," I tell him, and Duck laughs, patting his own wet-combed hair with a sheepish grin.

And then, amid the sparkling of dresses and the black mantles and the sprinklings of laughter, I feel the eyes of a single person on me from across the room. Unlike the others, he stands perfectly still. Waiting for me.

I kiss Duck on the cheek, like Crissa might have done, except for once her exuberance suits me, too. Then I turn and walk across the floor to Lee.

"Hey."

I feel a foreign boldness coursing in my veins as I stand in front of him and we look at each other. I take in the sight of Lee in dress uniform, so suited to it that he seems dangerous. And I take in the cool liquid tension, like discomfort but not quite, that comes with the feeling of his gaze on me.

"Better than the last dress you saw me in?"

The last dress he saw me in was a shift approaching rags. I hear myself make the Albans reference as if someone else dared it. Lee's smile becomes a grin. He lets out a soft laugh.

"Much better," he agrees.

And still, his gaze is on me. Surprised, like he's just realized something and is pleased by it. I feel the pitter-patter of recognition, of those eyes, that face—all the more familiar in a dragonrider's ceremonial uniform—but for this one moment I refuse to acknowledge it.

The Palace clocktower is tolling the hour. It's time to go.

Lee turns his elbow ever so slightly away from his body, and though it's not a gesture of politeness we've been taught, I understand. He's offering me his arm.

Heart in my mouth, I take it.

LEE

Even though all our training and security measures since the sighting have been implemented under the assumption that we'd be going against a sparked fleet, I've still, in the wake of meeting with Julia, felt uneasy. Unable yet to make any report that wouldn't arouse suspicion, I've been advocating for higher numbers of patrols along the northern coast, with a greater number of Guardians manning each one. But when it comes to the night of the Lycean Ball, my request for additional precautions is overruled.

"It's been weeks, we've seen nothing, and Atreus wants all of you there," Holmes tells me beforehand, during our meeting in his office in the Inner Palace, lined from floor to ceiling with maps of the Medean, of the North Sea, of Callipolis. "For all we know, they're not even sparked."

For a moment, I consider telling the Minister of Defense that I know better. But I'm fairly certain this man, this *hero of Palace Day*, would drop his avuncular tone pretty quickly at that news.

Not an option. I'm only safe—and only free to act—as Lee sur Pallor, from Cheapside.

So I bite back the answer that I can't give and deliver the one I can. "I thought the policy is to plan as if they *are* sparked."

Holmes gives me a hard-eyed stare, then lets out a bark of appreciative laughter.

"I like how you think, Lee. But it's just one night. Try to enjoy yourself, all right?"

By the night of the ball itself, I've almost persuaded myself to listen to Holmes. As we make our way to the Hall of Plenty at sunset, its lingering warmth enough for the breeze to feel like a caress, the tension left in me from Julia's threats slides reluctantly away. It's hard, on such a night, to remember fear.

Especially not with Annie's arm folded in mine. She lingers beside me as we make our way through the Palace to the Hall of Plenty, and her continued presence is something I marvel at. Duck walks a few paces ahead, sucked into conversation with Rock and Lotus, though occasionally he twists back to look at us. Each time he does, his eyes find and fixate on Annie. I can't tell if she doesn't notice or is just acting like she doesn't.

Though the occasion has changed, much about tonight's feast feels familiar from the old days: the elegant figures making their way to the candlelit Hall of Plenty; the sound of muffled laughter within echoing in the courtyard without. As a child, I used to wander here with my cousins and siblings after dinner, throw rocks in the ponds surrounding the statue of Pytho the Unifier, and climb the marble dragon's back to touch old Pytho's nose. Pytho is gone now, destroyed in the Revolution, but his dragon remains.

Outside the hall, ministry officials are pulling aside guests who will make up the opening procession: the Lyceum graduates; followed by the Guardians according to flight ranking; and finally the professors of the Lyceum, robed for the occasion in their academic caps and gowns. I can hear the sound of hundreds of people inside, talking, laughing, waiting for the meal to begin. Annie, standing beside me at the rear of the Guardian section, sucks in a breath and then exhales.

I turn to look at her, and as I do, I can't help taking it all in again: her gown, a burnished aurelian red, settling just off her shoulders; the curls of auburn hair arranged atop her head in an elegant cascade; the pale expanse of skin between, rippling with the burn scars of a dragonrider. She's at once as beautiful as what came before and something else entirely: something powerful. The women of the old order have been surpassed, and so too has the cowering child I once met in an orphanage.

But I take in her expression and realize that, absurdly, despite her transformation, Annie is still intimidated by a fancy dinner.

"You're nervous?"

Annie nods. "I don't exactly belong in there," she mutters, smiling grimly.

I wonder if I'm imagining that she puts an emphasis on *I*.

ANNIE

Stained glass sparkles high above, stone pillars as broad as the tables themselves rising to support a vaulted ceiling shrouded in smoke from the fires that line the hall. Candlelight warms the faces turned toward us, sparkles on jewels and gowns, and glints on the golden wristbands on every wrist. I am aware of the eyes of the hall on us as we make our way down the central aisle. Our seats, along with those of the other members of the Fourth Order, are at the high table.

Once everyone is seated, Atreus rises.

"We are gathered today to celebrate the accomplishments of those Lyceans who have completed their education and are now entering our society as colleagues. Some might wonder, in this time of crisis, whether such ceremony and celebration still has a place: To them I answer, now more than ever. On the brink of war we do well to remember what we fight for. We do well to remember that Callipolis has a future that shines brightly, and these young people deserve a better world.

"The graduates we honor today will not only inherit the world we leave them: Some of them will be on the vanguard fighting for it. Tonight, in a very special addition, we also welcome the thirty-two Guardians who have reached the final stages of their training.

"Lyceum graduates, please rise when I call your name."

Atreus proceeds to read from a roll: the student's name, their specialty, and, where applicable, their government posting. After about forty young men and women have risen from their seats, scattered up and down the long tables that fill the hall, they are applauded and sit down. Atreus proceeds:

"Will the Guardians of the Thirty-Second Order please rise when I call their name."

He begins with the lowest-ranked of the dragonriders, whose ranking was determined in qualifiers before the public tournaments began. Their names are followed by drakonym instead of surname, and modified by dragon breed. After the riders of the Thirty-Second Order have been listed and applauded, Atreus proceeds to the Sixteenth. Lotus and Deirdre are among those who rise. Then the Eighth, those who made it to the public quarterfinal: Duck, Rock, and Crissa are among them. Crissa's squadron leadership is noted after her dragon's breed. Then the Fourth: *Power sur Eater, Stormscourge. Cor sur Maurana, Stormscourge squadron leader.* And finally Atreus says, "Last but not least, our finalists for Firstrider."

Antigone sur Aela, Aurelian. Lee sur Pallor, Aurelian squadron leader.

The applause is, by now, shockingly loud; I can feel it

thrumming through my chest, sending tingles up my spine. Lee is staring hard in front of him. Atreus nods to us, we resume our seats at last, and he raises his glass.

"To the future."

We raise our glasses and drink. My mouth has been uncomfortably dry for the last half hour. I'm surprised by how pleasant my first taste of wine is, like grape juice but richer. I take another sip, and Lee leans over.

"It's strong. Don't use it to quench your thirst."

I nod, but can't help thinking that if my mouth keeps drying out at the rate it has so far, my throat might just close up. Lee takes in my expression and frowns. He twists and makes a minute gesture at one of the servants moving along the table, who swoops down at once to hear Lee's request. An iron wristband, I note, with muted discomfort. Around us, roast goose is being sliced and served, steaming vegetables are being piled on plates.

Lee tells the servant: "Water for the table, please."

The servant bows. "At once, milor—"

He catches himself. Lee smiles politely, not acknowledging the slip, and the servant backs away, embarrassed. I take a gulp of wine, on purpose.

Aside from Miranda and myself, there's only one other woman at the table present for reasons other than marriage: a steel-haired, middle-aged woman with jewels glittering silver against the warm gold complexion of her neck. When Atreus introduces her as Dora Mithrides, I realize I know about her already. For various reasons related to a dead husband and an inherited financial empire, she's one of the most powerful citizens on the Janiculum, an honorary alderman on their council, known for investments that were critical to getting the Revolution off the ground. When she speaks, it takes a moment to figure out why I don't understand her right away. Then I realize she's speaking in Dragontongue.

Hane drums her fingers on the table, lines appearing between her eyebrows at the sound of the language; she glances at Mitt Hartley, the chairman of the Censorship Committee, who lifts his eyes to the ceiling. The foreign minister, Legio Symmach, and Dean Orthos, head of the Lyceum, smile almost guiltily; Holmes's forehead wrinkles like he is parsing.

"Callish, Dora," Atreus chides gently. "Many of our guests don't speak Dragontongue."

Dora *hmphs* and reverts to heavily accented Callish. "Including your four Guardians, I take it? I've noticed that no riders from the Janiculum made it into the Fourth Order."

"I'm from the Janiculum," Power says.

Dora, who is sitting next to him, pats a ring-crusted hand on his arm. "You'll forgive me, boy, I mean to say Janiculum *blood*. Patrician blood. You are adopted, are you not?"

Power blanches. Cor chokes on his wine and nearly spits it out. Even Lee has to hide an inhaled snort that he turns into a cough.

Adopted? Power, who spends all his time lording his birth over commoners like me?

Power gives Lee and Cor a look of venom, the color of his cheeks deepening nonetheless. And when he catches me struggling to keep my mouth in a line, he juts out his chin, glaring at me.

I hide my smile in my wineglass and return my attention to the adults, who have noticed none of our exchange.

"I thought we were agreed," Atreus is saying to Dora, smiling with the strained patience of an old argument, "that blood is precisely *not* how this regime would select its elite."

"You mistake my point," Mithrides answers promptly. "I have no classist complaint to make. My concern is *military*."

General Holmes's eyebrow lifts with a look of incredulity, but he continues slicing his goose without engaging.

"Oh?" Atreus asks, with reservation.

"With regard to your sparking problem."

Holmes puts down his knife.

"Madam Mithrides, there *is* no sparking problem."

Mithrides snorts.

"You need dragonborn blood to spark your fleet. The patricians have dragonborn blood in them. Too many generations of intermingling not to. All I'm saying is, if you had a few more patrician riders—"

Hane and Atreus look at each other, expressions not entirely masking surprise, seeming to be silently conferring. Stephan Orthos, the dean of the Lyceum, responds first, his tone irritable.

"Yes, I know that theory is all the rage right now," he says, "but there's no science behind it, Dora. Just misapplied literary criticism. The *Aurelian Cycle* is a work of fiction, not a military manual. Whatever people down at the club are saying."

Orthos does not notice how his words generate another exchange of glances between Hane and Atreus, or its alarm.

"I'd like someone to please explain to me this *theory* that the Lyceans are discussing in their club," says Holmes.

Holmes is, I realize with a start, the only exception to the class-gold guest list. Either consciously or not, he flicks his wrist as he speaks, so that his sleeve covers his silver wristband.

Hane speaks first, her tone hesitant.

"As I understand from my research department, the theory Dora refers to is one that's cropped up on and off over the years and found a small resurgence recently because of the pressures on our fleet to spark. The usual blood-supremacy argument about dragonriding families, based on the *Aurelian Cycle*. Because it depicts dragonlords as godlike, the theory would say that there's a blood difference, a blood superiority, between the dragonborn and their subjects. Of course it's a completely— unsubtle—reading of the text . . ."

There is distaste in Hane's tone.

"And how is that?" Mithrides asks icily.

Lee's voice is quiet, but he has no difficulty drawing the attention of the table, even though he's speaking for the first time.

"Because the hubris of the first Aurelians was their downfall. You could just as easily read the *Aurelian Cycle* as a condemnation of the dragonlords." Lee nods at Atreus, acknowledging the interpretation that we have discussed in class, and then adds: "You could even read it as a condemnation of dragonriding itself."

This last part is an extrapolation Lee seems to have made on his own. Atreus's still face flickers as he studies him, the briefest trace of surprise. But Hane, nodding wordlessly in Lee's direction, doesn't notice.

"In recent months the theory has taken on new elements in certain circles," she explains, "claiming specifically that dragonborn blood is tied to dragon bonding and sparking. It's all completely unfounded, but the problem is, of course, that sparking itself remains such a mystery. What causes it? How to trigger it? We don't know. In any case I'd thought"—here, Hane gives Dean Orthos a questioning look—"that the blood-superiority theory had only fringe popularity and that most of its proponents had been apprehended by the Reeducation Committee. I would not have known it is *all the rage* down in the club."

Orthos shifts in his chair. He is a middle-aged man, graying, venerable, even when wearing an academic cap. At her glance he is, suddenly, full of discomfort, as if realizing that what he'd assumed was common knowledge was in fact something he has just, in fact, divulged. When he speaks, his tone is apologetic, appeasing.

"Well, you know how it is, Miranda," he says. "Conspiracy theories find fertile ground where people are frightened."

Hane takes this observation with a gracious nod of her head. "That is undoubtedly true."

And then, when she looks up, it is at Hartley, the chairman of the Censorship Committee, who has not yet spoken. He returns her gaze with matching gravity.

Though neither speaks, it's the first exchange in this conversation that actually alarms me. Hartley's committee determines what literature to restrict, ban, or confiscate; an exchanged glance with him has the power to change a library's contents.

Dora Mithrides has turned to Lee. "I take it you are studying the *Aurelian Cycle*? Where are you from, again?"

Lee's lip curves. "Cheapside."

"So you have learned Dragontongue in school."

There is unmistakable skepticism in Mithrides's tone. Lee nods.

"Well, you discuss the work very comfortably, for one who lacks a native appreciation for it."

Hane actually lifts her eyes to the ceiling in exasperation. Atreus is watching Lee and Dora with a look of muted curiosity; the corner of his lip has lifted in a mild smile.

Lee nods and inclines his head, graciously accepting what Dora seemed to intend as a compliment.

Then he smiles and answers in Dragontongue.

This is our work; this is our labor.

It's a quote from the *Aurelian Cycle*. I recognize it because we translated the line a few weeks ago. Lee has changed it slightly, so that the line makes sense in context. His accent is perfect. Cor and Power swing around to stare at him in surprise; Lee has always been notably unwilling to contribute during Dragontongue class. The rest of the table, who have already been watching him, are shifting and exchanging glances.

Atreus looks from Lee to the faces turned to him, picks up his wineglass, and takes a drink. Dora's eyes are still on Lee, though she speaks to the First Protector instead.

"I see what they're talking about, Atreus."

LEE

As dinner progresses, I grow more and more tense. I'm beginning to feel as though, at every turn, I'm about to expose myself.

Their hubris was the Aurelians' downfall, and it will be yours, too, if you keep showing off.

But this room, these people, this setting, spurs me to a recklessness that only a conscious effort at self-control can contain.

After dessert, Atreus rises and offers annual awards of accomplishment to class-golds who have made significant contributions to Callipolis. Recognition is given for civic virtue, for technological and economic innovations, for military service, academic research, and artistic achievement. Lotus's father, Lo

Teiran, is awarded the title of Callipolan poet laureate. When he rises to receive the laurel Atreus presents, he turns out to have Lotus's same wiry hair and lanky build.

In the half-hour break before the opening dance, the Fourth Order riders are taken around the hall to make introductions. Miranda Hane escorts Annie, General Holmes takes Cor, and Dean Orthos takes Power. Atreus escorts me. The conversations I have at his elbow with class-golds around the room soon run together.

"Lee sur Pallor! Pleasure to meet you at last, we've heard so much about you . . ."

"That's kind, thank you."

"Training up for the Firstrider Tournament? Between you and me, you are our—favored—finalist. Mustn't let us down, my boy . . . Not with these Pythians on our backs."

The man's voice is conspiratorial, the *we* seemingly referring to the Golds generally, whom Atreus has informed me he represents on the Gold Advisory Council. I give my answer smiling, though my thoughts are of Julia and her urging to betray; and to Annie, on whom this man's praise casts oblique aspersions. Of course he has no way of knowing, as he confides *between you and me* with a dragonborn, the irony of his preference.

He also has no way of knowing that, as I look at him, I recognize him. Not from rounds in the new regime: from court in the old.

Because while the small talk required by Atreus's introductions is not difficult, ignoring the disconcerting familiarity of many of the faces is.

What would Julia say, if she saw me shaking hands with the people who betrayed us?

But I already know the answer to that.

Her answer would be that we should make them pay.

ANNIE

Miranda Hane turns out to be the one who will accompany me around the hall making introductions. It doesn't ease my nerves. But I've been replaying the lines of introduction, in either language, over and over in my head for the last few days and know them cold. I'm startled when one of the first couples I'm introduced to, middle-aged and graying, beams at me.

"You, my dear," the man says, squeezing my arm, "are the light of the nation. This is what we once only dared to *dream* of."

I thank him, a little unnerved. As we move away, Hane smiles.

"The Bertrands were some of our earliest supporters," she tells me.

But they're not all like this. When Hane introduces me to another of the guests, a towering, elderly judge who serves on the Janiculum Council, he regards me with unchecked amusement. His tunic is long, intricately embroidered, and, like many of the vestments tonight, reminiscent of the old regime.

"So this is our highland rider!"

"How do you do," I say, curtsying.

Instead of bowing or even replying, he turns to Miranda. "Only a trace of a highland accent," he remarks, with admiration, in Dragontongue. "And she's clearly been given a good scrubbing—"

I can feel a flush blooming across my chest where it would usually be hidden beneath a uniform. Tonight, in the scooped neckline of my ball gown, it's exposed. When Hane doesn't crack a smile, the man wilts and switches to Callish.

"It was just a *joke*, my dear Miranda . . . Sometimes it seems one can't make them anymore . . ."

Hane looks sideways at me, as if to see if I have any rebuttal. I think of Lee, pulling out a line from the *Aurelian Cycle*, in Dragontongue, for a table of onlookers. But as at the Lyceum Club, when I stared down Power and realized words had fled me, I have no such rejoinder. When Hane realizes I don't, she makes an exiting remark and steers us on. I am still nauseated with shame as she introduces me to the next set of guests.

Once would have been enough, but they keep coming, these compliments that feel like insults, the airy condescension that purports itself as kindness. When I'm introduced to Darius's parents, who turn out to own a shipping and trading company that takes up half of Harbortown, they actually turn away from me while I'm still mid-curtsy.

"Is this her?"

By the time this voice finds us, I'm so exhausted that I turn only with reluctance at the sound. The man is younger, in his mid-twenties, his tunic simple but well-cut. It takes me a moment to realize what I noticed about his voice: a highland accent.

"Declan," Miranda says, with unmistakable relief. "Yes. Antigone, may I present Declan of Harfast, a junior advisor to the First Protector and one of the youngest members of the Gold Advisory Council. Declan was among the first graduating classes at the Lyceum."

"How do you do."

Declan grins. He's fair-haired, long-faced, lanky like an overgrown teenager. "Surviving," he says. "They eaten you alive yet?"

I let out a startled laugh. As soon as I do, I worry I shouldn't have, but when I look over at Miranda, her mouth has quirked.

"They're just jealous of our brains," Declan tells me. "Don't pay them any mind."

Instruments have begun to tune in the back of the hall. The open space in the center of the floor has cleared; guests are gathering on its edge. Miranda nods to me.

"It's time, Annie," she says.

Time to get up in front of these people and perform.

My gown was designed to be light, for dance; but all the same, as I weave through the crowd to find Lee, I find its crimson folds hindering and the skin of my chest and back feel bare. The excitement I felt at the beginning of the night at my own reflection has died. I miss my uniform.

I find Lee on the edge of the floor. To my surprise, he looks as drained as I feel. His face is pale in contrast to the dark of his dress uniform, his gray eyes flat and unseeing.

"How was it?" he asks.

I just shake my head.

"Yeah," Lee says, exhaling. "These . . . people."

There's something more than distaste in his voice: a latent anger approaching fury. It is, for Lee, almost unprecedented. When he realizes I'm looking at him, he composes his face at once.

As accustomed as I am to wondering at all the ways this life comes more naturally to him than to me, I'm startled to feel myself swept by sudden compassion as I understand something I should have seen from the start.

Of course. Lee has reasons to find tonight hard, too. Probably even harder than I do.

I think I surprise both of us with my next words.

"It's almost over, Lee."

Lee's eyes meet mine, searching. Then he takes my hand in his and together, we step away from the crowd.

LEE

Annie's fingers hold mine tightly as we assume position, her brown eyes fixed on mine as though determined not to look anywhere else. I could count her lashes, the freckles across her cheeks and shoulders, her burn scars shining in the candlelight. The red of her dress, blending in color with her hair. For a moment the room is silent, the eyes of the guests trained on us.

And then the music starts.

I've known since rehearsal that the melody would be one I know; but it's not until this moment, in the echoing vaulted hall, surrounded by the glittering gowns and formalwear, that I feel the ache of it. The sound of a single violin, the notes throbbing like a human voice and then rising up, higher, impossibly high, painfully beautiful. The memory of this dance, another night, another life, my mother and father and sisters and a world that was their birthright, a world that's lost. And all that's left is a handful of revenge-bent survivors on a rock in the North Sea and this room full of the people who betrayed them.

Annie's hands leave their position and circle my neck; the slight pressure is enough for her to bring my face down to look at her. Her eyes are wide, clear; her gaze seems to see me, see everything.

"Stay with me," she whispers.

I reach up with a single hand to take one of hers down from my neck. At the cue I step forward, and Annie responds. Now it's my turn to keep my eyes fixed on hers, to forget everything but the sound of this, my parents' melody, my parents' dance, and the sight of Annie moving with me, the feel of her waist against my hand and the pressure of her palm against mine.

Annie smiles suddenly, breathlessly, at the completion of a turn, and I feel an irrepressible smile answer hers; and then the sorrow is transformed into something more, something beautiful, and this, this movement that is so tantalizingly close to flying, that's like the high notes of a violin, some mix of joy and pain, is part of that transformation.

It's a fragile balance and I know it can't last, but it seems as long as we're here, dancing the Medean, all of these things can be reconciled and held together as one.

The music descends, and in its lull the other two squadron leaders join us on the floor for the final movement: Crissa, with Lotus, for the skyfish squadron; and Cor, with Alexa, for the stormscourge. Echoing, for those who remember it, the Dance of the Triarchs—and for a moment, though the banners hanging overhead are still the new regime's, the colors streaking across the floor are once again the tricolor of the old: Aurelian red, Skyfish blue, and Stormscourge black.

And then the last turn, the last resolve, and Annie is back in my arms, still except for her heaving breaths. It's finished. She's standing so close that I feel the heat of her body radiating against mine; her face is upturned, the roots of her hair are glistening with sweat; my face is bent toward hers.

Then the applause starts and the moment breaks. We step

away from each other. Alongside the other two couples, I bow, she curtsies, and I lead her off the floor.

I am still strangely, painfully happy. And for one bright, oblivious instant I envision this moment continuing: her remaining with me, alone, and the night wearing on with no one but each other for company.

But then she points out Duck and Lotus. They're sitting in the semidarkness at a table on the edge of the hall, Duck waving.

The vision fades.

I tell her: "You go on."

Her fingers find mine, twist, and pull. "Come with me."

And all the hope comes rushing back. We make our way over. In the afterglow of the dance, it feels instinctive to guide Annie with a touch below her shoulder blades as we move through the hall, to allow my gaze to linger on her hair, beginning to trail in wisps from its bun, tickling her neck and glowing red in the candlelight. Duck scoots to the side to make room for us, and when we sit, Annie's side touches mine ever so slightly on the bench. Though I'm certain she must feel it, too, she makes no move to create distance.

I am aware of every inch along my side where we touch.

"We were admiring your dancing," Duck tells us, grinning.

All around the hall, men and women are getting up to waltz. Annie rolls her eyes to the ceiling.

"No, really. Loads better than my brother."

"Congratulations on your dad's poetry prize," I tell Lotus.

As I speak, I feel Annie's fingers find mine again, roll them into hers on our knees beneath the table, and a feeling like dizziness comes over me. Hours left. And we're still together, and she's *smiling*. Smiling while she holds my hand.

"Thanks," Lotus says. "It's been a long time coming. My dad had a bit of trouble finding patronage for his poetry after the Revolution."

At Duck's look of confusion, Lotus draws a finger across his throat.

"Dead patrons don't pay well."

I can barely hear him, mesmerized as I am by Annie's hand in mine. How long has it been since Annie touched me like this? Surely it was never like *this*, her fingers twining with mine as though she wanted to feel every line and burn scar with the tips of her fingers, a blush creeping up her cheeks as if she feels my gaze on her and it brings heat to her skin—

Could it possibly be this easy, this *simple*?

Lotus cocks his head, lowers his voice, and leans forward conspiratorially. He jerks his chin behind us. "Are you listening to this?"

The faces at the neighboring table are indistinguishable in the semidarkness, but their loud voices are unmistakably those of freshly graduated Lyceans, speaking in Dragontongue.

"You'd want him as the next Protector?"

"From the riders in the Fourth? Yes! Why, who would you pick?"

Annie's hand has stilled in mine, her smile frozen.

Lotus sits back, looks between me and Annie, and tips the wineglass to his lips like he's settling in to be entertained. Duck, whose Dragontongue has always been weak, looks mostly confused.

I begin, tentatively, to run my fingers over Annie's stilled hand, tracing the calluses on slender fingers, the trails of smooth scars across her palm. Like I'm willing it back to life. Back to me.

It's simple. It's easy. It's just like the dancing, please—

The boy's voice says: "*Not* Power sur Eater, because he's always been such a cocky ass—Cor sur Maurana *maybe*, but honestly . . . probably Lee sur Pallor. Especially if he wins Firstrider."

My hand stills, too. Holding Annie's, frozen.

"A slum rat?" the girl's voice scoffs.

"Did you *see* him doing the Medean just now? Or have you had a class with him? He doesn't act like a slum rat. Practically looks like a Stormscourge."

The last line is an afterthought that the boy seems to think nothing of. But Annie's whole body stiffens. And then her hand comes back to life at last.

She separates her fingers from mine and returns them to her lap.

The happy-dizzy feeling dies.

I reach for my glass with the hand no longer holding Annie's and begin to drain it.

You think it ever could stop mattering?

The next thing the boy says makes me freeze mid-swallow.

"Anyway, better than a former serf. I mean, it's a good sob story, sure—I'll grant she's a poster child for the Revolution—"

Annie's eyes flare wide as we hear their scandalized snorts of laughter. She begins blinking rapidly, her bare shoulders going up and tightening at the sound. Lotus looks down, lifting a hand to rub at his forehead; Duck's eyes travel between the three of us, his brow furrowed.

"What have you got against serfs ruling?" the girl teases.

"Nothing, I'm just not convinced it's a *qualification* . . ."

The conversation moves on; some of the graduates in the party are getting up to dance. Annie lifts her head like one waking from a dream. And then she seems to realize her body's position in space and that her side still touches mine. She shifts an inch sideways on the bench. Though it's a slight movement, the distance that suddenly separates our bodies feels like a chasm. There's a charge in the air between us, as if Annie is tensed for any attempt on my part to cross it.

Then Duck, who barely speaks Dragontongue, and whose only understanding of what's happened comes from what he's read in our faces, gets to his feet and extends his hand to Annie. The hair he slicked back in the boys' washroom a few hours ago is sticking up at the back in spikes.

"Dance with me?"

Annie lifts her eyes, wide and over-bright, to his face.

"You don't like dancing."

"I'd like dancing with you."

But still she hesitates, and with a slight shift of her head, her face angles toward mine. As if my presence informs her answer. An old desire wells up within me, its pain so familiar, it returns like exhaustion.

I would give anything to ease the hurt on this girl's face. Anything.

"You should go," I say. "You'll have fun."

Annie's eyes are wide beneath dark lashes as she searches my face. Then she nods.

She rises, takes Duck's outstretched hand, and follows him to the floor.

There's silence after they've left us; Lotus still seems a little embarrassed. He clears his throat and claps his hand on my shoulder.

"Still, good news for you, isn't it? The Golds' favor."

I watch Annie's smile flickering, laughing unwillingly, as Duck tries to dance. The pain is slowly receding from her eyes. I hear myself say: "Yeah."

There's darkness for a time after that. I'm aware of the night continuing, of Lotus's wandering off to visit with his mother and father, and of my sitting alone on the edge of the hall, unable to summon up the energy to leave. Annie is still dancing with Duck.

You thought she could be happy with you? That she could ever forget?

"There you are. We've been looking everywhere for you."

"What are you doing here, sitting alone in the dark?"

Cor and Crissa have taken seats on either side of me, Cor punching me in the arm. He follows the gaze that I'm too slow to retract.

"My brother's a horrible dancer," he observes.

Crissa looks at Annie and Duck, then turns to me, and puts her hand on my knee. "We've been talking, Cor and I. Have you been training for the Firstrider Tournament?"

I rouse myself. "You mean in all my free time?"

"Ha-ha. We wanted you to know—we'll train with you."

I look from one of them to the other, shadows in the candlelight but their faces turned toward mine, their bodies angled inward. Suddenly the only thing that matters is that they're *here*, on either side of me.

"You don't have time for that—"

"We'll make time. We want you to win, Lee."

It's surprising, after an evening of being told variations of this from old men of the Janiculum, how different it is coming from Cor and Crissa. A vote of confidence from within the corps that I hadn't realized that I needed.

"I'd . . . really appreciate that. Thank you."

The music changes; a new set has begun. The sound of highland pipes is filling the hall with a pounding rhythm; the violin has become faster, playful. It's the kind of melody that was never played, never wanted, at the balls of the old regime. Annie, about to quit the floor, has her hand seized by Rock. I watch her protest halfheartedly, laughing, then allow Rock to lead her in a few bounds back into the center of the floor. Most of its occupants are younger, alumni among the youngest generations of the Lyceum, cheering with enthusiasm to begin a different kind of dance. Around the hall, older faces are looking on with thinly disguised disapproval. But those dancing don't notice.

Annie and Rock have begun mimicking each other with shouts of delight, their fingers twined together as they lean back. Annie's hair falls free of its pins and tumbles down her back, but she hardly seems to notice. The highland rhythm is so powerful that it seems to catch you in your stomach, take hold of your legs, so that even seated all you want to do is move your feet. There's a swapping of partners, and now Annie dances with a lanky, straw-haired ministry official who beams as he swings her outward; and then she's back in Duck's arms.

Crissa takes my hand, squeezes, and I look at her. Her dress, blue as the Medean, exactly matches her eyes, and her hair glows warm and gold in the candlelight.

"I think it's time we took you for some fresh air," she says.

ANNIE

Duck and I walk back to the Cloister in the early morning, when the sky is no longer quite so inky black. Duck hums the last song, his coat swinging over one shoulder; I hold my shoes by their heels on the hooks of my fingers, the marble of the Palace walkways cool beneath my aching feet. Duck's voice echoes in the deserted courtyard.

"Can you *believe* we live here?"

The courtyard smells of cold stone and the cool water that burbles in the fountains. Columns along the arcade rise to vaulted overhangs above us, where tendrils of ivy hang silhouetted against the stars. Distantly, a gull cries.

"Can you believe we ride *dragons*?"

He rounds on his heel, takes a few steps backward. "Can you believe I just *danced*?"

I laugh aloud.

"And not too badly, by the end," I grant.

This, I realize, must be what giddiness feels like. Like escape. As though for a few short hours, as I danced until my hair fell from its pins, I left behind every bitter thought that haunts me and was free.

Most of all the memory of Lee's hand in mine, the rush of old comfort thrilling with new danger—and his face when I pulled away. Like I'd just pulled him apart.

We've reached the Cloister garden. The rippled glass of the solarium glows orange, a fire lit within: We won't be alone when we enter. I reach for the door handle, and Duck takes my hand, pausing it. I turn to him.

"Oh. Not so fast."

He pulls me back to him, and as I realize what is about to happen, I freeze.

And then, with dizzying speed, a hundred small incidents click into place like a narrative whose common thread I did not, until this moment, let myself *see*.

Oh, dragons. How did I not know this was coming?

"Duck, I don't . . ."

He stops, too.

For a moment we continue to stand close, frozen, and I feel the threat of an end rise over us: an end of something that could have started and that I was almost certain I did not want; and worse, more terrifyingly, an end now to what we already had.

But then Duck takes a half step back and lights a smile. And even if it's not quite as easy as his usual smile, it's close. Crinkling his eyes, spreading across his square face.

"Hey. It's—okay, Annie."

The lingering uncertainty as I take in the strain around his eyes: *Is it?*

"Let's go in?" I ask.

That's when the alarm bells begin to toll.

LEE

Early morning, Cor is asleep. Crissa and I are beside him on a deserted part of the Outer Wall where we had, originally, decided to climb for a view of the city. The fire that we'd lit has gone out. The stone is cold, Crissa is warm, and the wineskin that we were passing back and forth is long empty. I feel like I'm moving in and out of a dream. In the dream, her hands are in my hair, mine are around her waist, and her mouth is on mine.

Is that what it felt like for her, dancing with Duck? I wonder. *Did she feel free and forgetful with him, like this?*

Whenever I rouse from the dream and remember why it's something I shouldn't have, the conversations begin again.

"Crissa, this isn't—we shouldn't—"

Even in the near darkness, I can see her lips parting in a smile. Our faces are so close, I can see stars reflected in her eyes. "We shouldn't what?"

This time I'm the one to answer by pulling her closer, by bringing us both back under. Because though I sense, dimly, a future of guilt spreading out on the horizon, it still feels a long way off. And in the meantime, Crissa's lips have opened mine with need.

We break apart when the bells begin to toll. Crissa groans, lowers her face onto my shoulder, her hair still spread across us both. As I recognize the bell's tones, the blurred world snaps back into focus.

"How is it already morning?" she asks.

"Those aren't striking the hour."

Crissa stills. And then she places a palm on the flagstones to push her weight off mine. The chill of the morning invades the space between us. The east is pink below a sky rippling with low-hanging stratus clouds; a single beacon has lit on the northern tower of the Inner Palace; below it, the alarm bell rings. Beside us, Cor is stirring, wincing from the noise.

Cold dread rolls over me, dousing any lingering warmth from wine.

I knew it. I should have said something. I shouldn't have let us take down our guard—

Crissa and I get to our feet as one and turn our sights out, over the sleeping city. A trail of beacons mounted on dragon perches have lit through the neighborhoods, vanishing in the distance of the lowland plains, leading to the north coast. A trail of light leading to the source of alarm.

The bells are rhythmic, tolling in the patterned code we were taught to interpret as children but have never since had reason to use.

Dragons. Attack.

9

—

STARVED ROCK

LEE

The lull of the ball is sliding away; all at once, Julia's words are ringing in my ears. *We will strike first to spread fear.* My fault, my stupid fault for doing nothing, for letting Holmes make a call that I *knew* left us absurdly exposed—

But there's no point in self-recrimination right now. No time for it. I seize Cor by the arm and pull him to his feet, half woken. Crissa presses her hand to her forehead and inhales as the fullness of our unpreparedness rolls over her.

"We need to get into the air—and they're not even saddled—and I'm in *this dress*—"

She clutches her gown in disgust, for what good is such clothing against dragonfire?

Cor focuses at last on the tolling bell, the burning beacons, and begins to swear, like a chant, rhythmically. I shake him till he looks at me, then seek Crissa's eyes.

"We've drilled this."

Crissa shakes her head, clearing it. Then she hums, like a recitation: "Get to the armory and suit up while the keepers saddle the dragons. Summon from the arena gate."

We don't have far to sprint: The stretch of the Outer Wall on which we stand connects directly to the Cloister by means of a trapdoor and a ladder, which we scramble down, and then we hurtle through a single corridor to the armory entrance.

"Where do you want us—" Cor asks while we're running.

The question is directed at me, even though the three of us are, as squadron leaders, equally ranked. But only after I've begun to answer do I remember that, or feel surprised that he's asked me.

"Skyfish squadron ahead, aurelian and stormscourge half-squadrons coming in behind. We'll leave the other halfsquadrons covering the city; we can't leave it unprotected—follow the trail of beacons to the attack, but when you get there, limited attacks only, Crissa, hold them off until we can catch up with you—"

We've reached the armory; Crissa seizes my arm before entering, pulling me to a halt. Cor pauses, too, swinging on the doorframe. Inside, the armory is full of riders shouting, scrambling to suit up; many of them are, like us, still in formalwear.

"Lee, what're we—?" someone calls from within.

"We're going to give orders in the air, just suit up and get to the gate, you're fine—" I call, before turning back to Crissa.

Her hair falls in half-pinned clumps from what remains of her bun, loose around her shoulders; in the dark corridor, the blue of her dress looks black against her hair. Her eyes are wide, her chest heaving.

"And if it's too late?" she asks.

"What do you mean—"

"If it's an extraction." She's clutching the cinched waist of her gown, gasping to catch her breath from the sprint. Cor reaches out an arm to steady her at the elbow. "Lee, if they've already—"

If they've already landed fire. *A single dragon is still enough to level a town.* What will Crissa's skyfish find when they get there? Dragons waiting for them, or just the dragonfire they've left behind?

"If they've already come, get in wherever the fire's gone down and bring anyone still moving on the blazesite out."

We've drilled that, too. But all the same it seems hearing the procedure recited aloud is what Crissa needed; she calms once I've said it, her face hardening.

Inside, we strip. Those coming directly from the ball are lacking their usual underlayers, but there's no time for shame; Crissa wrenches her dress up over her shoulders as confidently as if she were in a room alone; I note in a half glance, with a kind of numb disbelief, that a trail of flushed skin spreading down her neck was my doing and that the memory already feels remote.

The door bursts open and Annie enters, followed by Duck. Her hair is disheveled, her sleeves low and uneven on her shoulders. I have a half second to wonder whether she and Duck were occupied as Crissa and I were before she's beside me in the aurelian row, seizing the flamesuit from her cubby next to mine, reaching awkwardly behind her shoulders for the clasp of her dress. She curses.

"Lee—" she hisses.

"Give me your bootknife."

I slice the dress open down her back; the luxurious fabric rips like paper. She shoves it off with vindictive fury and dives for her flamesuit, a flash of bare skin that I turn my back on at once. We shimmy into our flamesuits without looking at each other.

"You want me on left or right vanguard?" she calls over her shoulder.

I think of Crissa's white face as she said the word *extraction*. *We will strike first to spread fear.*

How many minutes have passed since the first beacon lit? How many since we saw the last? What is the likelihood, if any, that the Pythians will still be there?

Annie may be one of the fleet's strongest assets in battle. But for an extraction? For a *blazesite*? Annie, who clutched my hand so tightly at the sight of Duck injured by unsparked stormscourge fire that her nails left marks, facing in all likelihood a scene of devastation by dragonfire the likes of which she hasn't seen since Holbin?

No. That at least I can spare her.

The answer comes out curt.

"Neither. I need you and Power covering the city with your halfsquadrons. We can't leave it undefended."

I realize only after I've said it what Annie will take from this: Defending is traditionally the role of the Alternus. She freezes, midway through tightening her cuirass. For a moment her fingers open and close on the buckles in time with her breath. And then she lifts her head and looks at me.

Power speaks first. Unlike my and Annie's voices, his is raised for the room to hear. He stands two yards away, separated by the benches between the aurelian row and stormscourge, paused in the act of lifting his cuirass over his head.

"You're already ordering Antigone to defend? Is that a *joke*? Firstrider Tournament's still two weeks away, Lee."

Power is glaring at me, disgusted. The disgust isn't new; having it turned on me on behalf of Annie is.

He's picked hell of a time for it.

At his challenge, riders around us fall silent and exchange glances. Annie's brown eyes are still fixed on me, her lips parted. When she speaks, her voice is quiet, close to a whisper, as if determined, despite the scene Power seems bent on creating, to keep our conversation private.

"I want to be part of the counterattack."

My voice lowers, too. Hissing the words that I need to make her understand. *"We're already too late for a counterattack."*

Annie blinks. As if she hears, though I haven't said it, the word implicit: *blazesite.*

But whatever I expect her to make of that, it's not the contortion of her disappointment into a twisted smile of newfound realization as she continues to look at me. As if I have, somehow, just managed to hurt her in any entirely different way. Instead of explaining herself, she breathes, with that same expression, so twisted with pain and surprise, it almost looks amused:

"Yes, sir."

She turns away and continues arming with jerking movements.

Power, who's made no effort to disguise the fact that he's continued to listen, lets out a snort behind me that makes me practically jump.

"So *that's* what this is about," he says at full volume, sneering. "Annie's *history*? You've got a lot of nerve, Lee—"

Glances down the row are being shot, anew, in our direction by other Guardians; Cor, two cubbies down from Power, has actually stopped suiting up as he assesses the confrontation, and Crissa's frown in my direction makes it clear that as far as she's concerned, I'm on the wrong side of this argument. But by now I'm too angry to care. Since when has *anything* between Annie and me been any of their business—Power has *no idea* what he's talking about—

My fingers are tightening on my leg guards as I strap them on, my jaw clenching. But before I can answer, Annie lifts her head from her armor and turns it toward Power.

"We have orders. The Keep needs defending. Suit up."

To my surprise, Power doesn't argue with her.

Crissa has finished arming first from her squadron, and her voice is the next to fill the room. She's moved to the doorway where she bellows at the remainder of her riders:

"Let's move, people! Weapons, shields, canteens!"

Outside, in the growing light beside the arena gate, riders arrive two by two at intervals of thirty seconds; dragons emerge from the caves and barely land before their riders mount; keepers are ready at the mouth to help strap boots into stirrups and tighten girths. The skyfish squadron departs first; when they're off, Cor and I begin launching our own riders. And then at last I'm mounting Pallor, kicking off, and leaving Annie and her blank face behind with the defending halfsquadrons.

She thinks she can handle a blazesite? Fine. But she shouldn't expect me to wait on her pride when Callipolan lives are at stake. I have more to worry about than her need to prove herself—

In fact, I have *family* to worry about. Only in the air does that reality finally hit.

Yes, it might be a blazesite. But what if it's not? What if we aren't too late, or it's Julia waiting on dragonback or Ixion or some other long-lost friend or relative—

What will I do?

ANNIE

When Power and I land with our halfsquadrons on the ramparts to take watch, it's the first time we've ever alighted on Pytho's Keep for anything more than a training exercise. Tonight, in the growing dawn, all I can make out of the citadel and ramparts are rugged silhouettes against the gray sky. The city below us is toylike in the half-light, miniature spires over miniature rooftops; the river glints with the reflected sunrise; the lowland plains stretch out in rolling lines of blue toward the sea to the east, the highlands rise to the west. We watch the rest of the fleet follow the trail of beacons north, their winged silhouettes diminishing against the horizon.

I watch them, and remember Lee's face at our first sighting of the Pythian fleet.

And now that boy, whose face I've seen fill with longing at the sight of our enemy, has ordered me to wait behind while he goes out to face them.

He's right. We probably will be too late. And it would have gutted me to see it.

But that doesn't undo the absurdity of the fact that, under threat by dragonfire from people whom Lee counts as family, he just questioned *my* fitness to face them.

How often have I longed for this boy's comfort? How often have I remembered and missed how much easier it was, in Albans, when I could still seek it from him?

But now I know what that feels like, delivered unsolicited and unneeded.

Because it's one thing to be written off by Goran, by the

Minister of Propaganda, by every single teacher I've ever had or ministry official I've ever done rounds with.

It's another thing entirely to be written off by Lee.

And there's more to it than just my injured pride.

Will Lee's determination to keep faith with Callipolis hold, if they aren't too late and he does face family? And if it doesn't hold, who will be able to stop him if I'm not there to do it? Who else in the corps has even a hope of matching Lee, if it comes down to that?

I should be out there.

On one side, Power waits quietly beside me, and I sense his anticipation for me to break the silence. On my other side, Aela, her presence like a fire in the back of my mind. When I reach my arm out and lay it on her wing joint, she turns to look at me. Her horned face fills my vision, blocking out the ramparts and the city below and the pink horizon. And as I stare into her golden eyes, the memory rises, like a vision: my father, his voice flowing in my memory from another lifetime, gruff with an accent that my own voice lost long ago.

You see, Annie, they watch us kneel, they see the back of our heads, and they think we've given in. They don't realize you can think from your knees just as well as from your feet.

A calloused hand, large enough to cup my face, tilts my chin up to look at him as he crouches to my height. The lined eyes, the conspiring smile, of a man I once believed would always be there to protect me.

And then the vision fades, and I finally understand.

My father taught me the form of courage that he needed. The courage of thinking from your knees. That was what we had.

But today, as I stood in front of Lee sur Pallor, I realized I'm done with my father's kind of courage. I felt how those words tasted, *yes, sir* to a dragonlord's son, sour and familiar, like old milk turned. And I realized that if I don't like how those words taste, it's up to me to do something about it.

I'm done thinking from my knees. It's time to think from my feet.

All the while Power stands beside me, silent. Waiting. The dawn light renders him little more than an armored silhouette at Eater's side. A distant part of myself is angry with him. Furious. But the rest of me recognizes that, right now, how I feel about Power is irrelevant.

"When are you free to train?"

Power doesn't express surprise or triumph or make any remark at all. "Tomorrow. Before patrols. I've got a free block."

"Good. We'll start then."

LEE

The coastline has appeared, blue-gray in the early morning. For a heart-stopping instant I think the trail of beacons leads to Fort Aron and its town off Aron's Cove, one of the few population centers along the northern coast. But then I realize the beacons continue past it. A mile from the fort off the coast, a single island is ablaze. It fills the cove with the light of its fire.

And then nothing: gray sea to the horizon; no signs of hostile dragons, nor the streaks of fire that would show our skyfish locked in sparring matches with sparked dragonfire.

They lit the island and left.

And some part of me, some awful, cowardly part of me, is relieved.

As we approach, I smell it. Sulfurous and heady. A scent I haven't smelled in years: dragonfire.

I kick Pallor down into a dive, leading the aurelian and storm-scourge squadrons into descent. Winged black silhouettes are dipping in and out of the blaze, the skyfish already on the site; the island is tiny, sparsely populated, and the entirety of its few shacks are on fire. A fleet of rescue boats, a combination of civilian vessels and naval ships from Fort Aron, have congregated at a safe distance off the shore, and Crissa's skyfish dart back and forth from them to the burning island, ferrying whomever they've been able to find to safety.

I slice my boot straps to leap off as we descend. On the ground, flames are still licking the buildings around us, wood snapping and cracking, and other Guardians are calling frantically as they search. Even protected by a flamesuit and the filter of my visor, the heat makes me light-headed, and once I begin coughing, I can't stop.

"Lee—here—"

Lotus and Duck are struggling to lift fallen beams, still partially afire, from the entryway of a burning building. As we clear it, a crash comes within: a floor falling through. Duck raises his arm over his visored face, preparing to go in, when I seize him.

"It's not sound. No."

"There are people in there, Lee—we can hear them—"

He's straining against me as, with another crash, the roof collapses in flames. I have to haul him backward.

"It's *too late*, Duck."

ANNIE

The sun rises as I look out over the city, simmering with the feeling of my own powerlessness. Surely there is no hell like this *waiting*. This *wondering*.

What are they facing? And *who will return?*

The sun is high in the sky by the time the fleet reappears on the horizon. In the interim, my imagination has had time to work, and so when we see them, my relief spirals into unexpected exhaustion. They're all right. They're safe.

I assign a lingering guard on the Keep and the rest of us descend. Once back in the caves, my feet take me, not up to the armory, but down the cave corridor. I find Duck in the sky-fish nests, where he's unsaddling Certa with shaking fingers, his pupils still dilated from spillover. He's blackened from soot and reeks of sparked dragonfire. The smell is enough to awaken memories that bring bile to my mouth.

"Annie . . ."

"Are you hurt?"

It's difficult to believe that, mere hours ago, we were laughing together as we tried to dance, or that for a few heartbeats I looked up at him and feared that I was about to lose him over something as trivial as a kiss.

Duck shakes his head.

"Lee and some of the others are still there," he manages, as if forming the words costs him. "Collecting accounts from . . . survivors—"

And then his face, soot-blackened, crumples.

And that's enough for me to know what happened. They saw

no combat; Lee faced no one. But what they did see was almost certainly worse.

I'm not surprised by the memories that rise with my understanding; but I am surprised by the calmness that settles over me as they do. The sudden, rooted sense of place. This is familiar. This I know. These are the paths I've wandered, in and out of sleep, for a lifetime.

LEE

The island, called Starved Rock, is one of the handful of vassal islands on the northern coast of Callipolis, named for its barren landscape and a legendary tragedy that took place on it during the Aurelian invasion. Because of its sparse population, it wasn't provided with additional fortification in the last month; it was assumed to be too close to the greater target of Fort Aron to be endangered.

In the end, the casualty count is low. Seven, out of a total population of twenty-six. The accounts confirm two storm-scourge dragons and one skyfish, who departed after setting fire to the buildings, rather than remaining to finish the job. Those who woke in time to escape the fires were not pursued.

Except for one, who finds me on the galley where survivors are being counted and their burns tended. The day has dawned gray and clouded, the deck of the ship rocks gently on the swells.

"Are you Lee sur Pallor?"

The boy, fair-haired beneath soot, has a blanket around his shoulders and a mug of tea he doesn't drink between still-shaking hands. He's risen from where he was sitting on the deck with his parents and sister.

"Yes."

"I was given a message from—Julia Stormscourge."

The deck is already quiet, despite the number of people on it; but at his words, it falls completely silent. The lapping of waves and the gulls overhead are all we can hear. The sound of Julia's name on this stranger's tongue fills me with numb dread.

"For—me?"

The boy nods.

"For the Firstrider," he says. "For the Firstrider and the First Protector."

The boy's voice is too strained for me to think of contradicting him. Beneath so much soot, his expression is indiscernible, although it makes his eyes appear white-rimmed. Crissa and Lotus, crouched nearby to go over accounts from other survivors, have risen to their feet. Crissa has lifted her hand to cover her mouth.

"She landed, spoke to me, made me memorize it, before . . ."

He leaves the sentence unfinished. My voice comes out hoarse.

"Go on."

The boy inhales, then recites: *"Consider this a taste. This was the work of three sparked dragons, but soon there will be more. We will continue until Callipolis is ours again, and the next time, we won't be so merciful. You have until Palace Day to change your minds. Do you really want to make more—"*

But here the boy pauses, eyes scanning my face as if remembering something about me, and it makes him hesitate.

"More?"

"Do you really want to make more orphans of Callipolans?"

10

SPARRING PARTNERS

The boy and the girl were the only children from their orphanage who scored high enough on the metals test to be invited to the Choosing Ceremony. On the awaited day, the boy was alive with excitement. Somehow, against all odds, he was back in the Inner Palace. And he was about to attend a Choosing ceremony. His birthright.

The girl did not share his excitement. They were on the threshold of the Hall of the Triarchs, standing in the line of waiting children about to be presented to dragons, and she was shaking from head to foot. "I don't want to go in there."

After a year of unease about the idea of this test, of commoners attending Choosing ceremonies, the boy's only thought now, when he looked at the girl, was that something extraordinary was about to happen and he didn't want her to miss it. Without pausing to consider it, he took her hand.

"We'll do it together."

Inside the hall, high above them, on the balcony, the boy could see a few adults gathered, watching the ceremony. The boy himself had stood there when his brother had been presented at a Choosing. Now, looking up at the balcony, the boy spotted the man who had saved him.

They passed the first hatchling, a slender, purple-tinged sky-fish, dog-sized. Its eyes passed over them without interest, and they continued on.

"See? Easy," he murmured to the girl. "They're just babies. Can't even breathe fire yet. Unless they Choose you, they don't even notice you."

She didn't ask how he knew this. Her eyes were fixed on the exit at the other side of the room. They passed another skyfish, then a third. He thought they were doing quite well until he felt her freeze beside him.

They had reached the stormscourge section. For an instant, his only thought was, Finally.

His family's dragons. He was home.

But then he looked at the girl and saw her face crumpling with fear. Looking at the stormscourges—his stormscourges—with such terror on her face that tears began to pour down it.

He felt as though something inside him was breaking apart.

"Come on," he said.

He wrapped his arm around her and pulled her forward, past all the great, beautiful stormscourges that he'd always dreamed of flying. Barely looking at them, because all he could focus on was the feeling of the girl's shoulders shaking as he led her on. "They won't hurt you, come on . . ."

And then it was over: He hadn't been Chosen, but it didn't matter, suddenly it didn't matter at all—

"See, we're done, it's done—"

He turned to her, desperate to see the look of despair gone from her face, ignoring the plummeting feeling of his own.

He was surprised to see something else. Instead of staring at her feet, the girl was looking up. Past him.

He followed her gaze and saw that she was looking at an aurelian, and that the aurelian was looking back at her.

He'd heard it said before that a kind of magic came with a dragon Choosing you—that the dragon bound you to it, that you formed a connection that was deep and full of an old magic. His father had always told him this was simply a myth, that it was a matter of imprinting and that there was nothing mystical about it.

But he couldn't help thinking, as he watched the girl's face transform, that he was seeing something unearthly. The girl who, a moment ago, had been cowering against him now released his hand as if she had forgotten it. She took one step toward the dragon, then another, never taking her eyes off the dragon's face. When they stood nose to nose, she stretched out a hand and laid it between the dragon's eyes.

The boy was so entranced that he didn't stop to wonder what was nudging him until he turned to acknowledge it. Then he looked up, into a pair of great, liquid black eyes, and everything around him stood still.

LEE

I sit across from Atreus while he reviews my transcription of the Pythians' message to the boy from Starved Rock. The tomes of Dragontongue lining the shelves of his office contrast with the careful austerity of his desk, of the chairs we're sitting in, and his simple, unadorned uniform. Lines form around his mouth and forehead as he reads. When he finishes, he laces his fingers together and looks up. It's early afternoon the day after the Lycean Ball, but it feels like a year has passed between last night and today.

"You handled this well, Lee."

The truth curdles in my stomach: I didn't handle this well. I let it happen. I let Holmes take down the aerial guard when I knew better and he didn't.

"How are we going to reply?"

Atreus's voice is clipped with distaste. "To the Pythians? We're not, for the time being."

"But our fleet hasn't *sparked* yet."

"It will. I'm confident of that. They give us till Palace Day? A great deal can change in three weeks. I'm happy to wait them out."

The next objection comes to my lips before I can stop myself.

"What if it's not worth it?"

Atreus tilts his chin. Untwines his fingers, lines them across his desk.

"What if what's not worth it?"

That boy's white-rimmed eyes, the smoking blazesite reached only a few minutes too late. "What if it's just—making more orphans of Callipolans? This war. If it even comes to that, if we even spark. Wouldn't it be better to—"

"To capitulate?"

"Compromise," I say hoarsely. "What if there were a way to compromise?"

For one mad moment it's on the tip of my tongue. I imagine saying it, imagine telling him the whole thing—*When I was a child, you saved me,* and *I believe in all of it, all we're doing,* and

Julia will listen to me, they'll listen to me, let me be the bridge—

Let me have some way out of this besides facing them in the air.

Atreus speaks first.

"It is difficult, knowing that your choices are ones whose consequences others suffer."

His voice is soft, understanding. As if, though I've said nothing of how it felt to arrive on the scene on the back of a dragon and still find myself powerless, he understands exactly the weight it bore.

"But that is the price of leadership. How exactly would you compromise with these people, Lee? They don't want our world. They want theirs. And that's something I will not allow. We are building something better."

Atreus's next words remove the possibility of uttering the truth like a candle snuffed of its flame.

"You are the future of this country, Lee. A leader chosen, not born. There can be no compromise on that."

What would you say if I told you I was both?

But that's not a question I dare ask. It's remarkable how, even this many years later, even trained in rhetoric myself, Atreus's words still have the power to make my spine tingle. Even as he damns my own people with them.

We are building something better.

Familiar. Calming. Atreus's vision, something to hold on to. Sweeping aside what came before it with such persuasive confidence. *Better.*

"The qualms you have expressed are not ones you alone will have," he admits. "Particularly if our fleet remains unsparked."

He taps his fingers together, scans the papers lying across his desk like he's surveying a land campaign from the air. His tone becomes brisk.

"It will be important that the people are assured. I'll speak to Propaganda about measures to be taken."

ANNIE

Power and I begin training the day after Starved Rock, following Atreus's speech in the People's Square. By that time, news of the attack has reached the capital from Fort Aron. The crowd is unusually quiet as Atreus describes what happened after the beacons lit. Standing beside Lee among the onlooking Guardians, I can't help but glance at his face as Atreus says certain words—*two stormscourge and one skyfish*—*survivor bearing a message from Julia Stormscourge*—*we will not capitulate. We are certain that our fleet will spark soon.*

I wonder what's going on behind Lee's masked expression. What he saw, what he's remembering, what he's thinking. It's from Lotus, not Lee, that I learned it was a surviving child who delivered the message. Does that name mean anything to him, *Julia Stormscourge*? What does he imagine, when he hears the word *capitulate*, other than the return of a world that surely must tug at buried desires?

And I wonder what is going on behind the eyes of the people who watch us. They're roaring by the end, roused by Atreus's words and voice, but even so—when Crissa and I take the footpath alleyways through Highmarket back to the Palace at the end of the address—the conversations whispered at street corners have a different tone.

"At least with the dragonlords we could defend ourselves—"

"Not to mention, with the dragonlords, my sons weren't getting paid a pittance from the Labor Draft Board—"

"Commoners and women riding dragons, fat lot of good that does if the fleet can't spark—"

Dora Mithrides's pseudoscientific rumor from the Lycean Ball seems to have trickled down to the lower class-metals. When they see Crissa and me, the huddle of whispering class-bronzes unfolds to observe us, making our way down the footpath in Guardian uniform, and while some elbow each other in sudden wariness, the most daring of them gives us a flourishing bow, baring a sardonic, ragged-toothed grin.

"Long live the Revolution, lady Guardians."

"Citizen," Crissa answers rigidly.

We round the corner to the echoes of suppressed, bitter laughter going up behind us. I'm shaking, unnerved by their anger; Crissa's lips are pressed tight, her fingers clenched to fists. Above us, the sign for the Pickled Boar swings over the tavern entrance: I realize with a start that the last time I visited this part of Highmarket, I was lifted on shoulders and offered free drinks. But now, when faces turn toward us, conversations slide into silence and lines form around mouths.

At the Palace gates we part ways, Crissa to the Inner Palace, and I to the Cloister and the dragon caves to begin training with Power. Aela is curled in her nest, asleep beneath a wing that encloses her like a blanket, and when I crouch down to wake her, I drop for a moment to my knees, take her head in my hands, press my forehead against hers. Her slitted eyes snap open and she lets out a rumble like a purr.

"When, *when* are you going to spark . . ."

But Aela has no answer. All the dragons have been subjected to test after test from their keepers and from physicians attempting to spark them, all futile; Aela's distemper at their visits reaches me all the way from the Cloister. She yawns, revealing rows of razor-sharp teeth, and shakes herself to her feet. I throw her saddle over her back.

"Time to go spend some time with your favorite storm-scourge."

The Eyrie is warmed with afternoon sunlight; beneath my flamesuit I begin to break a sweat. A thin blanket of cirrus clouds coat the sky high above us, washing out its blue and softening the sun's glare. Power waits for me, Eater lounging beside him, his wings flattened on the stone to warm in the sun. Aela growls and bucks at the sight of them, giving me a reproachful look. Eater remains where he lounges, but his head spikes flatten as he growls back at her.

"Don't look at me like that," I mutter, seizing her by the halter. "They're all right this time . . ."

"Hell of a speech," Power remarks, by way of greeting. "Nothing like a good dose of propaganda to start off your morning."

He eases himself down onto the stone next to Eater, rubbing him beneath the jaw, calming him. I sit, too. It feels strange to sit for a conversation with Power. Even with a few meters between us it seems dangerous, like laying down arms in front of an enemy. Aela gives a sniffle of incredulity and eases onto her haunches beside me, so close her side presses against mine, warming me through my flamesuit. Glaring at Eater, daring him to come closer. Her tail flicks back and forth, dragging on the flagstones. Power watches the hostile back-and-forth with lazy disinterest.

"We still heard people talking about wanting dragonlords back, afterward," I tell him.

Power's lip curls. "People can be stupid."

It's Power's usual condescension, but it reminds me, for the first time, of Dora's revelation about his parentage at the Lycean Ball. His anger, his defensiveness, about a fact that would have meant nothing to me if he hadn't spent years humiliating me for a low birth that it turns out we have in common.

I can't decide whether knowing the truth makes me like him more, or less.

He stretches, straining his arms above his head, the muscles in his shoulders rippling, like a cat arching its back. Maintaining eye contact the whole time. Then he shakes them out.

"If we're doing this, I want us to be clear on why. So. You tell me, Annie."

I tell him the truth. "I don't want to be Lee's Alterna."

Power nods, then gazes over the empty tiers of the arena stands, rising like the sides of a bowl around us, his brow furrowed. This late in summer, the sun has turned his face a deep brown. He says, "But I'm not asking what you *don't* want. I'm asking what you do want. I'm asking why you want to *win*."

And that's enough to stop me short.

Power lifts a hand between us and begins to count off on his fingers.

"Here are the facts. You're a finalist like Lee, his equal or better in every one of his classes, his only challenger in the air, his match on every count of trauma. You're every bit as qualified for Firstrider as he is, you're the only real threat he's ever had. But he doesn't see that. And I'm not sure you do, either."

At hearing my own abilities listed—without comment, or

anger, just flat facts—my discomfort rises, unbearable.

"I *do* see all that, but—"

Power waits, his lip curling, for me to finish the objection. My face is burning, but I resist the urge to avert it. And then I hear myself list the weaknesses that haunt me as if compelled.

"—I'm not—I'm not as good with people, I don't lead like he does—I'll never be as good at charming anyone or making speeches or—"

Power drums his fingers impatiently on Eater's scales. "Which might put you at a disadvantage for Protectorship, sure. But to be a good Firstrider, you just need a head for strategy, skill in the air, and nerves of steel."

For a moment, the shock of the words—their simplicity—prevents me from believing them.

No. Surely it's not so simple—surely I've not spent months doubting my place in the Fourth Order only to realize what I should have seen from the start—

When I say nothing, Power leans forward.

"Tell me where you came from."

For a moment I tense, primed for the disparagement of my background that he's usually so willing to give. But then, as Aela's tail tightens its coil around me, I understand. Power isn't asking about my birth, or my poverty, or my lack of polish.

He's asking what I did in spite of them.

My answer comes in a whisper.

"I watched my family get taken by dragonfire at the age of six, and I learned to ride anyway."

Power's brown eyes are raking over my face. The same way they've always done when he asks me about stormscourge fire. But today, I experience it as something besides cruelty.

Admiration.

"Damn right you did," he murmurs.

He leans forward, placing his palms on the sunbaked stone of the Eyrie floor. "Now tell me again why you want to make Firstrider."

My fingers are wound tightly around Aela's horns as I clench them. I let myself say it the way I should have said it from the start.

"Because I'd be good at it."

* * *

Aela and I don't know how to spill over intentionally. When Power learns this, he rubs at the line between his eyebrows and squints at me.

"Of course you don't," he mutters. "You really keep everything close to the chest, don't you, Annie?"

"I'm going to take that as a compliment."

Power snorts, like he didn't mean it as one. Then he gets to his feet, dusts his hands together, and I get to my feet as well. Facing each other, standing on the Eyrie, it feels like we're back in familiar territory. Opponents. Eater and Aela have tensed, sensing a change in the air.

"So what was it like, watching my match with Duck?"

After years of Power's goads, I can see where this is going. I feel a ripple of closeness to Aela, who's risen on her haunches beside me, as my anger rises.

"Don't—"

Power presses on, relentless. "Did you feel *powerless*? Were you *scared* for him?"

Aela is so close, I can practically feel her mind tickling my own as my breathing accelerates. My repulsion beginning to do its work on us, even as this becomes a game I no longer want to play.

"Stop, Power, this isn't—"

Power lets out a bark of laughter. "What's the matter, Annie—did you think I was a nice person, because I said I'd train with you? Do you want me to tell you how *I* felt, during that match?"

His own pupils are dilating. Eater rises to his haunches, lifts his head to the sky, and roars. They've spilled over; Power's smile has the frenzied energy of a dragon's influence.

"*No—*"

He leans forward, lowers his voice, and it cuts across the windswept Eyrie. "I felt bloody fantastic. Because beating Duck has *always* hit the spot. Sometimes, you've just got to kick a dog."

My fury bursts into Aela with such force it feels like a pot bursting from steam. There's a sudden, rushing relief as my emotions flood into her; her wings burst open, her horns go flat, and she bellows ash. She and Eater are pawing the ground as they eye each other, poised to attack.

Power, abruptly clinical, searches my eyes for the same pupil dilation I can see in his.

"Good," he says, seeing it. "Don't let the connection close. Let's get in the air."

I scramble onto Aela and we kick off from the ground like it's hateful to us.

Sparring under spillover is hyperreal in the moment but difficult to recall with clarity afterward. Power gives feedback in the air, rather than on the ground, and his words come through the fogging haze of Aela's emotions and my own: *That was sloppy.*

Do it again. Now again. Still, for all his corrections, Power concludes the first practice with, "I knew you'd be suited to it. Same time tomorrow?"

I am still too sick with Aela's and my anger, dulling but still hot, to answer, and can only nod.

When I return to the Cloister, I find Duck in the courtyard, hunched on a bench. For a moment, all I can think of, looking at him, are Power's words, and a fierceness like fury rises up in me again. But then I remember that in the last twenty-four hours, Duck has shouldered burdens heavier and harder than Power's bullying. Of the eight civilians the skyfish first responders helped rescue, I learned from Lotus, Duck saved five of them. His neck is bandaged beneath his uniform from burns he sustained in the extraction.

"How're you doing?" I ask.

Duck pulls his shoulders together in a shrug and straightens. In the wake of the attack I've been surprised by his ability—one I never had, and from what I can tell, Lee has never had either— to talk about the things that haunt him rather than keep them shut up inside. But that doesn't mean he takes any of what happened less hard. Duck hasn't talked about the ones they saved: just the ones they didn't. The burbling courtyard fountain and the trees rustling with songbirds are things he would usually point out to me, but today, he doesn't seem to see them.

"I'm . . . okay. How was training?"

Duck's the only person I've told about my decision to train with Power, and he asks in a tone that suggests he can't imagine anything but the worst.

I consider my answer, thinking of those things Power said. *A dog to kick.* Even as my rage pushed me and Aela to new heights, through new boundaries, I hated him. And in that way, training with Power *was* the worst.

But then I think of the single sentence Power elicited from me moments before he provoked the anger that changed everything.

A head for strategy, skill in the air, and nerves of steel.

I'd be good at it.

I don't have to like Power for him to be right.

For the first time since the tournaments began, I let myself imagine it. My name, appended by the single word that is both a title, a position, and a rank.

Antigone sur Aela, Firstrider.

I can't help feeling as if the mere act of imagining these words together, let alone of believing I'm worthy of wanting them, is defiance. Defiance of every lingering prejudice of Callipolis, of its ministry and their notes, and maybe most of all, defiance of myself.

But the seconds lengthen, and still I dare it.

"Training was good," I tell him.

LEE

It's begun to feel as if the New Pythians' ultimatum is hanging over the city like a knife. Late summer is a time of year I've learned to dread, associated as it has been, for as long as I can remember, with memories of Palace Day. But this year, for the first time, the city shares my unease.

I can't shake the feeling that, however Callipolis responds to the Pythians, I'll feel responsible. Because Atreus may not have read it that way, but Julia's message wasn't just intended as an ultimatum for Callipolis. It was also intended, very specifically, as a final chance for me.

A final chance to seek a solution short of war.

And with an unsparked fleet how can we in good conscience not consider—

"Lee. You need to train."

It's Cor who forces me to commit to a time and a place for him and Crissa to begin training me. I agree to it with a kind of disorientation: The Firstrider Tournament, to take place the weekend before Palace Day, has faded in and out of my awareness since the Starved Rock attack.

Partly because my growing anxiety about Palace Day overshadows it.

But also partly because, when I think of the tournament, Julia's words return with all their seductive force: *Do you want Firstrider so much you can taste it?*

Annie will be a challenging opponent. But my real opponent, my real challenge, is Palace Day on the other end of it, and Julia, daughter of Crethon, waiting for me to change my mind.

The Firstrider Tournament isn't what I'm worried about.

But I'd be a fool not to train. The first day we all share a free block, Crissa and I arrive at the Eyrie before Cor. It's the first time we've been alone since the Lycean Ball.

"Crissa, that night . . ."

Crissa puts up both hands, like she's holding me off, and offers a strained smile.

"Whatever you're about to say, I'm pretty sure I already know."

For a moment we look at each other, and then, to my surprise,

Crissa ducks her head and laughs sheepishly. And then I do, too.

"It was really nice."

She smiles tentatively. "Yeah. It was."

I mean it as an ending, a moment of closure. But all the same when she sits down beside me, just a little bit closer than usual, my stomach skips, and the moment doesn't feel so closed.

"Sorry I'm late."

Cor has landed. He dismounts from Maurana, sends her back into the air to circle with Phaedra and Pallor, and takes a seat on my other side. Crissa clears her throat and produces a calendar, on which, ten days from today, is circled the date of the Firstrider Tournament. A week later, Palace Day.

"I brought a schedule," she says. "Thought it would help us plan."

Only ten days.

Ten days to train.

And a little over that to call the Pythians off.

And if not . . .

And if not we'll see the full force of their wrath and we, unsparked, will have little choice but to bear it.

"Lee, what do you want to focus on? We can map out a drill schedule based on what you need."

I rouse myself, then hesitate. With most opponents, it's easy to home in on the best ways to beat them—but the fact is, Annie has no convenient weaknesses to exploit.

Cor speaks first.

"Spillovers. Word is, Annie's training with Power."

It's the first news that has been able to surprise me since the beacons lit the night of the Lycean Ball. Annie, training with *Power*?

"Since when?"

"Since . . . since Starved Rock, I think."

Cor's hesitation before giving this information is not lost on me; nor is the way Crissa suddenly busies herself with her calendar, rubbing her forehead with the tips of her fingers. Her shoulders are drawn together with unspoken censure that I feel like a cold draft of air.

"It was that bad?" I ask them, looking between them. "In the armory."

I've already felt the answer to this question, but ask in the dim hope that they'll say otherwise. They don't. Cor squints; Crissa lifts her shoulders. Her answer is hesitant. "I can see why you made the call. But I can also see how she might have found it . . . patronizing."

Starved Rock has begun to feel like the name for a catalogue of all the mistakes I could make in a single night.

"Anyway," Cor says. Abruptly, with the air of barreling out of the silence his news has created. "My point was, maybe you should give spillovers a try, too?"

Crissa is nodding. Shrugging off her disapproval, suddenly brisk, and tapping her pen on her calendar. "Cor's right. They might work for you."

I shake my head. "I don't do spillovers."

Cor hums, frustrated.

"Why—?" Crissa asks.

"I like to stay in control."

Crissa turns and looks at me. Her eyebrow lifts. I blush.

Cor glances between us, searching.

Crissa goes back to her schedule. "Well, at any rate. You should be prepared for styles of attack associated with spillovers.

We can make a list of good drills for that and then we'll just cycle through them."

"Don't forget contact charges," Cor adds, knocking his shoulder and fist against my side to demonstrate. "It'll be a same-breed match, they'll be fair game."

Crissa and Cor alternate running drills and playing opposite me. Their experience as squadron leaders means that both manage drills comfortably and well, attentive to intensity and pacing. I break a sweat almost immediately; Pallor is soon burning hot with exertion, and the hour passes before any of us know it. It's almost possible, training under their guidance, to stop thinking about Starved Rock, and Julia, and everything I've done wrong. Everything I might be *about to* do wrong.

After training, I finish unsaddling Pallor and go to the skyfish caves, to Phaedra's nest. Crissa is alone, scrubbing Phaedra down, her golden hair stained with sweat and half falling from its braid.

"I just wanted to say. I shouldn't have—"

The *shouldn't have* on the tip of my tongue is about Annie, a confession of guilt in the face of Crissa's muted disappointment, but then other *shouldn't have*s crowd in as well.

A *shouldn't have* just for Crissa: I shouldn't have kissed her on the Palace ramparts just to feel less alone. Even if she's pretty and makes me laugh and is so clearly interested—

And the worst one, that I can't undo, can't even confess, whose magnitude has the power to make the edges of my vision blacken: I shouldn't have let Holmes take down the aerial guard the night of the Lycean Ball.

Crissa pauses, looking at me, Phaedra's brush dripping ash-dark suds down her mother-of-pearl side. And then she doesn't ask what I mean, or even try to disagree with me.

"No. You shouldn't have."

The relief I feel to hear it said eases the breath from my lungs.

Crissa sets the brush down, in the bucket, and approaches me. Until she is standing close. Too close. Close enough that I remember exactly what it was like to kiss those lips, to wrap my fingers in her hair. Behind her, Phaedra lets out a sigh like a purr, her back arching, wings widening—and then stands very still. As if every nerve of her arched body is alert. Like Crissa, looking at me.

It's the language of the dragon's body that makes my mouth go dry, even if it's Crissa's murmured breath that I feel when she speaks.

"People do that. Things they shouldn't. Mistakes. You make them. And so do I."

A half hour later, I let myself into the boys' washroom with still-hot blood to find Cor alone, scrubbing ash slowly from his neck over a basin of water. His hazel eyes find me in the reflection of the mirror.

"I'm not an idiot."

I freeze on the threshold.

"I'm going to say one thing. And then have it your way, and we won't talk about it. I would *kill* anyone who ever hurt my sisters. You're my friend, Lee, and I'd follow you into hell as my fleet commander. But I think of Crissa like a sister. And *she deserves better than to be your fallback plan.* Do you understand me?"

Maybe it's because I understand exactly what he means. Maybe it's because, sick from so many weights of guilt I'd only just found some relief from, I'm not inclined for more. Or maybe most of all because, half an hour ago, Crissa looked me in the eye, as good as called me a mistake, and then kissed me anyway. I hear myself give the kind of answer I've seen Cor punch people for.

"If you're worried about Crissa getting hurt, maybe you should talk to her."

Cor snaps the towel back on the drying rack and exhales. I feel myself tensing, my fists clenching, suddenly *wanting* the fight. But then all he does is shake his head. His shoulders slump with defeat.

"I did."

I train with Crissa and Cor almost every day. Afterward, if there's time, while my blood is still singing from flight and exertion, Crissa and I find each other. In Phaedra's nest or Pallor's, their presence an edge of unreason that makes it just a little easier to forget better resolve. Because I share all Cor's reservations until the moment that I disregard them. Then I lose myself, for a few lingering moments, in the kind of oblivion that approximates happiness. Always later, but with slowly decreasing conviction, I tell myself that Cor is right, and that it has to stop.

And the rest of the time the world spins with uncertainty. I move from meetings with naval officials to coastal patrols to morale visits with unease that I am unable to voice. *What* is waiting for us after the Firstrider Tournament and Palace Day? What greater bloodshed for Callipolis that the Pythians hold over our heads?

Every spare moment I weigh it, the price of fighting versus the price of turning. Every time the calculation comes, more or less, to the same conclusion Atreus made so unforgivingly in his office after the attack: that no compromise is possible. Not from the Pythians. And not from Atreus.

But though the calculation comes out the same every time, I still feel doubt clouding it.

If I have even the chance of preventing more violence and don't pursue it—what will that be if not more blood on my hands, further Starved Rocks to regret?

ANNIE

I've begun spending every spare second in the arena, training my answer to every jittering nerve and rise of anticipation. Every other part of my life fades as I focus on the one point of my future that remains in my control. I have the feeling of being increasingly, tantalizingly close. Victory within sight. Racing the clock of my own courage and resolve to make it over the finish line before I falter.

Power and I practice daily after class. It is as though Aela and I are unlearning everything Goran taught from the ground up. We learn to rely not on the stirrups and rein and bit to communicate, but on the wordless impulses that move between us, unfiltered. In the moment it's exhilarating, to trust another being so completely; afterward, the exhaustion hits, with a memory of vulnerability. It becomes difficult, in the extricating, to distinguish Aela's memories from my own.

But the days add up, and even as our connection deepens, still we can't initiate spillover independently. Which means I continue to rely on Power for provocation. The beginning of training becomes an increasingly excruciating kind of ritual, evolving as Power and I work our way back through memories. Though spillovers can be provoked by positive feelings, they're not the ones readily available to our mining. At Power's prompting, I talk about my botched morale visit to Holbin, about the memo from the Ministry of Propaganda before the Fourth Order tournament, and then we start on memories from our earliest years in the corps. The things that used to happen, before Lee reported Goran to Atreus.

Power's take on these memories is different from mine.

"Do you remember," Power recalls, "how Goran used to call off drills before any of the girls or peasants got to practice, then humiliate you for not being able to do them later? I always thought that was hilarious . . ."

"Do you remember that time I got Duck's own dragon to bite his leg? Probably the crowning achievement of our first year. Even if it meant Cor and Lee beating the hell out of me later. Duck was hobbling for days . . ."

"Do you remember how Goran always put you on dragon-dung-shoveling duty? What was the reason he gave you for that one?"

Power is grinning as sweat trickles down his forehead, as if he already knows the answer. I give it anyway, hating Power as I always do in these moments, aching for the spillover that's just out of reach:

"He said I cleaned better."

"He was right, though," Power points out. And that's enough to send me over.

As much as I come away from these sessions furious—furious with Power, furious with the memories, *furious*—there's also triumph. Because for the first time in my life, the old wounds are useful. The fury gives me Aela; and when we're together, like this, we're powerful. At such a price, the memories of weakness finally serve a purpose, and once used, they never hurt with the same strength again.

Eventually there comes a day when Power asks: "Do you want to try going all the way back?"

I'm caught off guard.

"What?"

"You know. Your family, what happened to them. It always works for me."

My look of confusion must betray me, because he adds, impatient: "Not my adopted family. My real one. When my dad left my mum pregnant to die in a poorhouse and I got taken in by the people she cleaned for."

"Oh."

It's the first time Power has brought up the past that Dora alluded to at the Lycean Ball, but now that he does, he refers to it as if it's something I've always known. He flashes a grin at me, too wide, and lifts his fingers to massage the damp stubble of his hair as the late summer sun beats down.

"I always figured you were pissed, too," he says.

Aela is snorting, nuzzling my side, and I move my fingers up to scratch behind her horned jaw. I consider, searching myself for the emotions Power describes. Though I do find the memory of anger and pain, I also find that the emotions themselves have faded.

"You're not," Power observes, watching me.

I raise and lower my shoulders.

"It happened a long time ago," I say. "It's just . . . over."

There is something liberating about that realization, even if it leaves me feeling strangely empty. *Over.* Time has left me with— if not peace, at least a dimmer kind of pain. Not the kind that has the power to bring Aela close.

A strange expression is on Power's face. His usual scorn mixed with something else: almost jealousy, or bitterness.

"Good for you," he says.

But from his tone, I'm pretty sure that's not what he's thinking.

An hour later, our training finished, I make my way in exhausted silence through the aurelian cave corridor back up to the Cloister and stop at the sound of disturbance. It comes from Pallor's nest; the lanterns inside are lit. I round the corner unreflectingly, then stop dead. All at once the sounds I heard, which I should have understood immediately, make sense. A girl's voice giggling, murmured half words, an inhaled breath. Lee and Crissa, braced against the cave wall, wrapped in an embrace.

For a second longer than I have reason to, I find myself looking at the way he holds her, one hand moving down her hip, tightening on the leather of the flamesuit, the other winding in her hair to tilt back her head as he kisses her neck. As in his sparring, the same rough purpose guided by gentle precision, the same complete control.

Mouth dry, face hot, I flee.

And then alone, I learn that *this* is what is meant by desire, this lingering awareness of my own body, this ache to find him again, to *feel* rather than to see those hands and those lips—

—the blasphemy of it, to feel it for *Lee*—

And this is how it hurts, to want someone, and see them in the arms of someone else.

I spend the next two days *watching*, like some gossiping Lyceum girl, and hating myself for it. Watching every interaction he and Crissa have, whenever they smile at each other or laugh at each other's jokes or brush against each other in passing. I watch and I try to decide if I'm imagining that Lee, whose mood has darkened since the Starved Rock attack to almost unbroken silence, seems happier at least in her company.

And I try to tell myself that it's good if he's found a reason to smile, and that the thought shouldn't hurt. That the Firstrider Tournament is all that matters and that this is a shallow, superficial distraction—

It's Crissa who eventually stops my agonized speculating.

"Annie. I need to tell you something."

She's found me in the dorm, alone. I know from her tone at once what it will be about. She has dispensed with her squadron-leader voice, and sits on the bed across from mine, looking grave. For a moment the only sound is the gulls crying outside the open window. Then I decide to spare us both.

"I already know."

Crissa tilts her head, her grave expression faltering.

"You do?"

I nod.

"Well, I was going to ask if it's . . . okay with you."

I think of the way it felt, like a knife twisting up into my ribs, the sight of Lee's body pressed against someone else, his lips on another's skin.

"Why wouldn't it be okay?"

My voice is like ice. Crissa sounds tired.

"You know why, Annie."

"Lee's free to kiss whomever he likes. You're as good a choice as any."

Crissa stiffens as if I'd slapped her. "That was unkind," she says softly.

I feel the force of her reprimand like a lash. I remember the evening after making finalist, when Crissa opened the door to my infirmary ward and brought a party with her; of the hours she spent with me on the arena ramparts, coaching my public speaking at the cost of her free time; of the care she took, in the lead-up to the Lycean Ball, to ease my discomfort.

Crissa doesn't deserve this anger.

She goes on, with forced calm, "I am trying to say this. If you don't want—if this upsets you—I will call it off."

If this upsets you.

I think of a boy from another lifetime, making sure I had enough to eat, teaching me what it felt like not to be hungry. The years I spent, sparring with that boy daily, honing his abilities as I honed my own. Those few minutes in the middle of the Lycean Ball when we danced and my world stood still.

And then I remember that it is this same boy whose face so often, when I look at it, chills me with the shadow of another's, and that I've been training for the Firstrider Tournament as I've never trained in my life because of the burning desire, finally discovered, to step out of his shadow and into the light.

"Lee doesn't belong to me," I tell Crissa. "And if this is what he wants, he should have it."

I wait until she's gone before I break down.

* * *

Increasingly desperate headlines in both the *People's Paper* and the *Gold Gazette* predict that our fleet's sparking is imminent. State-sponsored editorials enthusiastically reaffirm the new regime's superiority to the rule of the dragonlords—one half of an argument whose other side Crissa and I overheard in the streets after Atreus's speech. The doubt implicit: *What good is an aerial fleet ridden by commoners if it can't defend us?*

The Ministry of Propaganda's answer is made clear enough, though I learn of it not from the paper, but from our poetry professor, four days before the Firstrider Tournament.

Dragontongue Poetry is one of the few courses to have continued into the summer months. Guardians have been expected to keep up our studies, although with our wartime obligations expanding, it's difficult for the professors to get work of any quality out of us anymore. Tyndale hasn't been understanding about it, and today he turns out to be in an especially foul temper.

"No, that's not quite right, Cor," Tyndale says, five minutes into the lesson. "In fact that was—all wrong."

Power lets out a snicker that he doesn't even bother to suppress. The sound of his voice, which I now associate with goads to the point that it makes my stomach jump, reminds me that we'll be on the Eyrie together again to train within the hour. Cor has folded his arms, scowling at Tyndale. In his Guardian ground uniform, with ash still caked to the back of his neck from a naval drill that ran late into the morning, he has the look of someone who has no time left for poetry or poetry professors.

"Antigone, fix it."

I look down at Cor's line with misgiving. Most of the time I can make sense of the *Aurelian Cycle*, but I haven't had time to properly prepare a translation in weeks; what free time I've had hasn't been spent on homework. I start to sight-read a translation of the line, but Tyndale stops me before I can get halfway through.

"That will do. Is any Guardian still capable of making a passable translation these days, or are you all too busy giving speeches to frightened class-irons?"

By now, a few Lyceum students have their hands in the air, some like Hanna Lund glancing at the Guardians anxiously, but Tyndale ignores them. "Lotus!"

Lotus has been slumping, flushed from the summer heat, over his desk. He lurches upright and starts reading his own translation, but he barely translates two words before Tyndale cuts him off, too.

"Lee," he says, with finality.

I know—because I've been keeping track—that this is the first time Tyndale's ever called on Lee.

Lee, who's been reading along in the primer with his forehead resting on his palm, reacts slowly. He lowers his palm, raises his head, straightens up. And then he stares at Tyndale. His fingers press hard against the open primer, the tips going white, and he doesn't reach for the notebook lying beneath it.

Since I saw him with Crissa in the nests, I've stopped speaking to Lee altogether, even as I have become aware of every shadow of his body's definition discernible through his uniform, as if a switch has been flipped in my thoughts that can't be turned back off. But now I notice also how Tyndale's attention has made Lee tense from head to foot. He hasn't appeared so alarmed in Tyndale's class since our very first day.

"I didn't do my homework," Lee says. And then he adds, with contempt bordering on anger: "Like you said. I was too busy giving speeches to frightened class-irons."

A ripple of surprise goes around the room at his tone. When Tyndale speaks, his voice is crisp, carefully enunciated.

"Well then, why don't you try sight-reading?"

Lee curls his hands into fists and looks down at the text beneath them. For a moment he's silent, but then he starts listing words aloud, throwing out the Callish equivalents of each word without any effort to make sense of them:

"The enemy, has, walls, rushes, in the deep, away from, summit—"

Tyndale throws an eraser at Lee's head.

Lee ducks, and the eraser sails past. There's a thud as the wooden side hits the far wood-paneled wall, powdering it with chalk. Tyndale is still bearing down on him, and now he stands right in front of Lee's desk. Neither of them is pretending anything but fury now.

Despite all the reasons I've stopped speaking to Lee, at the moment, as I watch Tyndale approach him, it's Tyndale I feel hatred for. Knee-jerk, fierce, protective. As if a poetry professor's triumphant sneer were danger enough to wipe every other grudge from my mind.

Stay away from him.

"No," Tyndale says.

Lee seems to be paralyzed, wide-eyed, waiting to see what Tyndale will say next, and Tyndale himself seems to be struggling to decide.

And then, as I watch them, as I hold my breath, the case of a single elusive noun becomes clear in my mind. And just like that, I realize I have it.

My voice is clear.

Alas, flee, dragonborn, you and your family. Flee from the flames. The enemy has your walls, the City falls in ruin from its height.

For a moment, the room is strangely still. The sound of my own voice, so unusually loud in my ears, lingers in the air. The tragedy of the line washes over me, beautiful and heartbreaking.

Then the moment passes. Lee closes his eyes and sinks back in his seat. A strange expression fills his face, tightening it. Tyndale seems to deflate. He turns from Lee, disoriented, and looks down at the books spread across his desk, gathering his thoughts.

"Yes," he says, distantly, moving away from Lee. "Yes, yes. Very good, Antigone."

Behind his back, people are glancing at each other, exchanging confused looks. Lee lowers his face into his palms and exhales.

"I should tell you," Tyndale says, turning back to us abruptly. He holds up his own copy of the poem, an old leather-bound version that looks like he's had it since his own school days. "The *Aurelian Cycle* was officially banned today, by the Censorship Committee."

I feel the pulse of the line in my ears again, the terrible beauty of it. Lee lowers his hands from his face and straightens slowly.

Lotus speaks up hesitantly. "You mean, banned for the lower class-metals? Restricted to the Lyceum library?"

"No. It was already restricted. Now it's being purged."

"Why?" Lotus asks.

Tyndale grimaces. "It was . . . decided . . . that the poem promotes values that are contrary to the national interest."

I remember rounds with Ornby in the censorship office, over a month ago, telling me, *Don't want to give the lower class-metals these kinds of ideas, they'll start wanting the dragonlords back. They can't handle nuance like you can . . .*

Wasn't he right? I've heard the murmured discontent in the streets, I've seen the editorials in the *People's Paper* urging reason . . .

But even as a newcomer to Dragontongue literature, even

as someone who hasn't grown up hearing the *Aurelian Cycle* quoted as readily as speech, the idea of banning it is unthinkable. It's taken too much of my heart already, in this class alone.

Even if some fools are misinterpreting it—how could Atreus allow such a thing? He enrolled the Fourth Order riders in this course. He quotes the *Aurelian Cycle* in class with us, effortlessly. Clearly he shares my love for its beauty, its tradition—

But that's not the same as prioritizing it.

I remind myself: Atreus led a coup against his own masters that resulted in their massacre. The same dragonborn that the *Aurelian Cycle* portrays as hubristic and godlike, Atreus brought to their knees. He doesn't have a history of standing on tradition. Even if he does have a taste for Dragontongue poetry.

"The official announcement will be in the *Gold Gazette* tomorrow," Tyndale says. "Raids will be conducted throughout the summer, and confiscated copies will be destroyed. Needless to say, the status of this class has become . . . uncertain."

Cor mouths *Thank the dragon* at Lee, whose face is slack, and doesn't return his grin.

Tyndale has us read a little more, but after hearing a few more lines of poor translations, he dismisses us. As we get up to leave, he goes over and stands next to Lee's desk, silent, but his meaning clear. Lee remains seated, his arms folded, as the rest of the students leave.

Power catches up with me in the corridor, breaking away from a group of Gold girls, and we exit into the Lyceum courtyard together. This late in the summer, the green would usually be full of students lounging on the grass and pretending to read, but in the wake of Starved Rock it's unnaturally empty. As if leisure under an open sky is no longer possible.

"That was fishy as hell," he comments.

I stop dead and round on him.

"What?"

Power pauses, too. Lifts an eyebrow. "You tell me, Annie."

For a moment we stand completely still as we stare at each other, and my heart begins to race as I take in his muted, sneaking smile as he regards my alarm and plays stupid. *What has he guessed? What does he know?*

This is dangerous. Power's made no secret of hating Lee, not since they were children, not since Lee put himself in opposition to every single one of Power's moves of assertion within the corps. I *remember* the sound of Power coughing while Lee held him and Cor punched.

Lee's identity in the hands of Power would be a disaster.

Power says, with a half glance at his own bare shoulder: "Oh, dragons. I forgot my bag. I guess I'll have to double back—"

His tone is unmistakable. He's *toying* with me.

But all I can think of, in this moment, is to make the move he's prompting.

"I'll get it for you."

Power just studies me, his smile widening. "Whatever you like, Annie. See you on the Eyrie?"

"Right," I answer, barely hearing myself.

I walk back into the classroom building, and though I should feel nothing, I'm sick with dread.

No, I think, as I approach. *No, no, no, I don't want this. I've never wanted this.* It was enough for him to say, *You're not a fool for trusting me*; it was enough for Tyndale to slip that name once, *Leo,* and never say it again. It's enough for me to want

Firstrider, and for that to have nothing to do with who he was once or where he came from. I don't need this now.

And the fear that is less rational, that is worse than any of that, that was, perhaps, the point of Power's game from the start: *What if I don't like what I'm about to hear?*

LEE

Julia's words, from our last meeting: *Watch and see when we exert pressure how this vision will splinter. Then we will revisit whether you find it noble.*

Is this the beginning of that splintering, this edict banning the words that have guided our people for centuries?

"It's been a while since we talked," Tyndale says, after he closes the door behind him. Dragontongue, again.

For the first time, I find myself glad Tyndale seeks a confrontation. My guilt has found a target and transformed to anger. I answer in Callish.

"Yes. It has. Was it you who told them that the Guardians would be in full attendance at the Lycean Ball?"

Tyndale, standing, leans his palms on his desk. The room is so warm, the heat in it so stuffy from the summer, that drops of sweat darken his white shirt beneath the arms. He tugs at the neck of his collar, loosening it.

"My dear boy. It's not as if the Lycean Ball or its guest list was a secret. And I'm not the only member of the Gold estate sympathetic to the Pythian cause." Tyndale nods to the *Aurelian Cycle*, lying dog-eared on the desk beside him. "After this, I imagine you can see why."

An image in my mind: smoke rising from a lonely island off the northern coast. If this is the vision splintering, it's still better than what the Pythians did to Starved Rock.

"There's more to civilization than poetry."

Tyndale sneers. He lifts a hand and flicks it, dismissing.

"Don't tell me a few dead fishermen were enough to turn your stomach."

"Unarmed civilians—"

"Casualties of war. An unfortunate price."

I stare at him, hatred coiling in my stomach. How dare he, this *academic*, this scholar who spends his days scanning verse and picking apart figures of speech, refer to what we saw on Starved Rock as a *price*, as if the loss of lives can be set on a numeric scale quantifiable like currency—

"But," Tyndale goes on, "if it's a price that makes you squeamish, now is your time to reconsider."

I'm shaking my head, as if with my body I can force out the thoughts that have already been plaguing my mind.

"I should report you," I tell him.

"I should report *you*."

For a moment we stare at each other, neither of us so much as blinking.

I get to my feet. Reach for my bag, sling it over my shoulder. Fingers shaking, though I will myself to calm. But as I turn to leave, Tyndale speaks again.

"Have you thought about what will happen if you refuse her? Not to the civilians. To *you*."

When I don't answer, Tyndale does for me. I've paused, half turned from him, my hand gripping my shoulder strap so tightly, the leather bites my fingers.

"You'll be in combat against your own relatives, your cousins. You'd be *killing your own family.*"

Tyndale drives the words home hard, like he's determined to jolt me with them.

"She's Firstrider, Lee. Their champion, their fleet commander. It won't just be them you'll have to go against. It will be *her.*"

He must find what he's looking for in my expression, because his own has become triumphant. "We await your next letter."

I have the feeling of ground slipping, and it's against this feeling that I growl my answer, with all the conviction that I wish I felt.

"I have nothing more to say to them."

I turn on my heel, wrench open the door onto the hallway, to find Annie standing on the other side of it. White-faced and round-eyed.

What did she hear?

What language were we speaking in?

Dragontongue.

Which she must have realized, but is also less likely to have been able to understand when muffled through the crack of a door—

"What are you doing here?"

"I forgot something," she says acidly.

"Shouldn't you be off playing spillover with Power?"

Her face colors. "Shouldn't you be off *sparring* with Crissa?"

I'd meant to pass her, but we've both stopped, and there's only about a foot between us. I feel like shaking her.

"You're in my way," I say, through gritted teeth.

Annie's eyes are bright. She lets out a soft laugh, full of anger.

"What are you going to do," she whispers, "*order me* to move?"

It's enough for me to jerk sideways, and for her to pass without a word.

ANNIE

We await your next letter.

Tyndale's words, Lee's low-voiced answer, the Dragontongue too fast for me to understand, the door bursting open and Lee's furious face draining as he sees me—

What was Lee's answer to Tyndale?

Out on the Eyrie, Power says, "Well?"

Our dragons wait for us, clawing the ground with impatience. Standing this close to Aela, I can feel the spillover a breath away. For the first time since we've begun training together, I realize the pathway is within my control.

At the same time, as close as I am to spillover, the part of me considering Power is completely calm.

"I got your bag, if that's what you're asking. Can we start? Call me a peasant, like you did last time. Let's see if that works."

Power scowls at me. Disappointed.

And then, as he starts hurling insults at me—first in Callish, then Dragontongue—I tune him out.

I let myself think everything that I've been holding in.

In contact with them. *Lee's in contact with Pythians.* Through our bloody *poetry professor.* How long has this been happening? Has it been happening all along?

After the sighting, he told me I wasn't a fool to trust him, and I believed him.

Aela's mind close to me, the barriers breaking, my fingers

stretching up to press between her eyes at the ridge of her amber-scaled temple—

Should I have?

I believe the words Lee said were ones he meant. But in the wake of a disaster like Starved Rock, and New Pythos's threat hanging over us like a storm about to drop—

In the face of almost certain violence and death against family—

If they're in *contact*—

Surely even Lee has limits for his stomach to hold fast.

The barriers breaking, Aela's mind sliding into mine, her slitted eyes the only thing I see . . .

In the last few weeks I've let myself want to win Firstrider. Let myself think I deserved to want it.

But what if there's more to it than that? What if I've *got* to make Firstrider?

Is Lee compromised?

Aela and I become one and we are ready to spar.

* * *

Afterward, head clear, ash scrubbed from my face, I take stock of the situation.

Tyndale is compromised. Lee is possibly compromised. And I've no idea what Power knows or guesses.

In almost certain threat of war, with such knowledge at my fingertips, what is my obligation?

I go to the Inner Palace, make my gamble, and file a single report.

11

THE FIRSTRIDER TOURNAMENT

LEE

The morning of the Firstrider Tournament, I wake from fitful sleep where memories blur with dreams. Sparring with Annie, when we were first learning how; planning our escapes, huddled in the closet in the orphanage; my father and his dragon, in flight. Weaving in and out of these, over and over again, Julia:

I pray to the long-dead gods that this tournament brings sense to you.

I sit next to Crissa and Cor at breakfast. Across the room, on the opposite side of the refectory, sit Annie and Duck. We haven't spoken since we met in the hallway outside Tyndale's classroom, four days ago.

The room vibrates with a barely suppressed excitement: The other riders seem to know better than to voice their anticipation in front of either Annie or me. Except, of course, Power, who takes a seat across from me to say:

"Do you know what Annie had me call her, so she could spill over?"

"Get away from us," Cor says.

Power tells me. Then watches for my reaction. Annie, across the room, glances over at us and then stubbornly away again.

How, I wonder, how could she have stooped to this, to train with this *imbecile*?

Without acknowledging either of them I drain my glass and rise.

"I'll see you later," I tell Cor and Crissa.

The armory is silent, empty. This time of year it collects heat during the day and never quite has time to cool off during the night, so it's already unpleasantly stuffy as I change into my flamesuit. I'm halfway through buckling on armor, beginning to think we won't overlap at all, when the door opens and Annie comes in.

"Hey."

"Hey . . ."

I can think of nothing else to say. And though Annie is one of the few people I've ever been comfortable with in silence, right now it's not the kind of silence that's comfortable. It's the silence of two people not speaking to each other.

Then, in that silence, Annie reaches for her flamesuit and freezes. Her back is turned: I can't see what she's looking at.

As gingerly as someone removing an unwanted insect from a plate of food, she pulls a sealed letter out of her cubby and rests it unopened on the bench beside her.

"What—"

"It's from the ministry," she says, her back still turned to me.

I straighten. Despite the residual cool that's distanced us since Tyndale's class, the news shocks me into anger. *Now? They're still pulling this on her?*

For a moment, I stare at her back as the discomfort creeps

in: Maybe the last time this happened, I was the person to say something—but today? Now? What is there possibly for me to say as her *opponent*?

But it turns out I don't have to say anything. Steel has entered Annie's voice like I've never heard before.

"I'm not reading it."

She yanks on her flamesuit without looking at the letter again, and when her armor is on, she heads out to the nests without me.

A half hour later we're both on the Eyrie. The blue of the late summer sky is blotted with billowing cumulus clouds, moving fast in a brisk breeze. They hang low, some of them even at the level of Pytho's Keep. Standing on the Eyrie, surrounded by stands that are completely full and cheering in a deafening roar, feeling the sweat begin to trickle beneath layers of armor and leather, I look up at the racing sun-swept sky and feel the first leapings of anticipation.

Skies like this are meant to be flown in.

At the mouth of the cave, we summon our dragons and wait together. There's silence again, but it's a different kind of silence: as if Annie, too, is aching to get into the air. Our backs are turned toward those watching on the Eyrie, and we face the stands that have quieted with expectation.

I feel that stillness awaken all my senses.

Yes. This is it. *Finally.*

After years of wanting and waiting and training, after dreams lost and regained, I am here. Vying for Firstrider as if the whole world hadn't changed since I first imagined winning the title.

Pallor and Aela alight on either side of us. Their anticipation fuels ours; Pallor is twitching with impatience to take off, and I have to yank on his reins to hold him still while I double-check his stirrups, his girth, his bridle. I mount, pull on my helmet, and place my hand on my visor. Before I lower it, I look over at Annie for the final check-in. She has mounted and is bent low on Aela's back with her head lowered, one gloved hand pressed against the side of Aela's scaled neck. Their eyes are closed.

A ripple goes through them both, Aela's wings twitch open, and Annie lifts her head. When she opens her eyes and looks at me, her pupils are dilated.

The familiar becomes alien, and my uncertainty becomes foreboding.

She nods at me, I nod at her, and we lower our visors.

Then we're off, into the air, at last. We leave behind the Eyrie, the arena, the Palace, and the city. The wind on which the cumulus surfs catches the wings of our dragons like sails snapping taut. We assume position, facing each other at a distance of ten meters, wings beating against the currents of air to stay in place. All around us, clouds are shifting and reforming in the summer light.

Distantly, through the roaring wind, we hear the bell ring.

We charge. Full speed, straight at each other. Adrenaline floods in, heady and familiar. We're close, closer, too close—

At the last second, as we veer and fire and swerve, and the heat of Aela's blast streams across my back as I flatten myself against Pallor to escape it and we ride a surging gust of wind out of range, I think:

I know this.

This is Antigone sur Aela. Every bit of them. They're not alien: They are simply more themselves.

And Pallor and I know them in our bones.

I rein him round to engage again and see Aela rising, gaining height, and at once we surge upward to race her for the advantage, and I can't resist a wind-swallowed cry of sheer delight. I've missed this.

This. This is how it's supposed to be.

She stalls on a hard gust and uses it to leverage a plunge down. Pallor and I roll into a dive. She follows, hot on my tail as we plummet through drifts of cumulus and ripples of turbulence, and my ears are popping from the kind of changes in pressure that only happen when the ground is something you're accelerating toward with all the speed you can muster. We roll again, come at Annie from the side rather than below, and hit Aela with a contact charge. Aela's descent becomes, from our momentum, a sideways roll as our dragons struggle in a locked embrace. It seems that the world spins: The horizon rotates on an axis, the cumulus churns around us as it streams past and reforms. Aela gains traction, sinks talons into Pallor's side, and he screeches and releases her. They take off, and we pursue.

It goes on. I could go on doing it forever; I want to. Annie and Aela's spillover makes their responses faster, their instincts surer, their assaults harder.

And I love it.

Pallor and I are pushing ourselves like we haven't in years, every nerve alive as we strain to match Annie and Aela. The challenge works on us like a drug. We're bursting through barriers that I'd previously thought of as our ceilings, and we push them back. Because even when they're flying their best, we know their mistakes; we know their weaknesses. We've helped them hone their abilities with drill after drill for as long as we've flown.

And they know us.

So it becomes a struggle to peel the layers back. To probe for weakness, to expose a mistake. A performance of something intimate. These are the things I alone can find in her, and she alone can find in me.

She finds my weakness first.

I risk opening my guard for a half instant, in order to take aim, a move I can usually pull off without the other rider even noticing—but today, Annie does.

Her shot sears across my exposed shoulder. A penalty hit.

It's the first penalty I've ever received in a public tournament.

The shock of it sobers me at once, and the breathless exhilaration I've been riding falters.

We reset. I open my coolant valves, easing the pain searing my shoulder.

Distantly, below, the bell rings. We charge again.

This time it becomes a contact charge at once. The dragons scrabble, fighting to get a clear shot at the other's rider; and then as we push off again, I catch Annie ceding just a little too much horizontal leverage, a classic Annie mistake, and I have her. She shies, it only grazes her, a penalty hit on the arm.

That's it.

We reset, Annie opens her coolant shafts, and we charge again. This time, when we ram, I head in sideways, hoping to gain centripetal momentum. It's not a move most riders know how to predict or respond to, but she responds just fine. She swerves, we misfire, and both leave ourselves exposed. In the opening, Annie fires again.

She lands a second penalty, across my leg.

It is full-heat, an intended kill shot: My leg sears with it and I let out a grunt of pain, which Annie hears.

"You all right?" she calls.

"Fine."

I'm furious with myself.

I back out of range to release coolant valves and reset, and all the while my mind is racing with a single panicked thought: We're on our second penalty.

For the first time, the reality really hits:

I could lose.

If we keep flying like we just did, I'm going to.

Annie could make Firstrider.

How is this the first time—though I've known all along that she'd be my most formidable opponent, that this would be my hardest match—that this thought really hits home?

Pallor ripples beneath me: The barrier between us has thinned as our emotions have risen. I can feel our anger at our mistakes, our tiredness, pushing us dangerously close to a spillover. I fight to stay in control.

The dragons are facing each other, reset for a charge. Pallor is heaving beneath me, the exertion of the match finally taking its toll. I can feel it wearing on me as well. Annie and Aela have been practicing at this spillover-induced intensity for a month; we haven't.

We need to calm down, refocus, and finish this. Before we're too drained.

But to do that, we need to buy time.

The bell rings. Annie surges forward, and instead of meeting her, I rein Pallor round to a retreat. He growls and resists, like he hates me for it, and I don't blame him, because I hate myself a little bit, too. We plunge into the nearest cumulus and keep going, through the heart of the clouds, keeping cover in their whiteness. I check behind my shoulder, over and over again, but see no sign of her. The cumulus have thickened as we sparred; we're in and out of seamless stretches of white, so much that it begins to feel like clear patches are the exception rather than the rule.

Have I lost her?

We burst into a clearing, free of clouds either overhead or beneath. The arena is far below; even Pytho's Keep is distant and small. We're surrounded on all sides by bulging white cumulus, shifting constantly in the wind.

Unbidden, Pallor grinds to a halt. I slam my heels into his sides, urging him back into the cloud cover, when I realize why he's stopped: He is shuddering with hawking, painful gasps, different from any he's ever made before. The sound fills me with alarm.

"Pallor," I say. "Easy. You're all right, just breathe—"

I feel him straining beneath me and at the same time his mind strains *toward me*, and I realize that the thin barrier between us is something he's fighting to break through. Pallor is straining for a spillover. Disregarding all of his training, all our habits of separation, all the distance that I've always asked him to keep. Through what's left of the barrier I can feel his anger at our weakness, his humiliation at the retreat, his horror at the idea of defeat, his determination, like mine, that we *must, at all costs, win*. Beyond all that, something else—a strange fear and excitement about something very close to happening, and with it the desperate need for *me*—

"Stop—stop doing that—"

He seeks the spillover desperately, his mind pressing with urgent need into my own, and I struggle to hold him out. He ripples and stalls and we hover, exposed, in this sun-pierced clearing amid the cumulus.

A shadow passes across us.

It's Annie, bearing down on us from above, Aela's wings close to her sides to speed her descent.

Pallor rears up to meet her, his whole body still convulsing, his growl half a hacking splutter, like a cat attempting to be sick.

There's a split second when Pallor and I realize that they're in range, that we're exposed, and that Aela has opened her jaws to fire.

We're about to lose everything.

The barrier between us shatters.

As the spillover floods my senses, understanding fills me at last.

Pallor's final convulsion spasms through his body and finds its release. Sparked dragonfire streams from his mouth.

We rock backward with the force of the blast.

I am consumed by Pallor's emotions, his exhilaration and fear and just a little pain; I am high with them. It is like nothing I've ever experienced, the rush of power, of ascendance, that I share with Pallor in his moment of sparking. As though the world were at our feet. Ours for the taking, and we will have all of it.

And as with gods the world quaked, to see them fireborne.

It takes me a gasping moment to emerge from the delirium, to rein him back and tell him to hold fire. But the damage is already done. Pallor's aim was true, and Annie sur Aela, surging toward us, was within range.

Fire has blanketed them.

Aela is stalling, her wings beating dully against the draft; Annie, astride her, is completely still. Her armor is blackened from head to foot. Steam and smoke rise from cracks of flame-suit exposed beneath as the cloud vapor evaporates and the outer layer of the suit burns.

Sparked dragonfire, undoused and at full heat, is enough to kill a rider. Flamesuit or no, armor or no.

I am, all at once, sick with fear.

"Annie," I call.

The high of the spillover is fading fast; Pallor is still with me, but now he's descending from his elation and beginning to feel my numb and growing terror.

Aela rocks on a gust, and Annie's helmeted head lolls sideways, limp.

I force myself to think. *Aela. Look at Aela—*

Aela's slitted eyes are still dilated, her snorts are full of anguish and fear: the signs of a dragon sensing its rider's pain. The signs of a dragon whose rider is *still able to experience pain at all.*

Annie's there. Unconscious, maybe, but alive.

Relief floods through me.

"Annie, wake up! You need to open your coolant valves!"

There's no response.

Fine, we'll just get to the ground fast, I think, reining Pallor in, nudging us down—

But Aela makes no move to follow us, and when I turn back to her, I realize she's convulsing now, too. Just as Pallor was, moments ago.

Of course. Because once one dragon in the fleet sparks, it spreads. And Aela's next.

My mind still melded to Pallor's, I feel his perception of her change on a level that's immediate and primal. He is suddenly *aware* of her, in a way he never was before.

And then—perhaps again it's Pallor noticing, or perhaps it's the sounds I myself hear—I realize that Aela's shudders and retches are not only frightening her, as they did Pallor; they're also hurting her. And I remember that sparking, in some cases and particularly with females, can hurt.

Aela is in pain.

And Annie is unconscious, tethered to her like a rag doll, her coolant valves closed, and the ground still far away. Every moment we lose, while Aela struggles to hack up the flames that her body spasms to produce, is a moment longer Annie goes without treatment for burns that could kill her.

The solution feels at once insane and inevitable.

I seize my bootknife from its sheath and cut the leather straps that hold my legs to the stirrups. They're the only protection I have, should I lose hold of Pallor, from falling to my death thousands of feet below, and I inhale sharply as a wave of vertigo hits me. The distance to the ground, the tiny city and arena and Palace below, that I'm used to thinking of only passingly, transform in an instant into something deadly.

Pallor has flown as close to Aela as I need him to, above her, as near as he can hover over to her without their wings colliding. Aela, twitching and convulsing, doesn't seem to notice; and Annie's in no state to notice anything.

I swing my left leg over Pallor's right side, both legs hanging down over his wing joint, ready to slide off.

And then I think, *This is insane, Aela will throw me, she'll throw me at five thousand feet—*

But in answer, something else inside me rises up, unbidden. A feeling that is at once new and feels at the same time ages old, like something I've always known but only now remembered: an echo of that delirious power that flooded my senses with Pallor's sparkfire. The line from the *Aurelian Cycle* reverberates, fortifying and intoxicating.

And as with gods the world quaked, to see them fireborne.

I steel myself.

"If she bucks me off," I tell Pallor, "catch me."

For the first time in my life, I've spoken to him in Dragontongue.

And then I slide from one dragon onto the back of the other.

Aela shrieks at the sudden weight, tosses her back upward in rejection of it, but I've landed sure, astride her behind Annie, and I'm able to seize the pommel of the saddle while she bucks. I wrap one arm around Annie—in the years since I've last held her like this she's grown from a child into a woman, but her body still, in this moment, seems too small, too fragile, and her armor is smoking, still burning hot—and then I lean forward and run a hand down Aela's neck, stroking her with firm fingers, willing her to calm. It feels wrong, deeply wrong, to touch another's dragon like this; and I know Aela feels the same about me as I do about her.

"Easy, easy, I'm trying to help her—*you know us*, Aela—"

Pallor circles beneath us, and through our lingering spillover, I sense his fear for us and his continuing elation at his sparkfire and still that humming, wild awareness of Aela; and I sense through him that she is aware of him, too, that his presence comforts her.

Aela's whimpering, but to my amazement, she doesn't buck again.

With one hand, trembling, I begin to open the coolant valves on Annie's helmet, her shoulders, her arms, her back. Annie remains unresponsive in my arms, light and limp, but I can feel the temperature of her suit lowering as the coolant flows through it. My other hand is still stroking Aela's neck as she balks with pain.

"It'll be over soon, Aela, I know it hurts—"

I think of Pallor, of his straining need to spill over, to be with me, for his release.

She needs Annie, and Annie's not here to help her through it.

"Annie, you've got to wake up—"

But it will mean waking to pain. I'm opening coolant shafts along her hips, her thighs, her calves. I can smell burning leather and under that, burning hair. Her braid, I realize with horror, is *gone*, reduced to a stub of charred strands visible beneath the neck of her helmet—

I've done this to her. To Annie, my Annie—

And the only thing I felt, as I did it, was euphoria—

"I'm so sorry, I'm so sorry—"

The words are choking out of me; the world around me blurs.

And then Annie stirs in my arms, just a little, and moans. Aela senses her rider rousing and cries out, a pleading screech, full of anguish. It is a profoundly intimate cry. I feel the hair raise on the back of my neck at the sound of it: I am, in this moment, only an intruder.

"Aela," Annie murmurs, through their pain, lovingly.

It's enough. Aela lets out a final, shuddering convulsion, and dragonfire fills the sky.

* * *

The arena, when we descend close enough to hear it, is roaring. I don't immediately understand why. And then I remember: Callipolis has a sparked fleet.

And a Firstrider.

Rematch, I tell myself. I'm clinging to the idea desperately; because the alternative, that this is how it has happened, that these were the terms on which I won, is too nightmarish. *They'll give us a rematch, they'll have to.*

I'm still riding Aela, and though I dare not attempt to guide her by rein, Pallor flies ahead of us and she seems content to follow. Annie, unconscious once more, is limp in my arms.

The cheering continues unabated as we land on the Eyrie. There, at least, people realize something is wrong. I descend from the wrong dragon, cut Annie free, and pull her off Aela's back. The medics are ready with a stretcher; I carry her the few feet to it and lay her in it. When we remove her helmet, her eyes are closed; and what remains of her hair is drenched in coolant.

"Lee, it's all right, she'll be all right—"

I only realize from the way people are saying this that I have lost all composure.

"Lee," Goran says quietly, "you've got to go up to the Palace Box, they're waiting—"

"Please let me stay with her—"

"You can find her as soon as you're finished. Right now Callipolis wants to see its Firstrider."

"No—we need a rematch—"

"That's not how it works, Lee."

"Please—*please, not like this*—"

The crowds are chanting: *Lee sur Pallor, Firstrider.* The title I dreamed of hearing as a child, appended to my name.

For a moment, the irony of my victory is so bitter, it is almost a taste in my mouth. That dream has come true now, years later, in a wholly different world and against all odds. But all I want in the moment is to undo it.

Goran grips me on the shoulder, and his tone hardens. "In the name of Callipolis, pull yourself together." I dry my face as I mount the stairs to the Palace Box.

* * *

Afterward, I make a single detour before finding the Palace infirmary. I go to the Lyceum, to Tyndale's office, and I slip a note under his door. The words I've written on it come with the ease of premeditated thought, and I write with the same blazing certainty that rose to guide me as I leapt from Pallor's back.

I was told you await my letter. Here it is. By the time you see this, you'll know that our fleet is sparked, and the Protector's answer. Callipolis will not bow.

You wrote me once that you hoped I would know the feeling of the might of the world at my feet. Today, I have known it.

Your choices are your own. My conscience is not your keeper.

Bring what fury you have and I will answer it with ours.

ANNIE

In and out of sleep I take in the nights and days of an unfamiliar room, a single familiar figure sitting at my bedside throughout. Dressings are applied and removed and time passes fitfully, through a haze of pain, but in one of the lucid moments I wake to a single half-heard sentence of Dragontongue parsed in its entirety by my sleeping consciousness and now fully intelligible:

Lee told Tyndale, *I have nothing more to say to them.*

I return to sleep with the utter exhaustion of complete relief.

When I finally awake, I'm in pain.

Slowly the world focuses; I know it after all. An infirmary room, where I've lain before, though never with bandaging this extensive or constricting. The window is open, letting in the summer sunlight and breeze. Vases full of flowers fill the space of my bedside table. Seated next to the bed, slumped over in an uncomfortable-looking chair, is Lee. Lines of care have smoothed on his face as he sleeps, though the bruises of exhaustion beneath his closed eyes remain.

How long have I been here? How long has *he* been here?

Memories of the match are returning in flashes: the gut punch at the sight of that letter from the ministry; the steel-hardened spillover with Aela; the aching relief of finally sparring with Lee sur Pallor again. The mounting anticipation of triumph. And then—dragonfire, like the memory of an old nightmare, and pain. And then Aela, needing me, and Lee, still there, holding me—

That memory is jarring, doesn't fit. *How—?*

But the memories are there, impossible: Lee behind me, astride Aela, his fingers fumbling for the valves of my coolant shafts, his hand on Aela's side, comforting her as she struggled to spark. Because it's not only my memories that contain him: Aela's do, too, and I remember her fear and anger at his intrusion and then, as he soothed her by touch and by words, her surrendering trust.

My throat has gone dry to remember it.

Then I realize *how* he must have done it, and exasperation battles with tenderness as I look at him.

You stupid, fearless flyboy.

Lee stirs, sits up with a start as his eyes snap open. The lines of care return to his forehead and mouth. He looks at me and sees I'm awake. His face fills with relief.

"Hey," he says.

But he says it bashfully, and I realize he's nervous, shame-faced. It takes me a moment to understand why.

"I'm all right, Lee," I tell him.

"I'm so sorry," he says hoarsely. "Annie, I never—"

I laugh and it hurts, so I stop. He notices, his eyes widening in alarm.

"It's not your fault Pallor sparked."

Lee is shaking his head, like that's not enough. "I asked for a rematch," he mutters, looking down. "But they wouldn't . . ."

I'm smiling, though this hurts in a different way.

"Why would they?" I ask.

Pain is filling Lee's face. "Because you deserved to win."

My throat tightens to hear the words said. To hear them said by *Lee*.

I struggle to put words to the feeling overwhelming me, to call it something other than disappointment. Struggle to explain the victory, stupid though it was, that meant everything to me. The little part of it that had nothing to do with Lee, or Callipolis, or anything but myself.

"It was good to really . . . want it. I didn't know I could— want something that much. And to believe it should be—"

Should be mine.

And now this is what it feels like, when you let yourself want something, fully, and fail to get it. I'm swallowing, willing my vision to clear. Lee is looking at his lap.

"Anyway," I add. "It's—probably for the best. You were the one they wanted."

Lee twitches, drags his fingers through his hair. And then he reaches into his pocket and produces a letter. Crumpled, seal broken, but I recognize it at once.

"I went back . . . while you were sleeping. It didn't say what we thought it did."

He hands the note to me. I open it and read the single phrase within.

> *Antigone,*
> *Go show them what you're made of.*
> *Miranda*

And that's how I learn that consolation has the power to hurt, too.

I hadn't imagined this bitterness of disappointment could intensify until it did. To see the words finally written, the affirmation finally given, that I've craved and struggled for as long as I can remember—and too late.

All I want to do, all my body wants to do, is pull my knees up against my chest, wrap my arms around them, lower my face, and sob.

Lee is staring at the floor, haggard with shame and guilt, and although I know he'd leave if I asked him, I also know there's more to say. So I run my thumbs under my eyes, gather my composure, and tell him what he needs to hear. The thing both of us need to hear, and remember.

"You'll be beautiful at it, Lee."

My exoneration, from its depths.

Lee's eyes are bloodshot as he raises them to look at me.

Beautiful: this boy who has grown into a young man, who is ready to become a leader, who's through it all been my best friend, and the bravest person I've ever known.

Whom I will trust to the end.

My voice is shaking as I add: "And it will be my honor to serve as your Alterna."

The past is behind us, the war ahead, and our fleet is sparked.

That's what matters.

Lee reaches out, and when his fingers take my bandaged hand, I don't pull away. For a moment, we're both still, feeling the pulse between our palms in the silent infirmary ward.

Lee speaks first. Now his voice is the lowest murmur.

"Annie. I need your help. I need you to . . ."

"Report Tyndale. I already did."

Lee blinks.

My heart is racing, but I keep my voice and my gaze steady. "After I overheard—I wasn't really . . . sure, what I'd overheard but I knew—" My fingers stiffen, still in his. "I knew I didn't want you talking to him anymore. To . . . them . . . anymore."

That was the gamble. Tyndale, not Lee.

And now I know I gambled right. *I have nothing more to say to them.*

He rubs his forehead and exhales slowly, through his mouth, realizing the danger narrowly missed in retrospect. As though realizing that I could have just as easily reported him.

"I put the report under my name," I go on, "and I filed it under speaking out against the ban, so it shouldn't . . . it shouldn't jeopardize you. The Reeducation Committee should process it within the week."

Relief is washing over Lee's face.

"Thank you," he says hoarsely. "I needed—I couldn't—"

"I know."

The next words seem to come choked out of him. "It's . . . going to get bad, Annie. Soon."

I wonder if he means for Callipolis or for himself. Because, I realize, looking at him, it will be both. Now that nothing stands between Callipolis and New Pythos but dragonfire. Lee's choices coming home to roost.

I can think of no consolation to give besides confirmation of the course.

"Then it's a good thing our fleet's sparked."

12

PALACE DAY

LEE

Annie is discharged from the infirmary a few days before Palace Day. Because I've been promoted to fleet commander, she's promoted to aurelian squadron leader in my place, and I hand her the badge for her uniform myself; the fleet commander's medal has already replaced mine. A bugle within the silver-and-gold-entwined circlets for the Firstrider; an aurelian dragon, wings spread, for the squadron leader. She accepts it with a gracious smile that doesn't hide her shuttered disappointment or undo my own clenching guilt.

Since the tournament, three more dragons have sparked. Though it's not enough to begin to consider offensive measures—particularly against New Pythos, so naturally well-fortified—it's still enough to change the mood of the city. Callipolis can defend herself again. The turn of sentiment, timed as it is with the arrival of Palace Day, means that the parade and its celebrations take on new significance for the Ministry of Propaganda: a chance to harness the hope of the people and cement it into readiness for war. But the parade is also the focal point of the Defense Ministry's security concerns.

Tyndale has vanished into the bowels of the prison that the Reeducation Committee shares with the Ministry of Information, indicted for sharing sentiments contrary to the national interest. Despite the fleet's sparking, the purge of the *Aurelian Cycle* remains in effect. Copies of the poem are confiscated across the city. Lotus's father's library is among those raided.

The Guardians' library is the only collection besides the Protector's exempted from the purge, but we still have to attend the bonfire. As I watch the flames turn pages into leaflike fragments rising on the breeze, the words of the Cycle itself return to me, bitter as smoke tasted on the wind:

> *To you, ashes and final flames of my own, I stand witness*
> *I who have escaped neither peril nor pain in your destruction*
> *If it is our fate to die, then by my own hand let me earn it.*

Three days before Palace Day, I'm shaken awake by Cor. Such was the nature of my dreams that I've lunged half out of bed, halfway to my feet with legs still tangled in blankets, before Cor pushes me back down.

"It's all right. You were just—"

Just waking people up, I realize. That doesn't happen much anymore, but around Palace Day, all bets are off. The dorm is unnaturally quiet, the usual snoring gone silent. The nightmares I've woken from are fresh enough that screaming is still echoing in my ears. The blankets are sweat-drenched; my face is wet.

"Thanks. Sorry. Was I—"

It's pressured speech; I have hardly any idea what I'm saying, but at Cor's whispered answer I sober instantly. His face and expression are impossible to make out in the darkness. "You were . . . you kept saying *no*."

I realize then that his hand is still on my shoulder.

"Thanks," I say again, shrugging it off.

In his class with the Fourth Order later that morning, Atreus passes out identical, battered booklets that all have the red stamp of banned material across the fronts. I read the title and feel myself break into a cold sweat.

A True Account of Palace Day and the Red Month, by R. T.

"Palace Day is an opportunity for great patriotism in our country," Atreus says. "A time for the people to unite around a narrative of a beginning that erases the past and starts again. But it is also a time for the four of you to consider the burdens that will be asked of you as rulers. While we encourage the rest of the city to enjoy the story of Palace Day, I would like you to consider the facts. The booklets in front of you, published not long after the Revolution and banned for the sake of political stability, provide a more than adequate summary. Please take a few minutes to familiarize yourself with the contents before we begin discussion."

There aren't enough booklets to go around. Cor and I are sharing. When I don't move, Cor takes the book and begins to flip through it. I'm determined not to look at Annie, or Power, or at the book at all, so I keep my eyes on Cor's face, watching his eyebrows knit together as his eyes travel down the page. His breathing hitches. He continues reading with his hand gripping his mouth.

By now, I've had years of practice sitting through classes about the Revolution and the Red Month. I've learned how to keep my face impassive and count the seconds. Anything can be survived for an hour.

But few teachers have spent any time talking about Palace

Day itself, and when they have, it's never been with the facts laid out so explicitly.

When Cor finally looks up, his face has gone green. He starts pushing the book toward me, in case I want to take a turn reading. I close it and push it back at him.

Atreus breaks the silence. "Cor, would you read from the top of fourteen, please?"

Cor flips to the page, and the others follow suit. He begins to read, hoarsely, about the fate of the Aurelian Triarch and his family. I feel the classroom fade in and out.

By time he gets to the second child, Cor's voice trails off.

Atreus doesn't ask him to go on.

Cor looks up. "Did you know? Did you know it would be like this?"

Atreus's smile is all steel.

"One never *knows*," he says. "But the course of popular uprisings are fairly predictable. We knew that the people would be difficult to control once they were allowed inside the Palace walls."

Atreus pauses, allowing the confession to sink in. Then he goes on.

"It went further than we wanted. I admit that. But even so, it was a risk I knew we were taking from the start. It was a hard decision, but it had to be made. Better these deaths, once"— Atreus drums his fingers on the booklet in front of him—"brutal as they were, than countless more undeserved deaths in the future. Do you agree?"

Silence. The pulse of blood in my ears, the sound of a room of people saying nothing.

Power speaks first. "I don't think it would have been a hard decision."

Atreus's response is cool. "You don't?"

"None of this is worse than what they did to us," Power says. "Blood for blood."

The words echo oddly in my ears. I can feel Cor glancing at me, and it is only after a moment of paranoia that I realize why. This is the sort of thinking that I usually push back against.

Then I hear her speak.

"You think they deserved this?"

I know Annie too well not to recognize the sound of her anger. Power says, "Yeah, I do. After what they did to us, they deserved it."

Annie snorts. "After what they did to whom, the *Janiculum*?"

Power hears the incredulity in her voice. His eyes narrow, his face suddenly contorting as he leans forward, his voice lowering. "My mother was from Cheapside. I'm a *Cheapsider*. The highlands weren't the only part of Callipolis that *suffered*, Annie. As far as Cheapside is concerned, the dragonborn got what they deserved."

It's the first time Power has ever outright admitted to being anything other than patrician, much less a Cheapsider. Cor's eyebrows have shot up as he studies Power's screwed-up face.

Annie's voice is shaking. "What they got wasn't justice. It was a massacre."

I raise my eyes from the stained oak table and finally look at her. Her hair is cropped now, the burned braid cut off after the match; it hangs in jagged chin-length spikes, like an urchin boy's. She's glaring at Power and has begun to flush.

I hear myself speak.

"You of all people should think it was justified."

Annie's eyes move to mine. Peripherally, I note the others shifting, uncomfortable, catching the reference as well as Annie has. Atreus clears his throat to intervene, but before he can, Annie speaks. Her voice is unexpectedly thick.

"What kind of person do you think I am, Lee?"

My throat closes.

Atreus breaks the silence, his tone impatient.

"Antigone displays—admirable—compassion for her ene-mies that Lee and Power would do well to imitate," he says. "It should never be easy to decide who dies. Even if, as in this case, they were guilty of terrible things.

"As you may know, before the Revolution, I was chief advi-sor to Arcturus Aurelian. The fates that Cor just read to us were those that met his family."

Annie inhales deeply and slowly as she understands. Atreus goes on with tranquil calm.

"Some wonder, knowing that connection, if I precipitated such violence against Arcturus and his people for personal reasons. If he had wronged me in some way, if it was an act of vengeance. After all, many revolutionaries were so motivated." Here Atreus nods, graciously, in Power's direction. Power twitches and eases back in his chair. Atreus's voice remains distant.

"In my case, it was not. In my case, in fact, I had every per-sonal reason to support Arcturus. He had been good to me when I needed help, sponsored my education, and seen to my advance-ment. But in the end, what he did for me personally was not enough to undo the wrongs he committed as a ruler. And on those grounds, I made my choice. The good of my people over the pull of my emotions."

Cor's fingers are drumming nervously on the table; Annie's eyes have widened; Power's lip is curling, his arms folded, as he looks at Atreus with what might be disgust. But the commonality between their reactions is horror. As if what Atreus describes—a cool reckoning unmotivated by personal vendetta—is the most unsettling of all histories.

I feel something else. Relief.

I'm not the only one to have chosen this kind of path. Once, long ago, Atreus did the same.

Atreus says: "I will live with the burden of Arcturus's death, and the death of his family, for the rest of my life."

Then he raises his eyes, and a hardness enters his tone as he adds, "That does not mean I regret them."

Atreus gives our silence a moment before making his final point.

"Much of what you'll be doing, as Guardians, will be deciding which is the lesser evil. Who lives, who dies. It will be—it *should* be—a terrible burden.

"Times may come when you question yourself. On those occasions, remember that these decisions are better made by you than someone else. If everything goes to plan, you'll be the most rational, the most well-trained, the most fit to rule. It will be *your* duty to make these decisions, to bear the guilt of them for others' sakes."

* * *

It's still a little strange to seek Crissa's company privately now that the Firstrider Tournament has passed and training for it no longer provides the excuse or the justification. But the desire to continue outweighs the reasons to call it off.

"Thought you wouldn't come," she says, when I find her in her dorm room.

The room is golden in the afternoon light. Crissa is seated at her desk, where homework and stolen refectory mugs are piled across the surface, folded into her chair as she leans over her reading. The other girls have obligations right now, and we have the dorm to ourselves.

"I had to . . . I went for a walk."

I throw my book bag on the floor next to her bed and sink onto it, leaning back against the mound of pillows and closing my eyes. The bed smells of the sea breeze and something just a little sweeter, a fragrance I've come to associate with Crissa.

"Is everything . . . okay, Lee?"

It's a checking-in tone, the kind I use with others but can't remember anyone ever having used with me. I'm so unprepared for it that I don't know how to answer.

"I just . . . I thought maybe it was because you were worried about Annie, after the Firstrider Tournament, but now she's better and you're still . . ."

She trails off. I have opened my eyes and am lying very still, looking at her, but she keeps her gaze on her reading.

"Still what?" I prompt softly.

"Sad," she says.

She does look at me, then.

"I know"—her words are careful, like delicate steps across ice—"that maybe there are things that happened to you that you can't—that are too hard to talk about. And I know that I know nothing—*nothing*—of what it must have been. But if there's anything you want to tell me, any way I could help you . . ."

The public bio, the one she knows, is that I lost my family during the Red Month. The triarchy created so many slum orphans in its last throes that the story has always gone unquestioned.

I imagine telling her: that the worst day I've ever lived is commemorated annually as a national festival and celebrated with a parade; that rather than taking comfort with what family remains to me, I've chosen to throw in my lot with their usurper.

When I say nothing, she rises and climbs onto the bed beside me. Although I make no move to turn to her—my body feels like it is weighted to the bed, like something apart from myself—she curls closer, fits her body against mine, and lays her head against my shoulder. She stretches her arm across my chest, spreads her fingers across my far shoulder. She is, I realize, holding me.

"One day," she murmurs into my shoulder, "when we're at peace again, I want to take a few days' leave and bring you with me. Home. To Harbortown, to see the beaches."

She's phrased it like this, I realize, so that it's not a question, so I'm not given the opportunity to say no. It sounds so nice that I hear myself answer before considering the words.

"I've been there, once."

"Really?" She sounds surprised. It takes me a moment to remember why.

"Orphanage field trip," I add numbly.

It wasn't an orphanage field trip. It was a family vacation. Sand in our hair, fiddler crabs under our feet, the smell of fresh fish roasting over a fire as servants turned the spit. My sisters buried me.

"You liked it?"

"Yes," I tell her. "Very much."

ANNIE

The day I'm discharged from the infirmary, a parade-planning meeting is held with Miranda Hane, General Holmes, Lee, Cor, Power, and myself, and concerns the question of national security during the parade. At the sight of Hane, my stomach does an odd flip, remembering her note. I'm still stiff from the many bandages beneath my uniform, sitting still is uncomfortable, and the feeling of my absent braid is disorienting.

"Did you know," Hane says, before the meeting starts, "that the title *Alterna* bears a feminine ending for the first time since our earliest poetry, because of you?"

Alterna is a Dragontongue loanword, and Dragontongue, unlike Callish, is a gendered language. Even though I did know it, I also appreciate Hane's bit of trivia, delivered softly and with a smile, for what it is: something between congratulations and condolence.

"Thank you," I tell her, and hope she knows I mean her note, too.

Hane begins the meeting by requesting as many dragons as possible in the cavalcade going down the Triumphal Way. General Holmes, though he maintains the need for air patrols during the event, is inclined to allow it. "The security of the city's my main concern for this event at any rate. Keeping the bulk of the riders armed and central will only strengthen its defense."

Lee has been staring with an arrested expression out the window at the Firemouth. The light is gray: a low layer of stratus has settled over the city, leaving those concerned with its air defense full of unease. Cloud cover like this is a defending dragonrider's nightmare. Lee never looks particularly well-rested even at his best, but at this time of year the bruises under his eyes are always especially dark, the lines around his mouth deepened, as if sleep is something he has forgotten.

"And the coast?" he asks Holmes, turning from the window.

Holmes nods, appreciative, and throws a grin at Hane. "Circumspect, our new Firstrider. I like that."

Lee responds with a twisted smile.

Hane and Holmes begin to argue over the breakdown of the coastal patrols. Lee doesn't interrupt them again. It is determined that two air patrols, one over the city and one along the northern coast, will be deployed simultaneously with the parade, each led by a sparked dragon.

"I'll lead one of the patrols," Cor says. "Don't much like parades, anyway."

The dragons who have sparked so far are in our highest ranks, Cor's, Power's, and Crissa's among them.

Lee says, "I'd like to take an air patrol as well."

Hane looks at Holmes and says, "That's not necessary, is it? I was assuming Lee would lead. Along with the Alterna."

"I'd lead what?" Lee asks.

"The parade," Holmes says. "That's fine, Miranda. Seems appropriate, for the Firstrider. All right, Lee?"

Lee's face has gone perfectly blank.

"Yes, sir," he says.

* * *

Palace Day dawns blue-skied. The fog cleared, the Guardians are approved to participate in the parade.

The booklet from Atreus's class has remained in my backpack, untouched, until the morning of Palace Day. Then at last I give in. The day is too incongruous: the excitement of the rest of the corps in anticipation of the upcoming parade; the feeling of festivity in the air; and the quiet composure with which Lee eats breakfast. He goes off on his own after that, as he always does on this day. As usual, I'm the only one who notices.

And I think, *I've had enough*. It's time. Today might be a day when the whole city pretends, but I, for one, am ready for something else. Lee has leapt from one dragon's back to another for my sake, is preparing to endure celebrations that have gutted him every year since we were children, and after this, his path will likely get harder. I owe him an end of pretense and acknowledgment of the truth.

The whole truth.

I go to an empty classroom, shut the door, and open the booklet for the first time since class. I turn to the page I've been purposely skipping every time I leafed through. At the top is a picture of the Drakarch of the Far Highlands and his family. My eyes are drawn immediately to the father, and I find myself staring, for the first time since it happened, at *him*. Even though the quality of the image isn't particularly good, I still feel the same mingled terror and hatred. He stands next to a woman and they're surrounded by children. They look happy and beautiful and proud. Pictured among his family, loving and fatherly, it's difficult to imagine him doing what I once saw him do.

I look at the text below the picture and search for the name of the youngest child. There: five years old at the time of the portrait, a boy named Leo. I stare at the name and for a moment I forget to breathe.

Then my breath returns in a rush; I search for him and see him there, grainy and unclear, but recognizable. The description may say that this boy is dead, but I know that he's very much alive.

Even though it seems like I've always known, it still hits me like a physical blow, seeing him there at last, pictured three feet from the other man. For a moment, the page blurs.

Then I blink my vision clear and force myself to read. I read about what happened to his mother, to his brother, to his sisters, finally to his father. I match every single face in the picture to the descriptions below. I slowly, meticulously imagine the scene that must have happened, on this day, ten years ago.

Then I look again at the picture, at the little boy whose face is just a few smudges of ink. Even with these limitations it's plain to see that he's smiling. Most of the rest of the family aren't—their expressions are solemn, dignified, befitting a formal portrait of a dragonlord's family. But it seems the artist made an exception for the boy; for an older sister, too, who sits beside him; they're both smiling merrily, as though they're about to break into laughter. I realize that, in all my time knowing him, I've never seen Lee smile like this.

It comes to me, then, a vision of what he must have been, once: a youngest child in a family full of laughter, at the center of their joy and attention. Affectionate, because he received affection; talkative, because if he wasn't, he wouldn't be heard; probably prone to mischief, because he could get away with it. It is easy to imagine him this way, though I only have a picture to base it on. After all, I was once the youngest child, too.

Then I imagine this smiling little boy losing everyone he loved in the span of a few heartbreaking hours. I don't need to imagine what the pain must have been like, because I remember it. In that moment, it doesn't matter to me who his father was or what he did to me. All I want is to find the little boy I knew in Albans and hold him.

"Annie?"

I look up. For a moment I think it must be him, and I realize the book is out, open, and it's too late to hide. But it's Duck.

"Hane's waiting," he says. "The pre-parade briefing, remember?"

"Right," I say.

He doesn't ask what I'm doing, though I see him glance at the book in front of me. Bewilderment crosses his face as he recognizes it. I close the book, put it in my bag, and get up. Side by side, we make our way to the oration room.

Hane is waiting to brief us at the sunken rostrum in the center of the floor. When Duck and I enter, I realize we must be late; everyone else is already in the elevated, rickety wooden seats that rise in concentric semicircles. Or, almost everyone is. Lee is missing, too.

"You didn't find him?" Hane asks Duck.

Oh, Lee, I think, *don't lose courage now. Not over a stupid parade.*

"No," says Duck, "do you want me to go—"

But before he can finish his offer, the door opens again and Lee comes in.

One look at him is enough to know that my fear was needless. If I notice that he's a little pale, a little tight-lipped, it's only because I'm searching for it. I'm struck instead by his marshalled self-possession: He's standing especially erect, his expression full of calm confidence. He's dressed in full ceremonial regalia, and he wears his cloak and armor as though he was born in them, the wings of the Fourth Order on his shoulder, the Firstrider's ceremonial bugle slung across his back. Instead of taking a seat like the rest of us, he goes to stand beside Hane. He doesn't apologize for being late; instead, he nods to Hane as if to indicate that the meeting may begin.

I look at him, quiet and dignified and in complete control, and I realize that the hurt, lost boy I remember is just as gone as the smiling one I never met. He's put both aside today, and he needs none of the comforting that I'd like to give him. The thought fills me with fierce pride.

Hane looks at him, once, measuring, and I can tell that she's noticed, as I have, the way he assumed power in the room as he entered it, and she's startled, though not exactly displeased. Then she clears her throat and begins to outline our route.

As she speaks, and I continue to regard Lee, I allow myself to see it. The resemblance that's haunted me, that I've resisted, for as long as I can remember, but that today I have confirmed past ignorance or denial.

I look at Lee and see Leon Stormscourge's son.

* * *

Atreus, mounted on a slate-gray warhorse, leads the way along the Triumphal Way, followed by the cavalcade of the crimson-clad Protector's Guard. Pallor and Aela come next, leading the rest of the aerial fleet not on patrol. Flashes of what I just read keep returning to my mind, and I find myself sickened by the festivity around me. The Callipolan flags waving, the banners and fanfare, the cheering crowds—all seems like more and more hypocrisy.

The crowds press close to us as we move forward, leaning against barriers constructed and maintained by the city guards, and we move so slowly that we have ample time to study the faces of the people cheering us on. Where once, I used to number myself among them, now I find myself looking upon them with the same aversion with which I once looked on the dragonlords. I watch them cheering themselves hoarse over a massacre and remember how, years ago, they hurled insults at a helpless dragon, even after it had been bound and mutilated, for the sheer pleasure of humiliating an animal that had only followed its master's orders. I remember being lifted on the shoulders of people in the same tavern outside which, a month later, my service to the city was mocked. I remember how it felt, the wet, cold splatter of a villager's spit on my face. Atreus's words, afterward: *The anger of the people can be often cruel and ill-placed.*

These are not my people; I am not one of them. Not anymore. These people understand justice only as revenge. They are undeserving, ignorant, and cruel.

It goes on, these thoughts, this mounting anger, until it crystallizes into one overriding feeling: disgust.

Then with a jolt I wonder: *Was this how the dragonlords thought of us?*

Next to me, Lee guides Pallor with agonizingly slow, careful steps, setting the pace for the whole parade. I glance at him periodically, every time seeing his still, calm face, masklike and hard. Only in his posture does any sign of strain show. He sits straighter and straighter as time wears on, stiffening a bit more every time the cheering swells with his name. By the end, he is rigidly upright. Others might perceive this as a sign of pride, but I know the truth. It is the posture of someone receiving a beating and determined to get through it on their feet.

The parade finishes in the People's Square, separated from the

Palace by the river and a wide stone bridge. By now, it's dusk; the parade was timed so it would end with the kind of light best suited to demonstrations of fire. Lee and I mount the dais where, years ago, Leon Stormscourge's dragon was beheaded.

Our dragons fire upward, into the deepening blue sky, then launch into the air; behind us, two by two, the other riders follow. We circle each other, the sparked dragons firing in formation, the others weaving round us; we can see the city stretched below, the masses in the main square, in the streets, gathered to watch us, cheering as one. Then at last it is over, and we depart for the caves.

* * *

Back in her nest, I take my time scrubbing down Aela, feeding her from a bucket of meat the caretakers left waiting for our return. Since sparking, she's developed a taste for charred meat, though half the time she overcooks it. When she ends up turning a leg of mutton into a big block of cinder, she attempts to eat it, gags, and then looks at me reproachfully.

"It's not my fault you can't figure out your own cook time," I tell her.

It's a relief, after the parade, to do something as familiar as having a staring contest with Aela.

"Hey, Annie?"

It's Duck's voice, from the cave corridor outside. The coastal patrols must be back.

"How'd it go?" I ask.

Duck shrugs. "Not so much as a sighting," he says.

He waits on the threshold of Aela's nest, a black silhouette against the tunnel's lantern light. "Some of the others are going in to town to see the celebrations," he says. "Do you want to go with them?"

No. The last thing I need is more celebrating.

"Or we could go for a walk," he adds, seeming to sense my reaction.

This, I favor: There's nothing like a walk around the Palace gardens with Duck to make everything a little bit better. "Okay. Let me just finish up here."

"Sure."

I turn back to Aela, registering his leaving the mouth of our nest out of the corner of my eye. It's only as I replay it that I realize Duck was heading off in the direction not of the armory, but of the lower caves.

I drop the bucket and take off after him at a run. I don't even stop to think why I'm running—all I know is that it's urgently important for me to stop Duck. More time has passed than I realized; he's just at the mouth of Pallor's nest when I stumble up to him. He's on the verge of looking inside when I catch him by the shoulder, silently, and twist him around to face me.

I'm shaking my head violently, and for a moment Duck opens his mouth in surprise and I think for a split second that he's going to say something and give us away. But before he can speak, another sound comes from within the nest. Retching, the splat of wet on rocks. Lee is throwing up.

Duck realizes what he's hearing and closes his mouth abruptly. I stand frozen with sudden shame; even hearing Lee right now seems like an invasion. For a moment, Duck's eyes linger on my face, and I sense the question there, unspoken: *Why did you expect this?*

We make our way in silence from Pallor's nest.

LEE

I had hoped the armory would be empty when I came up from the caves, but instead I find Crissa and Cor stripping along with the rest of the riders from their patrols, faces flushed and hair windswept. I summon up the energy for a single word.

"Anything?"

Crissa and Cor shake their heads.

I should be relieved, but instead I feel something almost like disappointment. Let them take us. Let it come. On Palace Day, I want the world to burn, and I care very little who sets it afire.

But aloud all I say is, "We should rotate out riders and send another guard up."

"I'll take it," Cor says. "I'm not tired, and you look like shit."

Crissa gives him a reproving look, and he shrugs, unabashed.

I know this is my cue to refuse and take my turn in the air. But tonight, in the wake of the parade, I don't have it in me.

After I've seen them out, I go to the Cloister library and pull the *Aurelian Cycle* from the shelf. It now bears a stamp of banned material across its front.

Aside from what we go over in class, I haven't looked at it in years. It's strange to read it; I remember it as something that was chiefly spoken aloud. Spoken aloud by *him*. When he told it to us, in riveting installments after dinner, before bed, it was always from memory. He never needed a book. Now, reading it silently in the empty library, I can hear his voice again. It's been a long time since I've let myself remember it.

Time passes and I hardly notice; I just keep reading, skipping to the parts I liked best, flipping backward and forward through the pages as I recall parts I want to revisit. I work my way inward, toward the part of the poem that's been most on my mind: the part where the lost island of Aureos is overtaken and burned, where the Aurelians are finally defeated and driven into exile. Sometime around one in the morning I summon up the courage to read it. I hear the words in my father's voice, and the voices of the characters become the voices of my family, till it's all a little blurred. But still with that separateness like a shield I feel the old grief and don't feel it, am caught somewhere in the middle, between these words and the real things. And then they are around me, half stories, half real, my family; though we are no longer in the part where they are being hurt; we've flipped back, to earlier pages, it's dinner, my mother is refilling my father's cup—

"Lee," she says.

But that's not my name, I think, and that's not my mother's voice.

Around me, the dinner is fading; my sister's laughter is growing fainter; and then I hear the name that is not my name again.

I open my eyes and look up. In the half second that it takes for Annie's silhouette to come into focus, when I've recognized her but not quite woken, there's a surge of the old bitterness. For that instant, I think, *It's always like this, you standing between me and them.*

But then the bitterness dulls, takes its rightful buried place. In the dim light of the lantern I've been reading with, I take in her expression. Her face is tense, set.

Her expression is enough for me to anticipate her next words. I close the *Aurelian Cycle* without looking at it.

"There's been an attack," Annie says. "South, over the Medean, under the cover of yesterday's fog. We've been summoned to the Inner Palace."

13

—

THE MEDEAN ATTACK

LEE

Despite the late hour, the windows of the Inner Palace are lit. Inside the Council Room, Lotus and Warren, the two skyfish riders whose patrol must have just returned bearing news, wait with Atreus, General Holmes, Miranda Hane, the Chief Treasurer, and the Ministers of Trade and Agriculture. I take the constituents as confirmation of my fears.

The Pythians didn't strike our military, our navy, or our aerial fleet. They didn't even try to attack our city.

They went for our trade fleet.

Atreus gestures for us to sit, not on the side of the room, but at the table with them.

"How bad?" I ask.

Holmes, with assistance from Lotus and Warren, begins to debrief us. Multiple air strikes, all within a window of about an hour yesterday evening, when the fog still hung low. South along the Medean trade routes between Harbortown, Damos, and Bassilea, where our patrols rarely venture. Given the number of attacks, their distance apart, and the descriptions returned by the navy, more than a half dozen sparked dragons were involved. Nearly our entire trade fleet was lost, and with them, most of this year's textile exports.

The casualty count of Callipolan civilians lost at sea will number in the hundreds; but that's only where the devastation *begins*, the Minister of Agriculture starts to explain. With so many farms incentivized from subsistence farming to textile exports, Callipolis no longer supports self-sufficient levels of food production to sustain its growing urban population, and with the exports destroyed, there are no profits by which to make up the difference. The Minister of Agriculture doesn't say *famine* because he doesn't have to.

So that's how it will go. Reaping fear not with dragonfire and blazesites but with the slow pressure of hunger through the winter. And we, with our half-sparked fleet, will be able to do nothing but endure it.

You wanted the world to burn? Now it's burning.

"We can borrow, can't we?" Atreus turns to the Treasurer.

"We're looking into it. Mithrides and others will help as much as they can, but many of them lost huge investments in the attack."

"What if we centralize our food resources for the winter and redistribute?" Atreus asks.

"It might be enough," the Minister of Agriculture says, looking frightened, "but there's really no way of knowing up front how much we would have . . . and that sort of operation is *very* difficult and has disastrous effects if mismanaged—"

Atreus asks, "Do we have alternative solutions for supporting the urban population through the winter?"

Silence answers him.

Atreus closes his eyes, his face twisted in deliberation. And then he opens them. He turns to Holmes. "Begin collectivizing resources immediately. I want every village, every farm, upturned for whatever it's made this harvest. We'll centralize resources and ration from the city center."

My mind latches on to a single word: *collectivize*. Surely he doesn't mean—

Atreus turns to us.

"Shift the skyfish to coastal patrols exclusively and keep a minimum of one sparked dragon accompanying them. Devote the aurelian and stormscourge squadrons to assisting with collections."

He does mean it. *Collections*.

A practice notorious in the old regime, that hasn't been implemented since the Revolution—and was, infamously, enforced by dragonfire. The dragonlords' preferred method for collecting their harvest taxes. My father's usual occupation, in autumn.

"You're asking us to—"

"The traditional methods. Speed will need to be our priority."

Traditional methods.

Words so easily delivered by Atreus, an order so dismissively given, that for a moment I don't even believe I've heard it.

Because, of course, for Atreus it's just that: two words. For me, for the other dragonriders, it will be something else entirely. Which is why Atreus is able to look so calm, while I go light-headed. Annie beside me is swallowing audibly, her hands clenching on the table, her eyes widening as the order washes over her.

Watch how this vision will splinter.

I hear myself say, "Yes, sir."

"How soon can you start collecting?" Atreus asks Holmes.

"First light," Holmes says. "I'll need to speak with the Firstrider and Alterna to arrange matters."

The general conducts the meeting with me and Annie in his office and on his feet. We agree to launch a strengthened guard tonight over the city; tomorrow morning, ground forces will begin collecting food from the countryside, accompanied by two dragons per visit.

"I think it's best if you go on the first collections, Lee," Holmes says.

For the first time since our meeting began, Annie speaks.

"No. I should."

She's white-faced, gripping the arms of her chair with tight fingers. Holmes takes in her expressions and his own softens.

"Antigone, collections are going to be very difficult—"

Annie's voice is faint but clear, each word spoken with crisp precision. "I know what collections are like."

Holmes blinks. The composition of his face shifts with understanding.

"As far as I know"—Annie twitches—"I'm one of the *only* Guardians who knows what collections are like. Lee's never—"

Here she stops and with a pang I understand her sudden hesitation: She's wondering if I've been on collections before, too. I shake my head.

I was always deemed too young to go along.

Annie inhales a catching breath and straightens.

"I know what you're looking for; I know what you'll need."

I feel a coldness entering my bones. Whatever Annie knows about collections, there's only one person she could have learned it from.

Holmes places his palms on his map-covered desk, and it creaks beneath his great weight as he leans forward. "Knowing what I need isn't the same thing as being able to do it. This kind of operation is only as successful as it can be harsh. They'll think we're lying about giving it back, that we're just collecting it for ourselves, as the old regime used to do. We're going to have to crack down hard, especially at first. I need riders who can do what it takes."

Annie's voice is faint but clear.

"I can do what it takes."

For a beat they stare at each other, this towering man, the girl a third of his size, eyes blazing. Holmes seems to find what he's looking for. He removes his palms from his desk and straightens.

"Good," he tells her. "Then you'll do the first ones, and begin training the others after that."

In the hallway outside, Annie stands stock still for a moment and wraps her arms around herself. Then she releases them, and we begin to walk. The Palace is quiet, dark, and full of the earthy smells of early autumn as we match stride through the courtyard arcades.

"Who do you want assisting you?" I ask.

Annie's answer comes without hesitation, as a murmur. "Rock."

Of course. Rock is a former serf, too. "You'll need to talk to him after I debrief the corps. And the two of you will have to begin training the rest after tomorrow."

"All right."

I realize the other thing that will happen tonight as if a stone has dropped into my gut.

"I'll also need to speak to Crissa first, before we wake the others."

"Why . . . ?"

"Her father is a trader, and he's at sea."

In the Cloister, I follow Annie to the darkened girls' dorm and count the beds to Crissa's. Then I say her name. She follows me into the hall, rubbing sleep from her eyes.

"Lee, what's . . . you nut, is this a *tryst*?"

In the sconce-lit corridor she turns out to be smiling. That easy, unlabored Crissa smile, that I've grown to cherish and am now about to take away. But I can't do it here, in the hall where she passes every day to and from bed; nor can I imagine doing it in the refectory, or the solarium, or the courtyard. Wherever we have this conversation, Crissa will remember it for that.

So I take her hand and lead her to an unused classroom in the library wing.

When I close the door after us, she's still *smiling*. "This is . . . pretty irregular, Lee. But I can make it work—"

"Would you mind sitting?"

The smile flickers. Doubt finally enters her expression. She sits, and I sit beside her.

"Has your father's ship sailed into port yet?"

"Not . . . for a week or so, I don't think. Why?"

In the time it takes for me to form the words, her face stills. Like all the pieces that didn't add up to a date are now adding up to something else. And then, as I knew it would, the smile goes out.

"No," she says. "No, no, *no*—"

I'd thought experience would be a kind of preparation for this conversation, but it turns out that there's no preparation for watching someone's face struggle to understand a new kind of pain.

"Nothing's certain yet. We only just got the news, we don't know anything for sure yet—"

"*What news?*"

ANNIE

When the Guardians are assembled, alert and curious, in the sconce-lit oration room, I ask Cor to come with me to find Lee. We can hear Crissa crying from the corridor. Inside, he is sitting with his arm around her on the old school pew, his face lowered into a hand.

"Annie, Cor," Crissa says when she sees us, and gets to her feet.

Cor's voice is rough. "Hey. How are you doing?"

"Not great."

Lee has risen with her. "Is it time?" he asks me.

I nod.

Lee tells Crissa: "I've got to speak with the others. Cor can wait with you here—"

Crissa wipes her eyes. "No. I'll come."

None of us are expecting this; when she sees our expressions, she lifts her chin. "I have a squadron that needs me. What do I have to hide? I'm not ashamed to be seen in grief."

Inside the oration room, she sits between me and Cor; the double takes that riders have when they see her tearstained face seem to make no impression on her. Lee takes his place behind the rostrum in the sunken center of the room. In the time it's taken to return to the oration room, he's become charged with burning energy, like a pent-up dragon finally released from its cave, and the corps notices. Silence falls.

"I'll keep this brief," Lee says.

It's the first time Lee has ever officially run a meeting with us as fleet commander. He explains what happened, what we'll be doing for the next few weeks, and what he needs immediately. It's over in ten minutes. He heads out with the first patrol, taking a third of the riders with him. The rest of us are dismissed to get some sleep.

I pull aside Rock to talk to him about tomorrow morning. When he realizes I'm asking him to assist in the first food collections, he pales.

"I remember collections," he says.

"I do, too. That's why we should do them first, then train the others."

Rock lets out a low, whistling breath. "Uriel's dragon," he swears slowly.

I tell him what I've been telling myself, ever since that conversation with General Holmes. "It won't be like before. We'll give it back."

"Even if we do," he says, shaking his head, "there won't be enough."

Rock keeps pretty well-informed about the state of agriculture in Callipolis, and the way he says this makes me nervous in a way even the Minister of Agriculture's predictions didn't.

"We don't know that yet," I say.

Rock grimaces, like there's something sour in his mouth.

"It's our best option. Even if there isn't enough, this is—fairest."

But even as I say it, numb dread fills me at the thought of what's going to happen tomorrow. Rock turns away, pulling at his mouth like he's working through something, and in the end he just utters a single expletive.

"When do we leave?" he asks me.

"Six in the morning. We should go to sleep."

Rock lets out a hollow laugh at the suggestion.

14

⎯

COLLECTIONS

The children were given a quarter of an hour after the Choosing Ceremony to say farewell to their parents. The boy and the girl watched from the side of the room as the others' parents wept, embraced their children, and made promises to write.

"Maybe we shouldn't do it," he said.

She looked at him like he was mad. "Of course we should do it. This is the best thing that's ever happened to us."

The next thing needed to be said very carefully, and he had been choosing the words for it all afternoon. "I know you think the people who used to have the dragons were bad," he said. "But what if the new people are bad, too?"

She considered this. "You don't think he's bad, do you? That man we met?"

She was referring to the First Protector, who'd talked with the Chosen children after the ceremony about the future they could expect in his new program. And the boy had to admit, he didn't think of that man as bad. That man had once saved him, after all.

"No, I don't think he's bad," he said.

But somehow, this didn't seem enough. She seemed to sense that he was still worried.

"Think about it this way," she said. "Even if they're bad, we'll be the ones with dragons in the end. We'll make the rules. And we'd never be bad, would we?"

LEE

I'm back on the ground by early morning and head to the Outer Wall with Cor to review alarm procedures. When we spot Annie and Rock descending into the Firemouth, back from their first collection, I return to the armory to wait for them. Annie comes in first, dumping Aela's gear on a bench and pushing past me for the washroom. She slams the door behind her and then I hear her sobbing.

"Don't," Rock says, grabbing me by the shoulder.

I look him in the face for the first time and realize it's ashen.

"What happened?"

Rock lets out a dull, horrified laugh, the kind of laugh I've never heard him make before. "We made an example of someone," he says.

The possibilities spread out before me. "You killed him?"

Rock shakes his head. "He wasn't in good shape, that's for sure."

"And then—?"

"It got results." His voice is dead. "Just like it used to."

Annie's sobs are drilling into me, that particular sound that

I'm primed, from so many years ago, to respond to. Hopeless, lost, frightened. The desire to go to her is almost overwhelming.

"She said she could handle it."

"She handled it," Rock says. "She was the one who did it."

Then Rock turns away from me and begins to strip off his armor. He moves with the exhaustion of an old man.

"When do you go again?"

I'm expecting him to say tomorrow, but he just squints like he's counting bell tolls. "An hour and a half? They want us to hit another village before nightfall."

So Annie's going to have to do it again, in a few hours. It seemed so clear, so simple last night, when she said she should be the one to do it, but it's less clear now, listening to her through the washroom door. *She asked for this. She wanted it.*

He leans forward, puts his head in his hands, and I know she isn't the only one feeling the weight.

"Rock. You did good. You did what you had to do."

"It sure as hell didn't feel *good*."

ANNIE

The sun has barely risen when we begin the first collection.

We wait in the makeshift, unpaved square, surrounded by a handful of crumbling, thatch-roofed buildings, while the crier makes the announcement to a straggle of villagers, many of whom our visit has woken. Then the troops start making house calls, and Rock and I wait, on dragonback, beside the collection wagons.

The villagers whose houses the soldiers visit are obliging enough, but I'm pretty sure they don't believe us about the Medean attack. I know my father wouldn't if a crier showed up and used it as an excuse to demand his harvest. Rock and I watch as the wagons are loaded, and together we compare inventories with maps of the village, shaded boxes showing fields, labeled with this year's crops. We realize soon enough that the soldiers—who are from the city and don't know better—are missing things. The village is producing less than it should.

We look at each other, and I know he and I are thinking the same thing; and after that, we know what to do, because we've both seen it happen before.

"Get the villagers into the square again," I tell the village leaders.

Though I've never met a single one of these people before, in this moment they all feel familiar: the men, built and browned from years of hard labor, with the same lines around their eyes that my father had, graying young; the women with their hair bound in the same kinds of scarves my mother wore, the children in their arms and at their sides, clinging, as I remember doing during these visits when my presence was required by our lord. I feel that I'm not so much looking at them as remembering them.

I tell the crier to reiterate the message delivered initially: that the welfare of Callipolis is at stake, that our need is imminent, and that food will be redistributed fairly once it's collected. I ask him to make clear that, upon assessing the collection results, we know we've been shortchanged.

The crier's voice is clear, stronger than mine would ever be on the wind, but the villagers don't look at him. They look at me and Rock, and our dragons.

When, at the end of his address, the square is silent, the rest of it proceeds like a script we all know by heart. Except now, my role is changed.

I already know which ones shortchanged us, so it's just a matter of picking one.

It should never be easy.

They all have families. One of them has older kids, though, they're nearly grown up, so that's the one I tell Rock to follow back to his property.

It takes Rock and the soldiers a while to find the hidden storeroom, but in the square, the villagers wait quietly, and fear hums in the air. I wait, my fingers balled to fists, feeling that fear focused on me and on Aela. I've dismounted and wait beside her. She senses my disquiet, and when I feel her mind seeking mine, seeking closeness, I expel her advance with such force that Aela whimpers.

No. I owe these people at least the fullness of my mind's focus, unfiltered by a dragon's comforting haze.

Instead I reach down, place my hand on Aela's haunch, and steady myself.

When Rock and the family return, the man is handcuffed. He's shaking, apologizing, crying. His wife begins to cry, too.

I tell one of the soldiers to escort his family back to his house. This, at least, is one thing we can do differently. Then I ask another soldier to fetch a bucket of water and a blanket. The village leaders begin to protest, and they, too, are led away.

Rock's eyes meet mine in a silent question. I nod once to

show I'll do it. Though, I suppose, I have to. Rock's dragon hasn't sparked yet. He could cause injuries, but for the full effect of this demonstration, we require flames.

"You'll all be given a second chance to remember if you have more food," I tell the murmuring crowd. "If there's more, and you fail to remember it, you will meet a fate similar to this man's. Bring him forward."

Soldiers push the man toward me. I feel as though the scene has begun to move in frames of stillness, each heartbeat matched to an image rather than a moving world: the man in front of us, standing; then forced to his knees, kneeling; Aela's wings half lifted in expectation as she looks down on him.

Your father would be ashamed of you, girl.

I tell Aela to fire.

The fire catches on his clothes and spreads as the man screams. I count the seconds. One for it to catch; two for it to spread; three for it to burn. I raise my hand at three, and the blanket is thrown over him, the bucket emptied, the fire smothered. More than that, four seconds, five, would cause burns severe enough to incapacitate him or endanger his life. Three seconds leaves wounds that heal.

The man crouches under the smoking blanket, gasping. I know what lies beneath: the reddened skin, the clothes that are mostly gone. It smells like it did the day my family died. Instead of vomiting, like I want to, I look past him, to the frightened faces of his neighbors.

"Let's try this again," I say.

We visit each house a second time, and this time, they give us everything.

LEE

I go with Rock on the second day, when he and Annie start training the rest of us. Annie takes Cor. I've drawn up a schedule with two goals in mind: that Annie and I never do collections together, and that Power never does them at all. It shouldn't matter, but I'm relieved the village Rock and I are going to is in the lowlands. Skyfish lands, not Stormscourge. It's one less thing to think about.

Although it's still not enough to keep me from thinking of my father.

"So, how long will this go on?" Rock asks me as we get suited up.

"Depends on how long it takes," I tell Rock. "A few weeks?"

Rock's thick fingers tighten on the laces of his boots as he yanks them. "Right," he says.

When we land in the village, Rock makes the announcement. The same rural lilt I've heard in his speech sometimes with Annie, but never around Lotus, softens his Palace-standard accent now. But Rock's appeasing tones don't stop the tired, unwashed villagers emerging from their cottages from looking alarmed at the sight of us. It's the first really cold day this autumn, and many of those listening are hunched to keep warm, clothes too thin to keep out the chill from the winds that blow relentlessly across the flat, rippling plains of Callipolis's eastern lowlands.

As the collection starts, Rock shows me the map of the village and explains how much we should expect of different crops by acreage. I remember my father explaining similar things to my brother, with similar maps, though I never paid attention then.

As the villagers make their contributions to the collections carts, Rock stands next to me and offers insights in a low voice. Who doesn't believe us, what they're holding back. Who we'll have to deal with later.

Deal with: the ambiguous phrase that Rock uses so matter-of-factly, but that I realize, with freezing blood, will be the part of this job that I've read about for years, *smelled* the results of on my father, and that Pallor and I are about to perform ourselves. *Deal with*.

"This village, they're being a little sneaky," Rock mutters finally. "We were hoping word would spread after yesterday's crackdowns, but I guess this one is pretty far from the villages we visited yesterday. Also, we're on Skyfish land."

I'm surprised Rock even knows.

"Meaning?"

"Meaning, Stormscourge villages know the drill. The Skyfish lords were more lenient when it came to crop taxes. All right, let's get this over with."

He shows me the map again, makes me tell him who's short-changed us so far. In another life, these would have been the exercises I'd have done with my father, and while we talk about it, I appreciate, with a kind of numb fascination, how *calmly* Rock and I are able to discuss this, these sterile words *deal with* and *shortchange*, divorced from the practice, legendary for its terror, that I'm about to perform in their name—

"Good," Rock says, after I give him my estimates. "And now we pick somebody."

He talks me through it beforehand, so I can carry out the entire procedure without asking him what to do. I recite it back to him with numb lips, and though I know I'm projecting the kind of confidence I've had years to practice faking, Rock seems to sense the truth. His deep voice softens as he impresses, a final time, the most important thing.

"Two to three seconds, Lee. Then you douse."

For a moment the protest sits on the tip of my tongue, as I stare back at Rock's wide face and kindly eyes, so clearly full of sympathy: *I can't do this.* But who is there to say it to? Rock, whom I outrank and must lead in resolve? Atreus, who gave me this order? Callipolis, whose citizens will depend on this food for winter?

No. There's no one to hear my protest, and there's no one to do this in my stead. Which means it can't be said, and must be done, and I must do it.

We walk a guilty farmer back to his house, kick around in the weeds until we find a hidden cellar, open it up. Then we bring him back to the square, make sure all his neighbors are present, and I give the order to Pallor.

A little later, we're standing to the side and watching as wagons are loaded with what wasn't offered on the first try. My heart is still hammering from the sounds of the man's shrieking. He's been carried away, his burns to be tended in one of the neighboring homes with salves that—I appreciate this with only more horror—we, on behalf of the Callipolan ministry, have brought and offered.

As if this somehow makes us better than the dragonlords from the old regime, who left burned serfs to their fates.

Pallor nudges my hand, like he can tell something is wrong, and I reach behind to rub his neck absently, warming my palm on his hide. It's clear that he shares none of my disquiet about what just happened, and even though I know it's not in his nature, I can't help wishing he did.

Rock, standing beside me, finally speaks. "I just keep thinking—I feel like a Stormscourge."

I remember Annie, falling apart in the washroom yesterday, and know that must have been her thought, too.

We're all thinking it.

"This was how . . . they did it?"

How *he* did it, is what I want to ask. But Rock wasn't from the Far Highlands; he would have had a different lord, though their methods would have been similar enough.

"Yeah."

I reflect that, even dead, with a revolution between us, my father has left a trail behind him such that I can still be trained in his methods, a degree removed, by the same people who suffered under them.

Trained to repeat them.

You believe his regime is better than what came before? Julia asked. *Wake up.*

But surely this is different, surely this crisis, our need, justifies what looks so terrifyingly like a repetition of past wrongs . . .

Rock rouses me from my thoughts. "Lee, you're in charge of the schedules, right?"

I nod.

"Do you think you could—make sure we don't have to do our own villages? I can do Annie's. And she can do mine. I just don't think I can . . ."

He trails off, as though he's a little frightened by his own request, and I recognize the look: the one people have when they want something from Goran badly enough to beg for it, but don't want him to realize.

"Of course," I say.

"Thanks," Rock says. Relief floods his voice, along with shame, and he turns away from me.

* * *

It's three days after the Medean attack when my schedule overlaps with Crissa's again. We share a meal in the refectory when she's getting off and I'm on my way out. I've been stewing in the horror of collections and the nightmares that follow them so deeply that it's a surprise—almost a relief—to rouse from them for a little while in concern for another's grief.

"How are you doing?" I ask.

Her eyes are sunk deep with bruises beneath them, her habitual smile gone. Even so, I note irrelevantly, she's beautiful, the flush of the Medean sun warming her cheeks and lips. She lifts both shoulders, spreading her fingers on the table.

"I've been keeping busy. It helps. I'm just . . . I'm really worried about my mum."

By now, lists of lost vessels have been drawn up; Crissa's father's went down under Stormscourge fire. But we've been stretched too thin, with collections, for Crissa to be allowed leave. She hasn't been home since the news.

"I'm sorry. I'll make sure they approve your leave as soon as we can spare it—"

"I know. Thank you."

She looks up at me. Her voice is quiet, but it doesn't hide her feeling.

"What was it like for you, after?"

The corps has always been pretty good about not asking this sort of thing, so I don't have an answer prepared. I think about it and then find myself telling her the truth.

"I didn't speak for months."

Crissa raises her eyebrows, like she isn't sure if I'm joking. When she decides I'm not, she says, "Oh."

"You're doing really well."

By the end of the week, scheduling has become a calculation of the riders' limits. Who can stay awake for another back-to-back shift, who can do with a little less sleep, who can keep their cool for just one more collection. The brunt of duties falls on the sparked aurelian and stormscourge riders; and then on the ones who can handle even more.

Which means I've begun scheduling shifts for myself, Annie, and Rock back to back. Neither of them questions it, and when the fatigue sets in, neither complains. The first indication that something is wrong comes not from Annie, but from Duck. He finds me in the spare classroom that I've been using as an office and eases onto the edge of the chair across the desk from me.

"So you know how Annie used to not . . . sleep? When we were kids? Just do homework all night?"

It was a strategy she used for avoiding nightmares. I found out about it because, when we were in Albans and too young to be embarrassed by such conversations, she suggested I try it, too.

"She's started . . . doing it again, I think. Not sleeping. No one's seen her sleep since the attack."

I feel like my insides are shrinking as they tighten. I've got Annie doing two, sometimes three collections a day, usually patrols after that; the days are long, grueling, and leave you ill with exhaustion. They are only barely doable on the allotted time I've given her to sleep here and there. But if she's refusing even that—

"I was just wondering," Duck goes on, squinting at the desk, "if you could maybe ease up on her . . . a bit? Take her off some of the collections?"

I remember Annie staring down the general as he attempted to dissuade her from this assignment, telling him in a tone of steel that she would *do what it takes.*

"This was her choice, Duck."

Duck's square jaw is clenched, twitching. "It's your call, too."

When the words weigh on me and I don't answer, he adds: "Surely it doesn't matter that much who—"

I shake my head, clearing it. "It does."

Duck's voice begins to strain. "Does it?"

"She and Rock are getting better results than anyone else. We need her out there."

But the numbers don't seem to make an impression on him. "Lee, it's horrible for her," he says. His voice has started to shake. "Come on. You know how her family—"

My patience snaps.

"I am aware of what happened to Annie's family."

For a second we stare at each other. I hold my face rigid, impassive; Duck looks so furious that for a moment, I wonder if he's going to hit me. I also wonder if I'll hit him back.

"Let me help you understand," I say slowly. "Callipolis lost almost everything in the attack. We won't have enough to make it through the winter, even if the collections go perfectly. People are going to starve. Right now it's just a matter of how many. Every bushel Annie extracts, every wagon she sends back to the depot, means we'll be able to spread resources further. We're talking lives, Duck. Your mother's, your brothers' and sisters'. With stakes like that, we can't afford to think about Annie's feelings."

By the end, I know that I've won. All the same, my insides are knotted, riddled with the thought of Annie—not this Annie, but the one from before, the child-Annie who used to let me take care of her—leaning close to whisper: *Sometimes when the nightmares get really bad, I just don't sleep. It's okay, really. You just get a little tired during the day—*

"Could you maybe just," Duck says, hoarse, "give me a few hours off at the same time as her, Lee? I haven't . . . I haven't seen her since it started. Maybe I could convince her—"

I've gone hoarse, too.

"Of course."

ANNIE

I'm emerging from the washroom when I hear a knock on the dorm room door.

"Who is it?"

"Me," Duck's voice says. "Can I come in?"

I've been able to avoid Duck all week without even trying, but there seems no good way to avoid him now. I open the door and am torn between wanting to pull him to me and slamming the door closed in his face.

"What do you want?"

"We've both got the afternoon off."

I turn away from him, take my towel back up, and resume scrunching water out of my hair. I've been bathing for at least a half hour, scrubbing every inch of myself until it hurt. It's late afternoon; the room is warm from accumulated sunlight. "You want me to do what, go for a walk with you? Enjoy the changing leaves?"

Duck's voice is soft, calm. "Of course not."

I've gone still, the towel bunched in my hair, staring at the contents of my dresser trays, unable to turn to him, though suddenly it's the only thing I want to do. And then he's taken a step closer and said my name, and I've spun toward him and he's wrapped his arms around me. The pressure that's been building in my throat and eyes mounts and reaches the breaking point.

"I'm sorry—"

He holds me, not speaking. It feels good, unutterably good, to have his arms around me. My face against his chest, my head cupped by his hand. As though he's holding me together so that I can fall apart. It's the first time we've embraced since the night of the Lycean Ball.

"Duck, I'm sorry," I blurt out. "I'm sorry—that night—I never wanted to hurt you—"

Duck's arms around me have gone very still.

"You're talking about the Lycean Ball?"

I nod, mortified. Duck inhales, then shakes his head.

"That doesn't matter right now, Annie. And you shouldn't *apologize* for it. Ever."

He speaks so forcefully, with such assurance, that it almost disguises the way his voice strains. But I'm too tired to focus on that. I sink deeper into his arms, squeeze my eyes shut, and will the world out. The dorm, the rows of crisply made beds and desks cluttered with the schoolwork of forgotten classes fade to nothing as I close my eyes.

337

But then that *smell* comes back.

"Can you smell it?" I whisper.

Duck's arms tighten around me. "Smell what?"

"Dragonfire. I smell like dragonfire. Even after I bathe. It's there when I eat and when I sleep and when . . ."

The words are spilling out like they're coming of their own accord. Duck makes a murmured noise of comfort, and there is pain in his voice, matching mine. Then he pulls away from me just enough to look me over, his tan face crinkled at the corner of his eyes with worry.

"Annie," he says, "you need to sleep."

When he takes my hand and pulls me toward my bed, I let him.

He tosses my discarded flamesuit to the floor and pulls down the covers, and after I get into bed he pulls the blanket over me, like he's tucking me in. And then he crawls onto the bed next to me, atop the covers. The blanket separating our bodies a message that is clear, if unspoken: *I'm here as your friend, and nothing else.*

Of all the ways Duck has ever been sweet to me, this is the gesture that seems sweetest of all, and that makes my eyes fill all over again. I curl closer, rest my head against his chest, and breathe in the smell of salt air, lingering from Duck's last sea patrol. It's the first reprieve from dragonfire I've had in hours.

"It's almost over, Annie," he murmurs, wrapping an arm over my shoulder. My face buried against him, my wet hair dampening his uniform, I feel the words rumble through his chest. I've calmed, by now, enough to let out a dull laugh.

"It's just begun," I answer. Can't he see that? "This is all there is. We're monsters, even if they call us something else."

Duck's breathing shifts. For a moment, its ragged rise and fall is all I hear. The arm he has draped over me shifts, as if, where I couldn't see, he's just reached up to wipe his eyes. But when he speaks, his voice remains steady.

"Did I ever tell you the story my mother used to tell us, of the time old Aron tricked the sun into lending him its fire?"

He's adopted the low murmur I remember him using at bedtime with his siblings, and already I can feel my shoulders loosening, my breath lengthening. I shake my head.

"Well then," Duck murmurs. "Listen closely."

15

THE LAST LETTER

LEE

There are a few days of relative calm after collections are finished. Inventories are being finalized in the depots, and in the meantime, aside from guarding the coastline, all we have to do is wait. Crissa secures leave to go home, an exception made to the usual proscription against traveling by dragon for personal reasons. Duck persuades Annie to go out to sea with him for a few patrols, and she returns looking the better for it. I catch up on sleep.

Then, for a second time, Annie and I are summoned to the Inner Palace, this time with Cor and Power. Now that we've taken stock, called in debts, and borrowed what we could, it's time to look at how distribution will work. Those sitting at the table are the same as last time, with an addition: Callipolis's chief physician is present, and the meeting begins with his presentation.

The physician describes the project he's been working on over the past week: finalizing a formula to predict survival rates based on ration amounts, fitted to the population of Callipolis. All of this seems fairly straightforward, until the physician explains the further way in which his formula works.

"As requested by the Council," he says, looking uncomfortable for the first time, "it can be broken down into—categories."

He rolls back a sheet of paper on the board he's been working on, and four numbers appear. If they were summed up, they look as though they would fit the population of Callipolis. But the smallest number is barely a tenth of the sum, and the largest is about half. I realize what they signify about the same time Annie does; next to me, she inhales sharply.

"This is the population of Callipolis broken down by class metal," the physician says, now looking decidedly hesitant.

Cor, who has been sitting on my other side taking notes until this point, freezes. His pen, poised on the next line, begins to bleed ink onto his notebook. Power glances at him and then past him, at me. Like he's challenging me.

The physician continues to explain, his voice becoming hoarse.

"Class Gold, the smallest, followed by Bronze and Silver at roughly twenty-five percent each, and then the Iron population rounding out at around forty. It's a foregone conclusion that full rations for all members of Callipolis, for the whole winter, will be untenable. And if resources are spread equally, the survival rates will be . . . undesirable. However, if *variation* in ration size is permitted, the figures change."

Atreus prompts coolly: "In other words, if some are given more food than others?"

"Yes. Large numbers of people can be saved . . . and heaviest losses can be contained within certain populations."

Certain populations.

I feel the horror of it rising like a tide, until I have to crane my neck to stay above it and breathe deep. No, no, surely I misunderstand—

Surely they're not going to base ration amounts on the *metals test—*

Surely we didn't just spend two weeks shaking down village after village for their harvests only to serve this further horror—

But though the faces around the table are grim, they show little sign of surprise. Only Power, Cor, Annie, and I, it seems, were not prepared. Atreus is particularly calm. "And what would those losses look like?"

The pen in Cor's hand is beginning to puncture his notebook.

"Well," the physician says, wiping his forehead. "That depends on how you adjust the numbers."

He flips to the next page. On it, at the top, his formula is written out, and below it, different numbers are plugged in. Power's expression is slowly filling with something like delight, while Cor remains frozen, staring at the inkblot spreading from his pen. Annie's hand begins to speed across her notebook as she copies the formula down.

"Here are a few of the proposed solutions."

The first gives full rations to classes Gold, Bronze, and Silver, and only one-eighth rations to Iron—for every full meal a Gold would be given, an Iron would be given an eighth the amount of food. Such distribution predicts survival rate for class-irons at around fifty percent.

"Less than ideal," Atreus observes, in the same calm voice.

"As thought I," says the physician, looking relieved. "As per your—aforementioned priorities—I have calculated a few other scenarios . . ."

He shows the second proposal, with Bronze and Silver receiving slightly less than full rations, Gold still at full rations, and Iron bumped up to quarter rations. Atreus dislikes this one, too, so the physician keeps showing him lower ration levels for Bronze and Silver, at eighty and then seventy percent of full fare, but even there the survival rate for the Iron class gets only up to around seventy percent.

Which looks *better* until you start doing that math: the number of weak and sick and young and elderly of the Iron population who would not be able to survive on such small fare.

But then the pull of the logic takes hold, even as it makes me feel ill with myself:

If losses are inevitable, where would it be better for them to occur? From skilled labor, upon whose farmers and craftsmen we rely? From the military, whose defense we need in a time of crisis? From the Gold elite, who govern our country?

Unskilled laborers—service workers, textiles and smelting, mining, quarrying—these would be the easiest workers to replace, the least-skilled contributors to lose—

No, no, *no*—I've had rounds among Iron workers, interviewed them privately to make sure they were well-treated, spent years attending their welfare, *Cor's sister* is an Iron worker—

I don't want these thoughts. I don't want to be weighing these choices. I don't want this *logic*—

Holmes speaks. "My soldiers need to eat, Atreus."

Atreus frowns, considering, and then nods. "Bring Silver back up," he tells the physician.

Which pushes the survival rate of Iron down again.

Cor clears his throat and murmurs, "Excuse me."

For a moment, I think he has something to say, but then I realize he's pushing back his chair to leave the room. Power's eyes follow him, lit with amusement; Atreus watches his departure impassively. Then he tells the physician, as though there were no interruption, "Bronze should also be as functional as possible. We can't afford to go below two-thirds."

Annie silently pushes her notebook toward me, on which, below the formula, she has scribbled the word *Gold?* For a second longer we look at each other, and I wonder whether my face has gone as white as hers.

I nod, because I had been thinking it, too. She stares at me, hard, like she's daring me to say it. I give in, turn to the physician, and ask, "Why is Class Gold at full rations?"

The physician glances at Atreus, and in the second that he does, I notice the gold wristband glinting on his arm. Around the room, others are shifting uncomfortably, glancing at each other. We're all Gold here, except for Holmes.

"The First Protector requested that we ensure maximum survival rate for Class Gold," the physician tells me. He looks embarrassed, but determined nonetheless, like this is one part of the plan he backs wholeheartedly. "They are, after all, the nation's most valuable citizens."

Annie speaks up, her voice quiet. "Surely they don't need *full* rations. Their work isn't usually physical, is it?"

The physician stares at her, like he doesn't quite believe a second underage person is volunteering out of turn. "Well, that varies by individual, but—"

"Lo Teiran does not need a full stomach to write poetry," I point out.

The physician is scowling at the two of us, like we're being smart-asses, but he seems unwilling to call us out on it. After all, as far as anyone here knows, Annie and I were poor and close to starving during the last famine—unlike any of them. This fact alone seems to lend legitimacy to our criticism. The physician looks at Atreus, as if asking him to speak for the class-golds, but Atreus does not. He and I are staring at each other.

"There are so few class-golds," the physician says, "it hardly makes a difference what they get. Statistically."

Atreus drops his eyes from mine. "Lower Gold to eighty percent full-ration fare and reset that as the baseline."

The physician swallows and nods.

We take a break around noon, though Atreus doesn't say what the break is for, as if the word *lunch* would be indecent to utter right now. For the last hour, the numbers have been fiddled with, manipulated, haggled over like a deal at the market.

Annie and I don't discuss where we're going when we leave the Council Room, but we seem to have one mind as we take the fastest route out of the Inner Palace. Outside, I exhale the breath I've been half holding and Annie puts her hands over her mouth. Then she screams aloud. It's muffled against her hand, and it only goes on for about two seconds, but it still makes me aware of open windows around us.

"Come on," I say, grabbing her by the arm.

I lead the way down the arcade, into the next courtyard that opens onto the Hall of Plenty. The leaves on the oaks have turned; the empty courtyard bursts with color. The sky hangs heavy with stratocumulus and the smell of coming rain.

"Did you know?" she asks me, spinning to face me when she sees that we're alone.

"No. But I should have."

It seems, now that I know, that I should have known all along. Of course there was more to the metals test than a free ride up the social ladder. After the thousands of ways I've seen the state act against Iron workers—in pay and labor and rights and information—should I really be surprised we came to this in the end?

Julia's words from our last meeting: *You believe his regime is better than what came before, just because it calls serfs by another name and teaches them to read?*

"I should have, too," Annie says.

This is what it was all for. These last two weeks of hell, of providing the muscle the state required, the dragonfire, the *traditional methods*—this was what we did it for. To give Silver three-quarters of Gold rations, Bronze half, and Iron a fourth.

Power has caught up with us, hands thrust deep in his uniform pockets. He takes in our faces and smiles.

"Good day to be Gold," he remarks.

Annie looks past him and points past me across the courtyard: "Cor."

He's hunched amid the fallen leaves at the base of a tree. His face has turned in our direction, but he makes no move to rise.

"Didn't his sister test Iron?" Power asks, with that same idle amusement.

Annie pushes past him, then cuts across the leaf-strewn grass toward Cor. After hesitating for only a moment, I follow. I'm pretty sure Cor doesn't want to talk to us, but I want to be in Power's company even less.

"She'll be okay, Cor," Annie says without preamble, when she reaches him. "We'll make sure of it."

"No offense, Annie," Cor says, sounding tired and not looking up from his knees, "but piss off."

For a second, nobody says anything.

He raises his eyes to us. "Neither of you even questioned it."

Annie glances at me, a mixture of confusion and shame on her face.

"It must be nice, not having a family," Cor goes on. He gets to his feet, brushing dried leaves off his hands, turning away. "Bet it makes this job a lot easier."

Annie seizes Cor by the arm. "Don't do this. You know I care about your family, they're the closest—"

But she seems too angry, or too embarrassed, to finish the sentence, and she gulps and stops. Then she just stands there, the line of her mouth rippling, as she holds his arm.

Cor's eyes travel down to her hand on his arm and he sneers. "You *care* about them? So that's what it looks like for you, caring about someone—assigning them a percentage chance of survival based on their *wristband*—"

"It's not like that," Annie says, and now she's starting to lose control of her voice. "It's not personal, it's—it's objective, it has to be, it has nothing to do with who you know—"

"And objectively, unskilled laborers don't deserve to live as much as everybody else. I get it, Annie."

Cor takes a step back, so her hand falls from him, and then he turns from us and walks away. The fallen leaves crunch beneath his feet as he goes.

Annie puts the hand up to her face and drags it angrily across her eyes.

"Did you question it?" she asks, without looking at me.

I shake my head. No.

I revolted at it. But I didn't *question* it.

And that difference is enough to make me want to crawl out of my own skin in horror.

"I didn't either," she whispers. "What does that make us, Lee?"

"Realistic," I hear myself say. "It's the best option. For the island as a whole. Unskilled labor is easier to replace."

"That was my thought, too," she says.

But she, too, seems horrified by this fact.

"Because it's the truth." My voice is hardening to shake her out of her doubt. "Most people might be too—soft or illogical—to admit it. But the truth is, we can afford to lose unskilled laborers. We can't afford to lose warriors or farmers."

I watch her close her eyes, watch her let the words sink in, and though her face is twisting like she's in pain, I know they're hitting home. And it leaves me wondering, just as it did after my interview with Duck, at this ability I seem to have, of convincing others of things I can no longer convince myself.

Though on some level, I think, Annie must want it. She must still be holding out hope that we're doing good, that we're an improvement, that Atreus is still right.

Of these things, I realize I'm no longer sure. During the second half of the day, we discuss how we'll hide the fact that each class metal gets different ration portions. We discuss how we'll publicize and lie about what we're doing, so the truth never grows to anything stronger than a rumor. And through these discussions, I sit in silence and puzzle over the same doubts I was so determined to cure Annie of.

Because even though the logic adds up, the calculation still feels *wrong*.

I think back over the last two weeks, of Rock's ashen face, of Annie's weeping after her first collection, of the cries of guilty farmers as flames caught and burned. I look around the room, at the stony faces of people who have taken it upon themselves to decide who deserves to live and die. Rock's voice echoes in my head: *I feel like a Stormscourge.*

I can't shake the suspicion that he's right. We're coercing food out of farmers with the same threats of dragonfire. We're about to endure another famine in which most of the people who die will be very poor. We'll lie about it, just as the dragonlords did. After that, are there differences? Do the justifications for our choices matter to those who starve?

For years I've told myself, if not always that the old regime was in the wrong, at least that Atreus is in the right. That his system is fair and good, that he has a plan worth following. Wasn't that the point? Just as Atreus once told us: *You only deserve this mantle as long as you can be more reasonable and more virtuous than what came before.*

I realize I'm no longer sure we are.

Julia's prediction, come full circle: *Watch and see how that vision will splinter, and then we will see whether you have the stomach for more.*

* * *

Back in the Cloister that evening, I head to the classroom I've been using as an office. There are memos from the ministry to process and schedules to write for riders accompanying rationing distribution. For the next few hours I'm virtually undisturbed; The only visitor is Power, who ducks his head in to ask for his patrol schedule. He never knocks.

"I'm working on it. I'll get it to you by tomorrow."

It's quiet for another hour. And then there's a soft knock on the door. A servant I don't recognize approaches my desk and hands me a note.

"A message, my lord."

"Thank you."

She's gone before I even register the title.

By the time I've risen and gone into the corridor, she's already turned the corner and vanished.

I lock the door with shaking fingers before returning to my desk.

The note is sealed with unmarked wax. It is written, of course, in Dragontongue, in the hand that I recognize.

> *Do you still think Atreus's regime is worth fighting for?*
>
> *We are Firstriders for opposing fleets. If you continue down the path you've chosen, there will be no forgiveness between us, only fire and death.*
>
> *One more chance: I will wait for you at the Riversource of the Fer, at sunrise, on the first day of the coming month.*
>
> *Maybe you can't betray them. But you can still come home.*

ANNIE

It's late after dinner when there's a knock on the dorm room door. It's a loud, hammering sound, like the person on the other side is slamming a fist, maybe an entire arm against the door. Crissa, who's closest to the door, opens it to find Lee.

He's drenched, rainwater dripping down his face and pooling between his boots, and he's wearing a flamesuit, as though he just got off Pallor and came here without changing. But that's not how I know something is wrong. It's his face: wild and lost and desperate.

Crissa bites her lip, and I know she's thinking he must be like this because of today's meetings, which I've just finished telling her about. She thinks he's upset about the figures, so callously calculated. But I'm certain that Lee is stronger than that, and this must be something more.

"Lee, what's wrong?" Crissa says, her hand still on the handle of the opened door.

He stares at her for a moment, like he can't even remember who she is, and then he croaks, "Annie. Annie, I need to speak to you."

I get to my feet. Crissa looks from him to me and says, simply and with dignity, "Of course."

He seems vaguely consternated as she leaves us, as though he hadn't meant his last demand to come out as a request for her to leave so much as a summons for me. But he's too distracted to bother correcting it, so he allows Crissa to sweep past him and then he steps into the room. Crissa closes the door behind her.

"What is it, Lee?"

Even as I say it, something in me already knows.

He takes a breath. His face contorts like he's in pain. And then he breaks the most important rule.

LEE

I'm on Pallor for hours. I circle the city, the outlying fields, pass over the villages whose food we've gathered. And then I take him south to the coast, past Harbortown, to the sea. The clouds are low and full over the Medean, but as the sun sets, it pierces through them along the horizon, doubled in the waves. And then the rain starts.

I watch, but I don't really see. The dam has broken again, the memories flash in a feverish, unrelenting storm: my sisters on Palace Day; my father's voice in clumsy, panicked Callish; Tyndale's bitter challenges. *I didn't sell out. I believe in Atreus.* The sound of men screaming as I set their clothes on fire. The numbers on the board, the percentages, the predicted deaths.

You can still come home.

And after hours of this, it's not so much a decision as an admission of defeat that I go to Annie.

She waits in the center of the empty dorm room, quiet and unassuming and trusting. Her bobbed hair accentuates her slender neck, her folded arms hug her sleeping smock close to her narrow frame. Dressed for bed, she looks more like the orphan I remember than the dragonrider I train with. We stand five feet apart.

"Your family," I say.

She sucks in a breath. We haven't talked about her family since our fight at Albans. It's too late now to go back, though, so I say it properly. Every word feels like another step down the plank.

"I need to know how they died."

"You know how they died," she whispers.

"I need to hear you say it. All of it."

The empty room, its rows of beds and desks, is so quiet that I can hear her breathing. When she answers, I hear no surprise in her voice. Only resignation. As if, on some level, she has been waiting for this, and is ready.

"All right."

The next question feels like a request for my own execution.

"Can you show me?"

She doesn't seem to have expected this. Her arms unfold, then refold, over her smock, as she swallows. "Yes. When do you . . . ?"

"As soon as possible."

"Well, you write the schedules."

"Tomorrow morning?"

"All right," says Annie, her voice faint. "Tomorrow morning."

16

—

HOLBIN HILL

LEE

It's still dark when we suit up. Annie's face is pale, with bruises under her eyes that she keeps rubbing, as if she slept as poorly as I did. We don't speak. In the air, Annie flies ahead of us, hugging close to Aela's back. It's quiet and clean after last night's storm, but the temperature has dropped, leaving the first bitter cold of winter in its wake. We land north of Annie's village, in a sheltered rock alcove farther up the mountainside where Pallor and Aela can rest, hidden and undisturbed, during our visit.

It's a half-hour walk down the sloping pastures to Annie's farm. As we walk, the sky turns gray, grows pink in the east, illuminating a highland skyline that I remember from my childhood—especially the distant, seaside peak on which lies the estate that once, before the Revolution, was my family's home. Farhall, seat of the Drakarch of the Far Highlands. Though Holbin is miles inland from the manor where I was born, the biting winds, the smell of heather, the fiercely sloping fields are the same as I remember.

And Annie remembers them, too. She picks her way through

the rocks and weeds nimbly, barely slowing, mindless of the winds that buffet strands of her cropped hair across her face. I stumble after her. She stops at last beside a magnificently gnarled oak, her fingers fitting into its crevices with the familiarity of old acquaintance as she rests her hand on it.

"It's down there," she says, nodding to the clearing below us. There's a small footpath, mostly overgrown, leading down to it. I look and see nothing but clumps of bushes, gnarled trees, weeds. Farther on, smoke is rising from the chimneys of the other homes of Holbin. Annie surveys all this and inhales slowly.

"I haven't been back since it happened," she says.

I have never been so hesitant of every word I say. "We can take it slowly. Do you want to sit here for a minute or two?"

She nods. I start to sit where I'm standing and then I feel her hand on my arm, the touch light, hesitant. "There's a good spot over here," she murmurs.

She tugs me over the roots, to a place closer to the trunk where one of the oldest, most prominent roots forms a kind of ledge. It's smoother than the other parts of the tree, like it's been the bench of many people before.

"It's a good place to sit," she says. "I used to come here with my sister."

"You had a sister?"

Annie's eyes dart to me, then back out over the sloping fields. "Two. And—three brothers."

I ask her for their names.

Annie grips the knees of her flamesuit at the question. I think of what it felt like, Tyndale and Julia pulling those names out of so many years of silence, the shock and the ache of it.

"Lila, Hettie," she says carefully. "My sisters. Hettie and I were closest, we always did chores together."

"How old—"

"Hettie was eight. Lila was twelve. My brothers were Rory and Garet. Rory was oldest—he was fifteen. He and Dad used to argue all the time. Garet was ten. And then the baby, he died before his naming."

"And your parents?" I prompt.

Annie squints away from me. "Silas," she says, her voice still careful. "And—"

Then she looks stricken.

For the first time, it occurs to me that her mother might have passed before Annie was old enough to know her given name. I hasten to backtrack, but before I can, she exhales a single word with sudden relief.

"Anthea."

She adds, with determination, like she is reciting it: "I have her hair."

When she speaks again, her voice has regained some of its strength.

"I can go down now."

She rises first and waits for me. Together we walk down the overgrown path, Annie pressing a hand against her cheek to hold her hair from her eyes. At the base, she looks around and swallows.

"It's here," she says. She points around us, and in the growing light I distinguish the foundations of a building emerging from the weeds. "There's not much left. The house—most of it burned down in the attack. And it's been years, it's overgrown now . . ."

Her voice is faint again. She turns away from me, then moves slowly toward the ruins like she's in a trance. She steps over the first row of bricks and says, "This was the front room . . ."

I step closer so I can see the rest of it more clearly, realize then how small her house was: Its entire floor plan would have fit into my family's vestibule.

"How many stories—?"

"One. And the outhouse was over there."

One fireplace, shared by the kitchen and the bedroom. One bedroom, which they shared. She shows me where the kitchen table used to be, where the beds were, where she slept with her sisters. It's all unrecognizable, this many years gone, whatever was left after the fire long rotted and devoured by vines. But Annie conjures up the furniture and habits of this house as if she can still see them. I'm struck by the reverence with which she describes a world that sounds pitifully poor.

After she's done walking me around the foundations, she turns to face me.

"Do you want to hear about the attack now?"

I shake my head. "Tell me about the Famine."

She nods, and I sense that she's gratified by the fact that I want to start there. "Come on," she says, turning from me.

About twenty yards from the remains of her house, she shows me a patch of land that looks, at first glance, like all the rest of the land around us. But then I notice the markers—wooden, not stone like those next to the Palace—planted side by side, one smaller than the other.

"Your mother and baby brother."

"You remember?"

"Of course . . ."

She tells me about the crops failing, the blight no one had ever seen before, the way her father tried to hide his panic after the tax. Then came winter, and during that winter she learned what it was like to be hungry. They ate things that weren't supposed to be food. She says it concisely like that, but I insist that she elaborate.

"I think we ate our dog," she says. "Dad said it wandered off, but I never believed that, there was meat on the table for the next week. My brothers tried dirt and got sick for a few days. I figured out how to . . ."

"How to what?"

"Worms," she says simply, her whole face glowing in humiliation.

The winter she's talking about, the first winter of the Famine, I only vaguely remember. There were fewer feasts than usual, and crop failure was the explanation offered when anyone complained.

"Anyway, Mum would have probably been all right, but she was pregnant again. Always, always hungry. It was horrible— so horrible—especially for Dad. When the baby finally came, it took a really, really long time, and she was just too weak. You could hear her, it went on for over a day. And then she went to sleep and . . . didn't wake up. The baby didn't live much longer before he passed, too."

By then it was springtime, new crops to plant, and the family pulled themselves together, though things were different now. Less laughter, more anger. Her father began to fixate on the fact that what little usable food their crops had produced had been taken by the dragonlords' tax. If they'd been able to keep what they had, his wife might have survived. As summer passed, the blight reared its head again. But this time, prepared by their last winter, the farmers of Holbin began to plan for the dragonlord's next visit.

By now, Annie's unlikely ability to read had manifested itself, and without the moderating influence of her mother to stop him, Annie's father began taking her to his meetings with the other villager leaders, and she listened as they planned their counter-moves to the palace decrees she read to them. Thus, when Leon Stormscourge visited their house in late autumn and accused Annie's father of conspiracy and withholding what was owed, Annie had no doubt of her father's guilt on both counts.

"Holbin was attacked twice," she says. "The first time was a warning. They knew my father was one of the ringleaders. The second came after the villagers still didn't meet quota. They set most of Holbin's buildings on fire. Then they took everything they could find, not just enough to cover the tax. I was living with another family by then, but after the second attack, they couldn't afford to feed me anymore, so they took me to Albans."

We're still by the graves, but she's staring down the hill at the village now. The sun has climbed over the horizon, enough so that the peaks of the mountains are glowing gold.

"And the first attack?" I prompt her.

Annie hesitates.

"Lee," she says softly, still staring out at the fields below us. "Are you sure you want to hear . . ."

I don't know if her hesitation to talk about it is for her sake or mine.

"I need to know."

She sounds distant, tired. "All right."

Annie leads me back to the house, then takes me about ten paces into what had been her front yard.

"This was where he stood."

She stops me, so I'm standing in the same place. She points behind me. "He'd dismounted from the dragon—it was waiting over there. And the soldiers, they were standing there, and there. We were over by the house. And Dad was talking to him. Here."

She stands about three feet from me, taking the place of her father. We face each other. And then Annie takes a breath and drops to her knees.

As a child, I watched countless people kneel before my father. But I think this is the first time I've ever really seen the act for what it is. A protest rises to my lips; my face begins to burn. But then Annie raises her eyes to mine, like she anticipates this, and at her look I fall silent. I asked her to show me, and this is what she wants me to see.

She lowers her head and remains kneeling for three long, measured breaths. I think she's counting them, just as I am. Her palms are flat against the grass as they support her weight. I stare down at her bowed head, the nape of her neck, her rigid back. It's a long moment. I have ample time to consider that, in another life, this is how we would have known each other.

Then Annie rises to her feet. A flush has crept into her face, matching mine. She continues her story as if there were no interruption. Her tone is relentless, as if now that she has begun, she's determined to get through it without stopping.

"My father must have been intimidated; he'd never spoken to one of the dragonborn before. This man, he seemed powerful, terrible and powerful. Like a god. Dad must have been frightened, too, because of the dragon. But he held his ground anyway. He was dignified. It couldn't have been easy, to be dignified while kneeling in front of someone like that.

"I couldn't hear a lot of what they said, and it was hard to understand Lord Leon's accent. But then Leon ordered the rest of us to go into the house. I knew something was wrong because Dad was crying. Leon asked Dad which was his favorite, which I didn't understand at first. Dad said he didn't have one. Then . . . my brother must have understood because he told me to walk toward the dragonlord, and I did, I didn't understand, not until it was too late—"

She sucks in a breath like she's running out of air.

"I wouldn't have gone if I'd understood, I didn't know—"

This is the refrain she must play for herself, on bad days and after nightmares; this is her refrain, and like mine, it is never enough.

"Annie," I say.

She locks her eyes on me and I know she's using this to pull herself back. When she speaks again, her voice is shaking.

"They made Dad go into the house with my brothers and sisters, and then the soldiers locked the door and went to guard the windows. They were quiet inside, Dad must have been keeping them calm. I still didn't understand. And then Leon turned to his dragon and said something in a different language, and the dragon fired."

She traces the path of the flame across the yard with a finger, so I can imagine it.

"I could feel the heat on my face, my arms. I watched the house catch fire and I started—asking—for him to stop it.

Because the soldiers had me standing here, right next to him."

She takes two steps closer to me and turns so that we're both facing the house. She's close enough to touch, barely inches from me.

"I started to hear—"

But she can't finish this sentence, and the panicked look has come back full force, like she can barely see anything but the things she's telling me. I make myself look at her, like this, take in the sight of Annie breaking apart.

"—I could smell—"

Her face convulses, and for a moment she trembles, facing away from me and toward the remains of the house. When she looks back at me, her face has set.

"I tried to look away. But he—" She reaches out and takes my hand in hers. Her eyes are fixed on mine. "He put his hand in my hair. Like this." She lifts my hand behind her head, places it on her streaming hair, and automatically my fingers clutch a handful. Her hair is soft, downy, like a child's. Her voice begins to lose control. "And he turned my head and made me watch until the screaming stopped."

I release her, abruptly, like holding her has burned me.

But the sight of it is seared into my vision, my hand gripping her hair like the scruff of an animal, like a dog whose face a trainer might force into its own excrement. She was small and weak and helpless in my hand.

Ruling came naturally to me, Leo.

"By the time he let me go, I was—upset. And he, he—" Annie inhales and then her voice, finally, breaks. "He comforted me. He held me and he comforted me."

I take a step back from her. Annie gets herself under control again, but barely. Then she says, "That's what happened, Lee," in the tone of an apology. "I'd like . . . I'd like a few minutes to myself, if that's all right."

"Of course," I manage.

I make my way up the hill, and as I start to move, I find I can't get away fast enough.

Which is your favorite. He comforted me. Lord Leon.

And the question that comes with it, since the orphanage, since the beginning, the agonized protest of betrayal that has no one alive to answer it, only memories of a man who was only ever kind and caring and my *father—*

How could you have done this?

I stop when I reach the oak again, and then I grab the trunk with one hand and double over, my stomach heaving as I gasp for air.

That's when I notice something glinting in one of the knots of the tree, deep down. I begin to work on retrieving it, with that single-minded kind of focus you only have when you're distracting yourself. My stomach calms, the gasps subside. I scrabble with my fingers, then prod with a twig.

When I get it out, I realize it's a woman's necklace, cheap and crude and rusted, and the nausea comes back. It would have been a lot better if Annie had found this, I realize. I do not want to be the one who gives it to her.

I look down the hill for the first time. She's kneeling, her head in her hands.

I busy myself with cleaning the necklace while I wait for her, not looking down the slope again. When she rejoins me fifteen minutes later, her eyes are bloodshot but she's wiped her face dry. I feel a moment of such tenderness for her, it hurts. My Annie, who doesn't cry in front of people.

She sits beside me, looking tired and drained, and silently I take her hand, turn it palm up, and place the necklace in it.

For a second she just looks at it. And then her whole body hunches, like all her muscles are tensing, like this is just one thing too much. I know from this that it must have belonged to her mother.

I wait for her to move, but she just sits there, paralyzed by a necklace so worthless that the women in my family would have thrown it away without a thought. Before I think about whether or not I should, I shift closer to her and take it back. I unclasp it and gently gather her hair into one hand so her neck is bare. She remains hunched forward, unmoving, while I fasten the necklace around her neck. I try to touch her as little as possible, but still my fingers brush against her skin, her hair, I can't help thinking that he too touched this neck, this hair—this beautiful hair, this delicate neck, this tiny creature, not tiny in the way women can be naturally, but tiny because when she was young, she was hungry—he touched her, and instead of recognizing her beauty he tore her apart.

She looks up at me when she realizes I've finished, and her face is wet.

"That bastard," I tell her.

After all these years, resisting it, avoiding it, I never thought it would feel like this. Good. Like I've been set free.

She swallows, wipes her face on her sleeve, and her fingers rise to touch the rusty chain around her neck. She tucks the pendant into her shirt.

"Thank you," she says simply. But she says it like she isn't just talking about the necklace, and she looks at me to make sure I understand.

I nod, because I cannot speak.

* * *

After that, we fall into silence. The wind cuts across us as we stare down at Holbin, at the skyline that holds, within it, the dragonlord's estate that I once called home. Though we could have moved apart, we're still sitting close together.

When she finally speaks, it's to ask the question I know she's been withholding. She sounds exhausted.

"What's going on, Lee?"

"They've . . . given me a final chance."

Annie processes this in silence for a moment.

"How?" she asks.

Meaning, now that she's turned in Tyndale.

"A servant I didn't recognize passed me a note."

I am reaching into my pocket for it as I say this, only to realize I don't have it. It was the first note from Julia that I didn't destroy immediately, because it was the first note I'd ever intended to show anyone else.

It's fine. It's in the office, and you always lock the door.

I push the rising worry from my mind.

"It said that even if I couldn't bring myself to, you know, bring Callipolis down from the inside . . . I could still just go home."

Annie swallows, hard.

I start to explain. "I've been telling them no for a while. Since—"

"Since we started having class with Tyndale," Annie realizes, her voice a murmur. "And you've been meeting with them, too?"

There seems no point in telling her anything but the whole truth.

"Just one of them. We've met twice. Once before the first attack. I was trying to dissuade her. And before . . . over Midsummer. I didn't mean to, I just . . ."

"You just missed them."

My throat tight, I nod. And then I struggle to explain.

"I've been telling myself it's not about that. I know it's not. There's so much more to it than whether Midsummer is hard, or whether Palace Day is—" I stop, because I can't think of a word to fittingly describe the depths. Then I say, "But it's gotten harder over these past few weeks."

"I know," Annie murmurs. "It's gotten harder for me, too."

I have been staring at my knees as I speak, but when she says this, I glance at her: Her profile is arrested, staring out over the glowing slopes of the highlands, her gaze unseeing.

"The thing that strikes me, now that I'm older, is that what happened to my family was . . . routine. All of it. I'm not the only child who survived a fire; there was a name for it. I was a *designated witness*. When it happened, Leon wasn't acting out of anger; he was completely calm. After all, he was just exercising his legal rights. Another day on the job, for a dragonlord."

Yes. Which leaves me to wonder which unremarkable night it must have been, when my father came home from one of his visits to our land holdings, smelling of the dragonfire that had just orphaned Annie.

"As much as I've hated doing collections these past two weeks," Annie goes on doggedly, "as much as I felt like a

Stormscourge—I also know it was nothing close to the worst of what they did. And so long as that's the case, this is the side you want to be on. Even if we're a little evil, we're still better than the evil they were, before."

The lesser of two evils. It's a far cry from what I hoped we'd be. And a far cry from what Annie once hoped for, as well.

I murmur, "Do you remember when you told me . . . that even if the people giving us dragons were bad, we wouldn't be?"

Annie smiles sadly.

"All the time," she says. "But . . . I also understand now that it's more complicated than that. The war's not over. When it is, maybe . . . there will be time to change the rules."

The sun has finally risen high enough for light to fall across us. The thinner wisps of Annie's hair are glowing as they blow around her face. Silence has fallen again. Annie seems to take it as a cue. She reaches into the pocket of her flamesuit, pulls out a piece of paper, and unfolds it on her knee. It's torn from the banned book about Palace Day, and the page she's flattening is the one with my family on it.

She folds the page in half, so that only the blurry black-and-white rendition of our portrait is visible, not the descriptions of their deaths underneath. Then she points at the youngest child in the picture.

"This was you?"

I nod.

I ask, "How long have you known?"

Annie's lips compress. "I've known you were dragonborn for almost as long as I can remember. The rest of it . . . I tried not to know for a long time."

I take the paper from her, press it on my own knee, and look down at my family. All six of us. My father, regal and careless. My mother beside him, her expression warm with pride, my hand held in her lap as I stand beside her; Laertes and Larissa, not an inch of difference in their heights, despite the years that separated them; Penelope, smiling from ear to ear, like she always did.

"You were with them, weren't you?" Annie says. "On Palace Day."

I nod again. I flatten the knees of my flamesuit, dredging the words up. Fighting the silence that overcame me like a brick wall as I sat with Julia, because I need Annie to understand that *I* understand.

"They made me watch, too."

As soon as I say it, I start to feel sick again.

The tips of Annie's fingers touch my knee, and remain there. "I'm sorry, Lee."

She sounds like she means it from the depths of her being. Like she really is sorry about what happened to us, no matter what my family did to hers first. I reach for something to say next and find myself still talking about *it*.

"Atreus is the reason I'm . . . He came in at the end. Saved me."

Annie's eyes widen. "So he *knows*—?"

I shake my head. "He doesn't. I used to hope he did, but he has no idea."

"But if he saw you that night, how could he not recognize . . . ?"

"I used to wonder, too," I say, "and now I think . . ." I grimace, knowing how this is going to sound. "That night, I think there was blood on my face."

Annie's fingers tighten on the leather of my flamesuit. I hand the clipping back to her, keeping my eyes on our hands, so I don't have to see her expression. She puts it in her pocket.

"And this . . . relative?" she asks, tentative now. "The one who's been contacting you?"

I nod. "Julia. Julia Stormscourge. My cousin. The one who left that ultimatum after Starved Rock."

A line has formed between Annie's brows that she smooths with her thumb. "I met her, I think. At the first tournament. She complimented my flying . . ."

After so much else that's passed, I feel barely surprised.

"She's been very persistent," I mutter.

"She must care about you."

"We were friends when we were little."

Annie's eyebrows draw together. "Is she highly ranked? In their fleet?"

She's hit upon the salient point surprisingly quickly, and though she's phrased it obliquely, the sense of the question is clear: *Will you have to face her?*

I let out a dull laugh and am unable to hide the pain in it.

Annie lets out a slow, half-whistled exhale. "Oh," she says, her voice filling with sadness. "Oh, Lee."

It doesn't make it any better, to know that she sees the choice for what it is, and that it fills her with sorrow to witness; but nevertheless it is, in its way, a balm to hear it marked aloud.

"We should be getting back," I murmur.

The walk to the dragons is quiet, drained. But it's the kind of drained that feels cleaner, cleared out. All the tension that I'm so used to feeling around Annie is gone. It was like the whine of a buzzing insect, low and continuous, the kind you forget even as it sets you on edge. Now that it's gone, I realize I must have lived with it for years.

Try as I might, I can't remember locking the office door at all.

17

—

ATONEMENT

ANNIE

Back at the Palace, we unsaddle Aela and Pallor in their nests, and walk together up the aurelian corridor of the caves. The entrance of the Firemouth glows distantly, several bending corridors out of sight, and torches light the way along the route. Though I remain empty of words, I find myself reaching for Lee's arm, wrapping my own inside it, and he returns the pressure.

And then we round a corner, and find Power and Darius waiting for us in the cave corridor's torchlight.

"Hello, *my lord*," Power says to Lee.

He's grinning from ear to ear, his eyes full of a cruel, frenetic energy that I associate with his spillovers.

For an instant the four of us stand frozen. And then we move. Lee and I raise our wrists to our mouths to summon; Darius launches himself at Lee, knocking his wrist aside before it can reach his mouth. Power has me on the ground in seconds; larger and stronger than me by half, it's easy for him to fold me over and twist my arms behind my back. I hear a soft click as he removes my wristband.

Three feet away, Lee struggles against Darius with an animal ferocity I haven't seen in him since Albans; Darius's grip on his summoning arm is loosening inch by inch as Lee pummels him with his free fist. Then Power speaks.

"Give him your wristband or I'll break her arm."

I'm not prepared for the sudden pain that shoots up my arm as he twists it, and I don't hold back the cry. Lee's eyes fly to my face. Though he's momentarily gotten the better of Darius, he freezes.

"Nothing personal, Annie," Power breathes in my ear. "For the sake of Callipolis, you understand." He raises his voice. "It'll be easy, Lee."

He twists harder; I inhale in spite of myself.

Lee releases Darius, unclasps his wristband, and holds it out. Darius snatches it.

"Hands behind your back."

Darius produces a length of rope, which he uses to tie Lee's hands together. When he's hauled Lee to kneeling on the cave floor, Darius takes a step back. Lee's jaw is clenched, his eyes staring so hard, they're white-rimmed.

"That's better. Trade, Darius."

I'm passed from one boy to the other like a sack of grain, then Power steps away when Darius has confirmed his grip on my arms. Power's eyes rake over Lee, kneeling before him with his hands bound.

"So. All these years. When I thought you were a self-satisfied, superior piece of shit—turns out I was onto something. Golden Boy is just a little too golden."

Lee's teeth are gritted. "Where is the letter?"

"Oh, I've got it. Ready to hand over along with you," Power says, smiling. "But we're in no rush to do that, Lee."

OSARIA MUNDA

Darius shifts, though his grip on my arms remains firm. "Power, I don't know if—"

"Scared to hit a dragonborn, Darius?"

I can feel Darius's swallow against the back of my head.

Lee's eyes flit from the faces of the two boys to me. His voice comes out a growl. "You want to stay down here hashing out schoolyard grudges, fine. But you have no grievances with Antigone; let her go."

Power lets out a delighted bark of laughter.

"So she can spill the beans to Atreus and cut our party short? I don't think so. And who says it's schoolyard grudges? Maybe I'm just feeling *patriotic*. Giving one last dragonborn what they should have got on Palace Day—"

Lee twitches. Power sees it and laughs again, softly. Then he demands, like the thought is of passing interest to him now that it occurs:

"Who are you, anyway?"

Lee's chest rises and falls with the sound of his breathing.

"Stormscourge, I'd say," Power goes on, his eyes narrowing as he studies Lee more carefully. "Must be, those eyes."

His gaze slides on to me, like a dragon tracking new prey. As if he senses my every nerve going on end at the sound of the truth exposed.

"And you've known it all along, you *lying, traitorous bitch*."

Lee flinches on the last word; Darius's arms tighten against mine to the point of pain, as if he's worried I'll be galvanized to make a renewed attempt for freedom.

"So who is he?" Power demands of me.

At my silence, Power nods to Darius, and Darius tightens

still further. And then the ratcheting pain in my arms trips into something else.

I can feel Aela.

She's almost out of reach; the aurelian nests are far down the corridor, and the cave walls are thick. But faintly, she is there. And her awareness is wakening to my pain.

Aela, please. Hear me. Come to us.

"Who is he?" Power says.

Lee's face has screwed up as he waits for the first blow.

I raise my chin, and though it sends renewed pain through my twisted arms, I plant my feet to straighten. Because these words will be not for Power but for Lee, and right now, it's all I have to give him.

"He is Lee sur Pallor, Firstrider of Callipolis."

Lee's eyes close, his breathing quiets, and his clenched jaw spasms as he swallows.

But it is my face, not Lee's, that Power watches. His smile becomes soft and cruel.

"Remind me of your dragonlord's name, Annie?" he whispers.

At my silence, the corridor stills. Darius's grip on me has gone slack.

"Leon, wasn't it."

Lee's eyes are still closed, like he's willing himself to shut everything happening out, but the ripple that goes through him is enough. Power's eyes glitter with a malicious mirth.

"Well, that's an interesting twist."

Aela, please—

Power turns from me, seizes Lee by his hair, then forces his head back.

"Tell me, Lee. Were they punished for it? The ones who were there *at the end*?"

Lee's eyes have snapped open. They fix, with hatred, on Power's face.

Power's smile grows. He leans forward, his mouth next to Lee's ear. "I thought not."

And then he slams his fist into Lee's gut.

Lee grunts. The force of the impact makes him lurch sideways. But before he can fall, Power seizes his shoulders, steadying him. Then he hits Lee again.

And again, and again. Lee begins to wheeze and splutter, not given enough time to breathe between blows—Power is laughing as he begins to pant from exertion—Lee dry-heaves—

Then, from above us, comes a blaze of light.

Aela.

Dragonfire fills the cavernous corridor, illuminating its soaring ceiling. The source of that fire is Aela, her wings outspread as she descends. She lands to my right.

Power freezes; I wrench myself free of Darius's slackened grip and he doesn't attempt to regain it.

My voice is shaking but strong.

"As Alterna of the Callipolan Fleet," I tell Power, "I command you to unhand Lee. Make a move to summon and Aela will fire on you where you stand."

As Power releases his grip on Lee's shoulders and Lee slumps, disoriented from pain, I catch him with one hand.

"The letter," I demand, from Power.

Power produces it and I pocket it, not taking my eyes off him.

"Wristbands."

They hand us back our own, and then I say: "And yours."

Power balks. "You can't be serious."

"For assaulting a fellow rider and a superior officer? For obstructing justice? I'll have both of you court-martialed."

"They're not going to court-martial us for mistreating a *dragonborn*," Power spits.

Aela bares her teeth and inhales, and Power decides not to argue further.

The bands click softly as they're unclasped; one by one, Power and Darius hand them over to me. I reach down, find the knot in the ropes binding Lee's hands, and yank it loose. I fit my own wristband back on my wrist, then Lee's on his. But he's still too winded to stand and remains on the ground, gasping as he leans against me. It's unnerving to feel the weight of his head, his shoulder, against my thigh.

I look down at this boy, vulnerable, at my mercy, and think, *To the ends of the earth I will protect you.*

"Lee," I murmur. "Tell me what you want me to do."

Tell me if you want to run.

My fingers are in his hair, feeling his shaking.

But his voice, when he speaks, is sure. The tone of someone issuing a final command.

"Take me to Atreus."

* * *

Aela escorts the four of us to the Palace entrance to the caves. I support Lee, my arm hooked tightly against his, Darius and Power in front of us. After we've left Aela and the caves behind, we make our way through the near-empty Cloister to the Inner Palace. In the anteroom of the Protector's office I turn to the two members of the crimson-clad Protector's Guard, stationed on either side of the door.

"Please ensure that Power and Darius do not leave this room."

Then I remove my arm from Lee's side, steady him as he sways, and hand him Julia's letter.

I follow him into Atreus's office.

Atreus is waiting, seated, at his desk. He takes in Lee's disheveled appearance and our harrowed faces. Even though Power and Darius landed no blows on exposed skin, the indications of a recent beating are apparent enough. Atreus straightens at once.

Lee crosses the office to the desk, his movements still a little stiff. He hands over the letter and stands silently while Atreus reads it. When Atreus looks up, his face rippling with confusion, Lee speaks. For the first time in my memory, he uses fluent, colloquial Dragontongue.

"I am Leon's youngest son. Ten years ago, you spared my life."

Atreus's eyes widen ever so slightly, then his expression smooths again. But the emotion that is left on his face is, unmistakably, pain.

Lee sees it, swallows, and plows forward.

"For the past few months, I've been in contact with my cousin, Julia Stormscourge, Firstrider of the Pythian Fleet, who has repeatedly sought my support for the Pythian cause. I have repeatedly refused her. You have in your hands our most recent correspondence."

Atreus's eyes flicker down to the note in his hands, then back to Lee.

"Why do you confess this?"

"To ask for mercy, and to plead my case."

* * *

I wait outside, in the anteroom with Power and Darius, while Lee tells Atreus the rest. Lee doesn't emerge until late morning. When he does, he speaks to me without acknowledging the presence of Darius or Power at all.

"I told him everything. He wants to question you now. I'll find you after—"

And then Lee looks down: One of the Protector's Guard has placed a hand on his arm. The arm with the summoning whistle on its wristband. Though the guard doesn't exert pressure, the gesture conveys a clear meaning.

Lee begins to shake again, this time violently. Looking at him, I find the memory of an old lesson from Callipolan history class returning to me, unbidden: that when, toward the end of the Red Month, the revolutionaries made their dragonlords hand over their summoning whistles, it was the beginning of the end.

We were always taught to think of that moment as a glorious turning point, but now I realize how differently Lee must remember it.

Lee unclasps his wristband and offers it to the guard. Power and Darius, seated across the room, look on avidly. The guard takes it, and his hand remains on Lee's arm.

"If you'll come with us, now," the guard says. And then he adds, more softly, as if some paternal urge overtakes him as he regards Lee's trembling: "It'll be all right, son. Just protocol."

Lee stands frozen for a moment. Then he raises his head to look at me.

What hollow comforts were they given, I wonder, when this happened ten years ago, that I will unwittingly echo if I give comfort now?

So instead, all I tell him is: "I'll find you as soon as I can."

Lee allows himself to be led away.

Power, sitting on the opposite side of the anteroom, catches my eye. "See?"

Instead of answering him, I raise my fist to knock on Atreus's door.

* * *

Atreus sits across from me, still and silent, while I speak. I start at the beginning, with the fact that Lee's father killed my family and that I've known about it for years. I tell him about Albans, everything I can remember, including the things Lee said that day we fought. He shows brief surprise, then, the faintest raised eyebrows, and they rise again when I describe our reconciliation.

I describe the months afterward, before the Choosing ceremony, when Lee took care of me—protecting me, feeding me, even holding me. The words come clumsily: I'm describing memories I've never discussed with anyone.

I tell him about our years in training, every detail I can think of to vouch for Lee's character. I speak of Lee's untiring efforts to coach the others, to keep Power in line, to prevent patrician kids from bullying lowborn riders, back when that was something anyone tried. I tell him about the care Lee has taken with his studies, the attention he pays to ideas of justice and virtue and all the things Atreus speaks about in class. The lines deepen around Atreus's mouth and he nods, as if he, too, has seen this.

I tell him that for the past few months, Lee has been solicited by his family repeatedly and has, at each turn, refused them.

And then I tell them about going to see Holbin Hill with Lee this morning, how he asked to go, how he told me about Julia's final offer, how in the caves we were confronted and assaulted by Power, and Lee asked not to be allowed the chance to run but rather to be brought to Atreus to make a confession.

Finally, I pull my mother's necklace out of the neck of my uniform, show it to Atreus, and explain how I got it. It feels like I'm undressing before him. Surprise shows on his face again. It is unclear if he is surprised more by what I am telling him, or by the fact that I'm telling it.

"Your account is as remarkable as Lee's," Atreus says. "He described something incredible, and you have confirmed it."

"He's loyal to you," I say. "He believes in you."

"I'm not sure it's me he believes in," Atreus says. "In any case, thank you."

As we rise, his tone becomes businesslike. "For the time being, please tell those who ask that Lee has been apprehended following charges of misconduct. Whatever more you choose to disclose to your fellow Guardians should remain within Cloister walls. Effective immediately, you are promoted to acting Firstrider and fleet commander."

A month ago, it would be a promotion I dreamed of, and a month before that, one I didn't dare to dream of. Today, it comes as a blow.

Acting, I reassure myself. *He said "acting."*

"What about Power and Darius?"

"I will speak with them next."

* * *

I set a meeting in the oration room for the evening, before dinner, where I'll debrief the corps. In the meantime, I cross-reference schedules, and at the hour I know everyone I need will be free, I round up the ones I'm most sure I can rely on: Crissa, Rock, Cor, Lotus, and Duck. In the classroom that's become the fleet commander's office—which I refuse to think of as mine—I tell them the full version of what happened, rather than the one I'll present to the corps later today. That Lee's been apprehended, that Power and Darius made an attempt at vigilante justice and are currently being questioned by Atreus, that Lee is in the stockade, because—

"Because Lee is the son of Leon Stormscourge," Rock repeats.

"Yes."

Here's where they've grown incredulous. But I'm determined to talk it through with the riders I rely on most. Not just for their loyalty to Lee: for their standing in the corps. And I want to give as much time as I can for them to grow accustomed to this truth.

"The *dragonlord* Leon Stormscourge?" Rock presses.

"Yes."

The office feels crowded with so many people inside it, the low ceiling beams even lower. I'm standing behind the desk, Lee's chair vacant beside me; the five of them are gathered in a loose ring around it, some leaning against the walls, some sitting. Rock sinks down into a chair, curses loudly and then, to my surprise, says, "This explains so much."

"What are you talking about?"

Rock's calloused hands open in a shrug. "He was always just so—"

"Good at everything?" Lotus suggests, from where he leans against the locked door, his arms folded.

"Yeah . . ."

Cor is hunched in the other chair, bent over his lap. He speaks for the first time since I've told them. "And now we know why."

I feel the beginnings of frustration prickle.

"Don't do this," I tell them. "Lee earned his place, just like the rest of us."

"Yeah," says Rock dubiously, "but it must have been—easier for him."

Although it's a thought I've been grappling with for years, I've no patience for it now. "It wasn't easier for him."

"Yeah, really? Name one thing that wasn't."

Crissa has been standing with her back partly turned to the group as she stares out the narrow window at the Cloister courtyard. "Palace Day," she murmurs.

Panes of glass cast small squares of light across her face. It takes the rest of them a moment to understand her meaning. Cor lifts his head. "He wasn't . . . ?"

I nod. "He was."

"Oh, dragons," says Cor quietly, placing his thumb and index finger against his forehead. "So all those nightmares— they were of—"

Cor's bed has been next to Lee's since we got here. It's the first time I've considered what that would mean. Cor's never spoken about it; none of the boys have. "Yes."

It's a moment before anyone speaks again. And then Lotus murmurs, "I always *thought* his Dragontongue was a little too good . . ."

It seems Lotus couldn't resist remarking this aloud. Crissa, still looking out the window, allows a watery smile, like she appreciates the moment of levity. Rock just snorts.

"*That's* what you're thinking about, of all things?" Rock puts his head in his hands and lets out a groan. "I just realized . . . I taught a Stormscourge how to do collections. Lee's uncle killed people I know."

A noise of impatience escapes me, and I realize immediately afterward I shouldn't have let it. It's enough to catch Rock's attention. He lifts his head from his hands and looks at me.

"No," he says. "*Leon*—that wasn't the one who—"

I nod.

"What's going on?" Lotus says, looking between Rock and me.

Crissa exhales slowly but sharply, so that it makes a small sound: like the realization she's made has caused her pain. Cor's eyes narrow, like he too understands. I look past them all to Duck. He has eased himself onto the floor, his back against the wall, his knees drawn to his chest. He alone of them all doesn't look surprised. I remember his expression, on Palace Day, as we listened to Lee vomiting and he asked nothing.

"Did you know?"

Duck stirs.

"I didn't . . . know, exactly. But you and him, you've always been a little strange around each other."

Crissa lets out an appreciative, shaky snort.

"That," she mutters, "is an understatement."

Her and Duck's eyes meet. For an unsettling moment, they exchange a flash of understanding. Then Crissa turns from the window to face me. The silhouette of her golden hair glows against the light.

"How long have you known?"

There is a certain relief in coming clean with her at last.

"Almost as long as I've known him," I tell her. "Stuff came up, at the orphanage . . ."

"He . . . told you?"

"No. It wasn't like that. There were just—things." I try to think of something other than the fight, or the fact that he used to ask for my help planning escapes to what I know, now, was New Pythos. "Like . . . he couldn't really speak Callish when I met him."

Rock lets fall an expletive. Cor's fingers reach up to clutch his hair.

"It didn't occur to you," says Lotus, "to report him?"

"I didn't think about it like that, I was just a kid . . ."

Rock says, "Let me get this straight. Lee is the son of Leon Stormscourge. *That* Leon Stormscourge. And you realized this. And it wasn't a problem for you?"

I shake my head. "It . . . couldn't be, not at the time." And then, knowing they need more, I take a breath and explain. "He took care of me. The other kids . . . He made sure they didn't take my food."

It's humiliating to admit this sort of thing to people I routinely beat in the air, and I can feel my shoulders draw together to confess it. I force them straight. If this keeps them on Lee's side, I'll say it.

Crissa's mouth is working like she wants to cry. Lotus clears his throat, uncomfortable. Rock scrutinizes me, his eyes narrowed. Cor's fingers continue to seize at his hair, his head still bowed. And Duck supplies, quietly, from the ground where he sits hugging his knees: "So you didn't think about it."

I nod. "I needed him."

Cor tears his hands from his hair and bursts out, "Dammit, Lee."

"And later?" Rock demands. "It didn't occur to you, later,

that him being a dragonrider wasn't a good idea for Callipolis?"

Cor has raised his head to look at me, too. As if he, like Rock, is demanding an answer. And I realize that after years of friendship, of trusting and following Lee, even Cor is on the verge of dismissing him now that he knows the truth about Lee's parentage. The realization fills me with fury.

"No," I say, "it didn't. Because there was never any reason to think it. And in the meantime, in case you've forgotten, he earned your trust, too. He was tutoring *you* after hours, Rock, so you wouldn't get punished for lagging behind. And he was helping *you* keep the patrician riders in line, Cor, in case you don't remember the stuff Goran was always turning a blind eye to. By the time Atreus made him squadron leader, he'd already started looking out for every single one of us."

I glare around at them. Even in the dim light of the single narrow window, I can see them struggling to find an objection.

"Look," says Cor finally. "You don't have to tell me Lee's a good person. But this . . . isn't about that."

"It seems like it's all it should be about," I say.

"It's not, Annie," Rock says quietly.

I round on him.

"Even good people don't get over things like Palace Day," he says. "That's just how it is."

"Right," Cor says, like Rock spoke for him.

"If people . . . if people did that sort of thing to my family . . ." Rock breathes in slowly, stares up at the wood-beamed ceiling, and clenches his fists. "I wouldn't forget it, ever."

Cor is nodding, grim-faced.

I think of this morning, of Lee's face when I showed him the picture of his family, the shutters closing behind his eyes. "He hasn't forgotten," I say. "But that doesn't mean he's plotting revenge, either."

I can tell from Cor's and Rock's expressions that they don't think this is even possible.

"Look, Annie," says Rock, and now he just sounds apologetic. "If that's not why he's here . . . then why is he?"

He means it as a rhetorical question.

But even as I understand this, and know that as far as Rock is concerned, Lee is already finished—I realize there's an answer. I don't think it's one Lee himself would make, and it isn't one I could ever put into words until this moment. But now that it comes to me, I am unshakably certain it is true.

"Atonement."

Cor and Rock look at each other, then back at me.

"Lee knows what his father was. What he did. He's known for as long as I have."

But Cor has only returned his head to his hands, and Rock's face has softened with what might be pity.

"Annie," he says, "even if that were the case . . . how could it ever be proved?"

* * *

The stockade is in the lowest level of the military wing of the Inner Palace, lining the arena, where prisoners used to be kept awaiting execution by dragon. I've only been down here once before, when Duck and I were young and exploring. It seemed like a dark place, forsaken for good reason, and we never returned.

"Lee?"

"Here."

I hold the lantern against the bars and peer in. The cell is tiny, its unpaned window letting in the cold air from the arena. Lee is lying on a cot in the corner. He pushes himself up onto one arm and looks at me with a hand shielding his eyes.

"What did Atreus say?" he asks.

"Nothing conclusive. I think he's still . . . deliberating."

He has, since I've left him, been stripped of his uniform and provided with a tunic and trousers. It's the first time I've seen him in plain clothes since Albans, and my first thought is that they don't suit him.

"I've brought you some stuff."

"Oh . . . thanks."

He rises and approaches.

"Ice," I say, handing that over first. "And there's a medical examiner coming to look at you in a bit."

"It's really not that bad—"

"I want him to be able to testify later."

"They won't care," Lee says.

I hear it as an echo of Power's goads, which have been resounding in my head during the few quiet moments I've had over the last hours. *Were they punished?* I tell him what I've been telling myself. "That's not true. The Palace Day perpetrators were locked up, they were executed, I checked ages ago—"

Lee's face is startled at first and then, at once, guarded.

He clarifies: "I meant they won't care because of the concerns for national defense. They can't afford to confine sparked riders, especially not one in the Fourth Order. Power's too valuable."

Then Lee clears his throat and adds, softly:

"He didn't say anything I haven't already had to think about for years, Annie. Don't worry about that."

He turns from me, slightly, pulls his shirt up, and holds the bag of ice against his abdomen. I stare at the web of burn scars across his back that don't entirely mask a different, older web of scars beneath. The ones he has never, not even in Albans, talked about.

The day, its disaster, lies shattered around us. All at once the only thing I want is to rewind: to yesterday, to hours ago, before everything went wrong. Before I had to see Lee like this.

"I . . . told some of the others. Figured I'd better, in case Power . . . anyway. Duck, Cor, Rock, Lotus. And Crissa. No one else."

Even with him turned, I'm able to see the knot of his throat move as he swallows.

"And they . . . ?"

"Some of them might need time."

Lee nods rigidly.

"I'm acting fleet commander," I go on. And add: "For the interim."

The interim before—what?

But Lee doesn't comment on this phrasing. Just says, "Good."

"I'm . . . going to need to talk to you about that. At some point."

I hear my voice do the thing I've been praying it won't do, then: jump an octave, go shrill. Lee hears it too and stills. And then he lowers the ice from his stomach and turns back to me.

"Hey," he says.

Only from Lee would such a simple phrase be enough to calm me like a caress.

"We can go over it now, if you want," he says.

I nod, mortified by my swollen throat, by the fact that in such a moment Lee would be comforting *me*. Mortified by how much I need it.

"Do you have something to write with?"

I nod again.

We sit together on the stone floor of the stockade, separated by the bars, as Lee holds the ice to his stomach and talks while I take notes. He tells me about the duties he's assumed as Firstrider—and then about more than that. Additional responsibilities he's taken on over the years, while doing his rounds with the ministry and the military. He describes the contacts he likes to check in with, the quirks of each task, the extra measures he likes to take to ensure the jobs are done well.

Lee's voice is contained, calm, steady throughout, even as my own breathing grows ragged.

When he's finally told me everything he can think of, he hands me back the mostly melted bag of ice. He's shivering, his leg damp from the ice bag's dripping water. I pull the blanket I brought him out of my bag and pass it through the bars. He wraps it around himself, murmuring a thank-you. I hand him, one by one, the remaining contents: a pillow; matches; a lamp; today's editions of the *People's Paper* and the *Gold Gazette*; and his copy of the *Aurelian Cycle*, in the original Dragontongue.

His eyes close as he takes this last from me, like he's receiving a benediction, and for a moment his fingers and mine touch over the book. Then the contact is broken, and we both get to our feet.

"I'll be back as soon as I can—"

"You've done enough. You need to prioritize other things right now."

I don't argue with that.

"Is there anything else I can bring—?"

Lee starts to shake his head and then stops.

"I don't know if he'd want to come. But . . . Cor?"

"He's not ready yet, Lee."

Lee's swallows, his face rippling with the effort to remain calm.

"And . . . Crissa?"

As soon as he says her name, he catches himself, shrinking as if he fears my anger. But it's not anger so much as sadness that settles over me, and not the kind he's anticipating. Because there's nothing so heartbreaking as the thought that, even in this way, he's at my mercy.

I look at him, standing alone in a cold, dark cell to await whatever fate he's offered himself up for, and I imagine how it would change, to have Crissa here, her laughter, her smile, her gentle humor a light in the darkness, her beauty something to blot out the barren ugliness of this place. Who am I to begrudge him the ways he's found to escape his darkness? I've been escaping mine with Duck for years.

My heart swelled with love for him, I say:

"I'll make sure she gets visitation rights."

Lee, for the first time in our interview, looks close to losing control.

"Thank you."

* * *

Crissa finds me outside the oration room where I'm about to hold my first meeting as fleet commander. I'm surprised when her greeting has nothing to do with Lee.

"You ready?" she asks.

I nod, my stomach leaping, and Crissa touches my arm. She stands so erect, her golden hair cascading down her shoulders, that I have to lift my head to meet her eyes.

"When Atreus made me squadron leader," she says, "the most important thing for me was confidence. Even if I didn't feel it, I faked it. I faked it *all the time*. And eventually, I'd faked it so long, I convinced myself. That's what you're going to have to do, Annie."

It's as if she knew exactly the doubts that have been wriggling in my stomach. Before I can even think how to thank her for sharing such a thing, she's stepped over the threshold of the oration room and left me to find her seat.

Power is waiting for me inside the doorway. He makes a flourishing salute.

"Congratulations on your promotion, Commander."

I stop dead.

"He let you off?"

Power shrugs. "Atreus gave us a slap on the wrist and suggested we keep our mouths shut for the time being. I'll do my best." He grins at me in a way that puts me on edge at once. Then he nods inside. "Better hurry. Looks like Goran's already staging a coup."

Goran has taken the rostrum, calling the room to order. At the sight of him, a weight like a stone thuds in my gut. I approach, watched by thirty of my classmates.

"I'll take it from here."

Goran looks at me.

"That's all right, Annie, there's no need."

We stare each other down. I think of how he must see me, a

sixteen-year-old peasant girl who doesn't know her place.

Even when you don't feel confident, you fake it.

I raise my chin, square my shoulders, and think of Aela.

And to my amazement, Goran steps aside. The corner of his lip raises and he makes a little shrug, as if to say, *Suit yourself, if you want to make such a fuss about it.*

I take his place at the rostrum. Then I turn to him.

"Thank you," I tell him, "you are dismissed."

Goran's half smile flickers. But even he recognizes the reality of rank when it's laid bare: He may be our drillmaster, but drillmasters do not outrank fleet commanders.

Without another word, he turns and leaves the room.

My classmates, watching us, have fallen silent.

Into that silence, I tell them that Lee has been apprehended on allegations of misconduct and is relieved of his duties until an investigation can be completed. I tell them that they will, in the meantime, take orders from me. Deirdre becomes acting aurelian squadron leader in my place.

I hold my shoulders back, speak from the diaphragm, and pace it slow. Like Crissa and I once practiced. And then, when I conclude with a call for questions, I intone it the way Lee does, *down*, like I'm not really asking at all.

Power raises his hand.

"I've got one," he says. "If it looks like a Stormscourge, talks like a Stormscourge, and walks like a Stormscourge—is it a Cheapside slum orphan?"

* * *

The damage control after that takes hours. It's only after Cor raises his voice at the Guardians interrogating me that I'm finally given a few moments' peace; throughout the Cloister, groups are gathered in discussion. Cor and I lock ourselves in Lee's office to confer.

"I'm backing you hard, as is Crissa, but you're going to have to be ready for gossip," Cor says. "Power's telling everyone that you've been covering for Lee all along. And—he's saying more than that."

After being on the receiving end of Power's birth-based slurs for the past seven years, I can readily imagine what more he's saying than that.

"I don't care what he says about me."

"You've got to. You're the fleet commander. And if you want them to hear your case for Lee, you'll need their respect."

Over the next few days, I hear whispers around the Cloister—theories about why I've stood by Lee, ranging from those that question my allegiance to those that say I'm a lovesick schoolgirl, to those that insinuate serving dragonlords is in my blood. The one time I overhear this last suggested, it's Crissa's voice that opposes it with fury.

"If I ever hear that you utter that old-regime blood-determinative bullshit again, I will report you."

To my face, no one opposes me at all. In the meantime, I figure out how to do Lee's job. Managing the details and the paperwork comes easily; for the rest, I use every trick I've learned from watching Lee and training with Crissa to project confidence. Aware of the murmured reservations of the corps—for me as a leader generally and now, specifically, as the supporter of a dragonborn—I'm conscious of the importance of showing them that I can do this job right. Not just for my sake, but also for Lee's. Those who doubt me and those who trust me alike follow my orders without question, but I sense that the calm is temporary: It's as though we all hang suspended as we wait for Atreus's decision. And in the meantime, we hear nothing more.

Lee reads about two books a day, brought to him by Crissa, and less frequently by Lotus and Duck. Cor and Rock haven't yet visited him. And I haven't gone back. Lee's right: I have other priorities, and I need to stay focused. I can't when I'm thinking about Lee.

In the meantime, my time is consumed by organizing ration distributions, which are to take place on a rotating basis throughout the winter from depots at major population centers across the island. Schedules for distribution are based on class metals, with each class metal collecting their ration cards on different days. The Inner Palace hopes to minimize discontent by minimizing comparisons, though it's acknowledged that people won't remain blind to what's happening forever. That's where dragons will come in, General Holmes tells us, in his briefing to the corps. He doesn't explain his meaning.

On the first day ration cards are distributed in the city, they're given to class-irons in the center of Cheapside. Cor and I accompany it. The location and class metal were chosen by the Ministry of Propaganda, to be heavily featured in the *People's Paper* the next day. The ration cards' equivalents in bread and potatoes will be meager, even by Cheapside standards, but no one in this crowd complains. For them, the miracle is that the food will be free. Discontent will come later. When they begin to realize just how little they've been given, when they come to see what others have.

"How is he?" Cor asks.

We're standing beside the ration distribution line off the center of the square, based out of the Cheapside guardhouse. The line winds around the square; guards are shouting at the crowd to have their left sleeve rolled up, ready to show their wristband. Aela and Maurana circle overhead.

"You could visit him," I tell Cor.

Cor squints away from me, up at the old Cheapside dragon perch silhouetted in the autumn light, and says: "I can't. I'm still too angry."

"He's still *him*, Cor—"

"I don't know what that is anymore."

When Atreus calls me into his office a week later, I'm relieved to find he's ready to discuss Lee's situation at last. But then, with little to no preamble, he introduces the solution he's considering. After he has described it to me, he says:

"I was not unmoved by your story, Antigone. And I believe— I am eager to believe—that you have certain insight into Lee's character. I would like you to use this insight to help me now. This is a risk I would not undertake lightly, without substantial reason to believe it would go in our favor. So I am asking you what you think the outcome would be. Answer carefully, for you take the fortune of Callipolis into your hands."

Though his solution does not, now that it faces me, feel surprising—in fact it feels as though it has been long coming, something I should have seen from the start—still, I am short of breath.

"Antigone?" he prompts.

"Do it," I say.

I'm sorry, Lee.

LEE

On Crissa's visits, we talk mostly about the newspapers, or books I've been reading, or the flying conditions, which I am able to discern through the window. But sometimes I ask her about the corps. About the others. About Cor.

"Does he believe Power?"

Crissa sits, cross-legged, on the opposite side of the bars, her hair glowing softly in the torchlight. Our hands are wound together in her lap. "No. Of course not. He's stood by Annie from the start. Rock, too."

Then why won't they come?

"It's hard for them, Lee."

"It isn't hard for you?"

Crissa pushes stray curls back from her face and shakes her head. "This? No. *This* isn't hard for me."

But as to what is hard, she doesn't say. When the Protector's Guard interrupts our visit to give me my summons to Atreus's office, she kisses me on the mouth, in front of them.

"Go be good and brave, as you've always been."

The guard escorts me to Atreus's office on either side. I'm acutely conscious of the differences between now and the last time I was here: I'm no longer in uniform and my wrist is bare. Still, it's good to stretch your legs after so many days in one room.

"Lee," says Atreus gravely, gesturing at one of the ornate chairs facing his desk, "please sit."

He nods to the guards to leave us, and then we're alone. The glass wall overlooking the Firemouth spills afternoon light across his desk.

"Are you aware of what day it is?" Atreus asks.

I've been keeping track, so I give the date. Atreus nods.

"Do you know what will happen in a day's time?" he asks.

I shake my head.

In answer, Atreus passes a piece of paper across the desk to me: the letter from Julia. In a day's time, I realize, she'll go to the Riversource and wait for me.

"You may already know that I have spoken to Antigone, as you requested. She confirms your story. You do seem to have led a life of . . . unusual allegiances."

I wait. This seems to be a reprieve, of sorts, but it can't be the end of it, or else we would have had this conversation a week ago, after she first spoke with him.

"Nevertheless," Atreus goes on, "one cannot help having reservations. I believe you have attachments to Antigone, and she to you. Considering your background, it is remarkable; though considering the exigencies that threw you together, it is also understandable. I also believe—and am impressed by—the fact that you have sustained contact with, but continued to refuse, the family that reached out to you from New Pythos.

"But I'm also afraid that mere refusal of your family is not enough. I cannot risk Callipolis's safety on the fact that you surrender me a letter and tell me you care about a girl whose family your father butchered. There is a war coming, Lee. Your family and their dragons will come again, by the end of this winter at the latest. When they come, every one of our sparked dragons will be integral to our defense. I need soldiers loyal to their City, I need Guardians loyal to an idea, and I need them ready to kill for it. In short, I need to know, not just that you can refuse those on the other side, but that you are ready to fight them. Do you understand?"

"Yes," I say.

Here it is at last, I think. Tyndale's question, on the table, to be pushed aside no longer. Julia's ultimatum, about to be laid bare.

"Good," says Atreus.

"What do you want me to do?"

I'm pretty sure I already know the answer, and when Atreus nods at the letter, I'm not surprised. Even so, the way he phrases it makes me flinch.

"I want you to take your dragon, meet their Firstrider, and return with two heads in a bag. If you can't do that, don't come back at all."

18

—

THE RIVERSOURCE

"My son," said Leon Stormscourge, in Dragontongue. "Please, Atreus."

"Leo will be looked after," Atreus said.

Then he turned to the soldier beside him and gave him an order.

The soldier, who'd been watching the boy, didn't hear it at first. The boy couldn't have been older than eight—though what little of his expression the soldier could make out beneath a mask of blood was not the kind of expression that belonged to an eight-year-old.

The soldier, who had grown up thinking of dragonlords and their sons as another race, another species, was surprised to find himself thinking that no child, not even a dragonlord's, should ever wear a look like this.

Then he heard Atreus's command. It had been said so quietly, the soldier thought at first he had misheard it.

"Take the boy into the hallway," Atreus murmured, "and slit his throat."

ANNIE

"He won't do it," Cor says.

"Yes, he will," I answer.

We're standing in the fleet commander's office, a desk between me and them, and the door is shut. My palms are planted, flat, on the desk's surface. Since becoming acting commander, I've organized and stacked all of Lee's papers.

"People don't kill their relatives," Rock says, like I need this explained to me.

"Lee isn't *people*," I tell them. "He'll do it. They're both Firstriders; he's always known what that would mean."

Cor makes a ticking noise of skepticism. His arms are folded.

"Annie," Rock says, his voice rising, "you understand what happens if he *doesn't* do it, right? You understand who will have to deal with him if he changes sides? You."

I answer with rising anger.

"Yeah, that's occurred to me, Rock."

"And you'll be able to do that?" Rock demands.

It is like a confession, to say it aloud after hours of pondering in silence. "Yes."

* * *

By evening, word has spread throughout the corps about what's supposed to happen the following morning. Dinner is quieter than usual, and when we turn off the lights in the girls' dorm, it's silent the way it can only be when people aren't sleeping. In the end I throw the bedcovers off myself.

"Crissa?" I murmur. Her bed is next to mine.

I have no idea what I'm about to ask her, but she doesn't make me find out.

"I've said my goodbyes," she says. "You should say yours."

It's all I need to hear.

Goran's office is unlocked. I let myself in and get his keys. At the stockade, the guards let me by without question. When I say his name outside the cell, I hear him stirring.

"Annie?"

He says it like he thinks he must be dreaming.

It's dark inside, well past two in the morning already, and I can only see his outline as he gets to his feet. I unlock the door, let myself in, and before I can even go to him, I feel his arms around me, pulling me to him. "You're cold," he says, "you're shivering . . ."

I hadn't noticed. He sits me on the edge of his cot and wraps the blanket I gave him around me, and then he holds me close again.

"I didn't want to wake you," I say.

Lee lets out a quiet laugh in the darkness.

"I wasn't sleeping."

No. I suppose he wouldn't have been. I put the blanket around him, too, so that we're sitting side by side, the blanket wrapped around us, and we're as close as we used to sit in Albans, when he'd put his arms around me in that closet on the third floor.

"Let me keep this vigil with you," I whisper.

In answer, he only presses me tighter. And then he winds his hand in my hair and lowers his face into my neck. It feels so *right* that a lump rises in my throat, and I lift my hand to cup his head to my shoulder, holding him there. I think of the glittering night from a world ago, where we held hands after a dance and it felt right, like this, but I pulled away. I can't remember anymore why I did.

He inhales slowly. "Well, here we are," he says.

Like *here* is the utter end, and he's seen it coming all along.

"Do you . . . do you know what you'll do?" I ask.

He lets out a laugh again, and it sounds a little like a cry.

"I know what I *should* do," he says.

Whether he can do it, is another question.

"I keep thinking," he says, his face still buried in my neck, "I keep thinking I should just take Pallor and run away."

So, that's how close he is to despair right now. To entertain the idea of turning his back on all of it.

But I know Lee better than that. And the one thing that I know, that has held true from the beginning, is that Lee doesn't run. Lee stays. Even when it hurts him most.

"No, Lee," I say.

He doesn't respond, just clenches and unclenches his hands in my hair.

"You know you can't do that."

"Why not?" he asks dully. Like he knows, but wants to hear me say it.

And so, even though the only thing I want is for this feeling of his face buried against my neck to go on forever, I pull back. He's forced to lift his head and look at me.

"Because you've been given this power, and you have a responsibility to use it. Giving it up—that's as bad as giving the other side a dragon. You pick a side no matter what you do."

Lee's still for a moment. Like the words have stricken him. Then he looks away.

"Let's talk about something else," he says, "okay?"

"Okay," I whisper.

We have about three hours before I have to leave.

For those three hours, we lie side by side, wrapped in the blanket, almost like lovers except it's something more intimate than that. We talk about anything we can think of to push away thoughts of tomorrow, and for moments on end, we succeed.

But the distractions work too well, and time passes quickly, and in the end three hours feels cruelly short.

"Annie," he says, when it's time for me to leave. "If I don't . . . if I can't . . ."

It's a question, even though it doesn't sound like one. I make the promise that he wants to hear even as it breaks my heart to say it.

"Yes," I tell him. "I'll do it."

He lowers his head into my hair, breathes in like he's taking a final breath, and says, "Good."

When I rise to leave, he seizes me, pulls me close, and hesitates. For a moment, as he stares at me with lips parted, I see the longing in his face.

Longing for *me*. So much longing that it looks like despair.

He lets out a groan so quiet it is barely audible, and with a tenderness that makes my eyes burn, he leans forward, tips my head down, and kisses me on the forehead. He quotes the *Aurelian Cycle* in Dragontongue.

You have given life to me.

As the touch of his lips on my forehead burns like a brand, understanding floods through me. I look up at him, taking in his face in the lantern light: the high cheekbones; the dark hair;

the eyes that look older than ever tonight, set against a pale and careworn face.

I realize he's never looked more like his father, and I don't care.

I lift my fingers to his hair, bring his face to mine, and close the distance. For a moment the cool shock of his lips' touch goes through me. Lee's whole body has stilled. For a fleeting instant, as he freezes, I wonder if I shouldn't have.

And then he inhales a shaking breath that I can feel, and his lips part on mine, and his hands go down from my hair to my waist. Still light, as if they dare not tighten on me—but then, as he begins to kiss me back, they do tighten. For a moment the kiss, too, is gentle, careful—I'm so conscious of my not knowing, of his knowing—and then he utters a sound so low in his throat that it may be a cry of need or perhaps sorrow muffled against my mouth. Then we're no longer gentle, and I no longer care that I don't know what I'm doing, because I know. My lips taste the first warmth of his tongue, my hands take in his chest and shoulders and neck as if they must make up time for all the years we haven't touched, and I marvel at the feel of his hands, *Lee's* hands, holding me so tight to him it's like he wills our bodies to crush together as one. The strength that I have seen in wire-toned muscles now folded around me, their power on my body heady as wine.

I step forward, pushing him back, so that when he backs into the cot, he sinks down onto it. For a moment we continue to kiss as I stand between his knees and gather courage. But it's too late to hesitate, too late now for shame, and so I do the one thing left I want to do. I climb onto his lap, fold my knees around him, and wind my arms around his neck to kiss him between drawn breaths. An echo of how we sat in Albans, when he used to hold me.

But this time, it's I who am holding him.

And all the while his shuddering breaths, and the taste of his saliva mingled, finally, with salt, and someone is saying, *I am* saying, *Come back to us,* over and over again.

Until it becomes, at last, *Come back to me.*

LEE

Annie leaves me wondering whether I've dreamed it.

All the same, for the immeasurable space of what must be a half hour between her departure and Atreus's arrival, the storms of my mind are stilled and all I can think, all I can remember, all that matters, is her lingering warmth.

Come back to me.

In the final hour, Atreus comes down the stairs flanked by two of his guard. He hands me my uniform himself. The armor glints a little in the growing light of dawn, the wingspread dragon with its four circlets of fire bold against the repurposed scales of the breastplate. Though the guards are bearing lanterns, their light is already weakening with the dawn.

When I'm armed, I ask him:

"Did you kill my father?"

Atreus is not expecting this, and for a moment we stare at each other. He is silhouetted in the lantern light.

"It won't change anything," I add. "But I need to know."

One more thing that, for years, I haven't let myself wonder. But it seems time to lay everything in the open.

Atreus answers curtly, though he meets my eye as he says it. "I did. Though I considered it more an act of mercy than anything else."

"Yes," I acknowledge. "It would have been."

Faint surprise shows on his face, and he makes the smallest gratified nod. Like it's I who have just offered him mercy.

"You're ready?" he asks.

"Yes."

"I'll be waiting for you on Pytho's Keep," Atreus says.

ANNIE

When I return to the Cloister, I find Power sitting alone, awake, in the solarium. The room is in shadow, the sky through the glass ceiling still dark. My hair is undone, my face damp, the taste of Lee's lips still on mine.

"Did you enjoy your tearful goodbyes?" Power asks.

It's the first time we've been alone in a room together since the day he confronted Lee in the caves. The bruises on my arms have begun to fade to yellow where he and Darius held them. When I start to turn away, he speaks again.

"Letter from the ministry. Just arrived. Addressed to the fleet commander."

He holds it out. The seal is unbroken. I open it and read the message within while Power watches me from his armchair.

PLEASE AWAIT FURTHER INSTRUCTIONS FOR THE CORPS IN THE CLOISTER. YOUR PRESENCE IS NOT NEEDED ON THE KEEP.

"Which does it say?"

I look up at him. *Which?*

"Do they want us there or not? When he gets back."

"Does it matter?"

Power smiles and leans forward. "Antigone, I'll admit it. I admire you. I admire how much shit you're willing to take face-first to get what you want. But it pisses me off when you're an idiot."

I fold the letter and return it to its envelope.

"What," I ask, "exactly, do you think I am being an idiot about right now?"

LEE

Pallor and I arrive first. The Riversource is in the heart of the highlands, a rocky clearing around a small, deep pool forming the hot springs of the River Fer. In Stormscourge lore, the gorge is said to be the place where the first stormscourge nests were found, where the first eggs were stolen, their hatchlings tamed by my ancestors. I've never seen the place before, but I've read of it. Looking around at the steep walls, the gorge famously impassable except by dragon, the intention behind Julia's choice of location becomes as apparent as if she has said it aloud.

This place is perfectly designed for a private duel.

The realization fills me with sudden relief—and then, as I mark the emotion, sorrow.

Julia sur Erinys appears alone above the northern ridge and descends. As they alight, Julia removes her helmet. Today, unlike our two previous encounters, she is wearing battle armor.

Emblazoned on the breast with Stormscourge heather, encircled by the three dragons of the triarchy.

The last time I saw such armor, I saw it on my father.

"Hello, Leo."

"Hello, Julia."

I take her in: the Stormscourge hair, the eyes, the face that in so many small ways is the closest thing to home I've seen since Palace Day. The armor that makes me miss my father like I've lost him all over again. I remember the feeling of her hands in mine on Midsummer as we grieved to have survived the same horrors and felt the same pain. I remember a childhood spent in laughter-filled play at her side, before we'd learned the taste of loss.

I see her and remember and it's not enough.

Because Annie's right.

There's a war, and I have to take a side. Palace Day and the ties of blood aren't enough to make me choose the wrong one. Whatever their claim on me, it's a fact that the dragonlords reigned brutally and killed indiscriminately. They're responsible for the deaths of thousands. They cannot be allowed to come back.

The prickles to my conscience, looking at Julia, only put me on guard. She is my kin; she was a girl I played with as a child; she has been, in these last months, the only tie I have left to the world I lost. But at this point, obeying instincts of tribalism or chivalry would be nothing but selfish. The reality is that she and I are both dragonriders. We're both weapons. And she must be destroyed.

Before this moment, I doubted I could do it. But now that I'm here, looking at her, there's no question. I'm going to do it. It's not that it will be easy: It will be horrible.

But that doesn't mean it can't be done.

The only thing left to be determined is how long it will take.

"Julia," I say, "I'm not sure how to say this, but—"

"You're not coming back with me, are you?"

"No."

"I didn't think you would," she says. "But I wanted to give you one last chance, in case."

"I appreciate that."

Though I'm suppressing the instincts, they nevertheless compel me to ask, awkwardly:

"Do you have others coming—?"

"No. I didn't tell anyone. I wanted to have the opportunity to settle it like this."

Privately. Without an audience. With dignity.

Because Julia, like me, learned the hard way to value a dignified death.

I tell her: "I came alone, too."

"Well then," she says, her tone mild again. It is clear that she understood the portent of my wording as well as I did, and that she knows what comes next.

For a moment, she fingers her helmet, though we continue to stare at each other. And then she lifts her fingers from it.

"You know," she says, "we needn't rush. Would you like to take a final walk together, before we do it?"

With anyone else, I would think this was cowardice or reluctance disguised as cordiality. With Julia, I know better. And even though it occurs to me that every minute longer I spend speaking with her will make this harder, I find myself desiring, against all reason, to have a final conversation.

"I'd like that," I say.

We dismount. Pallor makes a huff of consternation behind me; Erinys flexes and rears in impatience. They're sensing the upcoming fight, are eager for it. We ignore them, approaching each other slowly in the barren space between. We meet at the water's edge.

"Come," Julia says, and together we begin to walk around the pool.

I know instinctively that we can only walk around it once; that after we have circled it, we will return to our dragons. Her pace is slow, like mine, as if she has the same course in mind.

"Have you found happiness, cousin?" she asks.

It's strange to hear it put this way. I consider for a moment, if the last few years could be called *happy*. It's not a word I've often considered in reference to my own life.

Then I think of Cor's lopsided grin, of Crissa's rippling laughter, of Annie's lips on mine as her trembling fingers brought my face to hers.

"I have people I care for, who care for me in return," I tell her. "If that's what you're asking."

"I suppose, yes," she says. Then she asks, "They're the reason you refuse us?"

I sense her doubtfulness at the idea, and I realize that she doesn't consider personal attachments a good reason to choose sides, any more than I do.

"Julia," I say. "You know what our fathers did, don't you?"

We've stopped walking. Steam from the Riversource rises; through it, the blurred outlines of our dragons, waiting on the opposite side of the pool, ripple as they move on the water's still reflection.

"Yes," she says. "I know."

The way she says it, I know that I don't need to tell her that what they did was wrong. Somehow, despite being driven out of her own city, despite living in isolation among the bitter survivors of an old regime, despite never having met or cared for any child orphaned by her father's dragon, Julia already understands. Her face is pale, set, and sad.

I say, "Then you know why I've chosen as I have."

Julia says, "We don't have to be like our fathers. Our generation—we can be different. You and I, we already are."

We've both stopped walking.

I think of the civilians burned on Starved Rock, the unarmed ships destroyed on Palace Day. The question comes out raw with feeling. "*Are* you different, Julia?"

Julia's eyes flash. Instead of answering, she spits her accusation. "Are *you*? Your new regime is already failing. Athanatos has done nothing but fill the city with dirty workhouses and destroy our libraries—"

My answer returns cool, because my head, as Julia has grown angry, grows clear.

"He's trying to start again, and it's difficult. And what is censorship compared with your crimes? You attacked our fishermen, our traders. Civilians. They were *unarmed*."

Julia's face twists. She says, "We will do what it takes to regain what is ours."

I inhale the steam-filled air rising from the Fer and shake my head.

"Callipolis isn't yours anymore. The people have chosen. They don't want dragonlords."

A smile glints on Julia's lips at this, catches in her eyes, as she looks at me. She lifts a hand, gesturing, with an open palm, to me, then to Pallor waiting on the opposite side of the steaming pool, a silver smear against the rising karst.

"Are you sure?" she asks softly. "Look at you, Leo. Look how readily they gave it back to you. The dragon, the power, the respect. Is it true, you are Athanatos's favored successor?"

Julia's smile widens at my silence.

"You and I were born to rule."

There it is. The single belief that ruined all of them. From the dragonlords of the *Aurelian Cycle* all the way down to my father, and now Julia.

"No," I answer.

I had meant to add more, to explain myself, but I realize now there's no need. She does not agree with me; she will not. We've reached the bounds of reason and have come to the threshold of belief. I would not do her the dishonor of imagining that her beliefs have been any less hard-won than mine.

She seems to realize the same thing. She doesn't try to argue, to ask why. We resume walking the edge of the pool, but we're silent now. I have the sense that I've said what I needed to say; that she has, too. I also have the sense that we were both seeking this impasse. Now that we have found it, we're ready to finish what we came here to do.

There is a sadness shared between us, mingled with resolve.

"It's been good to talk with you these past months," she says finally, as we approach the part of the pool where we first started, where Pallor and Erinys wait for us, tensed, wings ready to spread. "Whatever our differences have been. It's been good to remember with you. I hope that, if ever we meet in any after-life, we will meet as we were, before."

As children.

The sadness mounts; it is piercing.

"My hope is the same," I answer.

We have reached our starting point.

We look at each other, exchange a final nod. Then we turn away. She returns to her stormscourge, and I return to Pallor. We mount again, replace our helmets, and set our visors. Neither of us hesitates before launching into the air.

ANNIE

"You are assuming Atreus is like you," Power says. "Willing to forgive the facts because of the feelings. But what if he isn't?"

The chill from the open windows of the solarium, letting in the early autumn breeze in the predawn light, is suddenly enough to make me shiver as I stand, facing Power. He's no longer lounging: Instead he grips both arms of his chair as he leans forward. As the sky outside lightens, the features of his face come into focus.

"Am I the only one *listening* in class with him? This is a man who authorized butchering every member of the dragonborn families down to the last man, woman, and child, including those who were his *friends*. He has rooted through a civilization of literature he loved and is destroying it, rather than let its values erode his city. Atreus doesn't follow his heart. He *works in spite of it.*"

The most important protest, the paradox that makes it all work, rises to my lips: "He once saved Lee's life—"

Power snaps his fingers and leans forward. "According to

Lee. Who was what, eight at the time, probably barely spoke Callish, and was senseless with shock?" He shrugs. "Ask yourself this. Is a man who ran a project of total extermination of a people really likely to change his program, just because he discovers a dragonborn rat ten years later who turns out to support his cause? Maybe. *Or* he's going to get what use he can out of him *and then discard him like the rest.* Quietly, with minimal fuss. Out of sight of those whose consciences would twinge."

I find my voice, and it's shaking.

"The whole point of Atreus's system is that *anyone* can be worthy."

Power's laugh echoes in the empty, glass-walled room.

"Maybe one day," he says. "But for now, I'm pretty sure the point is that some people aren't anymore."

He nods, once more, to the letter contained in my hands.

"Your move, Commander."

LEE

Julia flies her stormscourge the way I remember them flying in tournaments, when I was a child. The way stormscourges are meant to be flown.

Can I really do this?

Because it's one thing to resolve to on the ground; it's another to give your dragon the command to fire. Sparked dragonfire, undoused.

I know what's needed. I remember what it felt like, a month

ago, when I finally won against Annie in our final tournament: that eruption of violence that came with Pallor's sparking, the feeling of ascendance that left me sick from its darkness. It feels like I've spent a lifetime resisting it. But now, when I know that it's called for, I can't bring myself to give in to it.

But Julia can, and she is the one who does first.

I feel the blast sear through the left arm of my armor and flamesuit, burning skin, and for a moment—though we are not playing tournament rules, though we are not offering each other time-outs or resets—we both pause midair. I feel the burn, a full searing heat of sparked fire rage down my arm. As the pain makes me light-headed, as I fumble automatically for coolant valves, I lift my head and look at her. Our faces are visored; no expression is discernible on hers any more than mine. But as we look at each other, and the canyon stills and its echoes go quiet, I am certain that we are both making the same resolution.

There is no backing out of this. It will be finished, one way or the other.

I rein Pallor round, and this time, when the ferocity calls me, I don't hold back.

The world is a blaze of dragonfire and smoke and pain for a time after that. Everything we once imagined that dueling on dragonback would be. Except we didn't imagine then that it would be accompanied by a feeling, barely distinguishable from the searing burns that have spread across my body, of horror so great it feels like physical pain.

Julia's guard opens once, twice, three times, but never enough for a kill shot, and because I'm determined to do it with one blow instead of piecemeal, I let the opportunities pass.

I want to be Firstrider, you're always Firstrider, let me be it for a change—

Though neither of us is speaking, though there is no sound except the wind in the canyon and the hiss of flames, I find I can hear her, hear *us*, memories flooding in so long forgotten. From the Palace gardens, when they were ours.

What if I'm King Rada, of the Bassileans? Then we could fight each other, and we'd both be Firstrider.

She's lost her balance, just enough to expose herself, and through my blurring vision I notice the opening with Pallor at once.

A kill shot.

I feel like my heart is breaking.

Fight each other?

A sound fills the air: my own cry, wild with despair, in time with Pallor's blast. It feels as though I, like Pallor, am igniting.

He twists down, inhales, and fires.

There's a moment of perfect stillness, as the fire that filled my vision leaves me blinded, as the gorge becomes, for an instant, perfectly quiet. Then the silence breaks. An inhuman, hair-raising keen goes up, unearthly, alien, full of unbearable sorrow. Though it's a sound I've only ever read about, I know it at once. It is the sound of a dragon who has felt the bond with its rider break in the only way it can be broken.

It takes the breath out of my lungs.

Pallor recovers before I do, driving us forward, firing again to finish what we've started. The grieving stormscourge barely resists. It's as though she no longer has any reason to.

Same time tomorrow?

I'll try. Wait for me, Leo.

ANNIE

After my conversation with Power, I wake everyone. When they're dressed, full uniform, we convene in the oration room, where it's still dark enough outside for the lamps in their sconces to be the chief source of light. But already, birds are calling; dawn approaches.

"Do you agree," I ask, when all are assembled, "that if Lee completes the task Atreus has set for him, he will have proved himself trustworthy as a Callipolan and your leader?"

Around the room, Guardians look at one another, startled. Except for Power, who stands in the back, his arms folded, a strange, twisted smirk on his face as he watches me address the corps.

"Annie, it's more that we don't think—"

I cut Max off.

"For the sake of argument. If he does it."

"Of course," Deirdre says.

Others are nodding.

"Good. Then start suiting up. He's due back at Pytho's Keep within the hour. The Inner Palace wants us there as witnesses."

"Since when?"

"Since now."

The edge in my tone seems to be enough to prevent them from making further argument. As the rest get to their feet, I pull Crissa, Cor, and Lotus aside.

"I'm going to need your help with something."

And then I tell them the full stakes. I don't give them time for horror; instead I give them instructions. Cor to go to General

Holmes, Crissa to Miranda Hane.

"Go on dragonback, and tell them that you're there on the orders of the First Protector. Tell them that he requires their presence."

When they have departed for the armory, I turn to Lotus.

"How well do you know the houses of the Janiculum?"

Lotus gives me a startled look.

"That depends. For what?"

"Would you be able to identify Dora Mithrides's home from dragonback?"

Mithrides: honorary alderman on the Janiculum Council and wealthiest of Atreus's supporters, who was so taken with Lee at the Lycean Ball and so surprised that a boy of such polish could have emerged from the slums.

It seems time to make use of her lingering blood prejudices.

"Yes," Lotus says, beginning to smile as he understands. "I believe I would."

Twenty minutes later, he and I are circling above the Janiculum terraces in the half-light of early morning, the shadow of Pytho's Keep rising steep and black above us. Lotus points down, to a particularly ostentatious estate on one of the highest ledges of the hill.

"That one."

We descend and land in Dora Mithrides's front garden, inside her gate and guardhouse. It is, I realize, the first time I've ever set foot on the Janiculum. The dragons crunch on the gravel of a turnaround designed for long lines of carriages and horses; the grounds are still, save for a fountain burbling in the center of the turnaround and a mourning dove crying. I leave Lotus with the dragons and make my way up the great stone staircase to Mithrides's front door, overhung by an ivy-laden arcade. And then I pull the bell.

After a few minutes the valet answers, rubbing sleep from his eyes. I swallow my discomfort and speak as I've seen Lee do to servants in the past: without interest.

"Wake your mistress."

I'm prepared to add an official mandate, but the valet obeys without waiting for it. I don't know if it's because of my uniform or my tone.

When Mithrides emerges shortly afterward, she has dressed, though her graying hair is not arranged. Her lined face is alert and intrigued.

"By the dragon, girl," she says in Dragontongue when she sees me, and her eyes travel past me, to Lotus waiting on the gravel with his skyfish, Iustus, and my Aela.

In Callish, I ask, "Do you remember who I am?"

"Of course I do. You're the highland rider."

"And you remember Lee sur Pallor?"

"The Guardian from Cheapside with such an unusual grasp of Dragontongue poetry, and now our Firstrider? Of course. But I fail to understand why such questions merit a call at this hour—"

"Please come with me. There's something that you should see."

As Mithrides follows me down the stairs to the dragons, she remarks: "It's been a long time since I've taken a ride on one of *these*."

* * *

In early morning, Pytho's Keep is the first part of the city to clear the fog and catch the light of the rising sun. As Lotus and I approach, Mithrides clinging to my back with trembling arms, we're joined by the rest of the fleet, all who were present at my meeting in the oration room. From the air we are able to distinguish figures waiting on the plinth of the ancient Sky Court: Atreus, accompanied by the entirety of the Protector's Guard, a sea of crimson uniforms, who must have mounted the single winding stair carved into the karst on foot. Standing in the great, flat width of the open court, under the fullness of the dawn sky and lifted to such a height from the ground, Atreus and his guard look like toy figures.

"There's Lee," Cor calls to me, raising an arm toward the northwest.

A white aurelian approaches on the western horizon, returning from the highlands.

Relief fills me in equal parts with dread.

He's done it.

My Lee, what hell have you been through, to make it back to us?

"Let's descend."

Mithrides, astride Aela behind me, grips my sides with a sucked-in breath as we dive; all around us, dragons are gathering their wings for descent.

We land on the windswept flagstones before the Protector's Guard. Crissa lends her arm to Hane, Cor helps down General Holmes, and Lotus and I help Dora. The rest of the fleet have landed in a semicircle around us and the Guard. Today, with clouds hanging low against the karst, the dawn is diffused by pink mist. Old trees, hobbled by years of wind into little more than shrubs, border the ancient court and mark the edge of the karst's plateau. Three marble arches rise above the plinth on which the triarchs of another age sat, and the stone citadel rises behind them.

Deafened by the unrelenting wind, I summon up my courage to look at Atreus. He stands on the plinth, framed by the arches, his short gray hair whipping flat against his forehead. It is light enough, on the Keep, to see his face clearly.

For the moment, his eyes travel from face to face, lingering on Holmes's and Hane's and Mithrides's, and then to the array of riders, on dragonback, behind us. Like he's searching. But then I force myself to speak, and he looks at me. I have to raise my voice over the wind.

"As requested, Protector. Your witnesses."

It's like being drilled through to the center, holding Atreus's gaze. I think of my uniform, of the dragonrider's cloak flowing behind me, of the dragon that answers to me alone standing to my right.

"Thank you, Antigone."

"What is the meaning of this, Atreus?" Dora Mithrides asks.

General Holmes looks around the crumbling Sky Court in bewilderment, and then his eyes find the Protector's Guard behind Atreus, and he frowns. As if he's noted the presence of an armed force and the remoteness of our location, and begins to wonder at the combination. Hane merely looks with long, slow glances from me to the Protector, understanding what hasn't been said.

Atreus does not have the opportunity to answer Dora's question. On the edge of the court, silhouetted against the glowing sky, a final dragon has landed. Pallor no longer gleams silver-white; he's blackened with ash, each breath a hoarse gasp. When Lee slides stiffly to the ground, I realize that much of what darkens his armor is dragonsblood. His back is turned to us, his shoulders hunched, one hand gripping the ridge of Pallor's back for support.

"What on earth?" Dora breathes from behind me.

"Atreus," says Holmes, with mounting intensity but through barely moving lips, his words clearly intended for none but Atreus to hear, "*why is your Guard waiting on the Keep for our Firstrider?*"

I don't wait for Atreus's answer. Instead, I turn from them and go to Lee. I can feel the eyes of those watching on my back. I join Lee at the court's edge. Beyond it, the karst falls away below glowing mist and the Palace, the city, and the river still lie in shadow.

Pallor has begun to let out keening cries as Lee spills over. Lee, his face averted, doesn't notice my approach until I say his name. I wrap my arms around him, pull him close, breathe in the smell of dragonfire and blood. When he lowers his head onto my shoulder, he is for a moment completely silent—as if his distress, so uncontrollably demonstrated by Pallor, is still something he seeks to contain within himself. Then the moment breaks. A single cry of grief escapes him, muffled and defeated, as if it has been torn from him against his will. I feel answering sorrow surging up within me.

But I force it down. The time for grief must be later. I let him go.

"They're waiting, Lee."

He doesn't ask *for what*, just nods and straightens. He drags one arm across his eyes, and for the first time looks past me, at our audience. The sight of them seems to clear his head. Beside him, Pallor's thrashing begins to slow, his cries to lessen. With sudden decisiveness Lee turns from me and yanks open a massive satchel tied to Pallor's flank, dark with the outline of a human body. He pulls from it a stained, blackened helmet on which the Stormscourge symbol of highland heather is still barely visible.

With a final touch to Pallor's still-shuddering side and a nod to me, he walks toward the waiting onlookers: Atreus, the Protector's Guard, Holmes, Hane, and the other Guardians and their dragons. There is a moment of silence in which all we hear is the deafening wind.

Then Lee stops, two yards from Atreus, and flings the helmet to the ground between them. Before Atreus can say anything, Lee begins to speak.

"I was born Leo, son of Leon, of House Stormscourge. I hereby renounce that name."

Hane draws a sharp breath. Holmes's eyes widen. Lee's voice is clear against the wind. He is speaking in Dragontongue, in meter, according to the traditions of high oaths in the old courts.

"In the name of Callipolis, I have forfeited all ties of blood. In the name of Callipolis, I have forsaken both the traditions of my people and the laws of their long-dead gods. In the name of Callipolis"—Lee inhales, his voice breaks—"I have slain my kin."

He slides to his knees on the flagstone, lowers his head, and extends his hands, palms up.

"Let the blood on my hands be my offering; let the spoils of my battle stand as proof of my loyalty."

And then he places his palms flat on the ground.

"All that I have, I offer to Callipolis. I am at your mercy, to be kept or cast out, according to your wish."

Lee, head bowed as he waits, does not witness the silent

interchanges of his audience: how Holmes levels a gaze at Atreus with a long, deliberate exhale, eyebrows raised in a challenge; how Hane has raised her hands to the sides of her face and seeks Atreus's eyes with her own wide ones, bright and horrified; how Dora Mithrides has folded her arms as she glares at Atreus, her lips pursed. The Protector's Guard are gripping their spears slackly, uncertainly, looking to Atreus for further instruction. Atreus looks past all of them, at me.

Then, to my utter surprise, he smiles.

It is not a smile with any warmth: It is a lip curled, a lifted brow, as if, instead of feeling thwarted by my maneuvers, he is laughing at them. In that moment, his malice is palpable.

The triumph that has been rising within me falters. A coldness blossoms in my stomach. For one heart-stopped instant, as he steps forward, I think, *He's going to do it anyway.*

Then he looks down at Lee and speaks.

"Rise, son of Callipolis."

Breath returns to me in a slow exhale.

Lee gets slowly to his feet. Atreus steps down from the plinth and places a palm on Lee's forehead. Lee raises his head fractionally at the touch. He closes streaming eyes. When Atreus continues, his voice is soft, emotionless. Almost lazy.

"Do you swear to honor, serve, and protect the City, as long as you have breath?"

"I swear it."

"Then be Stormscourge no longer. You are Lee, of no father and no house."

Atreus's hand falls. Lee opens his eyes, blinking as if the dawn light blinds him.

Cor steps forward, producing from the pocket of his uniform

Lee's silver-and-gold wristband, retrieved from Goran's office before our departure. He holds it out to offer to Atreus, but Holmes steps forward and takes it instead.

"Affirm your vows," Holmes directs Lee gruffly, in Callish.

Lee inhales. Then he recites, without faltering, the words that we first said as children, seven years ago.

"I vow to serve as Guardian, from this day forward, till death release me. I forswear all worldly possessions and riches, that I be not corrupted. I forswear all family and the comforts of hearth and progeny, that I be not torn from my purpose. All that I am belongs to Callipolis. By the wings of my dragon I will keep her. Let my will be her protection. Let my reason guide her to justice."

Holmes holds out the band to Lee's extended wrist and snaps the wristband in place. The fingers of Lee's dominant hand reach for it automatically, confirming its presence.

When the wristband is secured, I unclasp the medal of the Firstrider and fleet commander from my shoulder and hold it out to him.

Lee reaches for it, looks at me, and his eyes focus. Then, instead of taking it, he closes my fingers over it.

"Keep it."

I stand frozen, my closed fist smeared with the blood and ash of Lee's hand. For a moment, I don't understand.

Then Lee turns from me to address those watching, lifting his voice over the wind.

"I have sworn my loyalty to Callipolis. I have shown myself willing to wage war for it. But it is not a war I can or should lead. I recuse myself."

His voice thick with a different emotion, he unfolds an arm, gesturing to me with the whole of it. "Instead, I will follow the one who should. Antigone sur Aela is next in rank to take my place. She has demonstrated herself more than my equal in the air and on the ground. I will follow her."

Pressure on the edge of my eyes is growing as Lee's meaning hits home. For a moment, all I can think is *no. No, I don't want this, I can't do this—*

But then I remember that I did want this. That I can do this. And Lee needs it.

And when I look past him, to those watching, to see if they raise the objections that are half swirling in my head, I find they are not. Instead, for the first time since Lee arrived on the Keep, Atreus's face shows surprise. His hand has moved, seemingly unconsciously, to cover his mouth, twisted with whatever realizations he has left to make as he regards Lee's arm proffered in abdication.

Then Lee turns to me. "Antigone, will you accept the mantle of Firstrider and Fleet Commander?"

The eyes of the corps, of Atreus and Miranda Hane and General Holmes are on me, but now my eyes are only on Lee. Covered in blood and ash, gray eyes blazing as he stands tall, dark hair rippling in the wind of the Sky Court. Every bit a dragonlord's son.

Waiting on my word, though it costs him all that's left of his resolve to do so.

My throat tight, I nod. And then I force my answer to be loud, and carry over the wind.

"I will."

Lee steps closer, takes the medal from me, and affixes it again to my shoulder. I am aware, while his fingers clasp the pin against my uniform, of my own light breathing as I look up at him, as we pass through this moment. A few heartbeats that take us from one order to another.

The medal again on my shoulder, Lee steps back from me and bends before me, full-backed, into a bow. Though his voice is strained, it does not break.

"I salute you as my commander and offer you my dragon's service as your Alternus."

19

REVOLUTION'S CHILDREN

The soldier went on after the Revolution to live a quiet life, retired from military office, and in the great scheme of his changing city, amounting to little.

He would never tell anyone about the time he disobeyed his commander's orders. The time when he carried a boy into a hallway and kept walking. Looking back on that moment, he tried to tell himself it had been a choice. A choice, for better or for worse, that had defined him.

The truth was, it hadn't felt like a choice at all. He had simply looked at the boy and seen, not a dragonlord's son, but a child like any other.

He tended the boy's wounds, took him to the orphanage, and left him with a new name: Lee.

ANNIE

Back on the ground I escort Lee to the infirmary and make sure he is given a private room. Lee doesn't question or confirm the choice; in the time it's taken to descend Pytho's Keep he seems to have moved past the point of speaking. He remains quiet throughout the nurse's tending, during which I wash what ash and dragonsblood I've been stained with off in a basin to the side of the room. Only after the nurse has left, the door closed behind her, and I have taken him into my arms does he finally speak.

"Atreus asked, but I couldn't—we'll have to return the body—"

"I'll make sure that happens."

But he barely hears me, because he has realized the word he has used—*body*—and it's enough to make him lose it. As I tighten my arms around him, as my heart aches at the sound of his anguish, another part of me, another part that woke when he pinned the fleet commander's medal on my shoulder, remains calm as still water and hard as steel. That part of me thinks only: *You are safe.*

I hold him until he's spent, and then I help him drink the sleeping draft the nurse left us.

"You need to sleep. I'll be back when you wake up."

Back in the Cloister I find Power, lounging in the leaf-swept courtyard, the winter wind rippling through his hair.

"Commander," he says, and his tone, though sardonic as usual, contains what I suspect is satisfaction.

One person, at least, who likes the idea of my promotion.

He smiles, salutes with his characteristic flourish, and leaves me alone among the leaves.

Inside the fleet commander's office, I stand for a moment and test the thought: my office. Then I sit and begin going through the list of meetings that I'll need to attend in addition to those already scheduled. I'll meet with Holmes, to discuss the matter of the body of Julia Stormscourge and Lee's request that it be returned to New Pythos; and I'll meet with Miranda Hane, to discuss what kind of propaganda will be needed to ensure Lee's safe reinstatement in the corps. But before all these, I find a message from Dora Mithrides, inviting me to tea.

For the second time today and in my life, I make my way up the Janiculum.

It's a quiet walk through the Palace gardens and up the winding streets to Dora's house, through the riots of fall colors and the blowing leaves, along streets lined with ornate fences and ivy-clad mansions and the occasional trotting carriage. Dora's porter lets me inside the gate, the valet into her home. Soaring ceilings, great chandeliers, a grand staircase winding upward greet me: It occurs to me that these are all the things I am usually intimidated by. But today they don't have the same power over me.

"Antigone. Welcome. We'll take our tea on the veranda."

Dora Mithrides has dressed properly, applied her rouge, and arranged her hair. Her neck is weighted once again with thick-beaded necklaces. She leads the way through the spacious house to a veranda, sheltered from the wind, that looks out over a private garden and the city. The concentric walls of the Inner and Outer Palace spread below, the arena leaning out over the winding River Fer, which encircles the Palace gardens and the lower Janiculum. Across the river lies Highmarket, bustling and bright; Cheapside and Southside, low-roofed and dirty; and in the distance the Manufacturing District, bleak and hazy with smoke. Beyond that the lowland plains, stretching out to meet the sea and a blue sky.

"Cream or sugar?"

We sit at a glass table, the china arrayed before us so thin light shines through it. There's enough of a chill in the air that Dora has wrapped herself in a shawl; the leather of my uniform is sufficient to hold my heat. Dora has spoken in Dragontongue, and I sense, this time, that it matters which language I reply in. So, careful of each word, I answer in Dragontongue as well.

"Neither, thank you."

There are rules to this process, and Lee would know all of them, but Lee is not here.

Even when you don't feel confident, you fake it.

I smile at the serving girl and thank her for my tea.

When we are alone on the veranda, Dora takes a long drink from her cup, returns it to her saucer, and tells me:

"That was quite an operation you just pulled off, my dear."

I sip my own tea and find my wrist steady.

"I am curious why you did it. Are you in love with the boy?"

I smile into my teacup. *That* is how she chooses to reduce it? And then I set it down and level my gaze across the table at Dora.

"I did it because I believe Lee is everything Atreus's test found him to be."

Dora hums softly, nodding to herself.

"Yes, I can see why you would think that," she says. She settles back, blinking at me with beady eyes. "And I can also see why *that* would make Atreus see him as a threat to everything he's struggling to build."

I open my mouth to tell her that Lee isn't, and no words come.

Because, of course, he is.

The realization is simple, obvious, and terrifying—until it's answered with a memory from another lifetime. Of a boy who was good to me, who helped me first and asked who my parents were after, who remained my friend in spite of learning truths that hurt.

Maybe Lee does embody threats that Atreus opposes. Maybe he is a part of the shadow of the dragonlords that we must crawl out of by any means necessary. But when we were children and our choices were what mattered, the choices he made were not of the old world, but the new.

"Even after today?" I ask.

Dora smiles.

"I think," she says, "that Atreus is capable of being shaken, and that today, what you and Lee did shook him a great deal."

She laces her fingers together across her plump abdomen and straightens against her wicker chair. Stretching, turning talk to business.

"It also attracted my interest. In the boy's future, and yours as well. And if I am interested, the Janiculum is interested. Do you understand?"

She does not have to say the words *Protectorship* and *succession* for me to understand her perfectly.

"I believe I do."

Dora smiles. She opens her gesture, taking in the tray of biscuits on the table between us, a luxury unaffected by the rationing program that I'm in charge of enforcing.

"Please," she says. "Eat."

* * *

I return to the Palace infirmary later that day, when Lee's sleeping draft is due to have worn off. I walk down corridors flooded with warm swaths of sunlight down to the final ward and stop on the threshold.

Lee is in bed, awake, and propped on pillows. He has two visitors: Cor, seated at the end of his bed, and Crissa, her chair pulled up close to him. They're doing most of the talking, passing the thread of conversation back and forth carefully, relieving Lee of pressure to contribute. Lee, between them, does not share their smiles, but neither does he wear the expression of raw agony that I left him with earlier. He has calmed, and even if he doesn't speak, he seems to take comfort in their presence.

It's with a pain that feels strangely distant from myself that I notice Crissa has taken his hand. The kiss he and I shared in a darkened cell feels like it already belongs to the lives of former selves, burned away in the fire. What's left beneath, still raw, doesn't know what claim to place on this boy, whom I've just sent to hell and back.

But then Lee looks past them, as their conversation continues. His gray eyes soften at the sight of me, and the beginning of a line appears at the side of his mouth, like something just a little sadder than a smile, and I know the words without their needing to be said.

Our claim on each other is the same as it's always been. The fires we walked through today were ones we've trained to walk since childhood. And today, the choices that began in childhood made us strong enough to defy two regimes, in the name of revolution.

Together we'll defy them, step by step through this fire, to the end.

AUTHOR'S NOTE

Fireborne was inspired by many sources, chief among them Virgil's *Aeneid* and Plato's *Republic*. I first read Virgil as a high school Latin student and remember being struck, like Annie, by the tragedy of lines that I only half understood. The translations I made then, particularly those recounting Aeneas's flight from burning Troy, became the adaptive source for many of the lines in *Fireborne* attributed to the *Aurelian Cycle*.

My love of the classics has always been amateur, and I'd be the first to admit that the resemblances between this Callipolis and Plato's are few. But for readers curious about the sources that inspired Atreus's regime, the basis for its political structure, propaganda, and censorship practices can be found in the *Republic*.

ACKNOWLEDGMENTS

This book owes its existence in greatest part to two brilliant women: my agent, Danielle Burby, and my editor, Arianne Lewin.

Danielle changed my life when she found my manuscript in her slush pile, and since then, my awe of her has only grown. Her wisdom, kindness, and superb professionalism have made working with her a delight, and her emails have an uncanny ability to unknot the thorniest of problems—and to brighten the darkest of days. She has been my champion, cheerleader, counselor, and friend.

The year we spent in revisions, Ari Lewin worked me into a state of advanced exhaustion, kept me going with her wicked sense of humor, and let me up for air about three drafts past what I had thought would be good enough. Ari redefined *good enough*—and for an author at the beginning of her career, there could be no greater gift. Ari modeled and inspired a perseverance that transformed my book, matured my writing, and set the bar for the kind of writer I want to be.

In the larger publishing world, I would like to thank Kristin and Brian Nelson and the entire team at the Nelson Literary Agency; my foreign rights agents, Jenny Meyer and Heidi Gall, for finding homes for *Fireborne* abroad; Alice Lawson, *Fireborne*'s film and television co-agent at Gersh; and those at Putnam and Penguin Teen who helped bring this book into the world, including Elise LeMassena, Tessa Meischeid, Anuoluwapo Ohioma, Lindsey Andrews, and Jennifer Klonsky, with special thanks to Kristie Radwilowicz for a truly revolutionary cover.

I count myself lucky to have met and been supported by other writers along the way: Jennifer Gilmore, my undergraduate creative writing advisor; Kristen Ciccarelli and Rachel Hartman, whose wisdom lights the way; and my fellow Novel Nineteens, particularly Bridget Tyler, Nicki Pau Preto, Joanna Hathaway, Malayna Evans, Mara Rutherford, and Crystal Smith. Closer to home, I'm grateful to the Chicagoland writing community, especially Lizzie Cooke, my first-ever writer-neighbor and cafe buddy; Jeff Bishop, who brought the party to Team Lewin; and Reese Eschmann, who made *Fireborne* a better book.

My road to publishing was rocky and long, and I would never have made it without the combined love and brainpower of the communities that saw me through. I'm grateful to the parents and teachers of CBECC, particularly for the support of Jeremiah and Marcy Flanagan; the Seton community, especially Beth Norman and Linda Zehren, who helped get me over the finish line; and Portsmouth Abbey School, for being my Hogwarts. I couldn't have asked for a better cheering squad than Laureen and Michael Bonin, Kate Smith, Kale and Dimi Zelden, the great McDonough clan, and Dom Paschal Scotti.

I would like to thank the following mentors, friends, and

readers who've made the difference along the way: Anna Stilz, Helen McCabe, Melissa Lane, and Elizabeth Benestad, for teaching classes that inspired *Fireborne*; Maggie, my first-ever Voice of the Youth, and Marina, my youngest-ever reader; Sandra Vazquez Ventimilla, Jackson Popkin, Lehman Garrison, Joseph Labatt, Paul Baker, and Chelsea Mueller, for giving their feedback and thumbs-up; Marie and Frederick Nesfield, who've been beta reading for me since we were ten; Alissa Spera, for answering every question and bringing two bottles of champagne; and Phil Dershwitz, who convinced me he really did like it when I needed it most.

I am grateful in particular for the friendship and support of my first two readers and forever-roommates: Katrina Hall, the wise witness to my journey in all its twists and turns, whose beautiful correspondence I treasure like gems. And Erin McDonough, painter of poetry and namer of dragons, who loves the great stories and understands why.

Last but really first, thank you to my family: Grandma, Pam, David, and Mary Beth, whose love is my bedrock. The Stone family, for welcoming me as a fourth daughter and sister. Lorenzo and Marie Laure, je vous aime pour toujours. My father, who dared to chase the American dream. My mother, who feared nothing and gave me everything.

And Robert, who has been my first confidant, my best friend, and my anchor at the end of good writing days and bad: I found the shape of this book in our conversations, and its heart in loving you.